T0279334

The
BLOOD
ORCHID

Books by Kylie Lee Baker

The Keeper of Night
The Empress of Time

The Scarlet Alchemist
The Blood Orchid

The
BLOOD
ORCHID

KYLIE LEE BAKER

HARPER

An Imprint of HarperCollinsPublishers

Library of Congress Control Number: 2024935584
ISBN 978-1-33-509175-8

Typography by Catherine Lee

First Edition

To everyone who watched *Fullmetal Alchemist*
as a kid and never recovered

CONTENT NOTE

During the Tang Dynasty, Chinese alchemists tried to create an elixir of immortality. This story is what might have happened if they'd succeeded. Because this is an alternate history that reimagines China as it might have developed a century after this discovery, many historical details have been consciously changed. As such, please do not use this book as an authoritative source on Chinese history or culture.

In particular, please note that while the alchemy in this book is based loosely on the principles and goals of eighth-century Chinese Taoist alchemy, the depiction is entirely fictional and is not reflective of historical or modern Taoist practices. This book also includes contemporary Mandarin and Cantonese words, which differ greatly from the Middle Chinese that was spoken during the Tang Dynasty. The author made this decision for the sake of relatability and ease of reading for modern Chinese speakers (as well as a reluctance to learn a dead language for the sake of a fantasy novel).

PROLOGUE

The Empress's blood tastes of light.

When she dies in my teeth, when I feel her heartbeat slowing through the arteries tangled around my tongue, I learn the taste of death.

Everyone thinks that I've forgotten that moment.

They never speak of it because it was for the greater good, because I survived, because all people want is a victory. They don't want to know what it cost.

But I've felt tendons snap and recoil between my teeth like zither strings. My tongue has scored the Empress's spine, my teeth have peeled back her white powdered skin. It is not a taste that one easily forgets.

The moment plays again and again in my dreams. Every night, I hold her face still, keep her quiet, keep her mine, drink the gold from her withering veins.

But some nights, she does not die.

Instead, she reaches out and clasps my jaw with her bloody hands, burning red qi on slick pearl. She turns my face toward her, and I obey because she is my Empress, because when you see something beautiful, you can't look away.

Then she leans close to my ear and whispers words I know are not a dream. They are a memory.

Whatever power you think you have is an illusion.

Whatever your dreams are, they belong to me.

And wherever you run, I am already there waiting for you.

She sinks her nails into my cheek.

A crack ripples across my face, a single jagged line of darkness that begins beneath my right eye and races across my body. I am a daughter born from clay, I am a glazed porcelain doll on a shelf, and with a quiet sparkle of sound, I fracture apart.

She cradles me in her arms even when I'm nothing but fine white dust and jagged shards, and even then, she won't release me. My thoughts scatter like faraway stars, but all I can think is that her bloodless, blue-tinged skin is a beautiful contrast to the scarlet running down her throat. She is the first bright light of morning that slices across the horizon, peeling it open. She is my Empress.

And then at last, she dies. Not because she is weak, or because I've truly defeated her, but because she made me a promise.

Wherever you run, I am already there waiting for you.

A resurrection alchemist should not fear death. But now I do.

Because I know that on the day that I die and wake up in the river of souls, the first thing I see will be a pair of bright, golden eyes.

CHAPTER ONE

Year 775
Lanzhou, China

My brother and I were very good at pretending we weren't dead.

Out in the desert, the harsh sun pulled redness to our cheeks and drew sweat from our skin. We gasped down breaths like we'd nearly drowned and had only just clawed our way to the surface of this golden sea—a convincing imitation of life, in my opinion. I worried a bit that people might recognize us as the Crown Prince and the last royal alchemist, but I didn't worry that anyone suspected we were reanimated corpses.

The ground whispered with snakes, the *pat pat pat* of tiny rodent footsteps, the sigh of sand dunes shifting slowly in the distance. The sky was the color of parchment, choked with sand.

In the north, they called this desert the Borderless Sea. The dunes around us swayed, the desert alive and flowing as much as any ocean I'd ever seen, though it could have been an illusion from the heat waves, or my slowly melting brain. All I knew was that I'd once stuck my hand inside my uncle's kiln back in

Guangzhou and felt heat that I was sure would boil my skin right off—this heat was like I'd stepped fully inside of the kiln and locked the door behind me.

Wenshu and I had left the palace in Chang'an a week ago on horseback, but we'd reached a part of the world so parched that it would have been cruel to bring horses any farther—their hooves would sink into the heavy sand like mud. We'd sold them in Lanzhou for an amount of gold that we once would have marveled at, but now it was only added weight in our bags that I briefly considered dumping in the desert.

But even this relentless heat was better than staying at the palace in Chang'an.

In the weeks since the other alchemists had died, I'd hardly slept. Whenever I lay down at night, shadows flickered just past my windows, shivering away when I opened the door. Whispers slipped through the cracks in the wood-paneled walls, entered through the keyhole, contorted themselves to the diamond shape of my lattice windows to slither through and invade my dreams.

And at every turn, my sister, Yufei, was there, wearing the Empress's face.

She asked me about dinner and scolded my brother in the same voice that had once told me, unflinchingly, that she'd burned my siblings alive.

Even though Wenshu was borrowing the Crown Prince's body, I never once forgot that he was Wenshu. But for some reason, the Empress's golden eyes haunted me, even though I knew Yufei was the one behind them.

Maybe it was because I'd killed the Empress, sacrificed my body and my betrothed to make sure she was dead, and yet she was still strolling around the palace asking for roasted chicken at all hours of the night.

The Empress's death, of course, had become one of the palace's many secrets. As long as her body was walking around, she was alive as far as the public was concerned. In many ways, it was like I had never killed her at all. Maybe that was the problem.

I hadn't truly felt like I could breathe until I'd left the palace with Wenshu and the gates of Chang'an were a tiny golden sparkle on the distant horizon. The city that was once my greatest dream had swiftly become my nightmare.

Wenshu had found us thin white cloaks with wide hoods to protect us from the sun, so the two of us swept across the desert like ghosts, our footprints quickly erased by the constant song of shifting sand around us, as if we'd never really existed.

There was someone out here who could help us, but he didn't like to be found.

"Quit kicking up sandstorms behind you with your giant feet," Wenshu said.

If there was one thing my brother was good at, it was reminding me that no matter whose face he wore, this was absolutely not the sweet and gentle prince Li Hong anymore.

"Then keep up," I said, not even glancing over my shoulder.

"Not all of us have legs the length of the Yellow River."

I groaned, tugging my hood down in a futile attempt to cover my face with more shade. "Please don't talk about water right now."

"Are you dizzy?" Wenshu said, suddenly beside me. It was a habit from when we were kids, when he had to worry about me passing out in the heat. But those days were long gone, the name—my real name—carved into my forearm a reminder of all that had changed.

My mentor, the Moon Alchemist, had preferred death to living as an undead abomination like me. But I had too much to do before I could die again. My soul was safely tethered to my body, my dead heart once again beating, draining colors from the world around me, pulling light and life and qi from anyone I loved.

But almost no one I loved was alive anymore. I'd made sure of that.

My brother and sister were just as dead as me, my parents long gone, my betrothed waiting for me at the river of souls, his body loaned out to Wenshu like an extra coat. My aunt and uncle who had raised me were still alive and well in Guangzhou, but we could never see them again. Being near us would kill them, our presence lapping up their qi like a wet rag until there was nothing left.

"I'm not dizzy, I'm *thirsty*," I said. "Aren't you?"

Wenshu winced as a hot breeze blew his hood back, spraying his eyes with sand. "Why are you complaining instead of getting us more water, then?"

"Do you have heatstroke already?" I said. "We've only been out here a few hours. There's no water in sand."

"Not *in* the sand. *Below* it," Wenshu said, rolling his eyes. "There's groundwater somewhere down there. How do you think cacti survive out here?"

"I don't know, rain?"

"Rain," he echoed, giving the searing sky a pointed glance.

I would have kept walking just to deprive him of the satisfaction of being right, but my mouth was papery dry, my heartbeat pounding in my ears, and we still had hours to go before nightfall.

I knelt down in the sand, a warm bath of gold around my legs, and reached into my satchel.

Durian, my alchemy duck, popped his head out of my larger

bag. My hands were a bit sweaty, but I managed to pull three waterstones out of my satchel and press them into the sand.

Alchemy rushed like lightning into the ground. It cascaded down the path of desert crystals too small for the eye to see, reaching for the image of water, thinner and quieter as it burrowed deeper into the ground. My palms began to sting as if sunburned, the alchemy aching through my veins, loosening my fingernails, cracking my skin with dryness. I guided the current around the long-buried bones of rodents and abandoned snake skin and, finally, the tangled web of cactus roots somewhere far away. I traced them down and down until at last, my hands grew cool.

Water burst up from the sand, a thin stream that caught the light in its transparent brilliance. It arced high, then sloped back down and clocked Wenshu between the eyes, sending him onto his back in the sand.

"Fan Zilan!" he said, moving out of the way as I caught the next arc in my water sack.

"You asked for water," I said.

"Yes, in my mouth would be ideal next time," he said. "I'm not a frog who drinks through his pores."

"Could have fooled me."

"This isn't even my real face!" he said. "You're just insulting your ugly boyfriend."

I shook my head. "Something about your personality just ruins his face," I said. "Like adding rotten meat to a stew."

Wenshu's hood blew back again, sand pummeling his face. He spit on the ground, scrubbing his eyes with a sleeve that was only marginally less sandy.

I set Durian down on my skirt in a cloud of cottony fluff. His feathers were coming in, golden fuzz replaced with smooth white from his chest up to his face, but still a puffy cloud from the chest down. Most of the time, he sat in my bag with his head peeking out, occasionally letting out quiet peeps that annoyed Wenshu to no end. I'd tossed a few activated waterstones in with him to keep him cool, but he seemed wholly unbothered by the desert heat, which was more than I could say for myself.

I drew up some more water from the ground and cupped it in my palms, holding it out to Durian while Wenshu watched sourly.

"You care for that demon duck with more kindness than your own brother," he said.

"Are you actually jealous of a duck?" I said, raising an eyebrow. "Did you want to sit in my bag too? Eat crickets from my hands?"

He rolled his eyes, hitching his bag higher on his shoulder, eyes red from sand.

"I could be in a palace right now pretending to be a prince," he said. "Instead, I'm eating sand and getting sunburned while you insult me."

"Consider it payment for resurrecting you twice," I said, taking a long, glorious drink of water.

As the sun grew cooler and sharp red sunset sliced across the horizon, the sound of our footsteps began to change. Each step forward produced a low echo somewhere below, like the world had become hollow.

Wenshu must have noticed it too, slowing to a stop. He pulled out one of the scrolls from his bag and unfurled it. I spotted a tear in his sleeve near his shoulder and yanked him closer to me so I could fix it.

"Quit manhandling me," he said, eyes still fixed on the scroll. I slipped my hand into my bag, gently nudging Durian aside as I pulled out a few pieces of opal—waterstones with healing properties—to repair the tear so Wenshu wouldn't end up with a sunburn across his arm. I clasped the stones in my hands, then pressed both palms to his sleeve.

My hands grew cold as the opal melted away, the pain in my fingernails crescendoing to a sharp point before one of my nails split. The severed threads of Wenshu's robe shivered like tiny snakes, twisting and knotting themselves back together. I shook the numbness from my hands and leaned over Wenshu's shoulder to read the scroll.

We'd brought as many of my father's notes as we could carry. The Moon Alchemist's study had been full of them, and we'd spent the first few weeks after her death reading and trying to make sense of his language. My father and the Moon Alchemist had worked together, so her notes in Chinese had helped us translate some of his writing.

Many of his earlier scrolls were about perfecting the art of resurrection—old news to both me and the Moon Alchemist. But it seemed that my father had come to Chang'an for an entirely different project: the search for Penglai Island.

Back when people believed in gods instead of alchemy, they spoke of a mythical island called Penglai, home to eight immortal beings and their elixir of eternal life. They lived high up on a snow-white mountain in a palace made of gold and silver with trees that grew diamonds and rubies instead of fruit. They knew no pain, or hunger, or winter.

What a joke.

I knew, because of the rules of alchemy, that such a perfect place couldn't be real. Peace and happiness required suffering in turn.

But legends often sprouted from seeds of truth. At least, that was what my father believed.

In order for this island to exist, the most fundamental rule of alchemy would have to be broken, he wrote.

The creation of good without evil.

Though the legends have been diluted by superstition, if there is even a speck of truth to them, they describe alchemy without limits or consequences. The power to do anything at all.

The next few sections described his theories of how to find Penglai, but one page in the middle had been ripped out, and no matter how I tore apart the Moon Alchemist's study, I couldn't find it. Luckily, the surrounding notes made enough sense for us to at least begin searching.

A place like Penglai shouldn't have been possible. It was the kind of thing that children dreamed about, a naive hope crushed by age as the years wore on. Maybe a wiser alchemist would have dismissed it.

But my father had believed in it, just as he'd believed in resurrection, which many had thought impossible as well. He did not fear alchemy the way others did. He saw the potential for greatness and seized it, no matter the cost.

Maybe he had been wrong, and all of this was nothing but a foolish dream. But I remembered the look on the prince's face as the Empress slit his throat, the wound yawning open, waves of blood rolling down the steps, and I knew that somehow, it had to be possible. If I couldn't fix this, then I didn't deserve the second life I'd been given.

My father's notes mentioned a map that would take us to

Penglai Island, but even after poring through the Moon Alchemist's study, secret drawers and all, we hadn't been able to find it. He might have taken it with him the last time he left the palace, in which case we'd never find it.

But luckily, he'd mentioned where he got the map in the first place.

I've spoken to a great alchemist who lives in the empty valleys beneath the Borderless Sea. He calls himself the Sandstone Alchemist, for he has built a palace of sandstone underground. He claims he has been to Penglai Island.

Unfortunately, my father hadn't been thoughtful enough to include a map to the Sandstone Alchemist's front door. But his journals mentioned entering the desert from Lanzhou, and from there, he couldn't have gone far. The desert was hardly kind to the people who had lived on its borders for centuries, much less to pale-skinned foreigners who didn't know its secrets.

Part of me liked the idea of following the ghost of my father's footsteps. Once, I'd sworn to master alchemy just to spite him for leaving my mother on her deathbed. But when the Moon Alchemist had shown me the truth—that he'd given the last of his life to resurrect me and had returned to her for a cure—that hate had quickly dissipated.

I imagined him, long and wiry, copper hair and eyes full of sky, striding into this golden sea so many years ago with nothing but a dream. I didn't much believe in ghosts, but in the haze of heat waves, at times I thought I could see him there, looking over his shoulder.

Wenshu stomped his foot, the ground echoing below him, sand shivering away. "Does that sound like an underground palace to you?" he said.

"It doesn't sound like a sand dune, that's for sure," I said, kneeling down. I grabbed three earthstones from my satchel and pressed them to the ground.

Slowly, sand whispered away from the space beneath my hands, forming pale clouds behind me. As the winds picked up, the ground began to sink beneath our feet, and we dropped deep into the mouth of the desert. We sank down, the sand growing cooler and darker beneath us, until at last my hands touched cool metal, my feet on solid ground.

A trapdoor.

"That's one way to stay cool in the desert," Wenshu said. "Burrow underground like a fox."

I knocked twice on the door, feeling a bit silly waiting to be invited into a hermit alchemist's secret lair as if we'd stopped by for tea. As expected, no response came.

"Well, we tried," I said, placing three firestones to the lock, snapping it off easily. *Amateur*.

Wenshu made an indignant sound, gaze following the discarded lock as the sand swallowed it. "Zilan, you can't just—"

"Out of all the awful things I've done," I said, gripping the handle, "I think I can live with myself for opening a door."

We dropped down into a cool, silent tunnel. I ignited three firestones in my palm, casting the packed sand walls in pale orange light. A network of thin silver wire braced the curved ceilings of the tunnels, the ground beneath us polished sandstone in ribbons of red and brown. I held the firestones ahead of me, but the light couldn't pierce very far into the sea of darkness. There was only a tunnel growing narrower as it faded into the dark.

"This has to be the Sandstone Alchemist's home," I said. "No one could carry this much sandstone this far into the desert without alchemy."

"Finding him isn't what I was worried about," Wenshu said, staring off into the never-ending tunnel. "He doesn't seem the type to appreciate visitors, if the buried door was any indication."

"Did you think we'd find merchants selling the secrets to Penglai Island in the town square for twenty gold pieces?" I said, glaring over my shoulder. "This was never going to be easy." I turned and headed deeper into the tunnel system, forcing Wenshu to follow me, as I carried our only source of light.

The sounds of the desert grew distant the farther we walked, which was how I knew we were heading deeper underground. The sand walls seemed denser, darker from trapped moisture. We drew to a stop where the main tunnel split off into three smaller tunnels.

"Which way?" Wenshu said.

I hissed in pain as my firestones burnt out against my palm, singeing my skin and casting us in sudden darkness. "Do I look like a map to you?" I said, reaching into my bag for more stones.

"*You're* the royal alchemist."

I tensed, grateful that Wenshu couldn't see my face in the darkness, couldn't tell how much I hated that title. All throughout Chang'an, and then China, the news of the palace massacre had spread through woodblock print flyers.

THE SCARLET ALCHEMIST, the print said at the top, with an illustration of a girl drenched in red, standing before a crumbled palace oozing with blood, severed hands and heads on the lawn, the sky a vicious red.

Scarlet had once referred to my own blood that I'd spilled for the dream of becoming a royal alchemist, but it had taken on a new meaning since that day. I was the last of the royal alchemists, the only one who had emerged from the palace, trailing bloody footprints behind me. No one knew what had truly happened, but most people didn't need the truth. They created their own stories.

The Scarlet Alchemist, who killed all her friends. The Scarlet Alchemist, who was so jealous of all the other women in the palace that she tore them to shreds. The Scarlet Alchemist, who refused to die like a little cockroach, not because she was strong, but because everyone else had died for her. I had given everything for that title, and within a month, it was no longer an honor, but a curse.

"And what sort of alchemy do you propose I do here?" I said, still fishing for more firestones in my bag. "Exactly what kind of stone do you think tells you the location of a reclusive alchemist buried underground?"

My fingers were already growing cold, the temperature of the shadowed tunnels a stark contrast to the burning, golden sun aboveground. My trembling fingers skittered across the smooth stones, unable to discern their type in the dark. Normally, I could tell them apart by touch alone, but with my fingertips numb from cold, I wasn't certain.

Wenshu must have sensed my hesitation, because he sighed and started rummaging through his own bag.

"Royal alchemist can't even make a torch," he said, striking a match, bathing the hallway in light.

A man stood before us.

We both flinched, Wenshu nearly dropping the match as the pale wraith of a man took a step closer, a curved knife in each hand. His skin had the blue hue of corpses and glowed with a thin layer of dew, his long black hair damp around his face. His eyes were the murky white of the sand-torn sky, tinged red from sand that gathered in the corners, on his lips, in his beard. Topaz and ruby rings glittered on his knobbed fingers. Could this be the Sandstone Alchemist?

I tried to recall any words in Lanzhou dialect to say to him, but before I could speak, a golden viper curled around his throat, baring its fangs at us.

At once, Wenshu and I stepped back, pulling our robes forward so the loose fabric hung in front of us. Auntie So always said that if a snake wanted a piece of you, you better make sure they got a mouthful of fabric instead of flesh.

But the snake didn't strike, instead hovering by the man's face, its piercing golden eyes brighter than the match in Wenshu's hand. I pulled my sleeve back so it draped across my bag, just in case Durian chose that moment to poke his head out.

The man said something in a language I didn't understand. I had never traveled to the northwest before, had never heard their dialects from a world away on the southeast coast.

Wenshu and I shared a confused look. The man sighed impatiently and tried again, louder, shaking his knives.

"Who sent you?" he said, in something that resembled the dialect of Chang'an, knives pointed at both of our throats. The emphasis on each word was unbalanced, so it took me a moment to understand.

"No one," I said, trying to enunciate in case he didn't understand. "We're looking for the Sandstone Alchemist."

The man let out a sharp laugh. "Then you're looking for a corpse."

I sighed, mentally running through how many chicken-blood stones I had left. His words probably would have deterred anyone else, but death was not the endpoint in the journey of a resurrection alchemist.

"How long ago?" I said.

The man frowned. "What?"

"When did he die?" I said slowly. I turned to Wenshu. "It's cold enough down here to delay decomposition. If his brain is still mostly intact, I can work with that."

"*Mostly?*" Wenshu echoed palely. "You want to interrogate a dead man with half a brain?"

"He doesn't need to recite Confucian texts, just point us to a map," I said.

"The ethical implications—"

"We can put him back down after."

"*We?*"

"He has been dead for centuries," the man said, louder, like he desperately wanted us to shut up.

"No," I said sharply. "He hasn't." I knew because my father's notes said he'd spoken to the Sandstone Alchemist, and my father was certainly not hundreds of years old. This man was lying because he had something to hide. There was only one person who had ever told me a convincing lie, and I had killed her.

"Here's what's going to happen," I said. "You're going to take us to the Sandstone Alchemist, or I will hack your snake's head off with a shovel and bury you under ten tons of sand."

The man only laughed, and a hot flash of rage burned through me.

"You see these wires?" he said, gesturing to the ceiling with one of his knives. "You see how they sparkle?"

I glanced up at the wires for a quick moment, not wanting to take my eyes off the armed man for too long.

"Yes?" I said.

He reached out and pressed a single finger to a loose wire dangling by his side. It came away with a bright bead of red blood on his fingertip. "The metal is not reflective," he said. "It shines because of its sharpness. These wires could chop you up like a peach, if I wanted them to. Your bones will become wall ornaments, because I'll never get them untangled."

Then he touched the wire again, and light bloomed in his fingertip.

The web of wires shivered as alchemy raced through them, illuminated against the walls of the tunnel. I grabbed Wenshu and pulled him close to me as one of the wires came free from the ceiling, lashed out like a whip, and sliced off part of his sleeve.

I reached for my satchel, but at once, the man released the wire and the netting fell limp and still. One of the man's ruby rings turned to black ash, falling to the ground. *Classic destruction alchemy, fueled by firestone,* I thought. This man was an alchemist.

"Who sent you?" the man said again.

"No one," I said, pulling out three firestones and elbowing Wenshu until he moved behind me. "Be careful with your threats when you're standing in the same tunnel as us, under the same wires."

"Go ahead and try," the man said, his snake sliding down his bicep, curling around his wrist.

I pressed the firestones to the wall and imagined alchemy rushing through the sharp wires just as it had rippled down the roots in the ground seeking water. But at once, my hand cramped up as the alchemy rebounded, scorching my palm. I yanked it away from the wall.

"What did you—"

"You don't even know what it's made of," the man said, smiling darkly. "Some alchemist you are."

I clenched my jaw, stretching my fingers to bring feeling back into my stiff hand. His words shouldn't have unnerved me. No one had ever thought of me as a great alchemist until I proved them wrong. But for some reason, his words settled deep in my bones.

Because he was right—if I were a great alchemist, I wouldn't be underneath the desert searching for a myth just to undo my mistakes.

"You're the Sandstone Alchemist, aren't you?" I said.

"I don't think you want me to answer that question honestly," he said. "If I say yes, you can never leave."

I clenched my jaw. Why had my father befriended such an evasive, unhelpful alchemist?

"We're not here to cause trouble," Wenshu said. "We're looking for Penglai Island."

The man narrowed his eyes. "Two children have no business on Penglai Island," he said. "There are reasons its secrets are down here instead of in the royal library. It's not public information for anyone who bursts through my door."

"I'm not *anyone*," I said. "I'm the last royal alchemist."

The title meant little to me anymore, but it was who Wenshu expected me to be, the person he trusted to bring us safely across the world and home again. It was a title this man should have feared, conjuring images of blood and corpses.

The man laughed, the dark sound thundering down the tunnels. "You think that you're the best just because the Empress chose you? You think there aren't more of us out there who are too smart to serve her?"

I hesitated. All my life, I'd measured my worth as an alchemist against the imperial exam, the dreams of rich children in the north. Alchemy was a way to make money, not a hobby. Why would anyone become an alchemist if not to serve the Emperor?

"You can leave now," the man said, "or you can feed my snake for the next month."

I took a steadying breath. I hadn't come all this way to return to Chang'an empty-handed. *Focus, Zilan,* I thought, looking back up at the wires. *Think like a royal alchemist.*

The man had clearly made some sort of metal compound that reacted with firestones. I'd assumed the wires were common steel, but the ache in my hand made it clear I was wrong. Part of being an alchemist—a good one, anyway—was knowing every material by sight, by touch, by scent. The silver strands above us looked like the mudwire that Uncle Fan used to cut clay, made from steel. But the sharp sparkle even in dim light meant they were probably coated in something else, some mysterious metal to cancel out any transformations attempted by foreign alchemists.

Luckily, out in the desert, there weren't that many stones to choose from. Not in this quantity, at least.

I reached out for the netting once more, pushing past the ghost of an ache in my palm.

"Zilan!" Wenshu whispered.

I ignored him, tugging down a loose stretch of wire and slowly, carefully, bringing it to my lips. I opened my mouth and ran my tongue across the wire.

"*Zilan!*" Wenshu said indignantly. But the man had already lowered his knives a few degrees, mouth pinched.

"It's rock salt," I said, licking the sting from my lips. "Steel and rock salt coating, isn't it?"

The sour look on the man's face told me I was right.

"We can try this again, and see who can cut the other up faster, but I have a feeling no one will come out as the winner," I said. "Or you can tell me what I need to know about Penglai Island."

"How do you even know about that?" the man said, running

a trembling hand across his snake, even as his eyes blazed. "Only a few people—"

"My father," I said. "His name was Laisrén."

I had learned his real name in the Moon Alchemist's notes. He'd taken on a Chinese name when he met my mother, but the Moon Alchemist had only ever called him Laisrén.

A strange look eclipsed the man's face, slowly taking in my appearance with narrowed eyes. Whatever he saw in me, he didn't like. He tightened his grip around his knives.

"Laisrén's daughter is dead," he said.

"Yes," I said, dragging down my sleeve, showing him the name carved crudely into my forearm, the soul tag that had dragged me back from death in the Empress's throne room. "I am."

His gaze burned my scar for a moment before he sighed, lowering his knives. "Where is Laisrén now?"

"Dead," I said. *Because of me*, I thought but didn't say.

The man's brow creased. The sand around his ankles began to whisper, lighting up like tiny constellations. In the dim light, I realized that the ground swarmed with yellow eyes, thin snakes the color of sandstone drawing closer. Wenshu drew back, but I stood still. The viper on the man's shoulder hissed again, its gold scales glimmering.

"Show us the map," Wenshu said, even though he most definitely was not going to be the one stabbing a viper if the need arose.

"You two could never find Penglai Island with only a map," the man said. "It's a place for the greatest alchemists that ever lived. You don't even know what you're asking for."

"I'm not asking," I said, sharpening one of my iron rings into a spike.

The man's shoulders dropped a fraction, and that was how I knew we'd won.

"You're just like him," he said, before turning and heading back down the tunnel, not waiting for us to follow. "Come on."

The Sandstone Alchemist had carved out an entire world below the ground. The chasms of sandstone looked bone white in the darkness, the heat of the desert a distant memory as we descended into the cold and lightless labyrinth. Every now and then, starbursts of golden light flashed past my feet—tiny snakes glinting in and out of the sand.

Through the many archways, I caught shadowed glimpses of sandstone dining tables and pools of groundwater and stores of meat, though I didn't know what kind of animals one could reliably hunt out in the desert. Over the Sandstone Alchemist's shoulder, the viper watched us unflinchingly as the air grew colder.

You're just like him, the Sandstone Alchemist had said. Surely he was talking about my father. My mind burned with questions I wanted to ask, but I knew none of them would be well received, and there was much more at stake than my own curiosity. *How am I like him?* I wanted to ask. *Demanding? Persistent? Smarter than you initially thought?*

Auntie So had only ever told me that my father looked like an uncooked jellyfish and didn't speak comprehensible Chinese. The Moon Alchemist had met him as well, but we'd had much more pressing things to talk about back then, and now I could no longer ask her anything. The Sandstone Alchemist was one of the only people left who'd known him.

We drew to a stop in a room full of sandstone shelves crammed with scrolls, a low table in the center of the room surrounded by scattered, dusty floor cushions.

"I will give this to you, for Laisrén," the Sandstone Alchemist said, kneeling down to ignite the candle on the table with a handful of firestones. As light filled the room, his shadow swelled behind him, like a great beast rising to its full height. He stood up and moved to the wall, and the shadow shrank back to a human size. "Then," he said, "you will leave me and never come back or tell anyone where you got it from."

"I have no intention of returning to the desert if I can help it," I said. "And I'm not going to send people after you. I have bigger problems."

The Sandstone Alchemist narrowed his eyes as if appraising me, then nodded and bent down to the lowest shelves, shuffling scrolls around somewhere in the shadows.

Wenshu shot me a deeply skeptical look, his mouth pinched into a grimace. It wasn't hard to guess what he was thinking: *This was too easy.*

This man looked like he'd been fermenting underground for years, clearly hiding from something—or someone—at the cost of all else. He would not give away his secrets before we'd even shed a drop of his blood. Whatever he was about to give us would not be what we wanted.

The question was, how would we figure out where he actually kept the map?

He had his back turned to us, which meant what we wanted probably wasn't even in this room, or else he would have watched us closely.

But I had ways to see without using my eyes.

Quietly, I pulled three waterstones from my bag, squatted down, and pressed them to the ground.

Just like in the middle of the desert, alchemy rushed through my fingertips, channeling deep into the ground, seeking webs of roots. I imagined the alchemy spreading out and feeling beneath the foundations of the sandstone palace, giving me a mental map of the building and any rooms with extra fortification. But I'd forgotten just how deep underground we were.

The alchemy slammed into a hard layer of stone beneath us, the whole world trembling with a heavy *thump* as the power dispersed uselessly. Sand and clay powder rained down from the ceiling as the whole building quaked.

The Sandstone Alchemist snapped his gaze to the left doorway, then back at me and Wenshu. Luckily, I'd already stood up, feigning surprise.

"Earthquake?" I said, raising an eyebrow. "Or do you have even bigger snakes down here?"

"I'd rather an earthquake than another visitor," he said, standing up with a scroll under his arm.

I chanced a glance at Wenshu, who I knew had seen what I'd seen.

When disaster struck, people always looked to what they valued most. It was an old trick that market commandants tried on merchants they suspected were hiding money to evade taxes. Back in Guangzhou, the commandant would break our windows in the dead of night, or punch holes in the thatched roof during a rainstorm, or set fire in the middle of the shop, then stand back and watch. They knew that when disaster struck, you looked for what was most important to you.

And the Sandstone Alchemist had looked to the room on the left.

"Here you are," he said, holding out a nondescript scroll in one hand. *Probably blank*, I thought, *or something equally useless.*

But the Sandstone Alchemist was already heading for the doorway, getting ready to kick us back out into the desert. There was no way he'd simply let us look around. Not without a good reason.

I reached into my bag and cupped a hand under Durian's belly, whispered an apology into his feathers, and set him down on the ground.

At once, he took off for the doorway, flying low, nearly knocking the Sandstone Alchemist off his feet.

"Durian got out!" I shouted, rushing forward and shoving Wenshu into the hallway. "Catch him before a snake eats him!"

Wenshu knew as well as I did that Durian was more likely to eat a snake whole than be eaten by one—I'd caught Durian disemboweling a carp twice his size from one of the palace ponds—but luckily Wenshu only rolled his eyes and took off running.

"You can't just run around in here!" the Sandstone Alchemist said, chasing after Wenshu. I jogged behind them for a moment before turning back to the room we'd just been in, rushing straight through it to the room on the left.

This room had no shelves or cabinets. It was nothing but four walls of smooth, polished sandstone, no cracks or seams. At least, nothing you could see if you weren't an alchemist.

I pressed my palm flat against the wall, my iron rings flush against it. Alchemy rippled through the stone, searching for something to bend, mold, break.

Alchemy curled around a thin, nearly invisible seam in the wall, pausing to gauge my intentions, await my command. *Is this what you're looking for?* it whispered from somewhere deep inside of me.

I'm not sure, I thought, *but let's find out.*

The alchemy flooded the seam in a burst of purple light. The stone crackled as dusty white particles swirled into the air, the seam carved wider. At last, a small door swung open, no larger than my satchel.

I slipped my hand inside, fist closing around a few sheets of paper. But there was no time to read them now—hurried footsteps were drawing closer to the room.

I stuffed the papers in my bag and hurried back into the hallway, where Durian narrowly evaded the Sandstone Alchemist's grasping hands.

I reached into my bag, pulled out a handful of dead crickets, and tossed them on the ground. Durian landed on top of them before I could even put the bag away, gobbling them up. I scooped him up as he quacked in protest, setting him back in my bag.

Wenshu and the Sandstone Alchemist had finally caught up, panting and glaring at me, though likely for different reasons.

"We're done here," the Sandstone Alchemist said at last. "Take your scroll and get out."

"Let me see it first," I said, because accepting it too eagerly would look suspicious.

"Get out of my home, then you can see it. That was the deal."

Wenshu crossed his arms. "But—"

"You're already pushing your luck," the man said, jamming a finger at Wenshu. The viper slithered down his arm, baring yellowed fangs. Wenshu swallowed and backed up, nodding.

The man brushed past us, charging down the hall. Slowly, the ground began to slope upward, the sound growing softer and brighter under our feet. We reached a trapdoor in the ceiling, which the Sandstone Alchemist shouldered open with a grunt, bright light and a gust of hot sand blowing through. He clambered out, then held out a hand.

"Is all of this really necessary?" Wenshu said as the Sandstone Alchemist pulled him up. "You really hate people so much that you need to be this reclusive?"

The Sandstone Alchemist shook his head, yanking me up. I slipped in the sand, keeping a firm grip on Durian. "I'm not here because I hate people," he said. "I'm here because people would use me for awful things. That is the cost of being a great alchemist."

At last, he passed me the scroll. I was ready to leave, but I needed to at least make a show of looking at it until he disappeared back into his dune.

I unfurled the scroll and scrutinized the detailed map of China, the sweeping deserts of the northwest, the mountains in the northeast, the rippling ocean border in the east. But there was no indication of anything resembling Penglai Island, just as I'd expected.

I turned to pose some feigned ignorant question, but froze at the sight of Wenshu on the ground, one hand on the side of his neck, the Sandstone Alchemist no longer beside him.

"Gēgē?" I said.

He pulled back his hand, trying to make some sort of gesture, but his fingers twitched and trembled. A single thin line of blood ran fresh across his throat, the mark echoed on his palm. It wasn't a deep wound and didn't seem to have bled that much. But his lips were tinged purple, his face drained of color.

I took a step closer, but before I could reach him, something stung my neck.

I turned to the Sandstone Alchemist, now behind me, a blade in his hand.

"There's something you have to understand about the desert," he said. But even as he spoke, I knew that he hadn't cut me with a normal blade. The wound seared as if cauterized, the ache rushing from my throat to my chest, blooming into my arms, cramping my muscles.

"The sand is alive," he said, his words blurring into heat waves. "It flows just like the ocean. There is no permanence out here. The landscape changes every moment because the desert breathes, and what the sand buries is meant to stay buried. The desert keeps its secrets."

I reached for my satchel, but my fingers were already cramped into a tight fist, too painful to move. The viper circled the man's throat.

Venom, I realized. He must have coated his knife with it.

I fell forward onto my knees, drops of blood staining the sand that drank it hungrily.

"Penglai Island is lost for a reason," the Sandstone Alchemist said, his voice already sounding so far away. "I won't let you unbury her."

CHAPTER TWO

The world thumped beneath my cheek as the trapdoor swung shut. Now it was only me and Wenshu, choking into the sand, the sun burning half our faces, far from anyone who could help us. I couldn't even turn my head to see him as lightning fired through all of my veins, my breath thin and choked, lungs seizing. Durian was making a high keening sound, trapped in my bag beneath my leg, but I couldn't roll over to let him out.

I clapped a trembling hand to the wound on my neck, drawing out some of the blood with my iron ring, but it made no difference. The venom was everywhere in me, and I couldn't simply drain all my body's blood to extract it. I didn't know how to separate the snake's toxins from my own blood, because I had no idea what the venom was made of.

How long did it take to die from viper venom? There were snakes in the south that could kill you in ten minutes, but others took hours. Judging by how my vision was already fractured, this wouldn't take long.

I turned my face to the sun, its bright halos searing across my vision, breaking it into hazy shapes. Was this really how I would die? Withered like dried fruit in the sun, felled not by a great monster or the Perpetual Empress but by a snake that ate rats and prairie dogs?

I wondered if they'd strip my title in death. Royal alchemists died fighting for the House of Li, not out alone amongst the tumbleweeds, swallowed by the desert.

My father's words buzzed in my ears, the low voice that always seemed to come to me when I was dying, too many times to count now. I saw the words of his notes painted in the sky.

If there is an elixir of eternal life, I will find it.

I will never stop until I can return to them.

He'd been talking about me and my mother, but the words might as well have been my own. Had my father died in this same desert, his flesh pecked away by rodents, his bones crumbled to dust, mixing with the same golden sands now filling my mouth and scraping my eyes? The heat waves in my vision spiraled, and the world churned like an ocean of gold, the ghostly white silhouette on the horizon shimmering closer.

Get up, Zilan, he said. But I couldn't, and in the next shimmering heat wave, the silhouette vanished.

In the dance of lights in my fading vision, I thought of the viper's eyes, the same golden glare as the Empress. The Sandstone Alchemist had caressed its golden scales like it was some sort of mythical dragon, not a common pest that lurked in tall grass. Ever since the fall of the palace, I'd thought that the last thing I'd see would be golden eyes, but not those of a snake.

My eyes shot open, my fingers clawing into the sand.

The Empress's eyes were not naturally gold. They were the consequence of a century of eating life gold made by alchemists.

The snake's eyes and scales were probably not natural either. The Sandstone Alchemist seemed to care greatly for his viper, so perhaps he'd fed it life gold.

Life gold filled your body, turned you to a jewel on the inside, impervious to aging. But it also meant that your blood ran gold . . . and the same was probably true for venom.

I clamped my hand down harder around my neck, drawing all my concentration into my firestone ring. It was red zircon, a firestone from Champa that I'd peeled from the prince's wall before setting off, the kind of stone meant for destroying. It was dangerous to turn destruction alchemy on my own body, but what choice did I have?

The alchemy surged through my veins, searching for every trace of gold in my bloodstream. It sensed the foreign substance, tangled up with another caustic chemical, something I'd never worked with before. I clenched my fingers and let the firestone break me apart.

Destroying was so much easier than creating. That was another one of alchemy's central tenets. It took great skill to create something new, but destruction only required rage.

My veins screamed as the firestone stung through them, wrenching gold from blood, forcing the current of my heart in the wrong direction as the gold raced back toward the wound. A pressure rushed up my throat, then a stream of gold and something that stung like acid poured from the wound at my throat, sizzling as it blotted the sand.

My muscles still ached, but I could already breathe easier, the burning sweat on my face suddenly freezing cold. As soon as my vision cleared enough to see my palms sunken into the sand, I crawled to Wenshu and turned him onto his back.

For a moment, I saw the prince's corpse.

Blue-lipped and pale and dead after the Empress slit his throat, burning blood beneath me.

But Wenshu was still breathing. At least, for now.

I shook my head, numb fingers fumbling for more red zircon, crushing the stones to Wenshu's throat. His body twitched, and he let out a choked sound as I ripped the gold and venom from his veins. It splashed across my dress, stinging my hands. His eyes shot open, and he gasped down a loud breath, sitting up.

I withdrew my hands, palms blistered, nails split, fingers so cramped I could hardly move them. But I needed that kind of pain, I clung to it because it was so much better than being dead.

Wenshu touched the wound on his neck with a trembling hand, looking from the dried blood to my face. "Are you all right?" he said.

I looked down at my blistered hands. My muscles still twitched as if shot through with lightning, and the dunes still swayed unsteadily in the distance, making it hard to stay upright. But I knew what dying felt like, and this wasn't it.

"Yes," I said. "You?"

Wenshu blinked hard, cuffing drool and sand from his lips. "I think so," he said. Then his unfocused gaze finally settled on me. "I think it's safe to say that man was not your father's friend."

I laughed, a single sharp sound, too weak even to my own ears. Durian popped out of my bag and hopped across the sand, sitting down in my lap. I set my hand on top of him, but it trembled too hard to pet him.

"This is the part where you thank me for saving you and praise my quick thinking," I said, trying to smile even though my lips felt papery and cracked.

"Did you get the real map?" Wenshu said, ignoring me.

I reached for my bag, a few feet away from me in the sand, and pulled out the paper with shaking hands. "Of course."

"Then let's see it."

I placed it down in the sand, and together we leaned over the paper that the Sandstone Alchemist had tried to kill us to protect.

For a moment, we could do nothing but stare.

"This doesn't make sense," Wenshu said. "This isn't . . ." He shook his head. "What are we supposed to do with this?"

I took the wrong paper, I realized, my heart sinking. With a new wave of dizziness, I worried that maybe the venom would kill me after all, if the shame didn't. The paper below us wasn't a map at all, but a single sentence penned in shimmering ink.

The dragon's white eye, the faceless night,
The song of silver, the serpent's bite,
The child of Heaven, the scarlet-winged tree,
Together at last, the shadow makes three.

"A poem?" Wenshu said, frowning.

I shook my head, hands tracing the silvery ink. "The Sandstone Alchemist wouldn't hide a poem. This looks like a very old transformation."

The Moon Alchemist had taught me that when alchemy was a new science, when even basic transformations had yet to be discovered, alchemists would encode their transformations so that other alchemists couldn't steal them and present them to the Emperor as their own.

I turned to Wenshu. "*You're* the literature scholar. What does it mean?"

"I studied Confucianism, not poetry," he said, frowning. "Surely it's referencing alchemy stones in some way. Shouldn't *you* know what it means, Miss Royal Alchemist?"

"I don't use dragon eyeballs for transformations," I said, rubbing cold sweat from my forehead. Even if we figured out what it meant, what good would it do? We needed a map to Penglai Island, not another alchemical weapon. Still, part of me wondered what the Sandstone Alchemist possibly could have prized more than a map to Penglai. Surely this transformation could rend the world in half, dry out the oceans, or flatten mountain peaks.

"Well, it's not as if we can go back and look around again," Wenshu said, glancing to the sand where the trapdoor had been. "Let's just get as far as we can before he realizes what's missing. There must be another map somewhere."

I doubted it, but I wasn't keen on having my veins ripped open from venom twice in one day. We helped each other to our feet, stumbling to the outskirts of the desert. I cast a glance over my shoulder at the shifting sand dunes that had already erased our footprints.

This had been our only lead.

Penglai Island was difficult to research because most people didn't believe it was real. Even my father had scarcely written anything about it, other than his intention to find it. The more time we spent withering away in the desert, the more it seemed that Penglai Island was nothing but a lost dream that had swallowed my father whole in his desperation, and now had come to devour me as well.

But I would rather have been lost in a dream than head back to Chang'an and pretend to be part of the royal court again. Even if I hadn't sworn to bring the others back, I'd already noticed certain . . . complications to cramming my cousins' souls into the wrong bodies.

Night was falling quickly, the desert temperatures dropping, frigid wind blowing straight through our thin silk robes. Durian kept up a constant song of peeps from inside my bag, probably hungry by now, but he'd already eaten through the stash of bugs and grass I'd packed, and I had nothing else to feed him.

We followed a distant light until we arrived shivering at a small outskirt village. We'd entered the desert near Lanzhou, but after navigating the Sandstone Alchemist's tunnels, I had no idea where we'd ended up.

The village had only bamboo stakes instead of clay walls, the buildings thatched together with thin sticks. Goats with twisted horns meandered out across the dusty plains, gnawing at wild onion flowers striped white and purple. Some of the store signs were written in Arabic script in bright gold, a more common custom along the western borders.

As we drew closer, the goats limped toward us, bleating and nudging their horns at our legs. The sand turned to gray dirt, tracked with deep footprints, splattered with rusty brown stains. We passed through the bamboo gates and entered an empty village where wind sighed between the slats of the thatched houses, our every footstep shatteringly loud.

More and more villages were becoming ghost towns, ever since Yufei had eliminated life gold.

None of us had thought the aristocrats would be pleased that they could no longer buy eternal youth made from the blood of peasants, but we hadn't anticipated the lengths they'd go to just to keep their life gold.

In the last few weeks, the wealthy had begun hiring private armies to ravage every city and village they could find, kidnapping aspiring alchemists and jailing them until they agreed to make life gold. It didn't matter that the Empress had killed every alchemist who knew how to make it. Everyone but me.

The things you want are only childish dreams, the Moon Alchemist had warned me. It had seemed so simple back then: life gold is made from the blood of unwilling peasants, so we can't produce it anymore. But abolishing it hadn't created peace. It had only created more bloodshed. Now innocent people were dying to protect their alchemists, and alchemists were being tortured in jail.

This was yet another town stripped bare by private armies—I could tell from the shattered doors and crumbling fences, walls splashed with blood, hungry and untended livestock.

Well done, Scarlet, I could imagine the Empress saying. *This is the new world that you lost everything for.*

I told myself that this was part of razing the world and starting again. You couldn't build a new dream on shaky old foundations, after all. This country would have to pay before we could rebuild. That was the hope I had to cling to.

Something struck the side of my face.

I whirled around, only to see an old man slumped against a wall, a small pile of rocks in his lap. His clothing was torn, scraps bound around bloody limbs as if barely holding the pieces of him together. He shouted something at me in a dialect I didn't understand. When I didn't respond, he threw another rock, which I swatted away. Why was anyone left in this corpse of a village?

The old man turned his head to the side, shouting something at the broken window behind him. A younger man appeared, wearing an embroidered cap, clutching a knife in one hand. The older man pointed at us, and the younger man turned to glare.

"We're just looking for a place to sleep," I said in Chang'an dialect.

"Not here," the younger man said, his words accented but

close enough to Chang'an's dialect that I could understand. "There's nothing left for you to take."

"Take?" Wenshu said.

The man's gaze raked up and down our clothes, the wind blowing back my white cloak to reveal the silk dress underneath. "You can't fool me. You're rich people from the capital," he said.

I barely held back a laugh. I'd been treated like a peasant while in Chang'an, but apparently I passed for a true northern aristocrat now. I didn't know which was worse.

"We're not from the capital," Wenshu said, stepping forward before I could speak.

This was another thing we made sure everyone knew, because everyone in the country was looking for us.

The last alchemist who could make life gold and the last heir to the throne of a crumbling kingdom. They would torture both of us until "the prince" permitted the production of life gold, or until I taught the other alchemists how to make it.

"My cousin and I are scholars from Lingnan," Wenshu said.

I hated to hear him call me his cousin and not sister, but with him borrowing the prince's body, we looked even less alike than before. "We came to Chang'an to study, but our ward was burned in the raids. We only want somewhere to sleep."

The older man said something to the younger man, who stepped around Wenshu, glaring at me.

"Your rings," he said.

I kept my expression still, fighting the urge to cross my arms and hide my rings, which would only look more suspicious. "Yes?"

"You think we don't know what alchemy rings look like?" he said. "You're an alchemist."

"I'm not," I said, too quickly.

"So the two of you survived in the desert and managed to crawl here from Chang'an on foot, without alchemy?" the man said.

More people peered from the broken windows of their houses now. It seemed the village wasn't as dead as we thought, only dormant, tricking travelers—or private armies—into walking away.

I doubted I could argue my way out of this one—the man was already convinced of what I was. I could have subdued him easily enough, but if I did, we certainly wouldn't be able to sleep here. That was, unless I also killed every survivor we came across. But I'd hurt enough people with my mistakes. I would rather stay out in the desert and pray I didn't become viper food in my sleep.

"We don't want any trouble," Wenshu said.

"And we don't need any more alchemists here," the man said, stepping forward.

"She's not an alchemist," said a voice somewhere behind me.

The three of us turned around.

A young man leaned against a withered tree, arms crossed. His coppery, sun-scorched hair fell in his eyes, tossed and twisted from the desert wind. Sun had turned his bare shoulders and forearms golden, but also stolen the color from his clothes, now only an echo of what I guessed had once been blue and green and yellow.

"I met her the last time I was in the city," he said, smiling at me. "She's just an aristocrat's daughter running away from an arranged marriage."

I carefully controlled my expression before responding. I was certain I didn't know this man, which meant he was lying for me. People only lied for others if they cared for them, or they wanted something in return.

I glanced at Wenshu, whose skin was still tinged gray from the remnants of venom, his hands trembling beneath his long sleeves. As far out as I could see on the horizon, there were no other villages, and the temperature was dropping swiftly. This place was our only hope of resting tonight.

"I'm running away from my father," I said at last, dropping my gaze as if ashamed. "He's already sent people after me twice."

The first man sighed, mumbling something to the old man on the ground.

"Fine," he said to the man by the tree. "They're your problem, Junyi." Then he turned to Wenshu. "You want to stay? Help us skin a goat for tonight."

"I don't know how to do that," Wenshu said, his voice wavering as he backed up into me. But that, like everything else about us, was a lie. Wenshu had once chopped up a man and shoved his severed limbs into a pillowcase. But he wasn't supposed to be Fan Wenshu the merchant's son coated up to his elbows in blood, he was a rich boy running away from Chang'an.

"We'll teach you, pretty boy," the man said, waving for Wenshu to follow him back out into the fields of onion flowers.

I didn't want to be separated, but normal rich girls didn't typically volunteer to help skin goats. They got their meals already skinned and cooked, arranged on golden dishes with fresh scallions and daylilies.

"I'll show you where you can stay," the man—Junyi—said to me.

I cast Wenshu a quick glance before turning and following Junyi. For now, this was as much good fortune as we could hope for—the armies were unlikely to come through a village they'd already raided, and we would have shelter and food for the night.

Junyi led me farther back into the desecrated village, into

a clay house with no door, scattered sticks and boards leaning against the front wall as if they'd been torn away. There was only one window on the western wall of the house, no doubt to keep out the rays of the setting sun. The tiled floor glowed warmly around my ankles, still clinging to the heat of the afternoon.

"What do you want?" I said, the moment I stepped inside. "Money?"

Junyi laughed, reaching for a pot on a high shelf, twisting in a way that would definitely injure his back if he wasn't careful. What kind of farm boy could be so reckless? "There are more important things than money," he said, setting the pot unevenly across the stove.

"Hardly," I said, frowning as he lifted a bucket of water from the floor and struggled to pour it into the pot. He set the bucket down heavily, water splashing over the sides, then tried to strike a match by rubbing it too slowly against his sleeve.

"You're going to set yourself on fire," I said, stepping forward and grabbing the bag of matches from him. I struck one against the clay front of the stove, tossing it into the woodpile, where it caught fire at once. I shoved the pot back to the center of the stove for good measure. "Have you never made tea before?"

He laughed stiffly, tossing two tea cakes into the pot, which was more than necessary for two people. "Forgive me for being a bit nervous in front of a royal alchemist," he said.

I drew back against the wall, one hand in my satchel. *There it is*, I thought. He probably wanted me to make life gold for him and keep it a secret from the rest of his village. "I'm not—"

"Do you really think no one knows who you are?" he said, breaking up the tea cakes with a wooden spoon. "The only surviving alchemist of the massacre, the hùnxiě girl from the south, tall like silver grass. You're kind of hard to miss."

"Then you should know that I could kill you easily," I said. I didn't exactly want to get kicked out of this village for murder, but I wasn't about to let a stranger push me around just for a couple hours' rest either.

The man didn't even turn around, staring into the water that was slowly starting to steam. "Of course," he said, "but you wouldn't do that. You don't kill people without a reason."

"Not wanting to be turned over to a private army is a pretty good reason," I said.

"What, those peasant boys with borrowed swords?" Junyi said, rolling his eyes. "Why would I waste you like that?"

He slammed two cups on the table, ladling murky water into them. He hadn't let the tea steep for nearly long enough. It was such an unimportant detail, but something about it only amplified the sense of wrongness that surrounded him. Something about Junyi made me feel like I was one foot into a dream. Someone who had grown up in this village should have known how to lift heavy objects, how to strike matches, how to make tea, but he seemed more like one of the clueless aristocrats I'd met in the capital. I kept my back to the wall, hand still clenched inside my satchel.

"Is there a problem, Scarlet?" he said. Something in his words paralyzed me far worse than viper venom.

"Don't call me that," I said.

"Pardon," he said, nudging the cup closer to me and taking a deliberate sip of his own. "Not poison, I promise. Come on, there isn't much water out here, and I've used some of it just for you."

Stiffly, I stepped closer and knelt in front of the table, picking up the lukewarm teacup but not drinking it.

Junyi took another sip, staring past me out the window at the empty paths. "My village is gone," he said, his voice low. "My mother used to do all of *this*." He gestured to the teacups. "So I'm sorry if I seem . . . unpracticed, but I never thought I'd have to learn, and then it was too late."

My fist unclenched in my satchel. I supposed that made sense. Maybe I was too used to looking for danger everywhere I turned. I laid my hands in my lap, staring at my reflection in the teacup. Did he know this village had been destroyed because of me?

"You're all that's left of the best alchemists in the country," Junyi said. "You're going to stop the private armies, aren't you?"

I looked away, his gaze too earnest. "It will take time," I said. "I'm not fighting armies single-handedly."

In truth, I no longer trusted myself to devise political schemes. Just plotting one person's death had wiped out nearly everyone in the palace. There was no way I could defeat several private armies all at once with only me and my brother. I needed the other royal alchemists with me, but their souls were still trapped in the river plane.

They were trained resurrection alchemists, so they knew to stay by the river as long as they could, to wait for someone to bring them back. But the river plane had a way of scrubbing your mind clean until your life was nothing but a hazy dream. They couldn't wait for me forever—soon they wouldn't remember why they were waiting at all.

Junyi leaned closer across the table, shifting out of the shadows of the shelves. The setting sunlight caught his eyes, a deep and warm brown with tiny—almost imperceptible—flecks of gold.

"How will you do it?" he said. The words were a reverent whisper, as if the question was a dark secret.

I thought of the Sandstone Alchemist nearly killing me for

mentioning Penglai Island. I certainly wasn't going to broach the subject with a villager I'd just met.

"You don't need to know that," I said.

"Tell me, and I can help you," he said. "I'm strong. Surely I'm more useful to you than that cottonweed trailing after you."

"That's my cousin," I said, frowning.

Junyi went still, hands tight around his teacup. "Your cousin?" he said. "Not the Crown Prince?"

I clasped my hands under the table, regretting my words. I hadn't thought any villager this far from the capital would recognize the prince's face.

"How interesting," Junyi said, leaning back. "And what have you done with the prince?"

"I haven't done anything to him," I said, standing up. But the man stood up at the same time, casting a dark shadow over me.

"Yet you're dragging his body around with you as a . . . souvenir? A memento?"

I turned for the doorway, but Junyi got there first, blocking my path.

"Move," I said. "I'm not here to hurt you."

"Oh, I get it," Junyi said, ignoring me. He tilted his head to the side, inspecting me. "You're going to resurrect him, aren't you?"

I drew my knife from my sleeve, pointing it at the man's throat. He didn't move at first, as if he doubted I'd actually use it, but I drove my elbow into his sternum and backed him up against the shelves, the blade digging into his skin and drawing a whisper of blood that trickled down his throat.

"Resurrect him?" I said. "Who said the Crown Prince was dead?"

But the man's sharp smile only widened, and then I was certain that this was not a normal boy raised in a desert village.

As far as the public knew, the palace massacre had been nothing more than a failed coup. All the royal alchemists had sacrificed their lives protecting the House of Li, and Emperor Gaozong had tragically died from his illness during all the chaos. Officially, Empress Wu and the Crown Prince were alive and well. How could they not be, when their bodies were so clearly walking around the palace?

There were only four people besides me who knew that the prince had actually died that day.

My siblings, who had borrowed the royal family's bodies.

Zheng Sili, the alchemist who'd tried to resurrect the Empress—last I'd heard, he'd run home to Guangdong, and this certainly wasn't him.

And of course, the Empress herself.

The man who called himself Junyi seized my wrist, but I held tight, digging the blade harder into his throat in warning.

That was when I saw it.

His sleeve slid up as he gripped my wrist, revealing two jagged characters branded into his forearm.

Wu Zhao.
The Empress.

CHAPTER THREE

My gaze locked with Junyi's, and for a moment, the walls of the sunbaked clay hut fell away. The harshness of the desert sun dissolved, replaced by frigid golden tiles, a throne room soaked with blood, pale sunlight cast across me in sharp diamonds through the elaborate lattice windows. I would know those eyes anywhere, even if the face had changed.

"Who said the Crown Prince was dead?" I said again, leaning into my knife, a desperate edge to my words.

"No one had to say anything, Scarlet," Junyi said, his smile glass-sharp. "I was the one who killed him, after all."

Then the Empress's grip tightened on my wrist. She shoved my blade away, and I couldn't even think to fight back, could barely even breathe. I had killed the Empress, ripped her throat out with my teeth. What kind of monster would have resurrected her? If she still lived, then everyone had died for nothing.

"You're creative, Scarlet, I'll give you that much," the Empress said, releasing me and crossing her arms. Her expression shifted, no longer the weathered and determined face of a villager who'd lost everything, but the proud glare of someone who owned the entire world.

I shook my head. "You're—"

"I've thought about it a lot, you know," she said. "The fact that you surprised me. There's very little that I don't foresee. In another life, maybe you could have been my adviser."

I couldn't bring myself to move, my feet rooted to the ground. *I'm dreaming,* I thought. *I dream about the Empress all the time. This is nothing new.*

"But the more I think about it, the more I realize that you couldn't possibly have planned all this," she said. She raised one hand to cup my cheek, her touch searing. "You couldn't have known what necklace I would wear, or that the pearls would roll in front of you. All that happened is you got very, very, lucky. Isn't that right?"

I tried to form words, but the Empress's touch was stronger than any venom. Distantly, I was aware of the knife sliding from my limp hand, clattering to the floor.

"You're not a great alchemist, are you?" she said, thumb caressing my cheek. "You were just struck with dumb luck and seized your chance. Good for you, Scarlet. Fate favored you this once. But victory is not a single moment."

The Empress leaned closer, and her next words came as warm desert winds whispered across my face, lips a breath from mine, speaking into me, through me. "This kingdom belongs to me," she said. "I earned it. I will die a thousand times before I let you take it from me."

Her grip tightened on my face, and something about the sting of her nails piercing through my skin shocked me awake. I took a step back.

"Then I'll kill you a thousand times," I said. "China belongs to Hong, not you."

The Empress's eyes widened, then she let out a sharp laugh. I kept talking, afraid I'd lose confidence at the Empress's next words.

"I don't know why you bothered borrowing a *peasant's* body," I said, "but you know as well as I do that you have no authority in any body but your own. No one will obey a farmer from Lanzhou who claims to be the Empress."

The Empress rolled her eyes and applauded melodramatically. "Well done, Scarlet. You could have been a first-tier scholar with that deduction. Luckily, I know for a fact that my body was one of the few that you didn't feed to pearl monsters. Shame about your friends, though."

My mind flashed to Yufei, alone in the palace. Wenshu had made sure she was surrounded by a ridiculous number of guards and made her swear not to leave the palace, but it was hard to dissuade Yufei from doing what she wanted, no matter how risky.

"You're not getting your body back," I said.

I pulled my second knife from my left sleeve and tightened my grip on it. The Empress wasn't worth wasting my last few stones on, and I doubted she knew much about hand-to-hand combat. I struck at her throat, but she dodged and wrenched my arm behind my back, forcing me to the floor. Even with no real skill in fighting, the Empress was wearing the muscled body of someone who worked in hot fields, taller and heavier than me, and she crushed me into the floor easily.

"You're not going to kill me," I said, as her weathered hands crushed my face into the tiles. "You still need someone to make life gold." *And deliver you my sister's body,* I thought, but didn't want to say it out loud in case she didn't actually know that Yufei was currently wearing her corpse like a dress.

"I'm not going to kill you *yet*," the Empress agreed, pulling my hair back and running a delicate finger across my throat, as if imagining all the blood that could spill.

I leaned down and bit her fingers.

I'd meant to snap them clean off, but only managed to break skin before her other hand yanked my hair and forced me away. I reached for my knife, which had skittered into the corner. The Empress lunged for me but froze as I pointed my blade between her eyes.

"Nine hundred and ninety-nine to go," I said.

She let out a sharp laugh. "Go ahead and kill me," she said. "Add me to your death toll, Scarlet. Along with all your friends."

My hand trembled around the blade, but I tightened my grip, determined not to show the Empress that her words could hurt me.

"You think this is the only body I have?" she went on.

I froze, my gaze dropping to the soul tag on her wrist. "You can't be resurrected into more than one body at once."

"*You* can't," the Empress said, a dark smile twisting Junyi's features.

I should have asked more questions, but she was leaning forward, brushing my blade away, and I couldn't stand the thought of her hands on me again.

I slammed my knife into the soul tag on her wrist, pinning her to the floor.

With a sharp gasp, her muscles tensed. Then her eyes went gray and she fell over limp in the dirt. Her robes had come untied in the fighting and loosened enough that I could see a wound in Junyi's stomach, crisp with dried blood. He must have died recently, probably in the raids.

Someone had come through this village and resurrected him for the Empress. But who?

I ripped my blade out of his arm, wiping it clear on a nearby rag. My white outer robe was stained with blood, so I balled it up and shoved it into my bag, even though it left my arms bare. Durian peeped in protest from under the fabric.

I stumbled back into the main road, retracing my path with numb feet until I found Wenshu, one hand covering his mouth as the other villagers skinned one of the desert goats.

"We're leaving," I said in Guangzhou dialect.

"What?" Wenshu said through his hand. "I helped kill a goat, and now you—"

"*Now*," I said, grabbing his arm. He clamped his mouth shut and followed me past the bewildered villagers.

"We have a problem," I said, as we walked back out into the lonely desert, the cold and borderless sea. "The Empress is back."

We walked all night across the silent desert, dunes painted gray and blue by nightfall. We didn't dare stop walking, for we needed to keep warm. My mind still hummed like it was full of sand flies as I remembered the Empress's eyes. Even wearing another's face, her gaze had held the same knife's edge of cruelty.

I didn't often feel dead, but at times like this, my mind was so loud and my bones so numb—the Empress had that effect on me, stripping away the colors from the world, the warmth from the sky. I thought of the faces of my friends, of Hong, of my cousins, whose real faces I hadn't seen in so long. All of them had died so that the Empress's reign could end. If she was still here, then they'd died for nothing at all.

She'd named me the Scarlet Alchemist, and now it no

longer felt like an honor but just another one of the Empress's cruel jokes. Because when it was over, I'd stood alone in a palace drenched in blood, having destroyed everything while the Empress laughed.

The memory of her voice kept me awake as the hours wore on, even when I could hardly feel my limbs anymore.

We arrived back in Lanzhou when the sky burst orange across the horizon. Wenshu was so tired he probably would have given the innkeeper all the money we had left in exchange for a few feet of empty floor to lie down on, so I took the coin purse from his pocket and called the innkeeper myself.

After a moment, he came out from behind a curtain and said something in Lanyin.

"Do you speak the capital dialect?" I said, putting down a few coins so he would understand my purpose if not my words.

He glanced at the coins, then looked between me and Wenshu. "Visitors from the capital?" he said in Chang'an dialect, already swiping my coins off the counter.

"Not from the capital, just passing through," I said, eyeing Wenshu warily where he was falling asleep leaning against a wall. "Do you have any rooms?"

"I have nothing but rooms," the innkeeper said. "You're about the only people heading this far north right now. Everyone else is going the other way."

"Where are they going?" I said.

"Chang'an," the innkeeper said, marking something on a sheet of paper and fishing a key out of a drawer. "Some sort of commotion at the palace."

"*Commotion?*" I said too loudly, startling Wenshu awake. "Why is there a commotion?"

The innkeeper shrugged, holding out a key. "My guess is it's something to do with another private army," he said. "You want the room or not?"

I thanked him and took the key, grabbing Wenshu by the arm and leading him upstairs. I didn't like the thought of a large private army congregating in Chang'an. It was one thing when local uprisings tried to draw out their own alchemists, but clearly someone wanted more manpower than what they could find in Chang'an alone.

There was little I could do about it from here. I could write to Yufei, but had no return address to give her, so there hardly seemed to be a point. I would have to trust that she was safe with her army behind the palace walls, and finish up this business with Penglai as quickly as possible so we could return to her.

I unlocked the door to a small room and found a single set of blankets folded up in the corner. Wenshu shook one out and checked it for bugs, then spread it on the ground and dropped onto it, face-first. I threw another blanket over the lattice window, blocking out the morning sun. I set Durian down on a windowsill, where he started pecking at a spider.

"I need to do something before you sleep," I said, tugging at the corner of Wenshu's blanket with my foot.

Wenshu groaned, brushing his hair back and exposing his scar as I knelt down beside him.

"Can't I sleep while you do it?" he said into the blanket.

"It might be fine, or you might never wake up again," I said, shrugging. "Your choice."

He grumbled something indecipherable. "Just hurry up. I've lost enough sleep because of your stupid boyfriend."

I knelt down and brushed a few more strands of his hair back, running my fingers over the glossy, gnarled skin.

範
文
書

Fan Wenshu.

Weeks ago, I'd carved the name onto the prince's body to bind Wenshu inside of it. The wound had healed, leaving raised pink scar tissue that didn't show any signs of fading. Wenshu had yelled at me the first time he saw it, saying, *Your handwriting is so bad that you almost resurrected someone named Fan Wénhùa!*

The fact that I'd been half dead at the time wasn't a good enough excuse for him, and he'd forced me to practice my stroke order until he was satisfied I wouldn't bind strangers to his dead body in the future.

I chose not to remind him that he was the one who taught me to write in the first place. I sensed that my handwriting bothered him far less than the realization that I'd chosen him over the prince.

Fans were not accustomed to sentimentality. We were the children of merchants, who were the children of farmers, who were the children of slaves. Sentimentality was for royal court poets and painters who could stare in longing at the night sky and contemplate the depths of their love, render their feelings in sumac tree sap and silk canvases. None of us knew how to accept grand gestures of love, because we simply didn't need them. We loved as we poured our uneaten soup into each other's bowls, as we stood in the sun to let the other rest in the shade.

But what I had done for Wenshu went far beyond that, and I was sure he knew it. I was equally sure that it was the only reason he was entertaining ideas of a mythical island on my behalf.

Whatever his reasons, he was here with me now, and I wanted to finish this up before he lost patience.

I steadied my breath, fingers pressing into the scar, and closed my eyes.

The sounds of the river rose slowly. At first, there was only a distant whisper of rushing water, its coolness numbing my fingertips where they touched my brother's scar. Then the water began rushing faster, its roar wiping away the sounds of the road just beyond our window and the low voices beneath the floorboards until there was nothing but the river's song.

When at last I felt the tepid water around my bare feet, I opened my eyes to the blank cage of sky above me.

I was standing in the in-between plane, where the world was only bones and darkness and qi—the life inside all of us that could fuel your alchemy if you only knew how to listen to it. I stood before the river of my brother's life, the dark waters of his qi rushing unstopped past my feet.

Back in Guangzhou, I'd made a living by unstopping the dams that blocked the flow of qi in the rivers of the dead. I'd dragged their souls back to the plane of the living like a deep-sea fisherman wrenching monsters back to the surface, even if they were never meant to see the sun. I hadn't cared for the consequences, only for the gold that their families paid me.

You shouldn't be here, the river said to me, as it did every time, the words an echo that hummed through my bones.

But I had already broken enough rules to send me to hell for all of eternity, and I wasn't going to start listening now.

I stood up straight, turning away from my brother's river and looking out across the shadowed tree line, the prickly leaves and stark white trunks like an army of ghosts daring me to pass through.

I closed my eyes and walked forward.

The trees parted for me as I passed, the edges of their leaves knife-sharp, scoring my face. The parched earth crunched and shattered beneath my feet as if I was walking over a bed of glass.

It didn't matter where I walked, because this plane answered to no map or compass or north star. Desire was what guided you onward, deeper into its maw.

Li Hong, I thought, repeating his name a thousand times in my mind, picturing the characters painted across the sky in gold.

I thought of the way he'd looked at me when he'd mapped every inch of my skin, tried to forge me into a treasured memory. I thought of the smile on his lips when he saw me, how it was so much brighter than the smile he gave other members of the court when he had to play the role of Crown Prince. And I thought of the pleading look he gave me right before the Empress slit his throat. That last memory always devoured the others—his eyes round with surprise, the black chasm of his pupils yawning wider until I knew he could see nothing at all.

With that thought, the forest pulled me in with urgency, the ground sloping downward, forcing me to run faster, until at last, the earth leveled out. I let out a deep breath as the night unlatched its jaw, releasing me. Slowly, I opened my eyes.

Hong was sleeping against a tree by the riverbank. He wore the same robes he'd died in, but their purple shade had grown fainter and they were splattered with mud. He did not breathe in this plane, his form so still that he resembled a painting.

I stepped closer, but my footsteps did not wake him. His mind was somewhere else completely.

The rope I'd fastened to his left wrist had come loose, revealing raw pink skin, the slack rope bundled in his lap. I'd tied the other end to the strongest branch of the tree, and now the bark was flaking away beneath the knot. *How hard has he been pulling at the rope while I was away?*

Hong was not an alchemist trained to understand the river plane, the way its words could infect your blood, the way it could pull you worlds away if your thoughts wandered too far. He had never taught his mind to withstand that kind of pressure.

Most of the dead lingered here for a week or so, clinging to latent memories in the scant drops of water from the riverbeds of their lives, clawing at the impenetrable dam that had sealed off the flow of qi. Eventually, they gave up and they wandered into the forest, where the darkness ate them whole.

I didn't know what happened next, but I knew that I didn't want Hong to go there.

It had been about four weeks since he'd died, and by all accounts, his soul should have been long gone. It would have been, if I hadn't tethered him here.

I pulled out three moonstones, healing the torn skin of his wrist, then whispered an apology as I tightened the rope once more.

He jolted awake, yanking his wrist away and grabbing on to the low branches of the tree as if trying to anchor himself in a typhoon. For a moment, he seemed not to see me at all, his eyes a flat plane of black, like the nothingness that awaited beyond the tree line.

"Hong," I said quietly, still kneeling in the dirt, afraid to make any sudden movements.

His gaze settled on me, his expression unchanged, and I wondered if today was the day when the darkness ate so much of him that he forgot who I was.

But then, slowly, like a flower unfurling in the early morning, the darkness left his eyes. He released the branch, a soft smile spreading across his face.

"Zilan," he said, the word echoing as if spoken inside an immense cavern. Everything about him looked faint and far away.

He held out a hand, and I let him pull me to my feet, even though the touch of his skin spread stinging cold through my fingers. He kissed me, his lips numbing mine, like I'd kissed a block of ice.

Every day, he felt a little bit colder, a little bit farther away. Souls weren't meant to linger in this plane for long. They could rot just like bodies, become echoes of themselves. More than anything, I feared that one day I would come to find him and would only see the tree, the rope snapped, his soul too far gone for me to call back.

"How do you feel?" I asked.

He hummed in thought, the sound like a low vibration of a zither string. "I'm not sure," he said after a moment. "A bit like I'm dreaming, to be honest. But there are worse places to be than in a dream, I suppose."

I said nothing, sitting down on a patch of dry grass and gesturing for him to sit beside me. He looked like a sheet of silk the wind might carry away. I needed him anchored to me.

I pressed my face to his chest and listened to the cavernous silence where his heartbeat should have been, his cold hands around me while I told him about the Sandstone Alchemist and the strange transformation we'd found.

I didn't tell him about the Empress. Not yet. He had died thinking it meant she would die as well, and I worried that his soul would decay even faster if he learned it had all been for nothing. He had foolishly believed in me, even when I was nothing but a míngqì merchant in Guangzhou. He saw me as a hero, a savior of the poor. What would he think if he knew the truth?

"We never even found the map," I said, tipping my head back against his shoulder, staring at the white sky. "I nearly died, and I have no idea where to look next."

"Why would he go to such lengths to protect a transformation?" Hong said.

I shrugged. "It must create something important, but it's useless if I don't know what it is. You can't do alchemy without intention. Besides, I don't even know where to start. What is *the dragon's white eye* supposed to mean? Am I supposed to find a dragon and scoop its eyes out?"

Hong laughed, but the sound felt far away. "Have you asked the Moon Alchemist what she thinks?" he said.

I turned, looking up at him. He had eaten gold up until his death, so his eyes still held tiny constellations of gold flecks, the brightest light in the dark sameness of this plane.

"She's gone," I said quietly.

He blinked hard, shaking his head as if clearing his thoughts. When he opened his eyes again, they were dimmer. "Sorry, I . . . I forgot."

I took his hand, lacing our fingers together, ignoring the biting cold.

Sometimes, it became all too clear that his soul was slipping away the longer he stayed here. His mind was a threadbare blanket, holes growing wider. At times, he murmured words that made sense on their own but were nonsense when strung together. His touch was already painfully cold, and each day it felt lighter, gentler, as if he could hardly touch me at all.

I looked into his gray eyes, and a question burned at my lips, but I could never voice it because I couldn't bear to hear the answer.

Do you forgive me for not choosing you?

With only one dead body left whole in the palace, I'd had to choose between the prince and my brother. I hadn't known which one I was going to choose when I entered the river of souls. But desire guided you in this plane, and when I found my brother's body on the riverbank and felt relief instead of regret, I'd known that was the only choice I could have made. He was my family.

But I still loved the prince, no matter how unfair it was to ask for love in return after leaving him here.

"I'm going to bring you back," I said, the words a quiet promise whispered into his collarbone.

"I know," he said. "I've never once doubted you, Empress."

I grimaced at the nickname, gently pushing his shoulder until he leaned back against the tree again, and I leaned against him so he couldn't see my face. I knew that for him, the name was a promise that he would return, that we would be married and I would be his empress consort. He'd promised to marry me on the day he died, and that was the one thing he hadn't seemed to forget even as the rest of his mind dissolved. To me, the name could only conjure images of gold eyes, of the woman who'd burned my cousins alive and slit Hong's throat. But I couldn't take away that small piece of hope from him, no matter how unsettled it made me.

"You're afraid," he said, his cold palm resting over my chest, my heartbeat that felt mockingly loud.

"I'm just tired," I said, because my fears weren't the prince's problem. I didn't need him to worry about me, I only needed him to stay.

"Rest here with me," he said, leaning back against the tree.

I shook my head, already standing up, untangling his frozen limbs from mine.

"Wenshu Ge wants to rest too," I said, looking away. "He can't do that if I'm down here."

Hong nodded. "He's taking good care of my body, isn't he?" he said. I was sure he meant it as a joke, but I could sense the worry in his tone.

"Aside from the viper venom, yes," I said. "He's so vain now, always brushing his hair. I think you might have to wrestle it back from him, when the time comes."

"I look forward to that day," he said. "Zilan—"

"Don't," I said, holding up a hand to stop his next words.

I would never let him say goodbye to me.

As long as he never did, we always had unfinished business. He would cling to the rope, waiting for me to return. He would never leave me without saying goodbye.

"I'll be right back," is what I always said instead.

"I'll be here," he said. "Always. For as long as it takes."

He did not kiss me goodbye, only gave me a small, sad wave.

It felt so unfair that I could turn my back on him and return to the land of the living while he stayed trapped in the dark, rotting.

It won't be like this forever, I told myself, and that was the only way I could bear to leave. *I'm going to bring him back.*

I walked through the forest, wanting a moment in the stillness of the night before heading back to Wenshu, who I was sure would notice the tears blurring my vision. The branches parted as I strode through them, releasing me into a pale, dark night, the moon a perfect crescent overhead.

I turned my face up to the sky, leaning against a tree. The

clouds parted and a cool wash of moonlight spilled across my face. At times, I imagined the Moon Alchemist reaching up and taking the moon from the dark sky as easily as plucking a soft peach from one of the trees that lined the streets of Chang'an.

Have you asked the Moon Alchemist what she thinks? Hong had said, as if I could simply knock on her door.

Even for a resurrection alchemist, it wasn't that simple.

I'd dropped by the rivers of the other royal alchemists just long enough to make sure they hadn't dried up completely, but I hadn't stopped to talk to anyone but the River Alchemist, too afraid of what they'd say. I could still see the flare of hate in the Paper Alchemist's eyes when she realized that everyone was dying because of me. Maybe hiding from her now made me a coward, but the next time I saw her, I wanted it to be with the elixir of life in hand, ready to escort her back to the land of the living.

I had never tried to find the Moon Alchemist's river. She had wanted to die, so she'd probably walked off into the forest the moment she'd set foot here, and I couldn't bear to see the parched dirt of her riverbed where her life had once been.

"What's the answer?" I whispered to the brilliant white moon, wishing she could hear me. "You'd know. You knew everything."

But the silent sky didn't answer me. She was dead because of me, and she would never answer any of my questions again. The Moon Alchemist was not in the sky, or on the moon, but torn to pieces in a muddy pit. I would have to figure out the transformation on my own.

The dragon's white eye, I thought, remembering the words scratched in ancient script across the parchment.

The words itched at the back of my mind, like scars of a

distant dream carved into my brain. I'd heard them before, but where?

Something tickled my hand, and I looked down at a tiny black orb-weaver, the kind that had always reminded me of the Moon Alchemist and her delicate, perfect sharpness.

She'd never appreciated the comparison.

I remembered studying in the palace, back before everything fell apart, when I'd watched an orb-weaver tickle across the low table covered in scrolls in the royal library, dancing over the beautiful, ancient calligraphy.

The Moon Alchemist's fist slammed down on top of it.

I lurched back. She wiped her hand clean with a cloth, scowling down at me.

"I left you here to study," she'd said.

I glanced down at the black stain where the spider had been, just below the character for *star*.

"I've been studying all day," I said.

"You were watching that spider for the last five minutes," the Moon Alchemist said. "I told you to study alchemy, not arachnids."

"These are all so old," I said, gesturing to the scrolls. "They don't make any sense to me. They don't even mention stones."

"They mention many stones. You just aren't reading close enough." The Moon Alchemist jerked a finger toward the words *western guard*.

"What guards the west?" she said.

I hesitated. "Soldiers?"

The Moon Alchemist rolled her eyes. "In mythology, Scarlet. Alchemists believed in gods back then."

Maybe the oldest alchemists had been raised to believe in gods, but in the golden age of alchemy, I certainly hadn't. Nor had learning about ancient history been a priority for a southern merchant girl. I only knew what I'd managed to glean since I'd come to Chang'an.

"The White Tiger?" I guessed, letting out a breath when the Moon Alchemist nodded.

"The White Tiger is associated with metals, so it's a white metalstone, such as . . ."

"Pearl?" I said hesitantly.

The Moon Alchemist smiled. The expression was so rare on her stony face. "Precisely," she said. She knelt down beside me, pointing to the next line. "And what about this one?" she said, her fingers hovering over the characters for *dragon's eye*.

I sucked in a sharp breath, the memory bleached away by the moonlight that now looked searingly white. I *had* talked about this with the Moon Alchemist. But trying to remember what came next was like reaching out into a thick wall of fog. I'd never been quite as good at rote memorization as Wenshu or Yufei, had only focused on remembering the most practical information, whatever would save me or help me win.

There were no other alchemists I could ask now, and all of the remaining alchemy scrolls were back in Chang'an, halfway across the country. I ground my teeth together, irrationally angry at the Moon Alchemist for always disappearing when I needed her the most. But of course, this was no one's fault but my own.

Have you tried asking the Moon Alchemist?

I swallowed, staring up at the canvas-white moon, a blank piece of paper. Maybe some echo of her presence remained at her river, some ghostly remains, anything. Maybe she knew I needed her and had held on. She always knew things, even before I could admit them to myself.

I realized, with a heavy pang in my chest, that I had never

learned her real name. Would I even be able to find her river?

But this plane was guided by desire, not semantics. She was always my moon, my teacher, the greatest alchemist of all time. She was the Moon Alchemist to *me*, and maybe that was enough.

I imagined brushstrokes against the papery white canvas of this moon at the bottom of the world, painting her name in the sky. Slowly, I began to walk deeper into the night.

CHAPTER FOUR

For a while, there was no pull at all, just the quiet murmurs of the forest, the cracked dirt beneath my bare feet, and the Moon Alchemist's name bright across the sky.

Please, I thought, tears burning at my eyes, cold as ice in the darkness. *I need you.*

All at once, the terrain shifted.

The wet dirt along the river turned to sharp rocks and grayed pine needles, spiny fish bones and white chrysanthemums with snapped stems—funeral flowers, soft beneath my feet.

The river expanded on both sides, opening up with a great sigh, wrapping around my ankles with coldness so biting that I stumbled to the side and tripped over pointed rocks. When I clambered back onto the riverbank, my footprints were oily crimson.

This was not what the Moon Alchemist's river should have looked like. She was long dead, and it should have been a weak stream at best, not a rushing river of grease and blood. Something was very wrong.

I walked along the sharp riverbank, an impenetrable line of

red pines on one side, the glassy river on the other, repeating the Moon Alchemist's name in my mind. But I couldn't sense her presence at all. If she had ever been here, she was long gone.

I drew to a stop, the blood on my feet running into the river, red swirling into the frigid water.

A hand closed around my throat.

Before I could react, I was face-first in the freezing water.

My cheek scraped against the sharp riverbed, my mouth flooded with ice, my open eyes searing with cold. I saw flashes of the red dirt walls of the western ward of Chang'an, the moon-bright surface of the alchemy compound, barrels of gold and trays full of blood.

This was the Moon Alchemist's river, I thought, *but whoever is here can't be the Moon Alchemist. She would never hurt me.*

I reached behind me, grabbing at silk robes, but couldn't break free from the grip that forced me down harder. I tasted the spice of qi, liquid gold on my lips.

I clawed at my assailant's face and wrenched myself back until I could gasp down a sharp breath of air. I tried to turn around, but their grip was firm, nails sharp against my throat. Another hand clasped my hair and shoved me back under water.

I tasted mud, my next breath knife-sharp as I choked on a mouthful of silt. The qi scalded my skin, a thousand tiny teeth devouring me. *Open your eyes*, it whispered.

I didn't like taking orders from disembodied sources of alchemy, but the sensation of cold water knifing up my nose was already fading away. My fingers traced over smooth wood, my feet pressed to solid ground, the smell of parchment and hot beeswax.

I opened my eyes.

I was back in the royal library, and the Moon Alchemist was standing over me, arms crossed. Her shadow contorted against the packed shelves full of scrolls behind her. We were in one of the study rooms in the royal library in Chang'an. I knew for a fact that this room had been destroyed by pearl monsters, that this could only be a memory.

"Think, Zilan," the Moon Alchemist said, jamming a finger into the scroll before me, the characters for *dragon's eye*. "We've talked about this before."

I shook my head—even if this was a memory, the Zilan from back then hadn't known the answer, and I certainly didn't know it now.

"That's not an acceptable answer for a royal alchemist," she said. "Should I go looking for that boy with a mustache? I bet he'd know."

"No," I said, closing my eyes, trying to push away all other thoughts. "I just need a minute. I need . . ." I trailed off, because my hands were sinking into the paper, the table turning to porridge beneath my palms. I realized too late that it was mud, and when I opened my mouth to speak, river water rushed down my throat.

I reeled back, my head smashing against someone's chin. Their grip on my hair loosened for only a moment before they pushed me back down again, the slap of cold water stinging my open eyes.

"*Well?*" the Moon Alchemist said.

The study was filling with water, a shallow pool of silt staining my skirts, but the Moon Alchemist seemed not to notice.

"Don't tell me you've never heard of the dragon kings," she said.

I picked up the teacup and emptied the rest of it into my mouth, but the tea only tasted like mud. Somewhere far away, I sensed the someone forcing me deeper into the water, the edges of the memory wavering, but I took a deep breath and tried with all my might to cling to it.

The dragon kings of the four seas were legendary weather gods who no one had believed in since the rise of alchemy. Auntie So had talked about them on occasion, but only as lost dreams from another world.

"The dragon kings are lords of the *seas*," I said carefully, "so *the dragon's eye* refers to a waterstone?"

The Moon Alchemist nodded. "Solve the problem like an alchemist," she said. "Find a theory and test it."

A sharp pain clamped at my throat. Water spilled past my lips and splattered over the parchment, but the Moon Alchemist didn't acknowledge it, so I gripped the edge of the table and kept talking, pressing my eyes closed.

"There's a golden fruit called dragon's eye," I said hesitantly, slowly recalling the words I'd once said in this other life, before everything had gone wrong. "Is gold—"

The Moon Alchemist shook her head. "Too obvious. Try again." When I didn't answer immediately, she sighed. "Dragons are pure yang energy, which means heat, light, courage."

I pinched at the fabric of my dress, desperately wanting not to disappoint her. The water had risen over my knees, sticks floating past me.

Most stones had either yin or yang energy, a power that was soft and dark or sharp and bright. Everything in the universe fell somewhere on that spectrum, but for alchemy stones, the strength of that energy mattered. Jade could have yin energy if its color was light and clear, but yang energy if its shade was dark. Both could be wielded by a skilled alchemist, but you needed to know what you were dealing with, how much power you held in your hands.

"If it's pure yang energy," I said slowly, the water spilling onto my lap, splashing onto the edge of the table, "it's potent and volatile. A waterstone that can be wielded for both destruction and creation, white like a dragon's eye."

The Moon Alchemist went very still, her eyes sharp and bright. "Such as?"

The hand on my neck ripped me from the water, slamming me back against crooked roots and jagged stones. I was staring up at the endless dark, the shadowed figure leaning over me dripping murky water onto my face.

I coughed, trying to sit up but feeling like a rotten piece of driftwood. A hand pressed down on my throat, the touch gentle now, almost reverent, but the threat of violence still clear.

"*This isn't your river!*" I said, shoving the hand away. "Leave the Moon Alchemist alone!"

The hood cast my assailant's face in shadows, but I could clearly see the two golden stars of their eyes.

Of course it was the Empress. I didn't know what she'd done to the Moon Alchemist's qi, but somehow she had bound her here against her will. The Empress never freed her alchemists, even in death. Once she chose you, you belonged to her forever. The Empress was probably keeping her around just to torture me, or maybe as a backup plan in case I wouldn't make her life gold.

I surged up and tried to grab her throat, scratch her eyes, anything at all. But her hand seized me, holding my wrist an inch from her face. The moonlight through the trees fell in strips across us both, as if slicing us into ribbons of alternating light and darkness.

As the moonlight fell over the Empress's hand, I stilled.

The hand closed tight around my wrist did not belong to the Empress.

It was too large, the knuckles too pronounced, veins too bright, nails too short. It looked more like the hand of an alchemist, nails split and knuckles bruised. I tried to peer past the shadows of the hood, but could see only darkness and gold.

I seized the sleeve, trying to yank the figure closer to me, but the person reared back, and I was left with nothing but a thin gold thread that had snagged on my ring.

The sight pulled me back to that morning, when I'd repaired the threads in Wenshu's sleeve.

Quit manhandling me, he'd said, while I pulled out three waterstones from underneath Durian. It was a stone with great healing properties, but also destructive ones, depending on your intentions. It was full of yang energy, bright white.

The dragon's white eye.

"*Opal*," I whispered.

The Moon Alchemist smiled. Her arms uncrossed, and in that moment I was certain she saw something more than a poor girl from the south who had stumbled her way into the palace through luck alone. She saw the Scarlet Alchemist, the girl who was supposed to save the kingdom.

"Well done," she said. "Now get back to work."

I opened my eyes.

This time, I was lying on my back on the cold floor of our room at the inn, staring up at the cracked ceiling. I clutched my throat as I choked down a sharp breath of hot desert air, melting away the stinging coldness.

I know what the first line means, I thought, regretting that I'd used up my last three opals on something as silly as patching up a coat. But opal was not a difficult stone to find. I might not have a map to Penglai, but at least I was one step closer to uncovering what the Sandstone Alchemist somehow thought was even more valuable.

When the memory of drowning began to fade, I rose to my elbows and looked over to Wenshu, who had fallen asleep.

"Gēgē," I said, giving his shoulder a sharp shake, "guess what?"

But he didn't stir. I grabbed his arm and rolled him onto his back. "Get up, we have to—"

My hands froze. Wenshu's eyes were open, the whites of his eyes swallowed by black, the night sky of the river plane.

He breathed shallowly, all his muscles slack. I'd only seen one person like this before—the prince's youngest sister, whose soul I'd failed to rescue from the river plane, leaving her body an empty husk.

I wound back and slapped him hard across the face.

When that didn't work, I ground my knuckles hard into his sternum, but still, he didn't respond. Durian had hopped down from the windowsill and was pecking at his fingers, probably hoping for more food.

"Not again," I mumbled, cracking my neck and standing up.

I should have been grateful this was happening now, rather than when we were crossing the desert, when I would have had to drag him the rest of the way. Or worse, when we were with the Sandstone Alchemist, who surely would have smelled our weakness and used it against us.

At times, Wenshu's soul simply blinked out of existence, leaving behind a hollow shell of a body. It began as moments in the palace when his spoon would freeze a few inches from his mouth, eyes clouding over before he blinked and continued eating like nothing happened. But then he started collapsing at random, the spells lasting for a few minutes.

I'd done the same, back when my own soul had been bound with the soul tag that said the wrong name. The Moon Alchemist had said it was because my soul was on too long of a tether, able to wander too far away.

Wenshu's soul tag was correct, for unlike me, he had only ever had one name. Even if my handwriting was messy, the fact that he was here meant that alchemy understood my intentions. But the body wasn't his, and surely that had consequences. I worried that one day, his soul would break free from the cage of the prince's body and never come back.

But not today.

"Get your butt out of the soul plane, you lazy jerk," I said, yanking off Wenshu's right sock. "We have way too much to do for you to abandon me now."

I gathered three firestones and ignited them in my palm, holding the flames up to the sole of his foot.

His knee jolted back. He let out a startled sound and sat upright, scrambling back against the wall.

"What are you *doing*?" he said, the darkness draining from his eyes, replaced by their normal deep brown.

"Waking you up," I said, blowing out the flame in my palm.

"Yes, how dare I get a moment of rest while you make out with your ugly boyfriend inside my brain?" he said, examining the sole of his foot and grimacing. "And stop burning me! It's not sterile!"

"I wasn't in your brain, and we weren't making out," I said, biting back harsher words. I didn't want to argue with Wenshu right now, but I hated it when he spoke so dismissively of Hong, whose infinite patience and understanding made me feel rotten in comparison.

Surely, if I'd resurrected Hong and left Wenshu to wait for me by the river, he would not have been nearly as kind about it as Hong. I knew that my brother resented Hong for putting me in danger when he was alive, but what right did he have to begrudge him now after his death?

"I figured out what the first part of the transformation is supposed to be," I said before he could complain any more about Hong. "But we'll have to go somewhere else for opal. I doubt we'll find it here."

"You figured it out inside my head?" Wenshu said, raising an eyebrow. "Even when I'm asleep, I'm solving problems for you." He sat up and stretched, glancing toward the sun through the windows.

"You can go back to sleep," I said.

He shook his head. "Postal couriers will open soon," he said. "I need to write to Yufei. If the Empress has returned, she definitely wants her body back."

"You don't think my wards will keep her out of the palace?" I said.

Wenshu shook his head. "I think Yufei will go out on a midnight snack run unless she knows her life is on the line."

To that, I had no argument. I sat back as Wenshu unfurled the paper, knowing he wouldn't talk to me while writing at the same time. He was so proud of his precise penmanship.

Durian waddled closer to me, pecking at my leg. I tried to scoop him up, but he dodged my hands and waddled away, quacking. Beneath the blankets, something gold shimmered. I crawled forward and pulled the covers back.

Three golden eggs sat beside the pillow.

I picked one up, turning it over in my palm. It was oddly heavy, like it was made with solid gold.

"Gēgē?" I said, holding one up to the light.

"A little busy," he said, swirling ink powder together with water from his satchel.

"I think Durian laid eggs," I said.

Wenshu frowned, turning around. "I thought Durian was a boy?" he said, jamming his brush at Durian accusingly.

"So did I," I said, setting Durian down and turning the egg over in my hands. I shook it gently, but I couldn't hear anything inside.

"So your demon duck laid golden eggs," Wenshu said, picking up another one and holding it up to his candle. "Great. What do you think is inside? Dynamite?"

"He's not a demon," I said, frowning.

"He's not a *he*," Wenshu said, glaring at me before turning back to the egg. "I wonder if we can sell these."

"No! What if more alchemy ducks are inside?"

"They're not fertilized eggs," Wenshu said slowly. "That duck lives in your bag. Where do you think it found a boyfriend?"

"I know that!" I said, snatching the egg from him. "I'm just saying, Durian isn't a regular duck. Stranger things have happened because of alchemy."

It was probably a good idea to get rid of the eggs, one way or another. Durian was born from alchemy, life created where there was none. *You cannot create good without also creating evil* was alchemy's principal rule. And yet, I'd created a seemingly normal duck that hadn't shown a single sign of evil . . . yet. There was no way these eggs could be a good thing.

I thought of the prince, how he would have insisted we keep the eggs on the slim chance that there were baby ducks inside. I imagined him tethered to the tree, the distant look in his eyes.

"Let's keep them," I said. "Maybe we can eat them or something?" I added, even though I had no intention of trying that, but maybe it would convince Wenshu not to sell them.

"You want to eat something that came out of a demon

duck?" Wenshu said, raising an eyebrow. "Whatever you want, Zilan. Just remember there won't be anyone around who can resurrect you."

He turned back to his letter, so I wrapped two of the eggs in my extra undershirt and set them beside my bag. There wasn't any more fabric to spare, so I slipped the third into the hidden pocket of my skirt, the kind Auntie So had taught me and Yufei to sew into our clothes in case we were robbed. It was hard to see the pocket among the folds of fabric unless you knew it was there.

Durian hopped down from my arms, burrowing into my bag. "Don't let it poop on the Sandstone Alchemist's papers," Wenshu said without looking up.

I rolled my eyes, dragging the bag closer to me by the strap, and pulled the papers out, Durian seated comfortably on top of them. I set him down on the bed and unfurled the paper with the transformation, running my fingers over the line that was no longer a mystery.

But what good does that do me if I don't even know what the transformation does? I thought, leaning against the wall and thunking my head back, glaring accusingly at the cracks in the ceiling.

I'd tried to prove to the Sandstone Alchemist that I wasn't an ignorant child, and yet I'd crawled from his home half alive with a bunch of useless scrap paper to show for it.

You two could never find Penglai Island with only a map, he'd said. And he was probably right. What had we even achieved besides accidentally killing an entire palace full of alchemists and servants, all to defeat an empress who apparently didn't see death as an obstacle? His taunt echoed again and again in my mind, his jagged words cutting deeper each time because I knew they were true.

But the more I replayed his words, the less sense they made.

The Sandstone Alchemist had spoken a dialect that resembled Chang'an's, but it had still been a struggle for me to make sense of, the rising and falling tones flipped and weaker than I was accustomed to.

I'd thought he'd emphasized *you two*, as if saying people like us could never find Penglai unassisted. Maybe because we were children, or poor, or because he hated my father.

But perhaps the emphasis hadn't been intentional.

You two could never find Penglai Island *with only a map*.

I sat up straight, flattening the paper.

I already knew of one place that you couldn't find with a map: the river of souls. No map in the world could bring you there—it was intention, a soul tag, and alchemy that opened the door.

"This is it," I whispered. When Wenshu didn't respond, I grabbed an orange from my bag and threw it at his head. "This is it, Gēgē!" I said. "This is how we get to Penglai Island."

"With a poem?" he said, rubbing his head where the orange had struck him. "Where is that supposed to take us?"

"Everywhere," I said. "Anywhere, it doesn't matter. It's not a place you walk to. It's a place you unlock."

I ran my fingers across the dried ink, the words that would bring all of the dead back to me.

"This is what we use to open the door."

CHAPTER FIVE

We left Lanzhou at dawn, tossing our bags into a creaky canoe that absolutely would not spring a leak and dump us in the Yellow River, according to the fisherman who sold it to us. I patched a few questionable spots with moonstone before we left, and by the time the sun rose, the river was drawing us north.

I read over the Sandstone Alchemist's transformation again once daylight broke, running my fingers over the words that would save everyone.

Even if I didn't understand the whole transformation, I knew the first ingredient. Opals were expensive stones imported from other continents, something we would never find in a desert village.

Baiyin, a day's boat ride to the north, was known for its copper and silver mines, so chances were good that stone trade there would be more diverse.

Maybe in Baiyin, I could find scholars who could help me figure out the rest of the transformation. No one would openly admit to being an alchemist now that private armies were everywhere, but that was the beauty of a transformation hundreds of years old—no one would know for certain that it was a transformation unless they also knew alchemy. No one could turn me in without incriminating themselves. I wondered if the first alchemists had ever imagined that one day, alchemists would need to hide their transformations not to protect their ideas but their lives.

All I need is one good scholar, and I could be on Penglai Island by the end of the week, I thought as the river curved to the left and Lanzhou disappeared behind the trees. That ember of hope flared bright inside me, filling me with warmth. Everything I'd destroyed could be repaired with only a few stones. It didn't matter what the Empress was planning, because I would reach Penglai first and have all the power in the world at my disposal. I didn't realize I was smiling until Wenshu told me to *stop thinking about your stupid boyfriend.*

The morning chill melted away, and as the sun rose over the Yellow River, we rode the current to the northeast, wide awake from the fear of toppling overboard, since neither of us could swim. We'd grown up on the Pearl River, but had never ventured past the shores—the children of clay merchants had no reason to go farther than the muddy riverbanks.

I steered us around patches of rocks and tall cordgrass, but no matter how I directed us, the waters drew us east, like it wanted us there.

After a few hours, there was nothing but sparse trees on either side of the river and searing sun overhead, baking us alive in the wooden boat. I'd set Durian on the seat beside me, but he'd stubbornly squirmed back inside my bag and fallen asleep.

Driftwood lay scattered across the banks, mixed with unsettled dirt and cracked Huyang trees. Villages like these—built too close to the river—were often swept away overnight in the summer floods, leaving behind nothing but ghosts and broken branches by morning. We passed through yet another shattered ghost village, the remaining trees creaking overhead, branches barely held upright by thin strips of split wood.

The quiet unsettled me. Even in the golden expanse of the desert, it hadn't been this silent, as if the world knew something that we didn't. I paddled faster than Wenshu, steering the boat too far to the left.

Wenshu frowned over his shoulder. "Would you relax?" he said. "I'm going as fast as I can, but your boyfriend didn't exactly have a ton of upper body strength."

"Don't say that like your body was any stronger," I said. Then, quieter: "This place feels strange."

"Well, we're leaving it. At a normal, sustainable pace," he said, turning the boat straight again. "Save your energy in case we see an alligator."

"Is that a possibility?"

I couldn't see his face, but somehow I felt certain he was rolling his eyes. "No, Zilan, I'm sure all the river beasts in the north are very polite and will step out of the water until we pass so as not to startle us."

Something thunked against the boat, rocking us to the side.

I jumped and yanked my oar out of the water, half expecting an angry alligator to chase after it, but the river was clear and still, save for the ribbons of water rippling behind our boat. I peered over the edge, but saw no sharp teeth or yellow eyes or muddy scales. Only a long, thin piece of wood embedded in my side of the boat, the end sparkling with gold fletching.

An arrow.

"Get down!" I said, grabbing Wenshu by his collar and yanking him backward to the bottom of the boat. He tried sitting up, but I lay down on top of him, jamming an elbow into his stomach and yanking Durian's bag off the seat beside me.

"What's happening?" he said, shoving my hair out of his face. "Is it the Empress?"

Something hit the opposite side of the boat, and a sharp pain bloomed in my ankle. We bumped into a cluster of rocks and the boat spun sideways, cold water lapping over the sides.

"Would you get up and *do something*?" Wenshu said, elbowing me in the ribs. "We can't sit here spinning in circles!"

"I like my body without arrows in it!" I said, shoving his face back down against the watery floor of the boat.

Do something sure sounded like a great idea in theory, but I'd only ever fended off archers with a bread basket, not with alchemy. How had I been so fearless only a few weeks ago, shoving the prince out of an arrow's path? What had happened to that Zilan?

More importantly, who was shooting at us? Maybe the Empress had possessed an archer like she'd possessed Junyi. Or maybe it was just bandits who had no idea who we were, and had only seen that we wore robes embroidered with gold. I burned up two of my iron rings, thinning them into a sheet of metal that I used to shield my face as I peered over the edge of the boat.

A sea of silver glowed along the shore, shimmering metal plates made up of tiny scales sewn together like iron dragons. I recognized the uniforms immediately because they were the same soldiers pacing the perimeter of Chang'an. What were they doing this far north?

An arrow flashed past me, scoring a line across my cheek. I ducked back down and clapped a hand over my face, pressing down against a bright flash of pain. At least it had missed my eye.

"Did they hit you?" Wenshu said, sitting up.

"Barely," I said. "Sit the hell down before—"

The words died in my throat as an arrow struck Wenshu's arm. Tiny sparks of blood seared across my face, the whole boat tilting as the force drove him backward. I reached out for him too late, grasping a handful of air as he fell into the water.

I threw myself to the side of the boat to pull him back up, but my weight tilted the boat too far to the side. All at once, the world flipped over, and I tumbled into the river.

I crashed into coldness and silence, flinching when the boat overturned on top of me. Sea plants tangled with my ankles, fish racing away, a rock formation scraping my arm. My ankle twisted around the strap to my bag, and I reached for it with a jolt when I remembered Durian was still inside.

I couldn't see Wenshu, but it wasn't as if I could have helped him when neither of us knew how to swim. I kicked toward the surface, clawing at the water as if it were quicksand, weighed down by the scrolls in my bag. The river tugged me farther away from the surface, and my back slammed into a rock formation, forcing the breath from my lungs. I inhaled without meaning to, and the freezing water stabbed through my chest like daggers.

A hand closed around my arm, dragging me upward. It hauled me onto a jagged, pebbled shore, my wet hair blocking my view as I coughed into the ground, cheek stamped into muddy gravel. I managed to swipe my hair out of my eyes and catch a glimpse of feathered helmets and shining breastplates before one of the soldiers pointed at me.

"She's got alchemy rings!" he said.

The men closed in on me, blocking out the white sky. I used my last firestone ring to sear the face of the first man to reach me, but another man seized my arms and twisted my wrists so hard I thought they might snap. The pain stunned me long enough for the first man to slip a cloth sack over both my hands. He tightened it with some sort of scratchy rope, using the excess to bind my wrists together.

My bag fell to the ground and one of the men grabbed it, but I didn't dare make a fuss and let them know anything important was inside. They'd probably roast Durian alive if they found him.

A few feet down the river, soldiers tossed Wenshu onto the shore, binding him up as he coughed and choked. The arrow in his arm had snapped off, leaving a broken shard of wood embedded just above his elbow. The water had washed away most of the blood.

Another soldier yanked on the collar of my dress, forcing me to my feet.

"Do you have any idea who you're manhandling?" I said, trying to elbow him. I outranked every single one of them. What did Yufei's soldiers think they were doing?

"No," the man gripping my collar said. "Why don't you tell us?"

"Don't," Wenshu said weakly before I could respond. "There's no insignia."

My gaze snapped back to the men. The shoulders that normally had golden cranes on them—the royal family's symbol for eternity—were blank. These weren't Yufei's soldiers.

"A private army?" I said to Wenshu, whose grim expression was all the confirmation I needed.

I'd seen private armies in passing, but usually only saw their aftermath—the villages turned to driftwood and embers, the cities that wouldn't open their gates to anyone, even travelers, for fear of who they'd let inside. The imperial soldiers had done a decent enough job at quashing any private armies that entered Chang'an, but there were few—if any—soldiers in the rural villages far from the capital. I'd heard that private soldiers made far more money than imperial soldiers, so many were switching sides. Part of me couldn't blame them for that.

But a private army was bad news for a runaway alchemist like me. Telling them my name was the fastest way to get acquainted with China's newest torture devices.

I groaned internally, remembering the fisherman who'd seen my rings when we bought his boat. There was a prize for turning in alchemists, but I hadn't thought an army was close enough to catch up to us once we were on the water.

"He's not an alchemist," I said, nodding toward Wenshu. "Let him go."

The man behind me laughed, finally releasing my collar and grabbing my arm instead. "Sorry if I don't take your word for it."

He tried to drag me toward the path, but I dug my heels into the sand. Wherever they wanted to take us, it would definitely be harder to break out of than this wide-open area. I grabbed fistfuls of fabric inside the bag around my hands and tried to tear it apart, managing to loosen the fabric before the guard struck me across the face. I bit down on my tongue, tasting blood as warmth rose to my cheek.

What a coward, I thought. He struck me with an open palm just because I was a woman. The Moon Alchemist had beaten me far worse than that.

I turned at the sound of Wenshu's sharp cry. A soldier had twisted the broken arrow in his arm, sending fresh blood streaming down his sleeve. I went still, forcing myself not to fight back as a soldier tightened the sack around my arms and dragged me up the incline. I would have to break away later, when Wenshu was safe.

They pulled us to an open-air cart, the kind that traveling merchants used to transport hay bales. A soldier shackled me to the baseboard with a short chain, then sat down beside me. I tried to scoot away from him, but five other soldiers piled into the cart, and I had no choice but to sit crammed between them. Across from me, Wenshu was squished up against a corner, trying with all his might not to touch the soldier beside him.

"Try to jump, and you'll be dragged under the wheels," the soldier next to me said. "We won't stop for you."

"Don't you need us in one piece to make all your gold?" I said, scanning the passing countryside for places to jump out without dying. But there was a steep drop leading to a river on each side of the path, nowhere to run for cover, no forest or city to disappear into. Even if I could unshackle us both before the guards could stop us, they would shoot us down with arrows before we made it ten feet.

"We need you alive," the soldier said. "There's a difference."

The carriage descended into forest backroads, pulling us deeper into the hills and valleys of the northwest. As the trees swallowed the river in the distance, the dream of Baiyin vanished along with it.

Slowly, the landscape began to unmake me. The air out here was papery dry, cracking my lips, pulling apart the seams of my skin. I had grown up in a world that always felt like a rainstorm, but this part of the world stole moisture from your lips and tongue, dried out your eyes, cracked the skin of your knuckles.

Wenshu looked like a drowned puppy across from me, mouth clamped shut, shooting me a dark look as if warning me not to talk. It was probably a good thing that we were both drenched, because it would make it harder for anyone to recognize Wenshu as the Crown Prince. My bag made a peeping sound, and I scowled at it until it stopped, begging Durian to be silent, lest he end up on a skewer.

They were almost certainly taking us to a prison for alchemists, to be starved and tortured until we made life gold. They wouldn't care if Wenshu swore up and down that he wasn't an alchemist—surely lots of real alchemists said the same. Once they tossed us in with a mass of prisoners, when there weren't so many eyes on us, that was when we'd escape.

The world began to slope upward, tipping me against a disgruntled soldier who smelled of fish, closer and closer toward the white sun. At last, the ground leveled and we arrived at a clearing among the tangled branches. A cracked clay building stood alone in the shade, its white paint so scratched and chipped that it looked like a serpent shedding old skin. It was large enough to be an aristocrat's summer house, if not for the disrepair and the perimeter of silver guards that watched us stonily as the cart lurched closer.

Another cart passed as we entered, heading out into the forest with cargo draped in stained white cloth. As it rolled by, I caught a glimpse of purpled hands and feet jutting out from beneath the fabric, long black hair drooping from the sides. The bodies jolted as the carriage drove over uneven ground, a woman's corpse tumbling out. The cart dragged her behind it, her long hair tangled in the wheels, her stiff limbs carving tracks into the mud.

Wenshu shot me an alarmed gaze, but I shook my head. *We won't be here long enough for that to happen*, I wished I could tell him. *I won't let it happen.*

The cart drew to a stop by the door, and the men unshackled us, pulling us onto solid ground. Wind raked through my wet clothes, goose bumps rippling over my skin. I hated that I was trembling from cold, sure it made me look like a scared little girl before the imposing guards.

Two of them opened the double doors as we approached, a dark, stale air wafting over us. They pushed us through, into a hallway of elaborately painted gold murals that had cracked into spiderwebs from the parched air, tiny paint flakes falling from the ceiling like a slow, golden snow.

We stopped before another guard, who grabbed me by the arm and tugged me forward, looked me up and down, then withdrew a knife and, in one sharp motion, sliced the strings of my alchemy satchel from my sash.

"Hey!" I said, but the guard ignored me, dropping my satchel in a metal bucket. Another guard bent my arms up at a sharp angle, twisting my wrists and removing the sack from my hands. My arms instantly went numb from the angle, and I couldn't stop them as they wrenched the rings from my fingers, including the gold ring that Hong had given me before he died.

"Not that one!" I said, trying to twist out of their grasp. But they only laughed and released my arms, which felt like they were made of lead. "That metal's too soft to even use as a weapon!" I said, but they ignored me, ripping out my hair clips, running cold hands up my ankles, seizing my shoes from my feet.

When they seemed satisfied that they'd stripped me of every possible alchemy stone, they shoved me through another door into a stone hallway. Wenshu shuffled close behind me, looking a bit like a disgruntled swamp creature, with his tangled hair hanging over his face, since they'd taken his hair clips as well.

More guards shouldered past us and unlocked a wooden door at the end of the hall just as the one behind us slammed shut, leaving us in a room of pure darkness. The guard knocked twice on a door I couldn't see, and another guard holding a candle opened it from the other side.

The guard shoved me through the doorway into a hall that

smelled of wet earth and salt. His candle cast pale light on rows of bamboo cells running along either wall, disappearing into the unseen darkness. White hands and dirty feet shuffled away from the bars as the guard drew closer, like cave creatures startled by light.

"You have room, right?" the guard from the last hallway said, lingering in the doorway.

The guard with the candle shrugged. "I'll make room."

The first guard nodded, then turned and shut the door. The remaining guard shoved me and Wenshu after the man with a candle, a bruising grip on my forearm. My feet already felt numb from the frozen ground, and the air only seemed to grow colder the farther we walked. I tried to peer into the cells, but in the darkness, the other prisoners were only jagged shadows pressed to the far walls.

At last, the guard drew to a stop.

"This will do," he said. Then he unsheathed his sword and thrust it through the bars without warning. "Back up!" he shouted.

Luckily, he seemed not to have skewered anyone, for his sword came back clean. He pulled a key ring from his belt and jammed one of the keys into the lock, swinging open the door with a piercing creak.

The guard shoved me inside, but I tripped over the lip on the doorway and fell forward, chin slamming into the ground with no free hands to catch myself. Wenshu fell on top of me, crushing me into the dirt. The door locked behind us, the footsteps receded, and all light vanished as they slammed the hall door shut.

"Get off me," I said, squirming as Wenshu tried to roll away without the use of his hands. I struggled to my knees, shaking my hair out of my face as my eyes adjusted to the ghostly faces of the other prisoners cast in darkness.

The other people in the cell watched us with dead eyes, slumped against the walls. Dirt and soot caked their faces, their eyes red, lips split, hair knotted. None of them tried to talk to us, as if new prisoners weren't a noteworthy event.

"Are you all right?" I said to Wenshu, squinting to inspect his arm in the dark.

"Well, I'm covered in filth, but I haven't lost a dangerous amount of blood, and it's not like this arm would be particularly useful right now, even if unpunctured," he said. "Though I'd feel better if you told me your brilliant plan to get us out of here."

"Give me a minute," I said, looking away. "I'll think of something. I just hope Durian is okay in my bag."

"*Durian?*" Wenshu said. "I'm more concerned about *us* than your demon duck!"

"I'll get us out of here," I said. "I just need . . ." I trailed off, taking stock of the cell. The floor was a dusty gray type of dirt that I'd never seen before. I bent down and tried to pinch it between my fingers as best as I could with my hands bound behind my back.

"It's made of recycled paper scraps," said a small voice behind me.

I turned to a girl who couldn't have been older than ten, her black hair so matted with gray dirt that she almost looked elderly, her lips chapped and colorless. How long had these people been down here, sleeping on the ground?

"There's no alchemy stones in it," she said when neither of us responded.

"How do you know?" I said. "Have you tried?"

The girl turned around, showing us her bound hands, wiggling her left hand, ring finger and pinky finger missing. "Each try costs you a finger if you get caught," she said.

Wenshu let out a wounded sound, thumping his head back against the wall. "We're doomed."

"We're not," I said. "I'll get us out of here." It was what he wanted me to say—what the Scarlet Alchemist was supposed to say—but the words felt paper-thin.

This soundless cage wrapped in cool darkness felt like a stark antithesis to the alchemist I'd been. I'd once stood proudly beside the Moon Alchemist in my crimson robes, having defeated the wealthy sons of scholars and been hand-chosen by the Empress. Now I was trapped in a paper box in the dark, everyone that had once helped me dead, stripped of my alchemy while the kingdom crumbled far away.

"I'll think of something," I said, more to myself than Wenshu.

"Keep quiet, would you?" called a man from the other side of the cell. "If the guards hear you saying that, they'll piss in our water. Again."

I clenched my jaw, running through my options.

It was impossible to completely strip a room of alchemical potential, because alchemy was in our bodies—the iron in our blood, the salt in our skin, the zinc in our bones. The problem was, most of it couldn't be used without a catalyst stone to activate it.

I ran my palm across the smooth walls, coated in a papery substance that wouldn't break when I dug my nails into it, no discernible stones inside. Whoever built this place must have consulted an alchemist.

"Back up!" a guard shouted near the door, nearly impaling Wenshu with his sword. Wenshu scrambled away and sat beside me as the doors swung open once more.

The guards threw a man into the cell. He landed on his face, groaning and spitting out a tooth. Even with his hands bound, I could make out the crooked angles of his broken fingers, the purple flesh where fingernails should have been.

"Better luck next time," one of the guards said, laughing with the other as he locked the door once more. A few of the prisoners helped the man sit up.

"Don't touch me," he said, twisting away from them. "I'm fine."

Even though his voice sounded parched, his words heavy with exhaustion, I would have recognized that voice anywhere. I stepped forward to get a better look at his face.

Our gazes locked, and he squinted at me through one swollen, purple eye. I knelt in front of him, because I had to be sure.

"Zheng Sili?"

CHAPTER SIX

The man went very still, like a rabbit passing under the shadow of a hawk. "Hùnxiě?" he said tentatively.

I looked him up and down, the dirt smeared on his face, skin colored with bruises, hair tousled and damp with blood. His offensively ungroomed mustache was thankfully gone, but in every other sense, he looked worse for wear. Like me, he had come all the way from Lingnan and been tossed into the jaws of the Empress and her political games. But while I'd tried to stop her, he'd helped her.

"*You piece of shit!*" I said, lunging for him.

It didn't matter that my hands were tied. I would rip his ears off with my teeth if I had to. I landed a kick against his jaw, and his head slammed back against the bars. He made a wounded sound, falling to the dirt.

"Zilan!" Wenshu said, but I ignored him and pressed my foot into Zheng Sili's sternum, stopping him from sitting up.

"Hey," one of the prisoners said weakly in protest, but I shot him a murderous look and he backed away. People in here were probably too busy surviving to insert themselves in other people's problems, and I doubted someone like Zheng Sili had made many friends.

"You tried to save the Empress!" I said. "After everyone died to stop her, you tried to save her because a couple guards pointed their knives at you? I could have you hanged if we were back in Chang'an!"

"*I know!*" he said, coughing as I switched my foot from his chest to his throat, pressing down threateningly. He looked like an overturned beetle, legs in the air. "I know, okay? Just let me up, and I'll explain!"

"*Explain?*" I said, grinding my heel down. "Let me *explain* my foot to your mouth!"

"Zilan," Wenshu said warningly, standing up.

I sighed. I really didn't want to pause to explain this all to my brother. "I was dying on the ground when this guy tried to save the Empress," I said, which seemed a good enough summary for the time being.

"Huh," Wenshu said, frowning. "Well, in that case." He turned and gave Zheng Sili a swift kick to the ribs, making him roll over and groan. "You can't kill him, though," Wenshu said. "What if they don't take his body out? It will smell even worse down here."

"Aren't you the prince?" Zheng Sili said, bloody drool pooling under his face.

"No," Wenshu said, sitting down.

I reeled back for another kick, but Zheng Sili jolted away, scrambling back against the bars.

"I'm sorry!" he said. "I'm sorry, okay? I didn't want to help the Empress, I swear! The guards threatened my family."

"Yeah, mine too," I said, glaring back at him. "They died so the Empress could die."

Zheng Sili winced. "I'm sorry," he said again. And for a fleeting, regrettable moment, I felt bad for him. He no longer sounded like the proud aristocrat who had torn my dress back in Lingnan. His gold molars were missing, his nose knocked off center, hair caked with blood.

"After you won the last alchemy exam, the Empress threw the rest of us in the dungeons," he said. "Half of us died down there from some kind of sickness. They left their bodies in the cell with me, rotting. I didn't know how long I was down there talking to corpses, but all I could think about was how I'd given my whole life to become the kind of person the Empress would respect, and she'd thrown me out like a piece of garbage for some peasant girl." He winced. "Sorry, I mean, no offense. But you didn't respect her the way I did."

"Because that's not what the imperial exam is about," I said. *And I'm a merchant, not a peasant*, I thought, but I doubted the distinction would mean much to an aristocrat.

"I know," he said, shoulders slumping. "I only got out when the alchemists took over the palace and set all the prisoners free. But before I could even go home, some guards found me and threatened to kill my little brother if I didn't help them. And that's . . . that's when you saw me."

The memory of that moment reignited the rage I'd felt upon seeing him. I could still taste my own blood as I'd lain half dead on the stairs of the throne room, thinking that when I died, at least it would have been for something that mattered. And then Zheng Sili had arrived, set his greedy hands on the Empress's dying body, and undone what I'd given everything for. Would her soul still be clinging to the river plane if it wasn't for him?

"You have no idea what you've done," I said, not sure if it was truly fair to blame everything on him, but the rage pulsing through my sore muscles felt so much better than the harrowing pity from only moments before.

"I didn't want to help her," he said, slumping against the bars of the cage, no longer meeting my gaze. "I didn't know what else to do, and I don't know if what I did was right. But do you want to know the worst part?"

"That all my friends and family died in vain?" I said, reining in the urge to kick him under the jaw again.

"Mine too," he said, letting out a dry, empty laugh that seemed to drain what little color was left from his face. Blood dripped slowly from the curve of his lips to his torn robes in a slow, dark rain. "A private army trampled my brother in a raid a week later. It was almost a relief when they captured me because I didn't have to figure out what to do next."

He looked so small in the darkness of the cell, withered into himself, pale from weeks without sun. I had long ago learned that sometimes people's souls died before their bodies did. You could see it in their eyes, an undertow drowning them slowly behind their irises.

But the world was full of sad stories, and Zheng Sili's was not the worst I'd heard.

I sighed, sitting down cross-legged and leaning against the wall. "This is exactly why you never became a royal alchemist," I said.

He looked up sharply, eyes narrowed. "*Excuse me?*" he said.

Maybe the rage in his expression, or even the blood dripping down his chin like a feral wolf would have scared some people, but I had seen far worse than angry rich boys.

"Your brother died because of a world that you helped to build," I said. "You know that, yet you still aren't sure if what you did was wrong? Do you know how many other people's brothers could have died because of what you did?"

Zheng Sili choked down a startled breath. "Listen here, hùnxiě—"

"*No,*" I said, raising my voice. "If you want sympathy, go back to your mansion and cry to the other sons of aristocrats who've never known suffering, because you won't get any from me. This is exactly why I beat you, Zheng Sili. Because people like you give up the moment life isn't easy anymore."

He ground his teeth together, sputtering out a few indignant sounds as if he couldn't decide the best way to insult me. This was the true Zheng Sili, the pathetic, sniveling boy I'd always known was beneath the aristocrat's exterior. I suspected that all the rich were like this just below the surface, but no one had ever dared to talk back to them.

"When you're done whimpering," I said, "I need to know if you have any pearl teeth left."

"*You knocked out my only pearl tooth when we were sparring!*" he said, face red.

I sighed, closing my eyes. *Just my luck.*

"Any other ideas?" Wenshu said, looking down at Zheng Sili like he was a piece of rotten fruit.

I nodded toward Zheng Sili. "Maybe if he cries enough, the salt in his tears will make us some quartz in a few hundred years."

"I'm not crying, I'm sweating!" Zheng Sili said.

"Would you shut the hell up?" one of the prisoners shouted. Zheng Sili obediently clamped his mouth shut and scooted back against the wall, shooting the man a dirty look. I sat down next to Wenshu, but something hard dug into my hip.

I tried to adjust it with my hands bound, but it only bit down harder, a bruising cold against my side. Had my pockets filled with river rocks when I'd fallen overboard?

Then I remembered.

My hidden pocket. *Durian's egg.*

"Gēgē," I said sharply, startling Wenshu. "Reach into my pocket!"

"You have a pocket they didn't empty?" Zheng Sili said.

We both ignored him as Wenshu bent down at an awkward angle, his hands still locked behind him. He used to help Auntie So make our skirts, which was technically women's work, but Auntie was never particularly impressed with how well Yufei and I could sew. He found the pocket and managed to slip his hand inside, pulling out Durian's egg.

"Incredible," Wenshu said. "You could have snuck anything in with that pocket, and you brought one of your demon eggs."

"Where did you find a gold chicken?" Zheng Sili said.

Wenshu started to answer him, but I elbowed him in the ribs. "Ignore him, and he'll go away," I said in Guangzhou dialect, motioning for him to pass me the egg.

"I speak Guǎngdōng huà!" Zheng Sili shouted, indignant. "I'm from Guangzhou!"

I had never heard Zheng Sili speak anything but the prim and proper dialect of Chang'an, fluent like any good aristocrat's son. He sounded like an entirely different person in Guǎngdōng huà, his voice much higher pitched and younger.

"It's a duck egg," I said, angling away so he couldn't see.

"There are trace amounts of copper in eggs," Zheng Sili said, ignoring me and moving around Wenshu to get a better look. "Crack it open, let's see what we've got."

I pressed back against the wall so Zheng Sili couldn't see the egg. "There's not enough copper for a transformation," I said, though I was sure he knew it was a poor excuse when we didn't have any better options. But I thought of Durian sleeping in my bag, the duck who had never even shown a trace of evil, nothing even remotely suspicious besides the eggs. Surely they contained some sort of evil, since Durian himself—herself—clearly didn't. Maybe the yolk was an acid that would burn the flesh from my bones, a bomb that would explode in my face? I had been careless back in the palace, and it had cost the other alchemists their lives.

"It's worth a shot," Zheng Sili said, trying to move closer. "What are you saving it for?"

Wenshu shouldered Zheng Sili back, making him lose his balance and fall awkwardly to his knees. "Don't touch her," he said. "We don't know what's in the egg. It could be dangerous."

Zheng Sili scoffed, turning around to show us his broken fingers. "More dangerous than these guards? Crack it open!"

"Back off!" I said. "It's not your decision."

"Actually, it's *mine*," said a low voice behind us.

I turned around. At the front of the cell, a guard held one of the prisoners against the bars with his sword pulled tight to her throat. It was the young girl I'd spoken to before, standing on tiptoes so the blade wouldn't tear into her neck. The guard reached his left hand through the bars, palm open. "Hand it over," he said.

I clenched my jaw, careful not to tighten my grip around the egg in anger. Against the cell bars, with the pale light gleaming wetly in her eyes, the girl looked so much like the prince's little sisters, who the Empress had thrown in the dungeon. They'd both looked at me with so much hope when I'd set them free, and then a few weeks later, one of them was nothing but an empty husk in my arms. That was the price they'd paid for trusting me to keep them safe.

Zheng Sili scoffed. "They don't even know each other," he

said. He turned back to me and gestured expectantly. "Go on, crack it open."

"*Now*," the guard said, tugging the blade tighter, a thin line of red spreading across the girl's throat and pulling a helpless sound from her lips. I thought of the corpses of children I'd resurrected back in Guangzhou, whose souls I found hiding in tall grass or curled up against trees, crying for their mothers in the dark. Children cried loudly because they thought someone would answer. I was supposed to be that person.

"Here," I said, rising to my feet, turning so the guard could see the egg in my bound hands. "It's just an egg."

"*Are you serious?*" Zheng Sili said. "Our only way out, and you're giving it up for a stranger?"

"She's just a kid," I said, my heart sinking as the guard reached through the bars and snatched the egg from my hands. He pulled his sword away, and the girl fell forward against me, scrambling away from the bars.

"*I'm* only eighteen!" Zheng Sili said. "You had no problem walking away and letting the Empress kill *me* after she made you an alchemist!"

"Yes," I said, "because you're an asshole."

Zheng Sili let out an indignant sound and finally—mercifully—shut up, sitting down heavily in the corner facing away from me like my very presence disgusted him. The girl had already left my side, retreating into the dark corners of the cell where the guards couldn't reach her. *You're not her savior*, I reminded myself bitterly. *You're the reason she was in danger in the first place.*

"How the hell did you sneak this in?" the guard said, turning the egg over in his hands. He pinched it between his index finger and thumb, holding it up to his candle. The surface crinkled with hairline cracks, then shattered in his hand. I stepped closer to the bars for a better look, praying that Durian had laid some kind of alchemical weapon.

But nothing but orange yolk and slimy egg white oozed down the guard's wrist. It was a normal egg after all.

The guard made a disgusted sound, shaking the goo off his hand. "You were hiding a rotten egg?" he said. "You alchemists are worse than . . ." He trailed off, staring at his hand, the glossy egg white like fish webbing between his fingers. He held up his hand, watching the translucent goo expand and capture the candlelight. Then he took one faltering step forward and collapsed face-first onto the ground.

Metal clanged as his helmet hit the dirt, his candle tipping over and extinguishing itself in a pool of hot wax, the hall cast in darkness again. The other prisoners murmured in confusion, some pressing close to the bars.

"I told you that duck was evil," Wenshu said, stepping around me to get a better look. "Is the guard dead?"

I knelt down, my face against the bars as I squinted through the darkness. The guard's chest rose and fell shallowly, the plates of his armor shifting from the movement.

"He's alive," I said. "Out cold, though."

I leaned closer, trying to make out the shape of keys in the darkness, but a sharp scent nearly cleaved my face in half, so strong that it felt like someone had jabbed a spear straight up my nose. I lurched back, falling against Wenshu, my eyes watering at the memory of the scent.

The egg smelled like durian.

Wenshu had always called durian "corpse fruit" because it smelled oddly similar to the scent of rotting corpses, which we knew all too well. But no durian—or corpse—had ever smelled quite this foul. No wonder the guard had been knocked out by the smell.

I tensed as the guard wheezed out a loud breath, but thankfully, he remained still.

"If you want to take advantage of this situation, now is the time," Wenshu said, squinting down the hallway. "I don't think any other guards have noticed his absence yet."

"Right," I said, blinking away involuntary tears and doing my best to wipe my nose against my shoulder. Before anything, I needed to untie my hands.

I sat down on the ground, this time holding my breath, and slid my leg between the bars. I prodded the metal plates of the guard's armor with my toe, dragging him closer. Steel was a metalstone, a catalyst that I could use to start reactions, so if I could only touch his armor with my hands, I would be free.

When he was finally close enough to the bars for me to reach, I turned around and angled my bound hands through the bars, twisting my wrists until my fingers brushed his steel plates.

The cool steel hummed beneath my fingers, all the tension in my muscles soothed away. Alchemy sang through my body, and for the first time since I'd left Guangzhou, I felt like I was home again.

I ran my fingers across the plates until I was sure I was touching exactly three metal scales, then let alchemy burn through me.

A chunk of the armor snapped off, the metal sparking and warping in my palms, contorting into the shape of a blade. I gripped it tight until I'd slid it back through the bars, then turned and offered it to Wenshu, who managed to cut my ropes from behind. My wrists screamed as blood rushed back into them, but I shook away the numbness and cut Wenshu's ropes, passing him the knife again.

"Cut everyone else's ropes," I said, holding my breath and reaching back through the bars, quickly transforming some of the metal plates into new alchemy rings. One by one, the untied alchemists joined me, ripping off gold plates and steel and iron from the guard's armor, forging his helmet into blades and batons, stripping the metals from him like vultures to a carcass. They nearly crushed me in their fervor, but I could hardly blame them after they'd been trapped down here for so long. I barely managed to snatch the keys before an overly eager alchemist could transform them into something else.

I turned as Wenshu cut Zheng Sili's ropes, perhaps deliberately saving him for last. Zheng Sili winced as his purpled hands hung limp at his sides, not even bothering to reach for metal with his broken fingers. He was such a far cry from the proud and polished alchemist I'd first met.

At the end of the hall, footsteps echoed down the staircase. I swore and reached around the bars until I managed to jam the key into the lock. The door swung open easily, and the alchemists flooded into the hall, shoving me against the bars on the opposite side.

Hands grabbed my wet clothes, yanking at my sleeves and hair. The prisoners in the nearest cell had latched on to me as if drowning.

"Please, let us out too!" the woman clutching my sleeve said. "Before the guards come back!"

"I need my arms for that," I said, slowly extricating myself and fumbling for the key as Wenshu appeared beside me.

"We have to go, Zilan," he said. I didn't have a chance to

answer as the lock clicked and the door burst open, knocking me into Wenshu. The alchemists rushed toward the end of the hall, not even trying to be quiet. The guards certainly must have known what had happened by now.

The other prisoners had all pressed close to the bars now, calling out for me, pale arms reaching and grabbing at nothing.

"Just toss someone the keys, and let's get out of here," Wenshu said, tugging my arm.

But I stayed rooted in place, the keys cold and impossibly heavy in my hands. I thought of the palace after the fall, corpses bobbing in the scarlet ponds, tile floors so blood-slicked they'd turned to crimson mirrors, gardens fertilized with entrails and teeth. The legacy of the Scarlet Alchemist who let other people fight in her place.

"Gēgē," I said, "get my bag and Durian, then come back here."

"Can't you just grab them on the way out?" he said, chasing after me as I hurried to the next cell, jamming the key in the lock. The stairwell at the end of the hallway lit up with bright sparks and a rush of fire, screams echoing across the stones.

"I'm a little busy here," I said, jamming the key in the lock of the next cell.

The door struck me across the face as the prisoners shoved it open, crushing me against the bars and nearly knocking Wenshu to the ground as they ran. Upstairs, I could make out sounds of screaming, the crackle of fire.

"Are you kidding? There's too many of them!" Wenshu said, hurrying along next to me as I unlocked the next door. "Zilan, did you see how many guards are outside? You want to be caught down here without any stones left when they come down?"

"*Then get me my stones!*" I said. "You're wasting time!"

Wenshu let out a frustrated sound and stormed off, disappearing into the dark.

I unlocked two more cells, not even halfway down the passageway. The desperate cries of the alchemists grew louder as they saw that I was coming to set them free. The scent of smoke spiraled down the staircase, the air growing gray and hazy.

With the next door that I unlocked, the crowd forced me to the ground, tripping over me, stomping on my fingers as they rushed out. I couldn't get up until they passed, the screams of the remaining alchemists somehow even louder now.

"Hey, hùnxiě!"

I turned around, facing the mouth of the hall.

Zheng Sili stood in the doorway beside Wenshu, who clutched my bag under his arm and Durian under the other. Zheng Sili held up a fistful of stones in a hand that looked slightly less mangled than a few minutes ago, which meant he'd found some waterstones to heal himself.

"Get away from the bars," Zheng Sili said.

"Or what?" I said, already moving to the next cell and struggling to find the key with my sore, trampled fingers. He had already ruined my plans once. Did he really have to do it again? "I don't take orders from you."

He shrugged, shuffling the stones in his hand, then pressed his palm to the nearest cell. "Suit yourself," he said.

Then all of the bars exploded.

I ducked, shielding my face as bamboo rained down with the hot scent of firestone and hiss of smoke. Hands closed around me, pulling me to the side as the rest of the alchemists ran for the door. The cell walls gaped open, bamboo turned to pale splinters. Through the smoke, I managed to make out Wenshu's face as he passed me my satchel, tucking Durian into his robes.

Zheng Sili stood beside him, shoving a few prisoners away when they crashed into him in their haste to flee. Maybe the other alchemists had trampled me into unconsciousness and this was a bizarre dream, because the Zheng Sili I knew would never have done anything to help me.

We'd just barely stepped onto the main floor when the ceiling cracked as if struck by lightning. The sizzling corpses of prison guards lay all around the tiles, charred black and dissolving into ashes inside their silver armor. Something in the elaborately painted wallpaper must have been highly flammable, because flames had scorched a path across the painted golden vines, the whole hall now a blazing lattice of flame. A beam had caved in across the front door, a wall of flame sprouting up in front of it, blocking our only exit. For once, I wished that destruction alchemy wasn't the easiest kind—maybe the other alchemists could have fought their way out without burning the building down on top of us.

I jammed my hand back in my satchel, but I already knew I was out of waterstones—I was supposed to restock when we reached Baiyin.

"What stones do you have?" Zheng Sili said.

I emptied the pitiful remains of my satchel into my palm.

"Three earthstones, six firestones, five woodstones, one button, and one soap bean."

Zheng Sili groaned, closing his eyes. "Okay, everyone shut up while I think of what to do."

He could think all he wanted, but there was no way around it—we needed waterstones. Either to put out the flames, or to strengthen the building supports before the roof fully caved in and crushed us.

I squinted against the sting of smoke and glared at the stones in my palms as if they would tell me the answer. *What would the Moon Alchemist do?* I thought. She could probably combine all the stones together into a waterstone, or some other high-level alchemy that would kill me if I even attempted it. I couldn't make stones change their element type.

Unless . . .

I picked up three of my earthstones—brown tanzanite—holding them up to the light. I'd bought the raw stone because it was cheaper, the brownish color rendering it an earthstone.

But if the color changed, the stone type could change as well.

The classification of alchemy stones was a complex science, but it was largely based on color. Green gemstones were usually woodstones, red were firestones, blue were waterstones.

But gem colors could change. It usually happened when jewelers treated them with heat. And trapped inside this golden oven, we had plenty of heat to spare.

I hurled my tanzanite into the flames.

"Do you have a death wish?" Zheng Sili said, gripping my shoulders. "We could have thought of something to use those for!"

"I did," I said, shoving him back and handing him three of my six firestones. "We're making some waterstones."

Zheng Sili took the stones, staring at them like he'd never seen a rock in his life. "You want to forge a waterstone from tanzanite?" he said slowly. "Do you have any idea how much heat that requires?"

"Luckily, we have the top two alchemists in Lingnan and six firestones between us," I said.

"Wait," Wenshu said, rubbing the sting of smoke from his eyes. "You're going to make *more* fire?"

"You should probably stand back," I said. "Keep Durian covered."

"Jewelers do this in ovens, not with open flames in their faces!" Zheng Sili said, cuffing sweat from his forehead as Wenshu hurried farther away.

The ceiling crunched ominously above us, and all three of us raised our arms for cover, but nothing fell except stray sparks.

"You have any better ideas?" I said.

Zheng Sili's face crumpled, and I already knew the answer. He was used to fairness, doing alchemy under perfect, scholarly conditions.

I turned and marched toward the door, standing as close as I could without actually burning myself. I crushed the firestones between my palms and closed my eyes.

Firestones had always spoken to me. It was a stone of destruction, calling on all the rage deep within my soul to raze the world to ashes. The stones began to heat up, so I held my open palms toward the flames, glaring at the tanzanite simmering on the ground. Fire bloomed from my palms, amplifying the heat and smoke of the room. It wouldn't burn me for now, as long as I stayed in control. I had no idea how long this would take, but I would have to bear it until it worked.

After a moment, Zheng Sili stood beside me. "If we get out of this alive, I'll buy you a drink," he said. "But if I melt myself to death because of you, I'm haunting you forever."

"If we die, I'll buy you a drink in hell," I said.

He laughed, the sound loud over the roar of flames. "At least you're honest about where we both stand," he said. Then he clapped the firestones between his palms, and released a blast of blue fire at the doorway.

I had almost forgotten how powerful his alchemy was. The first time we'd sparred, I'd been amazed at the way he wielded alchemy with the finesse of a zither player, while I used it more like a heavy mallet. I supposed that a lifetime of private alchemy tutors was worth something. But for all his skill, he had always lacked innovation, and in the end, that was why I'd been chosen by the Empress over him. But that certainly didn't make him useless.

The flames before us doubled, pulling sweat from my face, casting dizzy heat waves into the air around me. The fire stole all the words from my lips, all the air from my lungs. My palms began to ache, the fire brightening from a deep red to a clear orange.

But it wasn't enough. I could tell from the earthstones still lying dormant on the tiles, slowly paling but nowhere near the blue shade we needed.

I closed my eyes, trying to forget the searing heat on my palms. Firestone was fed by rage, so that was what I needed to focus on.

When I reached deep inside myself for a thread of anger, I saw the Empress.

Her eyes like sharp stars in the dead of night. Her delicate fingers coated in liquid gold, tongue lashing out to lick the substance from under her nails. Her throat pulsing as she drank red wine, a wall of fire in front of her, the tangy smell of burning flesh coating my throat as I entered the throne room where both of us would die.

The fire brightened again, the color lightening to an amber gold, the tanzanite beginning to glimmer with ghostly whispers of white and blue. Zheng Sili sank down to his knees, his hands trembling, but still he directed his flames at the door. We were so close now, but I was growing dizzy, could hardly breathe, and didn't know how much longer either of us could maintain the heat. Once these firestones burned out, we were doomed.

I closed my eyes and thought of nothing but the Empress, stoking the flames inside myself even hotter and brighter than the ones before me.

Her knife pulling across the prince's throat, the skin yawning open like a bloody scream.

Her honed fingernails tracing over my cousins' soul tags.

The taste of her blood on my tongue, the sharpness of her spine against my teeth.

At once, the fire blazed pure white, blasting back my hair in a surge of light. I leaned into the feeling, let it swallow me whole.

The taste of iron and gold, salt and death, pain and endings. Skin that splits like wet paper between my teeth, kindling bones, wire-sharp tendons, a hot rush of liquid power spilling down my throat. The Empress held tight and still in my claws, helpless as a mouse in the talons of a hawk. I wore a cage of pearl around me, an undead monster, an abomination that even the Moon Alchemist couldn't look in the eye, but I would do it all again just to watch her come undone. Her stuttered last breaths, the taste of her broken dreams, the salt of her skin.

When Zheng Sili released his fire, it was like snapping back into my body, doused with cold water. At first I thought he'd given up, but he dove straight into the fire, snatched the tanzanite, and pressed it between his palms.

The sudden spray of water knocked me off my feet. I crashed into the tiles, an icy rain pummeling me, glass-sharp in its sudden coldness. At the doorway, a geyser burst forth from where Zheng Sili had pressed the waterstones just beyond the threshold, drawing up a torrent from the ground. He'd extinguished the whole room at once, leaving us in sudden darkness and wet ashes, like we were inside a decaying corpse.

Wenshu lay on his back in a steaming puddle, looking stunned. Durian sat a few feet away, letting out unhappy chirps.

I tried to move to him, but the world slanted, and my cheek slammed into the ground. Wenshu appeared before I could try to get up again, hauling me up by my arm and pulling me toward the door. Overhead, the soggy rafters creaked, slowly folding inward. But it didn't matter anymore. Now we were free.

We emerged into the sunlight, where Zheng Sili was sitting heavily in a muddy puddle. It seemed the other alchemists had long abandoned the burning building and headed back home. All the guards' horses were gone.

We sat down a few feet away, too tired to move any farther. The sun was setting, and soon the freezing night would descend.

"You're alive?" Zheng Sili said tiredly.

"Seems like it," I said, reaching a hand out for Durian, who was waddling down the front steps.

"That's too bad," Zheng Sili said, wiping wet hair from his face. "I was hoping I could get out of buying you a drink."

CHAPTER SEVEN

"Some thanks we get for setting everyone free," Zheng Sili said, glaring at the horizon. "They didn't even leave us a horse. I swear, this is the last time I do a good deed."

"I doubt they knew we were inside," I said, shivering as a breeze ripped through the valley. We would need to head indoors soon, before night fell and the evening chill latched on to our wet clothes. I had no more firestones to dry us out, and it was a long walk to the next town.

I blinked hard, my vision still sparkling with gold flashes, the taste of blood still on my tongue. Even inside my own head, I couldn't escape the Empress.

"What are you doing out here, anyway?" Zheng Sili said, standing up and stretching. "Shouldn't you be in the palace?"

"Great question," Wenshu said wryly, pulling out waterlogged scrolls from my bag and grimacing at their state.

"None of your business," I said.

Zheng Sili rolled his eyes. "Oh, I'm sorry, is this royal alchemist business? Second-rate alchemists can't know?"

"If you're going to betray me the second someone points a

knife at you, then you don't need to know my plans," I said.

"That was weeks ago," he said.

I scoffed and turned back to Wenshu. "Just leave the scrolls," I said. "I can fix them when I get more waterstones. We need to get to another town."

"With what horse?" Wenshu said, grimacing. "How do you—"

He trailed off, a strange look in his eyes, the words stopping as if his air had been cut off. Before I could ask what was wrong, he folded forward, landing face-first in the dirt.

"Whoa," Zheng Sili said, taking a step back.

I swore and rolled Wenshu over, slapping him hard across the face. When that didn't work, I rubbed my knuckles across his collarbone and yanked at his hair, but he still wouldn't wake.

"Is he dead?" Zheng Sili said from behind me, not sounding particularly concerned.

"Shut up," I said. "He's clearly not."

"Nothing is ever clear with you."

I sighed, trying to bite back tears because the absolute last thing I wanted to do was cry in front of Zheng Sili. I was so exhausted that I would have slept right there on the muddy ground if not for the incoming cold that would surely kill me. Now I had to drag my brother to the next town.

"Where were you headed?" Zheng Sili said.

"Baiyin," I said quietly, afraid he would hear the way my voice trembled if I said any more.

"Sounds like a good place to restock on stones," he said. Then he squatted down, yanked Wenshu's arm around his shoulder, and hauled his limp body up, looking to me expectantly. "Are you going to help me or not?"

Stunned, I quickly tucked Durian into my bag and grabbed Wenshu's other arm.

"Why are you—"

"*Zheng Sili, best alchemist in Lingnan, leaves the Crown Prince unconscious to freeze to death with his poor, helpless concubine,*" he said. "That doesn't sound very heroic, does it? I would never find work again."

"He's not the Crown Prince," I said, tugging Wenshu's arm to force Zheng Sili to walk forward. "And I'm not helpless."

"Look, I know you think you're smarter than me, but I know the Crown Prince when I see him," Zheng Sili said.

I sighed. I supposed it didn't matter if Zheng Sili knew at this point. Who would believe him anyway?

"It's the Crown Prince's face but my brother's soul," I said.

Zheng Sili stopped walking. "And you were his *concubine?*" he said, expression twisted with disgust.

"*He wasn't my brother until a few weeks ago!*" I said, my face burning. "There wasn't exactly a wide array of corpses to choose from after the Empress's monsters ravaged the palace!"

"Corpses," Zheng Sili echoed. "So the prince is dead?"

I didn't answer, staring at my footprints in the mud. I hated saying it out loud. But Zheng Sili was perceptive, and my silence stretched on long enough that it became its own answer.

"Wow," Zheng Sili said. "And I thought *my* family was complicated."

I bit my tongue, too exhausted to keep arguing with someone with the emotional intelligence of a brick. I focused all my energy into putting one foot in front of the other as we headed down the incline alongside the river, following the current where it would have carried our boat had the private armies not overturned it.

"You're trying to get him back, aren't you?" Zheng Sili said after we'd walked in silence for a while longer.

I said nothing, staring at the rocky riverbank. Maybe if I ignored him, he would take a hint and stop talking. The sun was sinking lower, and we were losing light fast. I shivered, shaking hair out of my face.

"You seem the type," he said, when I didn't answer.

"The type?" I echoed tiredly.

He shrugged as best as he could with Wenshu's arm on one shoulder. "The type who doesn't leave anyone behind." He said it like an insult, lip curling. He turned his face to the sky, hefting Wenshu higher on his shoulder. "I suppose I could make time to help you."

"*Help me?*" I said, nearly dropping Wenshu. "Who said I needed your help?"

"*You* didn't. Your brother who spontaneously turns into a limp sack of potatoes certainly implied it," he said, nodding to Wenshu. "You don't seem surprised by this, which means it happens a lot. You already told me you stuffed your brother's soul into the wrong body, I'm guessing with some very high-level alchemy that you yourself don't even fully understand, which means you did a shoddy job and something went wrong, so this is going to keep happening. What would you have done if I wasn't here? Or if this happened when you were fighting someone?"

I grimaced, biting back a thousand sharp words that would take more energy than I had to spare. I forgot, at times, that just because Zheng Sili was rude, it didn't mean he was a fool.

"Why would you ever help me?" I said. "You hate me."

"I don't hate you," he said, raising an eyebrow and turning to me as if the thought had never occurred to him.

"You antagonized me at every round of the competition," I said.

"Yes, because it was a *competition*," Zheng Sili said slowly, as if I was the one being illogical. "I would have looked pathetic if a peasant girl won instead of me, and—lo and behold—I was right. When my father heard . . ." He trailed off, looking toward the sun, which had now burst into sharp orange on the horizon.

"I have no home to return to," he said quietly, the words so soft, so unguarded, that it didn't sound like Zheng Sili at all. "I went home after I escaped from the dungeons, but my father was so ashamed of me. He was very clear. I can return as a royal alchemist or not at all." He nodded to Wenshu. "And once you bring the prince back, you'll get married and become the new empress, won't you?"

"That's the plan," I said hesitantly.

"So you'll need a new crop of royal alchemists, won't you?"

I let out a sharp laugh. "You want to help me for *job security*?"

"Who would you choose, if not the person who helped you bring back the prince?"

"Oh, I don't know, maybe someone who didn't try to rip my dress off the first time we met."

"Are we really keeping track of petty things like that?" he said. "You knocked my tooth out."

I sighed, tightening my grip on Wenshu's wrist. "I'll think about it, okay? I'm so tired I can barely see straight. I'm not making any promises of employment at the moment."

Zheng Sili scoffed. "You're the most impulsive person I've ever met, and yet you're waffling over the easiest win-win situation that has ever been presented to you."

Suddenly, Wenshu twitched. He gasped down a sharp inhale and wrenched himself out of our hands, falling to the mud. He rolled over at once, looking up at me and Zheng Sili with wild eyes. He turned, looking at the river and the distant horizon, then sighed deeply, hanging his head.

"You couldn't have carried me the rest of the way to Baiyin?"

Just before nightfall, the land began to slope downhill, beginning the bridge between the desert and the mountains. Parched sand gave way to stony dirt.

The Yellow River curved through the city, the air wetter and plants more vibrant than in the golden sameness of the desert from where we'd come. In the distance, the jagged mountains captured the glow of the setting sun, a prickly row of golden spikes just beyond the flat waters of the river.

The city was named for its metal industry—*báiyín* meant *white silver*—and was a center for alchemical stone trading. At least, it had been before the private armies started rounding up alchemists.

We arrived at the outskirts of the city, all three of us shivering, nearly dead on our feet. I would have liked nothing better than to stumble into the closest inn and sleep for the next day and a half, but I forced myself to trudge to the town center until I found some stone merchants. I had fewer than ten stones to my name, and I didn't want to be caught unprepared again. I gave Wenshu some coins to find food, then started filling a tray with my stones, keeping an eye out for clear opal.

"I'm a jeweler," I announced to the stone merchant in Lanyin dialect, just in case he was thinking of turning me over to the private armies for suspicion of alchemy. It was one of the only things I'd learned to say in that dialect before we left Chang'an. "I use these to make bracelets."

But the merchant only waved his hand like he couldn't care less. I had been a merchant once, so I knew that as long as people

113

paid, there was little reason to pry into their business.

As I turned to the second row of stones, I tripped over Zheng Sili's foot.

"Quit standing so close to me!" I said, shouldering him back. But instead of stepping away, he only followed after me like a lost sheep.

"It would probably be wise to get me some stones as well, if you want my help," he said quietly.

I stared at him blankly, and it took me a moment to realize what he was implying. *He doesn't have any money.* I rolled my eyes and jammed a hand back into my bag, passing him a handful of gold. He caught it with both hands, frowning.

"That's it?" he said. "Aren't you spending the prince's money?"

"*Shut up!*" I said in Guangzhou dialect. "We just got out of jail. You want to go straight back there? And that's plenty to buy what you need."

"Are you being stingy, or do you actually think this is a lot of money?"

I rolled my eyes. "If you want more stones than that can buy, go dig some up by the riverbank," I said, slamming my tray down in front of the merchant. I caught a glimpse of opal behind the counter and held up three fingers, pointing to it. The merchant wrote down a number on a piece of paper and spun it around to show me.

It was nearly three times higher than what I'd expected.

"Are you serious?" I said before I could stop myself. The merchant must have understood the capital dialect, because his expression slid into a frown. I'd purchased alchemy stones for over ten years, and I knew how much something like this should have cost, even with inflation, which seemed to have evened out after the production of life gold ceased. "How much is the opal?"

"Everything is seventy-five apiece," the merchant said.

I clenched my jaw. He probably saw my clothes and thought I was some aristocrat from Chang'an who would toss her coins over unquestioningly.

"Look," I said, "I understand marking up the price for tourists, but this is robbery."

His frown carved deeper into his face. "I am not trying to swindle you," he said, "I'm making sure I'm not out of business by the end of the week. Same price for everyone. In a few days, my wife and I are melting down our gold and trading it for its weight in silver. That value has always held stable."

I blinked, taken aback. "That's . . . quite a risk," I said.

"The *risk* is trusting that gold will have more value than dirt by summer's end, with what's happening in the capital."

I went still. "What's happening in the capital?" I said quietly, careful not to reveal the apprehension in my voice.

"Riots," the merchant said, shrugging. "All of Chang'an's rich have pooled their money and are paying men from all over the country to knock down the palace walls and oust the royal family. We're standing at the edge of a new dynasty, and I'm not going to be sitting here helpless when gold loses its value again. My grandfather told me how it was when Taizong came into power."

So that's where all the men in Baiyin went, I thought. I'd assumed they'd been hired to draw out alchemists in hiding, but apparently the rich had given up on making life gold and were ready to take matters into their own hands. Yufei still had her army and a few alchemical traps I'd left behind at some of the palace doors, but would that be enough? She had always seemed so strong and unyielding, but then again, so had the Moon Alchemist. I could still see her lying on her back, skin sickly gray, teeth painted with blood while she begged me to let her die.

"Do you want the stones or not?" the merchant said. "I have other customers."

My hands felt numb as I dug into my satchel and pulled out more gold. It wasn't as if I had a choice. I passed him the gold and hurriedly filled my satchel, not waiting for Zheng Sili to follow. Hopefully I'd at least bought the right kind of opal—only the thought of reaching Penglai made that much money seem insignificant.

I found Wenshu at the end of the block, squatting by a corner, trying to wrangle Durian back into my bag.

"Jiějiě might be in trouble," I said.

"Yufei *is* trouble," Wenshu said. "Can you get your duck back in here?"

I snatched one of the apples from the bag in his other hand, bit off a piece and spit it into my hand, then held it out to Durian, who snatched it at once and finally sat still in the bag.

"There's a private army heading for the palace," I said. Wenshu hummed, his expression unchanged. "You're not worried?" I said after a moment.

"Am I worried about Yufei, who has never so much as let a man breathe in her direction if she didn't expressly allow it, who has an entire army and fortified palace? No, Zilan, I'm a bit more worried about us, seeing as all we have is a demonic duck and a failed eighteen-year-old alchemist to defend us. Yufei can hold her own."

I wasn't quite as certain, but there was little point in arguing with Wenshu when we couldn't do anything to help Yufei anyway. Maybe Wenshu truly couldn't comprehend the worst-case scenario in the way I could, simply because he had never been around for it. He had always waited by the river for me to resurrect him and clean up the mess I'd made. He wasn't the one whose failures were printed on flyers spread across China, whose name conjured shame and fear.

"If we go now, maybe Zheng Sili will get lost and never find us again," Wenshu said.

"I can only hope," I said, tightening the straps on my bag and heading down the street.

Zheng Sili did, unfortunately, catch up with us a block away, clutching a bag of stones in a green silk satchel. Together, we hurried to the first inn we could find.

The innkeeper looked at us for just a moment too long, giving away her suspicion. All three of us were still wet, with Wenshu and me wearing silk from the capital while Zheng Sili was so thoroughly caked in mud that it looked like he'd just climbed his way out of the tar pits of hell.

Wenshu shoved Zheng Sili out of the way and approached the innkeeper first. "Our servant overturned our boat," he said, glaring at Zheng Sili. "Please tell me you have somewhere we can stay for the night."

"Your *servant*?" Zheng Sili said in Guangzhou dialect.

I grabbed him by the ear and yanked him down to my level, forcing a sharp whine out of him. "Yes, because you're the one who bathed in mud," I said in Guangzhou dialect, already getting a fairly good idea what Wenshu was thinking—it didn't make sense for two men to share a room with a woman unless one of them was a servant, and we didn't want innkeepers to wonder what our story was. We didn't want them to remember us at all.

The innkeeper shot us one last look before telling Wenshu the price. He paid and waved for us to follow him upstairs. As soon as the door shut behind us, Zheng Sili crossed his arms and glared at me. "My father is a first-ranked magistrate in Lingnan, and I just had to pretend to be a slave," he said.

"A servant is not the same as a slave," I said, locking the door and wishing with all my might that we'd lost him in the town square. "And does your father's status really matter that much if he disowned you?"

Zheng Sili rolled his eyes. "At least *my* father didn't give me a servant's name."

I glared, but couldn't bring myself to disagree. *Zǐlán* meant *purple orchid* and was the kind of name more common among servants than scholars. The children of aristocrats had names that were virtues or dreams, carefully chosen characters that destined them for greatness. *Sīlǐ* meant *to think of manners*—a name for a man who diligently studied texts and applied their wisdom to his life. Zheng Sili was born to be a scholar, and I was born to be no one, and somehow we had both failed at our destinies.

Wenshu sat down heavily on the floor and pulled back his sleeve, grimacing at what remained of the arrow embedded in his arm. I knelt down in front of him and slapped his hand away. There was still a piece of wood lodged inside, so I pinched it between my fingers and yanked it out, then pressed three moonstones to the wound to heal it.

Wenshu gritted his teeth but otherwise didn't comment until I was done. He mumbled thanks, then rushed off to find somewhere to scrub the mud from his skin and clothes.

Zheng Sili was still hovering awkwardly by the door, so I dug out soggy handfuls of scrolls from my bag and dropped them on the ground in front of him.

"Make yourself useful," I said, gesturing to the wet paper. He wasted no time digging waterstones out of his bag and repairing the scrolls with a flourish of wholly unnecessary and ostentatious blue light. I repaired another handful, and at the cost of only a couple bruised fingers, my father's notes and the paper from the Sandstone Alchemist were once again dry and whole.

"This is one old transformation," Zheng Sili said, frowning at the Sandstone Alchemist's riddle. "What is this supposed to be?"

I tugged it away from him and rolled it up quickly, despite his protests. "Nothing that concerns you."

"Well, pardon me for reading what's right in front of me," he said, standing up and crossing his arms. "Have fun staring at your poems. I've been eating peasant food for months and need something of substance."

He stormed off and slammed the door behind him, finally leaving me alone.

I looked back to the scrolls, turning over my new opals in my hands. I held one up to the window, and as it caught the lamplight, I imagined the white eyes of dragons surveying the seas, looking down on this tiny bridge between the desert and mountains and all the lost souls inside of it.

It seemed that most of the city closed down just after nightfall. Though there were no wards in Baiyin that would lock us inside like in Chang'an, most of the shops were dark by the time Wenshu and I had both changed and headed into town. We left Durian sleeping on the bed and ventured farther and farther from the inn in search of light. Zheng Sili hadn't returned yet, and maybe, if we were lucky, he never would.

Baiyin clearly had not been spared by the raids. Half the buildings at the outskirts were little more than splintered wood and shattered clay spilled over cracked dirt. Instead of thatched roofs, only scorched black reeds covered the skeletons of houses, each gust of wind stirring up clouds of ash.

The center of the city had been more thoroughly repaired, a heart of golden light and loud voices that wiped away the unease of the ghostly outskirts. That was where we found a pub with candles still burning, the sounds of laughter rattling the lattice windows. It sat alone at the edge of one of the destroyed streets, boards hastily repaired with clay wires, cloth tarps thrown over the roof.

"Too noisy?" I said to Wenshu.

He shook his head. "I'm too hungry to be picky," he said, already heading for the door.

Wenshu attempted to buy us some congee while I claimed the corner of a long table, trying to make myself small in the large crowd. People this far from Chang'an probably had never seen the face of the prince or the royal alchemists, but I didn't like to stake my safety on a probability. I only wanted to inhale a bowl of soup, cram some food in my bag for Durian, and head back to the room to sleep until I felt less like a resurrected corpse.

The man at the bar must not have spoken Chang'an dialect, because I saw Wenshu pantomiming eating with a spoon as I sat down. He passed the man a few gold coins and crossed the room, sliding onto the bench beside me.

"I did my best, but I have no idea what he's going to give us," he said.

"As long as it's not life gold, we should be fine," I said. We'd eaten weeds and duck eyes and entrails that no one else wanted, after all. Anything served in a restaurant couldn't be that bad.

We waited in silence, the dim lighting and warm murmurs around us not at all helping me stay awake. I leaned into Wenshu and closed my eyes for what I swore would only be a few moments, but jolted at the sound of bowls hitting the table.

A server had placed two bowls of congee in front of us.

"Your pantomiming must have worked," I said, sitting up straight and grabbing my spoon. No matter how far from home we traveled or what delicacies we could have afforded, I always wanted congee when I was cold and tired. It made me feel like I was standing in the kitchen with Auntie So once more, back when I was too small to peer over the lip of the pot and could only smell the rice and marvel at the steam as I clung to her skirts.

"I think it's more likely that the word for *congee* is similar here," Wenshu said. "But maybe I'll have a career as an actor when this is all through."

I smiled and scooped up a heaping spoonful, blowing on it once before raising it to my mouth.

I hesitated, the spoon just barely grazing my lips, the white steam spiraling before me, shrouding my vision.

This didn't smell right.

There was a metallic undertone beneath the rice, brought forth in the steam. I had melted many metals down before with alchemy, so I knew the scent.

I knocked Wenshu's spoon out of his hand, spraying congee across his shirt.

"*Fan Zilan!*" he said, jolting back. "What are you—"

"Don't eat that," I said.

He tensed. "Why not?"

I leaned over the bowl and took a deep breath. The steam made my eyes water, and there it was, more pronounced—the metallic scent knifing up my nose. When I clasped the bowl in both hands, alchemy hummed through the ceramic, numbing my palms.

"There's an activated alchemy stone in here," I said in Guang-zhou dialect. I'd tried to feed the Empress an activated stone once . . . in the hopes of exploding her organs from the inside.

Wenshu sat up straight, trying to subtly glance around the room. "Who would do that?" he whispered.

"Maybe someone found out I'm an alchemist and told another private army," I said. "Maybe Zheng Sili sold us out for new shoes or something."

Wenshu sighed. "I really don't want to be punctured with any more arrows today."

I shook my head. "I don't want a fight either." I'd hardly slept at all, and my first meal in a day had just been snatched away. Another fight with a private army wasn't going to end well for us, alchemy stones or not.

"Shall we slip out quietly and run like cowards?" Wenshu said.

"It's a tactical retreat, not cowardice," I said.

"Of course," he said, nodding quickly. "You go first."

I cast one last sad glance at the bowl of congee that looked delicious if not for the likely poison, then pushed out my chair and headed for the door.

I had almost made it when a man wedged himself between me and the doorway, arms crossed. Another man appeared behind him, yanking the door shut and slamming down a wooden bar across the beams so no one else could enter. I took a startled step back, looking between them.

"Fan Zilan," the first man said, grinning darkly, "you're not going anywhere."

CHAPTER EIGHT

I just wanted dinner, I thought grimly, backing up against a wooden post as the man took another step forward. Was this the Empress and her pet alchemist, or just some soldiers from a private army? The strangers' eyes glowed, but we were standing right beside a light, and I couldn't tell if it was the reflection of candlelight or gold that burned from within.

I glanced over my shoulder at Wenshu, who had risen to his feet and was peering through the crowd to see what was going on, then I slid my hand back toward my satchel. But before I could reach any stones, someone seized my wrist.

A young woman stood behind me, wedged between me and the wooden post, my wrist clamped firmly in her hand. I couldn't see her well from this angle, but her long hair fell over my shoulder, the tip of her cold blade pressed delicately to my throat. If this was the Empress, just how many people had she convinced to help her?

"Three against one isn't very fair," I said, edging away from the blade. "Neither is trying to poison me. You really can't even capture me without all this fanfare? It's pretty embarrassing."

The first man shook his head. "We're not trying to capture you," he said. "We're trying to make you listen."

Listen to what? I thought.

"Zilan?"

Wenshu's voice cut through the crowd, and for a moment, both men turned toward him.

In their moment of distraction, I pressed my free hand to the wooden beam.

Alchemy rushed from my firestone rings into the post, bleeding through the wooden fibers. The beam crunched as the center weakened, spraying wooden splinters. The woman flinched at the sound, her grip loosening enough for me to elbow her in the stomach without letting her slice my throat open. I hurried toward Wenshu, grabbing another handful of firestones and praying the ceiling didn't come down on us.

Before I could throw the firestones, someone yanked me back by the waist and twisted my arm until my stones clattered to the ground. *How many people in this pub want me dead?* I thought as I tried to wrench my hands away. Everyone at the pub had gone quiet and turned to watch.

Wenshu called my name and rushed forward, but another man grabbed him by the collar and slammed him onto the table, overturning the candles.

Shadows rushed across tables and corners as the cold night enclosed the room. Only a few candles on the far side of the room remained, a thin breath of pale light in the pub that now felt more like a crypt. As the last two candles flickered, the eyes of every person in the room glimmered in tandem, their irises a warm gold.

A wave of coldness rippled down my spine. Surely not *all* of these people could be the Empress.

I twisted back to face the man holding my wrist. The moment our eyes locked, a dark grin spread across his face. It didn't matter whose skin she wore—I would know that expression anywhere.

"I really can't believe you put your dirty southern blood in the body of royalty," said the man holding Wenshu, now in crisp Chang'an dialect. "We'll definitely be leaving this part out of our history texts."

"I am not *dirty!*" Wenshu said, cheek pressed against the table.

I threw my weight forward, managing to free one arm, but another man grabbed it before I could reach for more stones. All around me, the customers at every table watched with vacant gold eyes.

"I suppose I must shoulder some of the blame," said the man holding me, "for allowing you into my palace in the first place."

"And to think Hong would have made you empress," said the woman who'd held a knife to my throat.

Everyone in the pub laughed in unison—a cruel, hollow sound, with no joy in their eyes.

"Don't talk about him!" I said, managing to elbow the man behind me in the nose. But the moment I broke away, more hands seized me.

"Oh, a sensitive subject?" the barman said, leaning on his elbow over the counter. "I suppose that's fair. I might be a bit touchy too if my beloved had died because of my incompetence."

"Zilan—" Wenshu tried to speak, but the man slammed him once more against the table and he let out a winded cough.

I ground my teeth together, my pulse pounding in my ears as I scanned the room for some sort of exit. I was decent enough at sparring, but fighting off an entire room of full-grown men and women was something else entirely. How could I incapacitate all these people? I could turn the floor to a sheet of ice, or release a smoke bomb, or set the walls on fire, but none of that was a good idea when I was trapped in the pub along with them. What would the Moon Alchemist have done?

She wouldn't have been in this situation in the first place, I thought grimly.

The man adjusted his grip on my arm, his sleeve sliding down to reveal his soul tag, the bright red scar tissue that spelled *Wu Zhao*. The same tight, precise script written on Junyi's arm.

Fighting off this many people at once was futile. I needed to take down the Empress, not her three dozen puppets.

But, luckily, I knew where I could find her.

I hesitated, glancing to Wenshu where he was trying to elbow a burly man back into the door.

"Can you carry me?" I shouted.

"What?" he said, wincing as a man bent his wrist back at a harsh angle.

"If you can't carry me, then drag me," I said. "I think I can give you about thirty seconds."

"*What are you talking about?*" he said, struggling against the barkeeper.

But if I said much more, then the Empress might start to understand as well.

I seized a knife from the table and raked it across the throat of the man behind me.

Hot blood sprayed across my face, salt stinging my lips. For a moment, I was in the throne room once more, clutching the Empress in my pearl-white hands, her pulse racing beneath my teeth.

The man fell forward and crushed me into the table, bowls

and bottles shattering beneath my spine, his blood spilling hot and fast across my chest.

A dozen other hands reached for me, but before they could tear me away, I grabbed the man's wrist and pressed three fire-stones to the soul tag on his forearm.

His blood rushed faster at my touch, a river soaking through my dress, rising up to devour the floor, drowning me in salt and crimson darkness. The table dissolved, the heavy weight lifted from my chest, and then I was falling into the silky night of the river plane.

Before I could even land on my feet, the landscape shifted beneath me, the river ripped away, dry land flashing past me as if I'd jumped out of a moving wagon. Desire guided you in this plane, and my desire was burning hot, lancing through my bones, cracking me open like scorched clay.

Wu Zhao, I thought. *Come find me.*

I crashed into wet earth and rolled down a steep incline, falling deeper and deeper into the woods. I sank my fingers into the freezing mud as I slid down, trying to slow my descent, but it parted like cream, and I only fell faster.

You want to find Wu Zhao? the world whispered through my bones. *Then fall.*

I crashed into flat ground, breath slammed from my lungs, mud on my lips. I rolled onto my back and gasped for air, the dark cage of the sky the same shade as the sludge beneath me, the whole world made of night.

Wu Zhao, I thought, the words as clear in my mind as the bright white coin of the moon overhead, *come out here and face me.*

But the Empress never took orders from anyone.

I didn't know if she could control other people's bodies while her consciousness was busy in the river of souls, but at the very least, I hoped I was making it difficult for her. After all, she was not some omniscient god, but a mortal clinging to the living plane through alchemy. The longer I could distract her, the more time I gave Wenshu to get us both out of there.

That was, if I could find her. She was here, that was certain—I had killed one of her stolen corpses, so whatever part of her soul had occupied him must have returned here.

I hadn't known souls could be fragmented in so many pieces. But of course, the Empress had never been scared to test the rules of alchemy. Anything could be done if you sacrificed enough.

I rolled over, trying to extract myself from the freezing mud that was starting to solidify around me, as if dragging me into a cold, wet grave. Who could have helped the Empress do something like this? What kind of powerful alchemist would have helped her? None of the royal alchemists, and they had supposedly been the best in the country.

Something whispered through the trees, a flash of light like the golden tail of a comet across the dark ground.

I rose to my feet. *The Empress should be here*, I thought. Perhaps I hadn't cut deep enough, and the man was bleeding out too slowly. Or perhaps there had been a nearby alchemist who had managed to heal him, and I was waiting for nothing while the Empress ripped my brother limb from limb.

The trees parted with a sigh of wind, as if welcoming me deeper. I stepped back, the ground now dry beneath my feet.

Fan Zilan, a voice whispered from the forest, a thousand miles away, yet somehow perfectly clear. It wasn't the Empress—the words were too bright and airy, like morning birdsong that the wind would carry away.

I knew that voice.

As the echo faded and the night fell silent as if waiting for my answer, I remembered darkness and fire, my name tangled with sparks and wet echoes and frantic heartbeats.

I blinked hard, rubbing my eyes as if I could scrub the images away. The last time I'd had vague recollections, it had been memories of my own forgotten death bubbling to the surface. I didn't like that my memory was now a tattered cloth, holes large enough for the night to whisper through.

I swallowed and backed up, away from the forest's edge, and thought of the Empress's name once more. This plane didn't want me here, and it was trying with all its might to devour me because it knew my mind was a labyrinth with no way out.

I imagined myself carving the Empress's name into the sky, each brushstroke firm and deliberate. The dry ground slipped away like a rug pulled out beneath me, and I fell to my hands in wet mud. Footsteps approached, and a pair of embroidered gold slippers stood before me, impeccably clean.

Slowly, my gaze traced up the line of shimmering gold fabric, and at last, there she was. A bright star in the dead, barren land-scape. The first blade of sunlight that rips that night open. Wu Zhao, the eternal.

My Empress.

"Scarlet—" she said, but she would never finish her sentence.

I lunged forward and wrapped my hands around her throat.

We rolled across the riverbed, our clothes snagging on twigs, sharp stones tearing fabric, yanking our hair. She reached for my eyes, her honed fingernails only a breath away, but I bit down hard on her hand until I tasted blood. Her scream scraped through my eardrums, echoing forever into the dark sky. I had never before heard the Empress's scream, even when she'd died.

Her fist crashed into my face. My teeth ached at the impact, blood filling my mouth. Her fingers scraped lines into my cheeks as I ripped her hair back, forcing her face away. She managed to shove me back just long enough to stand up, her foot planted on my chest. I grabbed at her ankle to topple her, but she stomped down on my face, and my vision exploded into red.

The real Empress was not a fighter, but the river plane was a game of minds, not physical strength. And the Empress had always been one step ahead of me.

"Let me tell you a story," the Empress said, and in the moonlight, looking down on me, her bright eyes glowed like those of a wolf stalking through the woods at night. "Once upon a time, the Crown Prince Li Hong was caught fleeing his country like a coward after his loyal citizens rebelled against his unjust laws. He was caught by a private army on the Mongolian border, and his corpse was dragged back to Chang'an, where the people hung his body from the city gates, along with his treacherous concubine."

"How imaginative," I said, the words coming out too weak and breathless, the way I had always felt around the Empress, now amplified in this in-between world.

"With no one else in the House of Li," the Empress continued, as if I hadn't spoken at all, "the kingdom then belonged wholly to his grieving mother, the Perpetual Empress Wu." At last, she looked down at me, shifting out of the moonlight, the glimmer dropping from her eyes, suddenly flat and black.

"This is the story that scholars will write down," she said, her voice low. "This is the only version that history will remember. This is the story you will help me create, Scarlet."

I clenched my jaw. "Why don't you ask your alchemist friend to help you?" I snapped. "Or do you expect me to believe you've been resurrecting yourself?"

The Empress stilled. It was only a moment, almost indiscernible, but quickly the cold smile curled across her face again. "*You* are my alchemist, Scarlet. You always were."

Her words curled tight in my chest. I felt as if she'd branded me just like the peasants whose bodies she stole. She'd made me the Scarlet Alchemist, so in a way, we were forever intertwined.

"Wu Zhao," I said, using her common name instead of her title because I knew she would hate it, "I am not yours. I never was."

The smile dropped from her face. Slowly, she sat back, turning her gaze toward the moon. Its white light spilled pale across her throat, and I remembered tearing it open with my teeth.

This had gone on long enough. I didn't come here to let the Empress push me around. I came here to distract her, break her mind in two.

I reached out and took the Empress's hand, lacing her fingers through mine, mud slick between our palms. She hesitated, frowning down at our entwined fingers.

"Scarlet—" she said warningly.

I tightened my grip around her hand as hard as I could manage. Then I closed my eyes and carved a new name into the sky.

The River Alchemist.

The ground flashed away, black mud sliding off the surface of the earth, replaced by needle-sharp grass. A thousand dark trees flew past us on either side, a great *whoosh* of air blowing over us as the world unfolded.

I dragged the Empress behind me, forcing her to cross the landscape with me or have her shoulder torn out of its socket. Her sharp nails sank into my wrist, drawing blood, but I only gripped her tighter.

We fell to the soft ground before a pale riverbed that had nearly dried up, a small clearing of silver grass that stole the moon's pale light, casting the clearing in ghostly white.

And there, pallid and wide-eyed in the grass, was the River Alchemist, her tattoos etched in gold across her skin, glowing like starlight around her face.

"Scarlet?" she whispered, the sound echoing as if whispered up from the bottom of a well. Her gaze fell to the Empress, and she took a startled step back.

Out of all the royal alchemists who had died, I'd felt the worst about the River Alchemist.

She'd helped me figure out how to poison the Empress when none of the other alchemists would dare discuss something so treasonous. She'd stolen my shoes to get me out of studying with the Moon Alchemist, brought berries and bugs for Durian to eat . . . and had died fixing my mistake.

I'd only visited her once in this plane, to tell her to hold on while I found the elixir, and to spread the word to the other alchemists, who I couldn't bear to face. She was the only one I knew wouldn't blame me for what had happened. When I'd told her my plan, she'd stretched back in the silver grass and looked up at the sky.

Take your time finding Penglai, she'd said. *I needed a vacation anyway.*

And now I had brought the Empress right to her. Once again, I was endangering other people with my impulsive decisions. But this time, it wouldn't be in vain. I would make sure of it.

The Empress tried to yank her arm away, pulling me to the ground.

"Help me!" I said to the River Alchemist.

The River Alchemist rushed forward and grabbed the Empress's free arm, bent it behind her, and used it to pin her to the ground by her shoulder. She turned to me, eyebrow raised. I hated how she hadn't even hesitated to trust me. I didn't deserve that kind of faith.

"Scarlet—"

"I don't have time to explain right now," I said. "Hold on tight and bring her far away."

"Where?" the River Alchemist said, frowning.

"Anywhere."

She shook her head. "If you and I aren't thinking of the same place, we'll be pulled—"

"In two different directions," I said, nodding.

The River Alchemist's eyes brightened with understanding, catching the light of the moon as the trees shifted overhead. A smile spread across her face. "Death by quartering," she said. "I like it."

"More like halving," I said, shrugging.

"Good enough," the River Alchemist said, turning toward the moon. "Hold on tight."

With her next breath, she was gone.

All at once, the Empress was dragging me across the sky, my shoulder tugging painfully at its socket as roots and stones scraped beneath my feet, the land flashing by so quickly that it blurred into a haze of gray. I had no destination in mind, so I was being tugged across the world along with the Empress.

I needed to choose somewhere else, but I couldn't decide where to go. I didn't want to bring the Empress to any of the other royal alchemists, and certainly not to Hong. It had to be someone I strongly desired to see, someone that would tug me in the opposite direction of the River Alchemist with just as much speed and force. What other dead people did I know, who the Empress could no longer hurt?

My father, I thought.

Before I had even fully decided, I'd slammed to a stop against the trunk of a tree, nearly losing my grip on the Empress in my surprise.

The River Alchemist stood on the other side of the tree, fighting to drag the Empress onward, her robes soaked in sweat. The Empress was struggling to break free of our hold, but with both her arms held apart, she couldn't do much more than kick at the dirt. We were no longer moving, suspended in place by the two opposing desires.

The River Alchemist's arm trembled, and then we were slowly moving in her direction once more, as if trudging through quicksand.

I turned away from her, trying to concentrate. This wouldn't work if it was only the River Alchemist dragging us across the world. I didn't want to simply carry the Empress, but tear her in two.

I closed my eyes and tried to remember what I could of my father.

Laisrén, the name I had only recently learned, that somehow felt like I had always known. I thought of his notes that I'd pored over by candlelight, the dream he'd ignited in me, first with my hate, then with my determination.

If there is an elixir of eternal life, I will find it.

I will never stop until I can return to them.

And if I found this elixir, if I completed his dream, maybe I could bring him back as well.

The ground began to shift, rushing faster beneath my feet.

My grip trembled on the Empress's wrist, her joints clicking and loosening as I fought to move forward, the dry grass turning to golden sand under my feet. The Empress was screaming, but I could hardly hear the sound over the rush of sand, the loudness of the world cracking apart, trees collapsing and sky unfolding.

My feet sank into sand, and I fell to my knees, still holding tight to the Empress's hand.

I remembered my father's low voice, the language I had lost. *Get up, Zilan*, he'd said. *Please.*

I trudged onward, even when I could hardly feel my shoulder at all, my nails piercing the Empress's sleeve.

I was in the desert once more, but this time the sands were gray, the trees lying in parched pieces around me. And in the distance, backlit by the sun, was a dark silhouette, robes fluttering in the wind.

I ran toward him.

I could no longer feel the River Alchemist pulling in the opposite direction, so my desire was probably pulling all three of us across the river plane, but I didn't care. The sands parted for me as I ran across the desert, the white sun swelling across the horizon, devouring the sky.

I was only a breath away, reaching out my free hand toward him.

I crashed down into hard dirt, my back slamming into crooked roots and jagged rocks. The sun overhead was only the distant moon, and my father was gone.

The Empress was on top of me, her face so drenched in sweat that her makeup was running in black streaks down her face, her perfect red lips now a bloody maw that dripped down her chin. Her face looked translucent, her whole body trembling, flickering in and out of existence. Both of her hands were free, which meant she must have broken away from the River Alchemist.

"You think you're clever," the Empress said, and even her voice sounded exhausted, far away and weak.

I turned toward the sky, as if my father might reappear on the horizon, but the world was dark once more.

The Empress grabbed my face with a trembling hand, forcing me to look at her.

"Do you remember what happened the last time you tried to play games with me?" she said.

Everyone died, I thought, her words pinning me to the cold ground.

"You have much more to lose than I do, Scarlet," the Empress said, her hand sliding down to my throat. "Wherever you go, I will always find you. You and I are tethered, and death can never sever that thread."

I tried to turn my head away from both her words and her burning gold eyes, but her other hand held my jaw tight.

Legends spoke of a red thread of fate, an invisible tether between souls who were destined to meet. I had once thought that Hong held the other end of my thread—the boy who had crossed the country and found me by the well in my broken city, only to meet me once again when I crossed the world myself.

But maybe the Empress was tethered to me in a different way, clawing against death to come back to me. Maybe we were always destined to destroy each other, for hate and love were equally sharp. She reached down to caress my face, and for a brief moment, I could almost see the scarlet thread tangled between her fingers—a curse, a promise.

I reached for her face to push her away, but my fingers tangled in her pearl necklace, only yanking her closer to me.

A blunt pain clanged through my head.

My vision burst with light, split halfway between the darkness of the river plane and a flash of candlelight. Something stung my cheek, and I heard Wenshu's voice far away, calling my name.

Wenshu.

I'd almost forgotten about him, left alone in the restaurant full of the Empress's puppets. That sharp spike of desire—to find him, protect him—ripped me from the river plane, still clutching the Empress's necklace.

I crashed onto my back on hard ground, Wenshu poised above me to slap me in the face. I shoved his arm aside before the blow could connect, gasping down a breath of night air. I was sitting on the ground outside the tavern, which Wenshu had barricaded with barrels. Inside, the people were yelling, tearing at the lattice windows.

I rubbed my forehead where I could feel a bruise forming and realized I was still clutching the Empress's pearls, coated in blood.

Nothing in the river plane was real except souls, so I shouldn't have been able to take it back with me. And yet I held four bloody pearls in my hand.

My head throbbed and I let out a groan, pocketing the pearls.

"Did you hit my head against something?" I said.

"Not intentionally," Wenshu said, looking away guiltily. "You're heavy, okay? I was in a bit of a hurry."

I forced myself to my feet and examined the barrier, then used some woodstones to reinforce the lattice windows with a solid pane of pine, blocking out the sound of yelling. I was tempted to just burn the whole place down, but that would draw attention to the restaurant and there was a chance someone would let everyone out.

"So much for getting some rest," I said, rolling my shoulder.

"This city obviously isn't safe. Let's grab Durian and get out of here."

"I thought we could at least get dinner before someone tried to kill us again," Wenshu said, already hurrying down the road.

I started to follow after him but hesitated after a few steps. "Where's Zheng Sili?"

"How would I know?" Wenshu said. "He's not a child. He can look after himself."

I glanced over my shoulder toward the city center. If the Empress had taken over a whole restaurant full of people, it was safe to say she had a tight grip on this town. She would probably recognize Zheng Sili, or at least would have noticed that we were traveling together. She might be pulling his organs out to make into sausages as we spoke.

I shouldn't have cared. But there was a difference between brushing someone off for rudeness and abandoning them to the Empress's whims.

"We have to find him," I said. Wenshu looked like I'd suggested we eat garbage, but he grumbled and followed me all the same.

We ran back to the main road in the city center, where the crowd grew dense once more. As we brushed past startled merchants and drunken men, I wondered if all of them were no more than actors in the Empress's charade, just background art for the stage she was setting to destroy me at her leisure. I prayed that whatever alchemy she'd managed to get her hands on hadn't allowed her to decimate this entire city.

I was about to run past a temple when Wenshu grabbed me by the sleeve, forcing me to a stop.

The Empress had found Zheng Sili first.

He was splayed across the steps of what looked like an

abandoned Buddhist temple, cheek crushed to the dirt.

I hesitated a few feet away, unsure of what to do. I'd never liked him, but I hadn't meant for the Empress to actually kill him. I shared an uneasy look with Wenshu.

Then Zheng Sili coughed, sliding down another step and groaning.

I stomped forward, yanking him up by the collar. His hair and clothes reeked of ale. "Are you *drunk?*" I said. "We've hardly been gone an hour!"

"It's none of your business," he said, words slurred, trying to pry my hands off but only managing to slap his wet fingers across my face.

I sighed and tossed him back to the stairs, where he lay down heavily, blinking as if just recognizing his surroundings.

"Hùnxiě?" he said, rubbing his eyes.

"Stop calling her that," Wenshu said.

Maybe it was the alcohol, or just the fact that it was another man scolding him instead of me, but he looked mildly ashamed. "Sorry," he said, "forgot your name."

I pressed a hand to my eyes. "The Empress is running around, and you're drunk."

"The Empress?" he said, eyes wide. He straightened up, but lurched unsteadily to one side and braced himself on the stairs. "It's okay, this isn't my first drink, there's alchemy that can help me sober up. Do you have any amethyst?"

"That's so expensive!" I said. "You use that to *sober up?*"

"Okay, never mind," he said, rising to his feet. "I have a faster way." Then he turned around and vomited behind the stairs.

Wenshu and I grimaced, looking away. When Zheng Sili turned back to us, wiping his mouth on his sleeve, his face looked papery white but his eyes looked slightly more focused. "Okay, what's the plan?" he said, looking between me and Wenshu.

I looked toward the horizon, where no other towns were visible as far as I could see.

"I think we're going to need a couple horses."

CHAPTER NINE

That night, the prince wasn't where I'd left him.

"Hong?" I said, winding deeper into the forest. I walked through the dark, silent woods, calling his name.

Part of me was terrified to venture back to the river plane, in case the Empress found me. But worse than that fear was wondering what she'd do to Hong if she found him first. She didn't even have to hurt him—all she had to do was cut his rope, and he'd wander into the woods and I'd never see him again. It was difficult for a non-alchemist to navigate this plane alone, but I knew better than to underestimate the Empress.

I walked deeper into the woods for several agonizing minutes until I found the rope, wearing thin against the tree. It pulled taut into the distant darkness, disappearing in the hazy fog.

I rushed forward, following the rope as it twisted around trees and branches, a web that only seemed longer and thinner the farther I went on. I hadn't remembered the rope being this long.

At last, I found Hong standing in the darkness, wrist pulled behind him, trying to walk forward but held back only by the tether around his wrist.

"Hong?" I whispered.

He didn't answer. His eyes were dark, his expression slack. I waved a hand in front of his face, but he didn't even blink. I sighed and wrapped my arms around him, pressing myself to his chest. After a moment, he stopped walking.

"Zilan?" he said.

I nodded into his chest.

He said nothing, but took a step back so the rope wasn't tugging on his wrist.

"I don't know what happened," he said, pressing his free hand to my back. "I don't remember walking here. Zilan, I—"

"Don't worry," I said, holding him tighter. I took his cold hand and tugged him back toward the river. We walked in silence for a few minutes, untangling the rope from branches and bushes along the way until we found a patch of soft grass. He bundled the slack rope in his lap, hands tugging at it anxiously.

"You're upset," he said.

I almost laughed. His brain was so rotted that he had nearly walked into his own eternal ending, and yet the first thing he wanted to talk about was my feelings.

I couldn't keep lying to him. The Empress was too real a threat, only growing more creative by the day. So I told him about how the Empress had spoken to me through Junyi, about the lost town of Baiyin, about all the bodies the Empress controlled.

He went very still as he listened, staring unblinking into my eyes. This was only his soul, not his true body, so he didn't need to breathe or blink, but the stonelike stillness unnerved me. When I finished, he sighed and leaned back against the tree trunk, tugging unconsciously at the rope.

At last, he let out a tired laugh. "Of course Mother would refuse to die," he said. "That's so like her."

"You're not upset?" I said.

He frowned. "I mean, I'm not thrilled that she's terrorizing you."

I shook my head. "But you died for nothing," I said.

Hong paused as if considering this, staring beyond me. He was still for so long that I wondered if he'd forgotten I was here. But then he shook his head slightly, reaching for my hand.

"I didn't die for nothing," he said. "I died for you, and you're still here, so none of it was a waste."

I knew he meant his words to be kind, but they only made me feel rotten. I didn't want anyone to die for me.

He squeezed my hand as if sensing my thoughts. "I would rather die a thousand times for you than watch you die even once, Empress."

"I'm not the empress," I said, regretting the words as soon as I'd said them. I never wanted to extinguish his hope, but I felt too drained to even pretend to be hopeful anymore.

"Of course you are," Hong said, frowning.

I shook my head. "I promise I'll get you out of here and become the empress one day, but right now I don't want to think about—"

"Zilan," Hong said, squeezing my hand. "You are already the empress. Didn't we discuss this?"

"No," I said, drawing my hand away from his. "I'm certain I would remember that conversation."

Hong grimaced. "I'm sorry," he said, gaze dropping to his lap. "I swore we already . . . My mind is a bit . . ."

I took his hand again. "No, it's not your fault," I said quickly.

His mind was a mess because of what he'd given up for me, and that could never be his fault. "What were you going to say?"

Hong went very still in the way he always did when he got nervous. "Well, before I died, I might have already filed some paperwork."

I raised an eyebrow. "What kind of paperwork?"

"It seems rather presumptuous in hindsight," he said, looking away from me, skin tinged pink with embarrassment, a shade I didn't know his face could turn after death. "I was trying to sort things out before we killed the Empress, since I thought we'd be so busy afterward and it wouldn't really be an appropriate time for that sort of thing, so I . . . might have already signed our marriage contract."

He winced as if expecting me to strike him, but I was too stunned to react. His words finally began to sink in, and heat rushed to my face. *"You married me before you asked my permission?"* I said, my voice far too loud for the silent forest.

"I would have withdrawn it if you'd said no!" he said.

"Aren't I supposed to be present for that kind of thing?" I said, gripping my hair.

"If we were commoners, then yes, but government workers don't tend to deny the Crown Prince what he asks for," he said. "So, though there wasn't a ceremony, if anyone checks the royal records, you are already the empress consort." He dared to look up at me, still backed away defensively. "Am I forgiven?"

"Have you apologized?" I said.

He smirked. "For loving you too enthusiastically?"

I punched his arm. "Try again."

He winced. "Okay, yes, you're right of course. I apologize for marrying you without informing you first. But seeing as I now know you would have said yes, am I forgiven?"

I did my best to glare at him, but it was no use. It was like glaring at a baby duck.

"Only because you're dead," I said. "You should consider yourself lucky, because if Wenshu Ge found out about this, he'd kill you."

Hong grimaced as if imagining. "Then perhaps we can keep this between us for the time being?"

I nodded. "I wasn't exactly planning to go back to Chang'an and sit on the throne anytime soon." I looked off to the horizon. "Though I do wish we could have brought the royal library up north. It sure would come in handy right now. I have no idea where to go next."

The best course would have been to find the Empress's puppet alchemist, to stop her from interfering at every turn. But that was just as much a mystery as Penglai.

"Do you know if your mother knew any other alchemists?" I said. "Someone must be helping her."

Hong grimaced, shaking his head. "I'm sorry, Zilan. She didn't confide in me about anything."

"You never saw or heard anything?"

"The Empress doesn't make mistakes," he said simply, as if it was an indisputable truth. He hadn't meant anything by it, but the words still made me shiver.

Suddenly, the prince sat up straight, eyes wide. "Oh no," he said. "I think . . . I think she might have a lot more bodies at her disposal than you think."

"Why?" I said. His panic was contagious, and my heart beat loud in my ears.

"A few years ago, she started branding peasants with her name in exchange for food," he said, looking away as if this was his shame and not hers. "I thought it was just her vanity, that she wanted to show that she owned them. But maybe this was always her backup plan."

I groaned, dropping my face to my knees.

Now that the prince had mentioned it, I remembered that campaign. The messengers had swept through Guangzhou wielding an iron brand and bags of rice. Uncle Fan and Auntie So had strictly forbidden us from participating, so I'd accepted a few more resurrection jobs than I otherwise might have, just to bury the guilt of not taking the food for such a small price. But many of our neighbors had no problem with it. They had suffered much worse than a small burn.

"She would still need an alchemist to activate the soul tags for her," I said. "A soul tag without an alchemist is just a name."

The prince shrugged. "I don't know, Zilan," he said quietly. "I'm sorry." Then his expression darkened. "You need to get out of here."

"What?" I said, drawing back.

"Check my body for marks," he said, gripping my wrist. "I don't think the Empress branded me, but you need to check. She's clever, so she might have knocked me out, or done it while I was sleeping, or when I was very young."

"If she could control your body, don't you think she would have done it by now?"

"How do you know she hasn't?" he said, eyes burning. "Zilan *go*, please."

I wanted to tell him that I knew my brother, that there was no way it was anyone but him, but his eyes were so panicked that I didn't want to deny him.

"Okay," I said. "I'll be back."

Then I turned away, my heart sinking the way it always did when I left Hong alone in the dark with no more than half-hearted goodbyes and unfulfilled promises. With every visit, I felt that my own heart was decaying just as fast as his.

I buried the thought and opened my eyes, blinking until the brown fabric ceiling of our tent came into focus. I was back with Wenshu and Zheng Sili, camped in an empty stretch of land a few miles from Baiyin.

After buying two horses and enough fabric for a tent, we'd ridden as far from Baiyin as we could manage before falling off our horses from exhaustion. Wenshu and I had pitched a tent while Zheng Sili watched us and complained, still halfway drunk. I'd set a couple firestones burning on a flat rock, casting the tent in warm light. Durian had curled up close to the stone, fast asleep.

Wenshu sat up, cracking his neck. "Finally," he said. "Took you long enough."

Zheng Sili, who was already dozing off in the corner, grumbled at the movement.

"Gēgē," I said, "we need to check everyone for soul tags. Starting with you."

"I have a soul tag," he said pointedly. "You know, the one that almost says Fan Wenhua because of your awful handwriting?"

"I'm serious," I said. "You could have an inactive one."

Wenshu looked exhausted and less than pleased with the suggestion, but he was a pragmatist if nothing else, and rolled up his sleeves to let me check. I checked all the usual spots for soul tags—the arms, the wrists, the back of the neck—but found nothing.

I leaned over and shoved Zheng Sili against the edge of the tent. He jolted awake, swiping out a hand to slap at me, which I easily dodged.

"Check each other for soul tags," I said. "I'll wait outside."

"What?" Zheng Sili said, rubbing his eyes. "Why do I have to do it?"

"Because you're both men?" I said, glancing at Wenshu, who looked at Zheng Sili like he was a pile of rotten fruit.

"Isn't it your boyfriend's body?" Zheng Sili said. "Shouldn't you know whether or not he has PROPERTY OF WU ZHAO burned into his skin?"

"How would I know that?"

Zheng Sili shot me an incredulous look. "Weren't you a concubine?"

My face burned. "*No!*" I said. "I mean, technically yes, but not like that."

"Can we please stop talking about this?" Wenshu said, looking pained. "I am going to jam knives into my ears."

I turned to Zheng Sili. "Wenshu Ge needs to check *you*, anyway, so call me when you're done."

"*Me?*" Zheng Sili said, eyes wide. "I am very obviously not the Empress, because *I can do alchemy!*"

When I didn't respond, he sighed and shoved his blankets away. "The Empress obviously takes people's bodies, not their minds," he said slowly, as if speaking to a child. "You think she could do the kind of alchemy I've spent a lifetime practicing just because she's wearing my hands like gloves? Don't insult me."

Wenshu shot me a questioning glance. I had to admit, Zheng Sili had a point. As far as anyone knew, the Empress couldn't do alchemy. I supposed it was possible that she'd learned in secret, but if she was any good at it, she could have learned to make her own life gold and wouldn't have needed me alive after all the other royal alchemists were killed.

"I think it's better to be careful," Wenshu said quietly. "Underestimating the Empress is dangerous."

Zheng Sili rolled his eyes. "Do you two really want to see me naked that badly? Fine."

"Don't flatter yourself," I said, but he was already untying his robes.

I hurried out of the tent as Wenshu made a strangled sound and shouted about how *you don't need to take it all off at once, no one wants to see that!*

After a few minutes, they determined that neither of them had the Empress's soul tag, which Zheng Sili was incredibly smug about. I was just grateful we hadn't been unknowingly dragging the Empress around with us for days, so I let him gloat for a moment before shoving him into the corner of the tent to make more room for me and Wenshu.

Zheng Sili grumbled and hugged his bag closer. "This is the thanks I get for helping you."

"You? *Helping?*" I said incredulously.

Zheng Sili's face slid into a frown, then he reached down into his sleeve and pulled out a crumpled piece of paper, staring at it blankly. "I could have sworn I gave this to you earlier, but—"

"But you were drunk out of your mind in the middle of the night?" I said, snatching it from him and shoving him when he tried to grab it. I managed to hold him back with one hand and unfold it with the other.

It was a flyer, a hole at the top as if Zheng Sili had torn it down.

WANTED: THE ARCANE ALCHEMIST
Dead or alive
Violent thief, beware of alchemy
Reward: 500,000 gold
Last seen in central Zhongwei

Beneath the writing was a scrawled image of the man. Strangely, where his facial features should have been, there was nothing but a blank space in the paper, like his face had been wiped clean.

"Your idea of helping is bringing me an unfinished wanted poster?" I said, turning to Zheng Sili.

He shook his head. "It's not unfinished," he said. "Some peasant selling goats gave it to me this evening. She said he's been stealing from nearby towns, but no one could describe his face."

"If she was *selling* goats, she was a merchant, not a peasant," I said. "Why is that so hard to understand?"

"Quit being pedantic and actually listen to me," Zheng Sili said. "You and I both know this guy is no royal alchemist, yet he's well-known enough around here that he has a title. What does that tell you?"

"That he's a thief who is really bad at not getting caught?"

Zheng Sili scowled and shook his head. "He must be good at alchemy, enough to be known for it, or else this would just say his real name."

Unfortunately, Zheng Sili was right. It was rare to find powerful alchemists anywhere but the capital, for few would spend their lifetimes learning such a valued skill if they didn't intend to make it their career.

The Empress couldn't have put herself in so many bodies without the help of a living alchemist, and there weren't many in the north skilled enough to pull that off. This one clearly didn't respect the law, and was good at hiding from the police, which made him a pretty likely candidate.

"You think this guy is the one who's been oh so kindly holding the door open for the Empress?" I said.

"Took you long enough," Zheng Sili said. "Do try to keep up with me. I know it's challenging at times."

I ignored him and turned to Wenshu. "If we can cut off the Empress and keep her in the river plane—"

"Our lives will become a whole lot easier," Wenshu finished. "But this flyer isn't exactly descriptive. How do you expect to find him?"

Zheng Sili shrugged. "Alchemists aren't typically good at being inconspicuous. But I have a few tricks we can try out."

"We need to find him," I said, digging a map out of my bag and unfurling it close to the firestones. It looked about a day's ride north, the farthest from home I'd ever been. To think that I'd once thought I'd live and die on the southern coast of Guangzhou, and now I was a world away, sweating in the northern deserts.

"And *I* need to sleep unless you want me to be hungover tomorrow morning," Zheng Sili said, kicking the corner of my map away with a blanketed foot.

"We don't want you to be here at all," Wenshu said.

Zheng Sili only rolled over, tugging his blanket. "Yeah, and people in the seventh layer of hell want a ladder."

Wenshu looked like he might keep arguing, but I shook my head. For once, Zheng Sili wasn't wrong—we needed rest. Tomorrow, we were going to find the Arcane Alchemist, dead or alive.

CHAPTER TEN

Early in the morning, we set off for Zhongwei.

Wenshu and I packed up the tent while Zheng Sili pretended to help but mostly folded and unfolded fabric, then the three of us rode toward the horizon, shivering from the early morning air that cut through our too-thin desert clothes.

At night, I'd dreamed of the Empress's hand at my throat, the two of us tangled in crimson thread. I woke long before the others and stared at my three opals for hours, imagining the beauty of Penglai. The opals' perfect clarity and smoothness somehow felt like mockery, because on their own, they were useless.

I'd tried clutching them and thinking only of Penglai while alchemy fired through my veins, but I couldn't conjure even a weak transformation. Clearly, something was missing, and the answer was probably encoded in the rest of the transformation. Perhaps another alchemist could help me figure it out—even if the Arcane Alchemist wasn't the Empress's pawn, maybe he'd know what the other lines meant.

But something told me a man on a wanted poster wouldn't be that benevolent.

About an hour into our ride, Wenshu slumped forward in the saddle. He started sliding off the horse before I could stop him, and when I grabbed on to his robes, I only managed to throw myself off with him, both of us crashing into the sand.

My shoulder hit the ground first, and Wenshu landed heavily on top of me. I curled into myself, trying to shield my face from hooves, my heartbeat thundering through my bones. I had already had my face smashed in once by a horse, and I didn't trust Zheng Sili to put me back together the right way if it happened again.

I heard the horse's steps slowing and tentatively sat up, wincing at the stiffness in my shoulder. I turned Wenshu over and frowned at the cut on his forehead, but it didn't seem that deep. Durian peeped and poked his head out of my bag—luckily we hadn't squished him in the fall.

Zheng Sili turned back and dismounted, hurrying toward us, our other horse lingering nearby.

"This is a very inconvenient place to crack your skull open," Zheng Sili said, squatting beside us and looking between me and Wenshu. "Can you still ride?"

"Give me a fucking minute," I said, rubbing my shoulder. My fingers felt numb, so I fumbled through my satchel with my left hand, pulling out a few moonstones and trying desperately not to think about how dangerous it would be for us to keep riding horses with Wenshu like this. It had only been a day since he had last collapsed. Normally we had more respite from the episodes. I pictured the holes in the fabric of his soul tearing wider, his soul wandering farther and farther from the river.

The cut on Wenshu's forehead had already stopped bleeding, so I turned my attention to my arm instead and pressed three moonstones to my shoulder. The pain ebbed instantly but didn't completely vanish, a muted current just beneath my skin. My fingertips grew colder, so numb I could hardly even feel them.

"You need to pop it back in first," Zheng Sili said, like it should have been obvious. "You're trying to heal something in the wrong place. It's like mending a cut on a severed arm."

"Excuse me?"

He pointed to my shoulder. "You can tell because it's lower than your other shoulder. You always had bad posture, but now it's even worse."

I grimaced, looking down at my shoulder, which did slope down a bit more sharply than it probably should have. I swallowed, nauseous, glad I'd at least numbed the pain before Zheng Sili pointed it out.

"I'll do it," he said, standing up.

"Absolutely not," I said, scooting back.

He sighed. "We have places to be, hùnxiě. You're bad enough at riding with both arms. If you fall off again, then you'll have two useless arms instead of one."

He reached for me again, but I kicked sand in his face.

"You're not touching me," I said, not really because of propriety but more because I didn't like the idea of being in pain in Zheng Sili's arms. "Wake my brother if you want to help so bad," I said. "He can do it."

Zheng Sili sighed, then wound back and slapped Wenshu hard across the face.

Wenshu sucked down a sharp breath, then coughed out sand, face turning red. He looked between me and Zheng Sili, then our abandoned horses.

"Shit," he said, running his hands across his chest as if checking for injuries.

"Don't worry," Zheng Sili said wryly, "your sister broke your fall."

He whirled around to face me, expression sliding into a frown as his gaze immediately locked on my shoulder.

"Just pop it back in for me," I said airily, far more confident than I felt.

He sputtered, shaking his head. "*Just pop it back in? Zilan, I'm not a healer.*"

"None of us are," I said. "You at least have fine motor control that I trust."

"Popping a shoulder back in isn't about fine motor control," Zheng Sili said, scowling.

"How do you even know this?"

"Because I'm not ignorant?" Zheng Sili said, shoving my other shoulder. "Lie down."

I clenched my jaw and tried not to make a sound as Zheng Sili wrenched my arm up and shoved it in with all the gentleness of a battering ram. I stared up into the desert sky, the sun a bright flash across my vision, and for a moment it was all I could see. I felt so small beneath the bright expanse of white sky, and tears burned at my eyes and I felt thoroughly pathetic, crying in front of Zheng Sili.

The Scarlet Alchemist doesn't cry, I told myself, sitting up and turning away, clenching my hand into a fist. *The Scarlet Alchemist has killed monsters, so she shouldn't be afraid to get back on a horse. Don't be ridiculous, Zilan.*

"Can we keep going now?" Zheng Sili said.

I wound back and gave him a solid punch to the arm. My shoulder stung at the motion, but at least I could clench my fist.

"The hell was that for?" he said, clutching his arm.

"Just testing out your repair," I said, standing up. "This will suffice."

"I'm glad," Zheng Sili said, shooting me a dark look as he grabbed the reins of his horse.

Zhongwei was the northwest's last stand against the encroaching desert, the sands sectioned with straw checkerboard barriers to keep the desert from swallowing the city whole. The city had no northern gate, because the world ended in the vast expanse of deadly, sweeping gold. How strange it was that Chang'an had paved its streets in gold, yet couldn't compare to the vast golden landscape of desert cities like this one.

We arrived at the gates by late afternoon, riding through the gravel fields of watermelon at the outskirts, our eyes scratched red from sand carried along the wind. Our horses seemed tiny in comparison to the camels that people pulled through the streets, spitting white foam, bulbous pink tongues hanging out of their mouths. The city sloped uphill, and just over the crest, I could make out the river bridging the city from the mountains, its water dyed sunset orange from all the red dirt and sand.

People stared at our horses as we passed, perhaps thinking us cruel for bringing them through the desert. I hoped it wasn't because they recognized Wenshu as the prince. Or maybe it had more to do with Zheng Sili scowling at everyone who passed by.

"You're scaring people," I said, shoving his arm. "You look too angry."

"I *am* angry," he said. "Thinking about anyone helping the Empress does that."

"*You* helped the Empress," Wenshu said.

Zheng Sili waved his hand dismissively. "I've redeemed myself."

"You're not the one who gets to decide that!" Wenshu said.

But his yelling was attracting even more attention, so I tugged a horse between him and Zheng Sili.

Wenshu sighed and snatched the reins from me. "I'm going to find a place to tie up and feed the horses so we stand a chance at blending in here," he said. "You two figure out some way to use alchemy to find him."

Zheng Sili wrinkled his nose. "Don't leave me alone with her! We're obviously not related, so people will think she's my wife."

"You should be so lucky," I said, rolling my eyes. Wenshu was clearly no longer listening to either of us, holding his hand out for gold coins, which I reluctantly passed him. He pocketed them, then led the horses away without another word.

Zheng Sili made an exasperated noise and started storming in the other direction.

"Is that your plan?" I said, hurrying after him. "Throwing a tantrum?"

"No," he said. "I'm looking for a stone merchant, since I apparently have to do everything around here."

"I see someone's not feeling hungover anymore and is back to being an ass," I said, following him into the town center.

Stones were harder to come by in Zhongwei, but we managed to find a merchant with a cart full of stones tucked between the cabbage salesman and another cart selling seaberries. I thought back to the opals in my pocket, still unsure what I could even do with them. But the solution couldn't have been that obvious, or else Zheng Sili surely would have told me just to make fun of my idiocy by now.

Zheng Sili filled a tray with a handful of lodestone and some desert kyanite, a blue stone I had never seen in person before, then turned to me for gold. By the time I paid the merchant,

Zheng Sili was already walking away, picking out a bunch of grapes and waving me over to pay.

"Desert grapes contain sodium," he said as I counted out coins.

"If that was what you wanted, we could have just bought salt," I grumbled, but didn't protest further, since I didn't have any better ideas for how to find the Arcane Alchemist.

Zheng Sili was already walking away, mumbling something about stones to himself. I caught up to him with the armful of grapes as he ducked into an alley, moving to the deepest part, hidden in the shade between buildings. He spread his stones out on the ground before him and closed his eyes as if thinking. I peeled a grape and bit it in half, holding it in front of my bag until Durian poked his head out and snatched it.

"I need those," Zheng Sili said, glaring.

"For what?" I said. "Care to explain?"

"You bought some ying waterstones back in Baiyin, right?" he said, as if I hadn't spoken.

I sighed and dug them out of my satchel, tossing them to the dirt, where he carefully arranged them in a pentagram with the other stones.

"I'm making a compass," he said at last. "It's a magnet that can point us in the direction we need to go."

"I know what a compass is," I said, frowning. "But I already know which direction is north. Why would that help us?"

"Because," Zheng Sili said, "instead of pointing north, it will point us toward the strongest concentration of alchemical energy."

I frowned. "So we need to catch this guy midtransformation?"

Zheng Sili rolled his eyes. "Transformations are like qi fireworks going off all at once, and the more powerful, the longer they linger," he said. "Did you really never learn this? You just knocked some stones together and hoped for the best?"

"Says the guy who never became a royal alchemist," I said, crossing my arms. In truth, I felt foolish for not thinking of this myself. Of course no alchemy stone could bring us to a man whose name we didn't even know, but it could bring us to other transformations. It would have been useless in a city like Chang'an that brimmed with alchemy, but this far north, where alchemists were few and far between, it could work. I supposed Zheng Sili's education hadn't been entirely wasted on him.

"Cover me," he said.

"Cover you with what?"

But he didn't wait for my response, resting his hands over the pentagram, blue light rising like small bursts of lightning between his fingers. I jumped to my feet and stood in front of him, doing my best to block anyone else's view into the alleyway with my skirts.

"I'm not a human wall, you know!" I said over my shoulder.

The crackling sounds died down, the light mercifully fading. "Not my fault you're a string bean," he said.

I turned around, frowning at the round compass clutched in his palms, a flat piece of black stone with a blue arrow that shifted in his hands, pointing toward the horizon.

"What are the grapes for?" I said.

"Oh! Right." He leaned over and popped three of them in his mouth. "I was hungry."

Before I could start yelling, he snapped the bunch in half and held the other half out for me. "I got you some," he said.

"*I* paid for them!" I said, snatching the grapes.

"Yeah, with the prince's money, so don't act all high and mighty about it," he said. "At least I gave you half."

"Half for you, and half for me and my brother to share?"

He shrugged. "I forgot about him."

As if summoned, Wenshu appeared at the mouth of the alley.

"Have the two greatest alchemists in Lingnan found a solution yet?" he said, crossing his arms and leaning against the wall.

"One of them has," Zheng Sili said, popping another grape in his mouth and rising to his feet, compass in one hand.

We followed the compass deeper into the city, but had to loop around the market to go where it pointed, not wanting to scale the walls of the ward with so many people watching. After half an hour, I started to suspect it was leading us in circles.

"Are you sure this is actually real?" I said, reaching out my hand expectantly. "Let me see it."

"Don't break it," Zheng Sili said, reluctantly handing it over.

At once, I could feel the hum of alchemy ignite in my bones, like I was holding a piece of the sun. I turned in the opposite direction and the arrow snapped back toward the direction of the sunset. It seemed real enough to me.

"How did you even make this?" I whispered.

"Intelligence," Zheng Sili said, snatching the stone back. "You want me to be your alchemy tutor, pay me."

"We're literally buying all your food," Wenshu said, but Zheng Sili ignored him.

We followed the stone even farther across town, down winding pathways, ducking around fruit carts and through stores. Zheng Sili seemed so singularly focused on the direction of the arrow that he saw nothing and no one else, and we had no choice but to follow after him, even when he brushed past families and ran through storefronts.

The sun set quickly after that, practically crashing into the horizon, a swift cold washing over the town. At last, Zheng Sili drew to a stop in the middle of a street. A sudden gust of wind blew my hair into my face, and I realized that one of my hairpins had fallen out somewhere along the way.

"Well?" I said, raking my hair out of my eyes.

He was glaring at his palm. "I don't understand," he whispered.

I sighed and grabbed the compass. This time, he didn't even fight me, but merely stared at his empty hand.

The compass arrow spun in dizzy circles in my palm, no longer settling on one direction. Wenshu watched over my shoulder, frowning. I held the compass up to my eye and squinted in the setting sunlight until I saw a crack straight down the center.

"It's broken," I said, handing it back to Zheng Sili.

He shook his head, not moving to take it. "That doesn't make sense. How could it break? It's made of strong stones, and it's not as if I dropped it."

"Well, can you make another one?" Wenshu said.

He shook his head. "I don't have any waterstones left. *Someone* wouldn't give me any more money."

"We can't use up all of our waterstones on your flimsy compass that brought us nowhere," I said. "Remember what happened the last time we were out of waterstones?"

Zheng Sili grimaced. He looked around at the street we'd arrived on, as if snapping out of his trance. We stood on a quiet residential road. Lanterns had burned down low, casting the street in soft darkness, edges blurred away by shadows. An old woman emerged from her house, shooting us a curious glance before dumping a bucket of soiled water into the street. There was a pub a few houses down with a fluttering banner of a panda eating a watermelon. It hardly seemed like a great hideout for a thief.

"Maybe you made it wrong," I said.

"How would *you* know?" Zheng Sili said, glaring. "You can't even make a normal magnet, much less one this advanced. Maybe we're in the wrong city."

"Well, can you make a rock that can take us to the right city?" Wenshu said from behind us.

Both of us turned to scowl at him.

"A *rock*?" Zheng Sili said threateningly, at the same time I said: "What kind of *rock* do you think can track elusive alchemists across the country?"

Wenshu put his hands up in surrender.

Zheng Sili let out a frustrated sound. "I'm hungry," he said, abruptly turning down a side street and waving us after him like servants.

We showed the flyer to merchants as we approached the city center. Most of them had some vague recollection of the Arcane Alchemist, but couldn't remember when, or what he looked like, or where he'd gone. Wenshu bought a few lamb skewers and congee and passed them out, which Zheng Sili somehow found a way to complain about even while eating as if starved.

"You guys are just cheapskates," he said, eating the lamb all the same. "It's not even your money."

"I didn't pack the entire palace treasury," I said. "The money will run out eventually, and then what? You'd have to eat weeds like a *peasant*."

Zheng Sili shuddered, licking the sauce off his skewer. He glanced down at his dirty hands. "Anyone have a rag?"

"Not for *you*," Wenshu said.

"Isn't everything you wear basically a rag?"

Wenshu made a face that I knew meant he would start yelling, so I reached into my pocket to sacrifice one of my rags rather than listen to them argue.

My fingers closed around a torn scrap of paper. I pulled it out, turning away from Zheng Sili and Wenshu and moving toward the light so I could read it.

"We don't have to take you with us and pay for your food, you know," Wenshu was shouting behind me, but his words barely registered as I read over the scrawled handwriting again and again.

"Are you forgetting who carried you to Baiyin?" Zheng Sili said.

"Zilan did that!" Wenshu shouted.

"Gēgē?" I said, turning around. When he kept shouting at Zheng Sili, I yanked his sleeve. They both turned to look at me.

"The Arcane Alchemist is back where the compass broke," I said.

"How do you know that?" Zheng Sili said as I passed Wenshu the note.

At the top, there was a hasty sketch of a panda eating a watermelon. Beneath it, a few crudely scrawled words:

Blue robes

Stain on right sleeve

Freckle near eye

"This was in my pocket," I said. Wenshu's expression softened as understanding dawned on him. Surely he recognized the handwriting.

"Did a child write this?" Zheng Sili said.

I shoved his shoulder, smashing him against a building.

"*What?*" he said. "I only—"

"It's *my* handwriting," I said.

"What?" Zheng Sili said, massaging his shoulder. "When did you write that?"

"I don't remember," I said. "I have no memory of writing this, which means—"

"That the Arcane Alchemist is here," Wenshu said. "We've already found him."

CHAPTER ELEVEN

We retraced our steps until we stood once more on the quiet residential street where the compass had mysteriously broken, the panda banner fluttering mockingly in the wind. Zheng Sili glared at it like it was the singular cause of our troubles, his shattered compass crushed tight in his fist.

I wondered if this was how Hong felt all the time—moments of his life wiped away as if they'd never happened, unable to trust his own mind. The once pleasant street now felt sinister, the clear sky foreboding. If I couldn't trust my own memory, nothing was safe.

The more I thought about it, the more obvious it became that we'd somehow lost time—how quickly the sun had set, how the compass had broken for no apparent reason, how I felt more exhausted than I should have. How much time had we spent with the Arcane Alchemist? What had happened when we found him? Judging by the broken compass, it hadn't gone well.

Zheng Sili looked ready to charge into the pub and raise hell for the crime of destroying his precious compass, but Wenshu grabbed his arm before he could.

"Don't go in there so angrily," Wenshu said. "If he's there and sees us looking like we know what happened, he'll walk straight out."

"So what's our story, then?" Zheng Sili said, wrenching his arm away.

"That we need to, oh, I don't know, *eat dinner*?" I said.

Zheng Sili shrugged. "I'm just saying, I'm not pretending to be your servant again."

"Then pay for your own damn food," Wenshu said, shoving the door open and waving me inside, slamming the door in Zheng Sili's face.

I made a conscious effort not to survey the entire room the moment we entered. Instead, I cast a quick glance around as if looking for empty tables, making a mental note of everyone wearing blue robes, which had apparently been one of the more salient details. It wasn't hard, because the pub only contained a dozen or so people, all men, several in blue robes, three of them with their backs turned. Of course this couldn't be simple.

I shuffled closer to Wenshu, who pretended to think carefully about which table to sit at. Zheng Sili slammed the door open and stomped inside behind us.

"This place is for drinking, not standing," one of the barmaids said, causing a few heads to turn our way. Wenshu distractedly slapped some coins on the counter, gesturing for me to sit beside him.

Zheng Sili cleared his throat, waving at the barmaid. "Do you have ox?"

Wenshu elbowed him in the ribs. "Do you have to order meat every time we go out?"

"Do I have to eat dirt just because you do?" Zheng Sili said as the barmaid set down some cups full of dark wine in front of us. Durian slid his beak out of my bag, but I quickly poked it back inside and tightened the drawstring. Setting an alchemical duck loose in the restaurant wouldn't exactly improve our stealth.

I took another slow sip and tried to look casually around the room.

One man in blue sat by the window, laughing and slamming down his cup as he talked loudly to two other men. That probably wasn't our alchemist—anyone with a forgettable face probably didn't have many friends.

Another man in blue at a corner table had a young boy in his lap and a woman by his side eating off his plate. I doubted the Arcane Alchemist had built a reputation as a thief and then started a family in the same city where he brazenly robbed people.

Another man in blue was reading a scroll at a dimly lit table by the opposite wall. He glanced up in irritation whenever his candle flickered too violently, his reading light shifting back and forth. With his back to the door, he didn't seem to have noticed us. I leaned slightly out of my seat, trying to get a better look at what he was reading.

As I leaned forward, I locked eyes with another man, who was slipping out the back door.

In the darkness of the far wall, it was hard to make out the hue of his robes. But as the candlelight flickered, I caught a bright flash of blue on his sleeve as he reached for the door.

We made eye contact for one fleeting moment, his hand an inch away from the doorknob.

He looked young, his face smooth and bright, dark eyes wide as he drew back at the eye contact. His hair fell over half his face, softening the harsh edges of his jaw. I was certain I hadn't seen him before.

Then the moment dissolved, and he turned back to the door.

On the side of his face, there was a single freckle just under his eye.

I leaped from my seat, ignoring Wenshu's and Zheng Sili's questions as I hurried after the man, nearly overturning a server. I couldn't let him out of my sight, or this would start all over again and we'd have no chance of finding him.

He was already heading out the doorway, but I grabbed on to his sleeve and stumbled into the alley with him just before the door could close.

"Hey!" he said, trying to pull his sleeve away from me. I held on tight, taking out my knife.

He raised his hands and backed against the wall of the building, jolting at the impact. His eyes watered as I drew closer, his hands shaking. The certainty I'd felt in the pub rapidly dissolved, weakening my grip around my knife. Could this startled deer of a man really be a great alchemist? His face certainly wasn't plain and unmemorable. In fact, I wasn't sure I'd ever seen a more handsome man, and I prayed Hong would forgive me for the thought. He had perfectly smooth skin and comet-bright eyes, his face somehow as delicate as an orchid yet thornlike in its sharpness.

Wenshu burst out of the back door, knife already in hand. The man in blue flinched, wringing tears from his eyes. He flinched again when Zheng Sili stumbled out the door a second later.

"I have a few coins in my pocket," the man said, hands still held up in surrender. "You can take whatever's there."

I looked to Wenshu, sure my expression gave away my doubt. "I don't remember him," I said, "but I wouldn't, would I?"

Zheng Sili frowned, stepping around me to examine the man more closely. "No alchemy rings," he said. He grabbed one of the man's hands, running his fingers over the smooth skin. He knew as well as I did that alchemists usually had calloused palms and broken nails from our transformations. "He doesn't look like an alchemist. He looks like a student who snuck away from his studies."

"I'm not an alchemist!" he said. "And my father can give you more if this isn't enough! Whatever you want!"

"We're not mugging you," I said.

"Unless you lie to us," Zheng Sili added. "We're not people you want to lie to." Then he turned to me expectantly. "Hùnxiě?"

I blinked. "What?"

"Show him," he repeated. "Go on." When I didn't move, he rolled his eyes and switched to Guangzhou dialect. "Go beat some answers out of him."

"We don't even know if he's the Arcane Alchemist," I said. "And why do I have to do it?"

"Isn't this how peasants solve problems?" he said. "By knocking each other's teeth out?"

"And what do the rich do instead?" I said, clenching my fists. "Bludgeon each other with their massive bags of gold?"

"We're wasting time," Wenshu said from behind us, arms crossed. "If you don't think it's him, we need to get back inside before anyone else in blue leaves."

I sighed, sheathing my knife with more force than necessary. Surely there were many men who fit the hasty description in my note, and this clearly wasn't the one. The man looked between us as we released him.

"You're really not mugging me?" he said.

"Just go," I said, massaging my forehead. What a waste of time. No wonder the Empress was taking over whole towns—we were never going to find her alchemist at this rate.

"Unbelievable," Zheng Sili said, crossing his arms. I didn't know if he was more frustrated with me or the man we'd almost mugged, but I didn't care.

The man bowed awkwardly, then turned and rushed off.

The Arcane Alchemist had probably left before we returned to the pub. He could be anywhere in Zhongwei by now, or maybe he'd even fled to another city. Just like with the Sandstone Alchemist, I'd rushed into meeting someone powerful without fully thinking it through and been woefully unprepared. I could almost picture the Moon Alchemist shaking her head in disappointment. I clenched my teeth against the sudden urge to cry, even though I would rather have eaten sand than cry in front of Zheng Sili. But as the cool winds of the north tore through my silk robes, I remembered once more how far I was from home, chasing after a myth, with nothing at all to show for it. What was I even doing here?

"If there's anyone else you want to interrogate, do it now," Wenshu said. "He seems the type to call the police."

"Right," I said, the word clipped so he wouldn't hear any sadness in my voice. The man was almost gone now, hurrying back to the street. A breeze descended from the mouth of the alley and gently nudged his hair over his shoulder.

There, on the back of his collar, a copper hairpin glinted in the moonlight.

I pressed a hand to the right side of my head, where my hair clip had disappeared that afternoon around the same time the compass had broken. As expected, my hair hung loose, the clip gone.

My hand fell to my side, my gaze locked on the man as he turned to look over his shoulder one last time. Our eyes met, and all at once, I remembered.

Zheng Sili's compass pointing straight toward the entrance of the pub.

A man in blue silk bursting outside.

Eyes like shooting stars, face as soft and white as a lily, a wicked pearl smile.

A swift argument, then Zheng Sili's compass crushed beneath his boot.

See you never, Scarlet, he'd said, waving goodbye, heading back into the pub.

But before he'd disappeared, I'd slipped one of my hairpins onto his clothes, praying we'd stand a chance at finding him again.

And it might not have worked, if I'd actually been an aristocrat from Chang'an—the rich wore gold hairpins, the same ones that held up this man's hair. Seeing one on the back of his clothes might not have meant a thing.

But I had always worn copper hairpins made from Wenshu's old scroll clips, ever since I'd used one to stab Zheng Sili at my first alchemy trial.

I was running before I even realized what I was doing, yanking the man back by the collar. I gripped him with one hand and unsheathed my knife with my teeth, then pressed the blade to his throat.

Wenshu and Zheng Sili hurried to catch up to us, watching me with wide eyes.

"I know who you are," I said.

All of his trembling stilled. He let out a sharp laugh. "That's impossible," he said, looking over his shoulder, his comet-bright eyes locking with mine, a dark smile spreading across his face. The timidness of his earlier persona had vanished, his words in crisp Chang'an dialect, each one like a thorn. "I'm no one."

Then he wrenched himself out of my arms and grabbed my wrist, twisting it backward. The knife slipped from my hands and clattered on the ground, and the man took off running.

I raced after him, clutching my bag to my chest so I wouldn't shake Durian too much. Wenshu and Zheng Sili quickly caught up, and the three of us chased the man in blue down the road, dodging merchant carts and ducking under camels. The man took a sharp turn down a side street, vaulting over a child playing with chickens in the road.

Wenshu had nearly caught up to him. Of course the prince's body wasn't any good at fighting but was fantastic at running for his life.

The man clambered over some abandoned crates, reaching for the rammed dirt wall that separated the city from the desert.

"Don't let him out of your sight!" I called. But Wenshu was way ahead of me, grabbing hold of the man's sleeve and yanking him back before he could jump over the wall. Zheng Sili and I made it to the crates and tried to help Wenshu drag him to the ground, but the man was already straddling the wall, and pulled the rest of us over with him.

I hit the ground and something crunched wetly beneath me. Judging by the pained sound Zheng Sili made, I worried I'd cracked his skull open. But as I rolled to my feet, my side plastered with pink fruit, I realized that what I'd actually destroyed was a watermelon.

We'd made it past the city walls and fallen into the gravel fields of watermelon spanning for miles into the horizon, the rocks sharp beneath my thin shoes. Wenshu was sitting in half a smashed watermelon, black seeds stuck to the side of his face. Zheng Sili stumbled to his feet, his skull thankfully not smashed open, though the watermelon beneath him hadn't been so fortunate. The man in blue had fallen a few feet away and was hurrying to untangle his ankle from a vine.

I reached for my stones, but Zheng Sili was faster. He seized the nearest watermelon, and alchemy raced through the vine like blue lightning. He was a breath too slow, and the alchemy only singed the man's fingertips as he freed himself and leaped to his feet.

"There's nowhere to run from us out here," I said. "The wall is too high to climb on this side, and we'll never lose sight of you in a valley like this."

"We don't want to hurt you, to be clear," Wenshu said, wiping sweat from his forehead.

The man rolled his eyes. "I know what you want," he said. "We've already met. That's how I know I have nothing to say to you." Then he slammed his palms into the ground.

The gravel, I realized too late. I'd thought the man was helpless with no alchemy stones, but we were standing in a field of rocks.

The world exploded into red.

I held my arm up against the barrage of sticky water and wet fruit. A thick chunk of rind hit me in the chest and knocked the breath from my lungs, but I managed to stay on my feet. My vision cleared, and we were standing in a decimated section of farmland, craters carved into the earth where the watermelons had once sat, the dirt mixed with pink fruit flesh and scraps of rind.

I whirled around, and as expected, the man was running back toward the city walls, probably hoping to loop around to the front gate.

"This is ridiculous," I said, cuffing watermelon juice from my face. "Hold him down," I said to Zheng Sili, who was spitting out watermelon seeds behind me.

"With pleasure," he said, reaching for the vines once more.

This time, four vines lashed out like serpents, each one seizing one of the man's limbs. He fell to his chin with a yelp, yanking at the vines to no avail.

I stomped toward him and picked up the nearest watermelon, holding it threateningly over his face.

"*Quit destroying the watermelons!*" I said. "Someone has to sell these, you know!"

"Okay, okay, fine!" the man said, trying to roll out of the watermelon's looming shadow. I set it down heavily next to me as Zheng Sili and Wenshu approached.

"Now," I said, "I would introduce myself, but we've already met, haven't we?"

The man shot me a defiant look, then let out a stiff breath and fell limp against the soil. "Look," he said, "I know you don't remember, but we've already done this part, so allow me to save us all some time. No, I am not best friends or secret lovers with the Empress, and she cannot blackmail me because I have no possessions or loved ones. I've never even met her, much less done her any favors, and I intend to keep it that way. She is very much not my type."

Wenshu opened his mouth as if to argue, but the Arcane Alchemist was faster. "*Sorry if we don't take your word for it,*" he said, mocking Wenshu's voice and rolling his eyes. "Sorry that I don't carry around proof that I *don't know* someone."

"You broke my compass, didn't you?" Zheng Sili said, frowning.

"Oh, your little toy that would lead the police straight to me?" the man said incredulously. "Yes, how cruel of me not to let you keep that. I thought it would at least prevent a repeat of this foolish encounter, but it seems today is not my lucky day."

I rolled my eyes and yanked at his collar, peering down his spine for some sort of soul tag.

"Oh, this part was my favorite," the Arcane Alchemist said. "The part where you three argued for ten minutes about whether or not it's ethical to force me to strip so you can check me for a soul tag, then I got so tired of your bickering that I stripped anyway just to shut you up. We can skip to that part again if you like?"

"Shut up," I said, at the same time Wenshu whispered, "That *does* sound like us." He turned to the Arcane Alchemist. "And why did we let you go the first time?"

"Oh, you didn't," the Arcane Alchemist said, shrugging. "I just ran into the pub when you thought I was putting my clothes back on, and you all forgot about me for a bit. But it doesn't change the fact that I didn't know the Empress an hour ago and I still don't know her now. So if you would be so kind as to release me—"

"No," I said. His story sounded fine on the surface, but I wouldn't let him slip away a second time. "Why should we trust someone who has no problem lying through his teeth every day? You've obviously had a lot of practice at it."

"But not enough practice at alchemy, apparently," Zheng Sili said. He gripped the Arcane Alchemist's chin, turning his face to the side to examine him better beneath the streetlight. The man let him turn him easily, looking oddly smug. "You have a nice face," Zheng Sili went on. "It's a shame about the rebound."

The man lifted an eyebrow. "Rebound?"

Zheng Sili crossed his arms. "You know, the small issue of no one being able to remember your pretty face the minute you leave a room? You can't fool me. You've clearly done way too much alchemy on your face and rebounded so badly you've practically wiped it clean off."

"Oh, that," the man said, relaxing. "No, that was completely intentional."

Zheng Sili frowned, looking to me as if I could explain it.

"You *wanted* to be forgettable?" I said.

He shook his head. "To be *arcane*," he said slowly. "Anyone can have a pretty face, but the most beautiful things are the most fleeting. If we lived in a world of perpetual sunsets and cherry blossoms, they would become common, and their colors would soon look dull. But for the evanescent moments that I exist, I am the most beautiful thing anyone has ever seen."

"You kind of look like me," Zheng Sili said.

I smacked his shoulder. "He looks nothing like you."

"I look like whatever is most beautiful to the person who sees me," the Arcane Alchemist said, smiling darkly.

"That makes sense," Zheng Sili said, nodding.

"And you think *you're* the most beautiful man on earth?" I said. "That explains a lot."

"I didn't know that was even possible," Wenshu said, ignoring us both. "To alter someone's perception with such precision."

"It shouldn't be," Zheng Sili said, turning back to the alchemist. "What stones did you use?"

The Arcane Alchemist rolled his eyes. "It's not something *you* can replicate, so don't bother trying."

"*What's that supposed to mean?*" Zheng Sili said. "Are you saying I'm a lost cause?"

I cast Wenshu a withering look and massaged my forehead where a headache was brewing. I was honestly starting to doubt whether this was the Empress's alchemist, only because she probably would have murdered him by now for his pompous attitude.

I shivered as a breeze rolled across the fields, my clothes now damp from watermelon juice. I crammed my fists into my pocket and huddled closer to Wenshu while Zheng Sili and the Arcane Alchemist kept bickering. My fingers crunched against the stiff parchment I'd balled up in my left pocket, the wanted flyer Zheng Sili had given me last night. I pulled it out, wanting to tear it up for what a waste of time this had all been.

But my gaze settled on the printed sketch of the Arcane Alchemist, the smooth expanse of nothingness where his face should have been.

The dragon's white eye, the faceless night.

I'd learned that *the dragon's white eye* meant opal, but perhaps *the faceless night* was just as important. Maybe the dragon's white eye was the stone, and the faceless night was where—or who—it came from.

"Did you use opal?" I said, loud enough that Zheng Sili and the Arcane Alchemist stopped arguing, turning to me.

"That was . . . one aspect of it," the Arcane Alchemist said, avoiding my gaze, "but as I said, it's not something you can replicate."

"What kind of opal?" I said, stepping closer. "Where did you get it?"

For the first time, the Arcane Alchemist looked genuinely angry. "What does it matter?" he said. "It was *my* transformation, and it can't be done again! Your questions are pointless."

Pointless? I thought bitterly. I thought of Hong waiting for me in the darkness, fading into a whisper of light. This man had clearly been in possession of an immensely powerful alchemy stone, and he'd squandered it to make himself beautiful. I took out my knife again and held the tip to his throat.

"*Where did you get it?*" I said again, my voice low. The Arcane

Alchemist had gone very still, Zheng Sili and Wenshu suddenly silent behind me, as if they could sense that this was no longer an idle threat.

The man swallowed, the motion tearing a pinprick of blood from the tip of my knife. "Somewhere you will never find," he said, the words quiet, almost mournful. The Sandstone Alchemist had said something similar to me once.

"Somewhere like Penglai Island?" I said.

The Arcane Alchemist went still, another drop of blood chasing the first down his throat. "What does a girl like you know about Penglai Island?"

"Only that I need to go there," I said, "no matter the cost."

The Arcane Alchemist let out a sharp laugh. I pulled my blade back a fraction so I wouldn't slit his throat by accident.

"You and me both," he said, "but that place is long gone."

"Gone?" Zheng Sili said sharply from behind me. "Islands don't just disappear."

"It wasn't just any island," the Arcane Alchemist said, his expression grave, gaze distant. "It was a fountain of alchemical power. Very little was impossible when it came to Penglai."

"You've been there?" Wenshu said, crossing his arms.

"Yes, of course," the Arcane Alchemist said, glaring back at him. "I have sailed back to look for it a thousand times, but there's nothing but dark water. And I promise you, a place like that is not something you simply forget how to find. It's gone."

The handle of my knife creaked warningly as my grip tightened. There was no way that Penglai was gone. If the Sandstone Alchemist's transformation was the key, then it wasn't a place one could simply sail to. He was probably lying to keep us away. He had to be.

Zheng Sili turned to me, expression pinched. "Then why was

that desert alchemist so protective of his stupid transformation?"

"Desert alchemist?" the Arcane Alchemist said, frowning.

I grabbed Zheng Sili's sleeve and yanked hard, but he kept talking, undeterred. "The Sandstone Alchemist, wasn't it?"

All at once, everything about the Arcane Alchemist's expression changed. It was as if dawn had broken in his eyes, his expression filled with warm light. "You found the Sandstone Alchemist?" he said, the words so delicate, so filled with hope. "He gave you a transformation?"

Gave *may not be the right word*, I thought. But it seemed the Sandstone Alchemist was no enemy to the Arcane Alchemist, so admitting that we'd robbed him was probably not wise.

"Can I see it?" the Arcane Alchemist said before I could answer, tugging against his restraints.

"No," I said, raising my knife again. "You know the Sandstone Alchemist?"

He nodded quickly. "Yes, we were childhood friends. Look, I think we may have gotten off on the wrong foot, what with you grabbing me and mugging me and all. I didn't realize you were his friends."

"And that changes things?" Wenshu said.

"Yes, of course," the Arcane Alchemist said impatiently. "I wasn't lying about Penglai—I have never been able to return. But I trust the Sandstone Alchemist. If he thinks there's a way back, it's at least worth looking into. He's a wise man."

"A wise man who tried to kill us," Wenshu mumbled in Guangzhou dialect.

"I can give you the opal I used," the Arcane Alchemist went on, ignoring Wenshu. "Straight from the rivers of Penglai Island. That's what you wanted, right? Whatever you need it for, it's all yours. It has served its purpose for me. And in return, if you find a way back to Penglai Island, bring me back with you?"

"That's a big *if*," Zheng Sili said.

"Why do you want to go back?" I asked.

The Arcane Alchemist let out an incredulous laugh. "If you knew anything about Penglai, you wouldn't be asking me that question."

He winced as I pricked his throat with the tip of my blade. "You're going to have to be a bit more specific," I said. For all I knew, he wanted to wield Penglai's power to overthrow the government and burn the country to the ground.

"I . . . may have overlooked certain . . . *disadvantages* to my gift the last time I was there," he said, glaring at the ground.

"He's broke," Zheng Sili said. The Arcane Alchemist glared at him but didn't deny it.

"That's all you want?" I said incredulously. "What, a fountain of eternal gold?"

"Something of the sort," he said, nodding. "It would be in everyone's best interest. I wouldn't need to pickpocket anymore. It's beneath my dignity, I know, but it's not as if I can get a job when everyone forgets me. You would be doing the public a great service by—"

"All right, *fine*," I said, sheathing my knife. If he gave us the opal, I didn't much care what he did next, as long as it didn't cause more harm.

The Arcane Alchemist grinned. "It's in my home, just beyond the fields," he said. "So if you wouldn't mind . . ." He glanced pointedly at his restraints.

Zheng Sili looked less than pleased, but bent down and dissolved the vines with a couple firestones.

The Arcane Alchemist sat up and rolled his shoulders, then rose to his feet and brushed watermelon seeds from his robes, striding confidently toward the horizon. "No time to waste!" he said.

We walked a few paces behind him, the gravel crunching noisily beneath our feet. Zheng Sili looked thoroughly uncomfortable with his hair matted by watermelon juice, a constellation of seeds still spread across his left cheek, which I had no intention of telling him about. Wenshu looked like he'd eaten something sour, glaring unsubtly at the Arcane Alchemist's back as we walked.

"I don't trust him," he said in Guangzhou dialect.

"Oh, he's full of shit," Zheng Sili agreed, "but we need his opal, don't we?"

"Right," I said. "We don't have to trust him to make a deal with him, as long as he delivers first."

The Arcane Alchemist glanced over his shoulder at me, winking in a way that made heat rush to my face. "Gossiping?" he said. "How impolite."

"About as impolite as setting off watermelon bombs in our faces," Wenshu said.

The Arcane Alchemist rolled his eyes and faced forward, walking faster toward the horizon.

The sound of gravel grew quieter as we walked, the stones sparser as we reached the edge of the farmland, where the desert rose up to meet us at the end of the valley. Golden sparks of sand spiraled toward us, stinging our eyes. There, right where the desert began, stood a circular tent covered in wool felt, the fabric swaying dreamily in the desert winds, revealing whispers of darkness inside. The soul of this desert felt different than what we'd walked through in Lanzhou—the sands there had felt full of life, like the desert was a great golden beast with a beating heart deep in the groundwater. But this desert felt cold, lonely.

"I can see why you need money," Zheng Sili said under his breath. "This isn't much of a house."

The Arcane Alchemist glared over his shoulder. "My inheritance was paid in copper," he said bitterly. "As you can imagine, the age of gold has not been kind to me."

Wenshu frowned. "Nothing has been paid in copper since the Sui Dynasty," he said. "You can't possibly be over one hundred and sixty years old. That predates life gold."

The Arcane Alchemist only shrugged. "Who needs life gold?" he said with a wink. "The waters of Penglai are potent."

Wenshu and I exchanged a startled look. "Is that a joke?" I said.

"Are you laughing?" the Arcane Alchemist said. "My jokes are always funny, so if you're not laughing, there's your answer."

"They do call it Penglai *Immortal* Island," Zheng Sili said under his breath. "Are you really immune to death?"

The Arcane Alchemist shook his head. "Oh, definitely not. Just immune to aging."

"Like life gold?" Wenshu said.

The Arcane Alchemist grinned. "Exactly," he said. "Where did you think the idea for life gold came from?"

"The Moon Alchemist," I said, frowning.

The Arcane Alchemist laughed and shook his head. "That's what the House of Li would love for you to think, but she wasn't even born then. You can thank the Sandstone Alchemist for life gold. It just looks a bit . . . unflattering to the royal family if the person to discover it isn't a royal alchemist, you know?"

The Sandstone Alchemist? I thought. No wonder he felt the need to hide so far out in the desert. Surely the Empress had done everything in her power to end him so he couldn't take credit.

"But no, I am assuredly not immortal. I know at least several of my friends who also drank the waters have since perished."

"Friends?" I said, grinding to a halt. "Wait, how many people have been to Penglai Island?"

The Arcane Alchemist pursed his lips, looking up as if counting. I knew the answer deep in my heart before he said it out loud. "There were eight of us in total," he said.

Just as my father's notes said.

The myth of Penglai was tangled with the myth of eight immortal beings and their elixir of eternal life. I hadn't been certain when I started this journey just how much of the stories were true, for myths were only seeds of truth before they grew into legends. But the farther north I traveled, the more it seemed that the legends of Penglai were real.

At last, we reached the yurt at the edge of the desert. The wind grew louder as it rolled across the dunes, the tent fabric shuddering in the breeze.

"After you," the Arcane Alchemist said, pulling back a heavy tent flap. Inside, I could see nothing but darkness.

A strangely cold breeze from inside the tent wound in ribbons up my ankles, and a buzzing sound rose in my ears.

"Go on," the Arcane Alchemist said. "I know it's messy, but it's not that bad. No need to embarrass me."

The breeze sighed up from the shadowed sand within, the scent of wild orchids that I knew from the outskirts of Guangzhou. The buzzing sound grew louder, and all three of us turned to Zheng Sili, the source of it. He patted down his pockets until he pulled out the compass, the arrow now spinning wildly, humming like a forest of cicadas.

I looked back to the Arcane Alchemist, and that was when I understood.

At the beginning of my journey with alchemy, the key had always been listening.

To the world, the undercurrent of life running through and beneath it, tangled in everything and everyone. To the river and its waters of life lapping over my feet. To the qi that vibrated through the universe like the echo of a zither string, humming with life and warmth.

Transformations are like qi fireworks, Zheng Sili had said. They had to be, because qi was what powered all of our transformations. And right now, the Arcane Alchemist was practically glowing with qi. I could hear the rushing current of blood flowing through his body, the frantic beat of his heart, his every breath a tempest of alchemical power. Behind him, the darkness within the tent pulsed with qi.

"You can change people's perception of your face," I said slowly.

The Arcane Alchemist nodded, gaze sliding into a frown. "Yes, we've already established this."

"Can you change people's perceptions of anything else?"

He hadn't expected the question, and his startled eyes told the truth before he could speak a single word of protest.

He held up his hands in surrender. "Whatever you think I've done, you're wrong," he said. "How many times in one night will you accuse me of something with no evidence?"

With his hands raised, my attention focused on the center of his chest, just beside his heart, where the qi was concentrated, loud as the ocean. My gaze followed the silver chain just barely showing beneath his collar, disappearing into his robes.

I stepped forward and grabbed the end, yanking the chain toward me.

The Arcane Alchemist stumbled forward, surprised by the

action. As the chain spilled into my hand, the pendant on the end slid down toward me—a silver ring encasing a cool white gem.

Opal.

I closed my fingers around it just as the Arcane Alchemist seized my wrist, and the world dissolved.

The tent fabric disappeared, as if devoured by the night sky. Wind rushed up from the valley below, carrying the sharp scent of orchids as it tore through the space where only moments ago there was solid ground. We were standing at a precipice above a valley, a steep drop into a rocky chasm below.

Wenshu and Zheng Sili lurched away from the edge, but I ground my heels into the stone and held out the hand gripping the opal pendant. The Arcane Alchemist had been pulling away from me and stumbled at the sudden lack of resistance, wavering over the edge. He grabbed my wrist, and the two of us balanced precariously between land and sky, a thin silver chain taut between us.

"I don't think we need to go inside," I said. "I think everything we need is right here."

He clutched my wrist, his grip sweaty as I extended my arm out another inch, leaning him farther over the edge.

"My ring won't make you beautiful," he said, eyes alight with dark fire. "*I* made the sacrifice for it. Its powers don't transfer. Whatever you want to use it for, you'll have to pay the price."

I took a step closer to the edge, yanking the Arcane Alchemist forward. "*There is nothing I wouldn't pay,*" I said, surprised by the raw anger in my words.

The Arcane Alchemist cast a nervous glance at the valley below. He clutched desperately at my wrist, his nails drawing blood. "That's what the Sandstone Alchemist thought too," he said. "And then he nearly destroyed everything."

My hand tensed around the ring. "What do you mean?" I said.

Before he could answer, the chain snapped.

The Arcane Alchemist clawed his fingernails into my forearm, yanking me forward as he fell backward over the edge. The valley yawned open beneath me as the balance shifted, my stomach dropping.

Then arms closed around my waist, pulling me back so sharply that it knocked the breath from my lungs. Zheng Sili was grabbing my arm, tearing it away from the Arcane Alchemist while I fell back against Wenshu. The Arcane Alchemist's sweaty fingers slid down my wrist, our fingertips brushing for a moment, qi bright and sparkling in his palm.

Then he slipped over the edge, into the darkness.

I couldn't hear the sound of him hitting the ground over the roar of the wind, but I could sense as his alchemy fizzled out, a candle extinguished in a single breath.

Zheng Sili released me and peered over the edge, grimacing. "Oh, he's definitely dead," he said.

I sat up stiffly, leaning toward the edge.

"You actually want to *look*?" Wenshu said, tugging my sleeve, face curled with disgust.

"I have to," I said, pulling away.

Far below, where the desert bled into the rocks, the Arcane Alchemist lay crooked on the sand, his head a bright burst of scarlet. An odd warmth spread through my chest, my heartbeat loud in my ears, and for a moment I thought I might cry. I had wanted this man's ring, not his life.

Ever since I came to the palace, I'd only wanted to save everyone, and yet innocent people died every day because of what I'd done. How had this become my legacy? *The Scarlet Alchemist* had once meant that I'd given my own blood for a dream of peace. Now it was the name of someone who walked through a kingdom drenched in red, the crimson of her robes hiding every bloodstain, devourer of all those who stood in her way.

I had made too many mistakes to be the hero that I'd once wanted to be. Maybe it was time that I stopped seeing myself as anything but a curse. Alchemists had to destroy in order to rebuild, after all. I would save them all in time, but my hands hadn't been clean for ages, and I might as well stop pretending they were.

I looked back at the ring, which hummed within my closed fist, like I'd grabbed hold of a shooting star. I opened my palm and held it up to the moonlight to get a better look.

The opal swirled just beneath the surface, like a snowstorm encased in glass. In the darkness, it shone brighter than the moon overhead, casting a circle of light and warmth around the three of us.

The dragon's white eye, the faceless night. I'd been a fool to think that any old opal would be the key to Penglai. Here, with this stone singing alchemy through my bones, I was certain that this was the first piece of the puzzle. And if the Sandstone Alchemist's transformation was correct, then there were two more pieces.

The dragon's white eye, the faceless night,
The song of silver, the serpent's bite,
The child of Heaven, the scarlet-winged tree,
Together at last, the shadow makes three.

The first stone had been forged in the waters of Penglai, carried by one of the Eight Immortals who had found it, so perhaps the other stones were the same. It seemed we were no longer looking only for loose stones, but for the immortals who carried them.

I slipped the ring onto my middle finger. The alchemy echoed through my bones, and all at once I felt as if I were a fallen comet, a ball of brilliant white fire. I closed my fist, and the feeling settled, energy whispering beneath my skin, waiting.

"Let's go," I said, looking back toward Zhongwei in the distance, so far away and small beneath the endless sky.

CHAPTER TWELVE

Wenshu didn't even make it back to the city gates.

We'd only walked a few minutes through the watermelon fields when he wordlessly passed me the bag where Durian was sleeping.

"I have to be the brawn *and* the pack mule?" I said, taking the bag anyway. Wenshu had stopped walking, staring off into the distance.

Zheng Sili realized what was happening a moment before I did. He grabbed Wenshu's arm just as he fell forward, managing to slow his descent and lower him gently onto his back.

"Come on, don't do this right now," I said, kneeling in the gravel beside him and shaking his shoulder.

"This is becoming more frequent," Zheng Sili said, as if that wasn't already painfully obvious. I ignored him, hooking Wenshu's arm around my neck and trying to stand up.

My shoulder flared with white-hot pain. I clenched my jaw so I wouldn't make a humiliating sound and quickly knelt back down, my hand trembling with the effort not to drop Wenshu flat on his face.

"That's what you get for riding a horse with someone who turns into a corpse at random," Zheng Sili said, frowning down at me. Then he squatted down beside Wenshu. "Put him on my back."

I was too breathless for harsher words, so I did my best to manhandle Wenshu upright with one arm, draping him over Zheng Sili's back. He rose unsteadily to his feet, swaying into me. He took a few halting steps, then fell back to the ground with a pained sound.

"Did you fall off a horse too?" I said, glaring down at him. "What's your excuse?"

"That your boyfriend's body is stupidly tall, and therefore heavy," he said.

"You made a big deal about how I'll need your help when this happens, and now you can't even carry him?"

"Yes, I said I could *help*, not do it all by myself," he said, managing to shrug Wenshu off his back, letting him flop down in the dirt. "I have never claimed to have that much physical strength. And need I remind you that I've been imprisoned for the last month while you were playing princess? How much do you think they fed us there? I'm not exactly in my prime here."

"*Then what good are you?*" I said, the words angrier than I intended. Zheng Sili flinched at my tone. I had criticized him often enough, but I didn't think I had ever sounded so furious, not since that time in the prison.

It wasn't his fault that Wenshu was an empty shell, that we were out here in a destroyed watermelon field instead of running a kingdom, that everyone was dead. But if I didn't yell at *someone*, I was going to explode like one of those watermelons.

"I'm an alchemist, not a wagon," Zheng Sili snapped, reaching for his satchel and pulling out a few firestones. The light in his gaze sharpened the way it always did when he had an idea. "Give me your arm."

"Why?" I said.

He rolled his eyes. "It's covered in blood, and I need something to write with."

I looked at my sleeve, which I hadn't realized was still bloodied from where the Arcane Alchemist had scratched me while clinging on.

"Before it dries," Zheng Sili said, waving me closer.

I'd already learned that he wasn't keen on explaining when he was in alchemy mode, so I sighed and knelt down beside him, holding out my bloody sleeve.

He grabbed it in his fist, wringing out some blood until his hand was coated in red. With his other hand, he rolled up Wenshu's left sleeve on the arm without the soul tag. With his finger, he quickly painted two characters in blood.

李
弘

Li Hong.

"What are you doing?" I said.

"We're alchemists," he said simply. "We shouldn't be dragging a corpse around when he can just walk by himself."

He cast a quick glance over his shoulder as if to check for witnesses, and then, before I could truly process the meaning behind his words, pressed the firestones to Wenshu's chest.

Red light surged from between his fingers, like he'd grabbed handfuls of molten lava. Immediately, Wenshu gasped and sat up so fast he nearly smashed his forehead into Zheng Sili.

He whirled around like a caged animal, edging away from the

red embers still clinging to Zheng Sili's hands. When he turned to me, his eyes went wide.

"Zilan?" he said.

I opened my mouth to say something like *obviously,* or *thanks for deigning to walk back to the inn by yourself,* but something about the look in his eyes stopped me.

The way he'd whispered my name sounded so scared, the way you spoke when you were afraid of what the other person would say.

"Is it really you?" he said, moving closer. The blood from the mark on his arm was dripping down his palm, but he seemed not to notice, raising a bloody hand to cup my face, looking at me with reverence, the way only one person had ever looked at me before.

You will never look exactly like this again, he'd said. *I want to remember this moment forever.*

"Hong?" I whispered.

He reached for me, but his fingers hesitated a breath away from my cheek. As if a door had slammed shut, all the reverent light in his eyes vanished.

He wrenched away, landing on his hands in the dirt, all the muscles in his neck taut, swallowing hard. His fingers curled, scarring marks into the dirt.

Then his hands shot to his throat.

Zheng Sili and I moved at once, each grabbing one of Hong's arms and trying to pull it away. But Hong fought against us, fingers white and tense around his throat, feet kicking up gravel.

"What did you do to him?" I shouted, barely dodging an elbow to the face.

But Zheng Sili didn't have a chance to answer, because the next moment, Hong surged forward and grabbed Zheng Sili by the throat, pinning him to the dirt.

"Don't *ever* do that again!" he said, and I knew at once from the tone of voice, the hard slope of his shoulders, the rage in his eyes, that he wasn't Hong anymore.

I hated myself for the pang of disappointment that wrenched through my chest.

"Don't kill him," I said half-heartedly, tugging Wenshu's arm until he released Zheng Sili, who sat up and coughed.

"Hey, it worked," he said, backing away when Wenshu glared at him. "You're back, aren't you?"

"What the hell did you do?" I said, trying to scrub the blood off Wenshu's throat with my sleeve, because if he noticed he was dirty, he might actually kill Zheng Sili.

"Well," Zheng Sili said, turning to cough as he massaged his throat, "you have one body with two souls who have a claim to it. One of them vanished, and the other is sitting around waiting, so I figured we could just . . . borrow it for a bit?"

"You tried to *resurrect him?*" I said, my grip tightening on Wenshu's sleeve.

He shook his head quickly. "It wasn't a resurrection," he said. "That would obviously require a huge sacrifice. I used jasper."

I clenched my jaw, not liking where this was going. Jasper was a firestone used to draw blood back into meat served to the royal family, essentially making it fresher, winding back the clock. Transformations with jasper were always powerful but short-lived.

"So it wasn't a resurrection as much as . . . holding a door open for a bit to see who wanders through," Zheng Sili said, looking absurdly proud of himself.

"Where did you learn how to do that?" I said incredulously. "Who the hell would teach you that?"

He shrugged. "It made sense in theory, so I thought I'd test it."

"On *me*?" Wenshu said, and he probably would have choked Zheng Sili again if I hadn't held him back.

"I know, I know," Zheng Sili said, rolling his eyes and wiping off his robes, "only your sister can do dangerous, experimental alchemy on you."

He started walking, waving us after him like animals. "Come on," he said. "Let's get back to the inn before you go boneless on us again."

Wenshu still looked ready to commit murder, but I tugged him to his feet, hurrying after Zheng Sili.

"Are you all right?" I whispered.

Wenshu didn't answer for a moment, still glaring at Zheng Sili's back. "I think so," he said at last.

"Why did you choke yourself?"

"I don't remember that," he said quietly. "It just felt like . . . I was fighting to be myself. Suddenly someone else was alive inside my bones, and I had to get them out, no matter what."

Zheng Sili looked over his shoulder. "Probably because you wanted the body more."

Of course he was eavesdropping, I thought. "How would *you* know what he wants?"

"Because he's *here*," Zheng Sili said. "Alchemy is about intention."

Unfortunately, I understood what he meant. Hong had resigned himself to waiting patiently to get his body back and never would have fought my brother for it. But to Wenshu, the body now belonged to him as much as mine belonged to me. It was no wonder he'd seized it back within moments.

My mind wandered back to the look in Hong's eyes, the first

time I had seen him in the real world in so long. But treasuring that moment felt like a betrayal, so I clenched my teeth and tried to focus on the scent of watermelons and earth, the chill of the desert wind, the alchemy ring bright and warm on my finger . . . anything but Hong.

We reached our inn just before sunrise bled across the horizon. Wenshu dropped off to sleep right away while Zheng Sili stared broodily out the window, but I stayed awake clutching the opal ring, watching the swirling clouds inside of it.

I huddled closer to the window and its pale light, quietly unfurling the Sandstone Alchemist's scroll. I read the second line even though I knew it by heart, fingers tracing over the characters that were supposed to save us all:

Song of silver, the serpent's bite

I had no idea what it meant. All I knew was that the first line had pointed me to a stone held by one of the immortals, so the second line was likely pointing me to a different one. Perhaps *song of silver* was a stone, and *the serpent's bite* was the person holding it? Silver was a metalstone that I'd often used in transformations, but that felt a bit too obvious for such an esoteric transformation.

I drifted off to sleep for what felt like only a brief moment, but the next time I opened my eyes, the light had shifted sharply in the room. Zheng Sili was gone, and the door was cracked open.

I sat up, checked that Wenshu was still breathing, and took the opportunity to change now that Zheng Sili was gone. I'd been sleeping less and less lately, but it hardly seemed to matter, my body running on pure, glorious hope, the delirious dream of Penglai.

I reached into my bag for Durian, but my hands only brushed across dry scroll paper.

"Durian?" I said, sitting up sharply. When he didn't appear, I tossed back my bedding, then forced Wenshu onto his side to check that he hadn't squished Durian in his sleep. He made a grumbling sound of protest and flopped over, but Durian was still nowhere in sight. My gaze snapped back to the open door.

Zheng Sili left the door open, and Durian got out.

What if someone found him and decided to eat him for dinner? My heart raced. I threw my shoe at Wenshu, who groaned in protest.

"Durian's gone," I said, already tugging on my robes.

I didn't stay long enough to hear his answer, shoving open the door and running out into the street. I hesitated at the door of the inn, staring out at the quiet street, the morning tranquility that didn't match my panic at all. I couldn't just run down the street calling out the name of a fruit that smelled like corpses. People would think I'd lost my mind.

I hurried down the street as quickly as I could without drawing too much attention to myself. I paused to ask a clay merchant if he'd seen a duck, and he gave me directions to the butcher, which only made me want to cry. I couldn't imagine telling Hong that I'd somehow lost Durian, that he was probably on someone's dinner plate.

A sandstorm must have passed through the city, because the air was thick and hazy, stinging my eyes and leaving a metallic taste on my tongue. I squinted, bumping into people in the market as I kept my gaze locked on the ground for a duck caught underfoot.

At last, I spotted Zheng Sili at the end of the street, squatting on the ground in front of an armory.

"Zheng Sili!" I shouted. My voice must have sounded too panicked, because half the street looked up at the sharp tone. Zheng

Sili glanced over his shoulder and stood up, a piece of twine in his hand tethered to . . . Durian's foot.

I came to a stop a few feet away. Zheng Sili held one end of the leash in his left hand and a couple of marinated quail eggs in his right. A few more peeled eggs sat on the ground, where Durian pecked at them. I looked between the two of them, Zheng Sili's face bright red as he fidgeted with the string.

"Were you *walking* Durian?" I said at last.

He crossed his arms, leaning back against the wall of the armory. "It's not my fault your stupid duck is so spoiled! He was so noisy I couldn't sleep anyway. And if he stopped you two from sleeping, your brother would just collapse more often, which is already hugely inconvenient—"

"You made him a *leash*?" I said.

"Well, I couldn't use your bag! It smells like a wet cow!"

"He's a duck! You just pick him up!" I said, resisting the urge to slam my head against the wall. I bent down in front of Durian and scooped him up with one hand under his belly.

Zheng Sili looked down at Durian, eyes burning with resentment. "Pardon me, but they don't teach us duck handling in alchemy school."

I rolled my eyes, tucking Durian under my arm. "Let's go back before Wenshu Ge comes running out here in his pajamas."

"Fine," Zheng Sili said, uncrossing his arms and pushing away from the wall. He moved away one second before the window exploded.

A slab of steel crashed through the window from the inside, punching both the paper and lattice frame out with a sudden *crunch*. Wood chips flew in every direction, the scent of fire and molten metal wafting over us. Zheng Sili yelped and leaped back before the steel could crush his toes. Inside, men were shouting over each other, the whole building trembling as more metal hit the ground.

Zheng Sili scowled and moved in front of the now-empty window.

"*You could have killed me!*" he shouted. "Have you lost your mind?"

No one inside acknowledged him, except to toss an iron hilt out the window, which Zheng Sili barely dodged.

"Okay, that's it," he said, storming toward the door.

"Have *you* lost your mind?" I said, grabbing his sleeve. "Isn't it a bit early to pick a fight?"

"It would have been such an embarrassing way to die!" he said. "They should at least compensate us now! My father would have them shut down if he were here."

He yanked his sleeve away and stomped inside the armory. I sighed and tucked Durian into my bag before following. Picking a fight with a merchant was an easy way to get skewered, and I would need to do damage control if I didn't want to drag Zheng Sili's corpse back to the inn.

Metal covered every wall of the armory, alight with the reflection of the fire burning at the center. There were gleaming bronze plates sewn into lamellar shirts, twinkling chain mail hanging from hooks, gold-plated helmets on shelves. Two men stood in the corner, one of them holding up a red-hot poker that he seemed to have pulled from the welding table. An older man stood in front of them with a sword held threateningly above his head. All of them turned as Zheng Sili and I entered, frowning at us before quickly looking back to each other.

Zheng Sili's bravado seemed to drain out of him at the sight of weapons. He stepped to the side, just slightly behind me, as if I was the one who'd decided to storm in here.

"They're trying to rob me!" the older man said, jerking his sword at the younger men.

"With iron pokers?" I said, crossing my arms.

"No one asked you," one of the younger men said, waving the poker clumsily in my direction. He probably expected me to flinch, but I only frowned and watched errant sparks spiral to the floor.

I crossed the room and grabbed his wrist, dodging a half-hearted swing at my face. He lurched back, but I held tight to his arm and twisted it until the poker clattered to the floor. It was easy to tell the difference between someone who actually knew how to fight and someone just throwing a weapon around. The merchant clearly knew how to wield a sword—he'd forged it, after all.

"I have sympathy for people stealing food," I said, twisting his arm a fraction farther and pulling a pained cry from his lips, "but I can't imagine why you need armor badly enough to pick a fight with someone who could cut you in half."

"It's our master's orders," the other young man said, backing farther into the corner. "If we don't listen, *he'll* cut us in half."

"He ordered you to hold up a blacksmith with a fire poker?" Zheng Sili said, raising an eyebrow.

The man in my grasp shook his head. "He just said to prepare for a journey south by sunrise, but everyone knows what he means. If we don't have proper protection, we'll be dead."

"*South* as in Chang'an?" I said, my lips pressed into a tight line.

Both men nodded. "He wants to stake his claim to the throne."

Zheng Sili rolled his eyes. "The royal army is better trained than you fools," he said. "They'll cut you down where you stand."

"The royal army is all but dissolved," the merchant said.

I turned around, releasing my grip on the young man. "What?"

The merchant sheathed his sword. He reached into his pocket

and pulled out a folded piece of paper, handing it to Zheng Sili. "The crown may be up for grabs," he said, "but that doesn't mean my armor is."

"The crown is not 'up for grabs,'" I said, turning to Zheng Sili for explanation.

But he had gone very still, his knuckles white around the paper, angled so I couldn't see it. "Where did you get this?" he said, turning to the merchant.

"The flyers were posted this morning, came up from the postal carriers, straight from the capital."

"What does it say?" I said, stepping closer. But Zheng Sili took a step back, pressing the flyer to his chest.

"I don't think you should—"

I tore the paper away from him and flipped it over.

It was an illustration, the ink faded from a stamp pressed down too many times, but the image still clear.

The gates of Chang'an, a hanged woman dangling from the center, wispy robes shifting like ghosts in a soundless breeze, long black hair, bare feet.

At the top, in bold, black ink:

THE EMPRESS IS DEAD

Zheng Sili came up behind me, clearing his throat. "It says—"

"*I can read!*" I said, angling away from him, a strange coldness washing over me as I kept reading.

Empress Wu hanged in front of imperial palace after siege by private armies. Crown Prince Li Hong and concubine Fan Zilan reported missing. With no surviving members of the House of Li to be found, the future of the crown is uncertain. The Tang Dynasty may have come to an end.

Slowly, I folded the paper in half and tucked it into my bag.

Everyone was staring at me, but I felt very far away. *So this was why they were robbing this man,* I thought. *Their master is going to Chang'an to claim the throne because the Empress is . . . Yufei is . . .*

Behind me, Zheng Sili shifted from foot to foot. "Are you . . ." he trailed off, the unasked question hanging in the air.

I felt like I'd fallen into a frozen pond, like the world around me was suspended in slow motion. Yufei was never someone I had to worry about. Out of the three of us, she knew how to protect herself the best. Leaving her had felt like the most logical decision, something none of us had thought twice about. But we'd left her to die alone.

"I need to get to the river," I said, tightening my grip on Durian and shoving through the door.

If it hadn't been too long since the Empress's body was hanged, maybe I could still find Yufei at the river of souls and tether her there like Hong until we could reach Penglai Island. Yes, that was what I would do. Death was only temporary for a resurrection alchemist, after all. Yufei was only a little bit dead, and soon she would be perfectly fine once more.

But news traveled slowly across the country, even something as important as this, and I knew that unless Yufei had the mental fortitude to try to hang on, she would be gone within a day. I'd only just managed to tether Hong before he wandered off, and I'd done that only hours after his death. Surely for something like this to have been printed and reached the northern borders, days had to have passed.

I ran faster, ducking around families and merchant carts and old men while Zheng Sili hurried behind me. Up ahead, a cart turned sideways blocked the road, a crowd of people gathered like a dam in the river. I tried to shove my way through, but the crowd was too dense.

When I came close enough, I saw the wheels of the cart lodged in the mud, the horse trying futilely to pull it through. I shoved Durian into Zheng Sili's arms and started fishing through my bag for stones.

"Are you sure you want to do that?" Zheng Sili said, his voice high-pitched and nervous. I ignored him, pulling out three earth-stones and sinking my hands into the mud. With a warm pulse of orange light, the mud rose and swayed like ocean waves, lifting the cart out of the pit before solidifying beneath my palms. The horse raced forward at the sudden lack of tension, the crowd parting at once to not get run over.

I held my muddy hands out for Durian, who Zheng Sili passed me without comment, his expression pale. People were staring at us now, but I had never cared less about being a spectacle. My mind was already halfway in the river plane, writing Yufei's name again and again across the sky. Once I was back in our room, with Wenshu as a conduit, I could save her.

I tried to force my way through the dispersing crowd, but a hand closed around my arm and yanked me to a stop.

"Let go!" I said, expecting Zheng Sili.

But I caught Zheng Sili's startled gaze a few feet away, his bag of quail eggs clutched protectively to his chest. A man in a sol-dier's uniform glowered over me, grip tightening around my arm.

"Most alchemists are a bit smarter these days," he said.

Another man in the same uniform appeared beside him, shoving Zheng Sili into the mud.

"I doubt a stupid little girl like her can make life gold," the second one said, "but we get paid either way."

Stupid little girl? I thought, the words burning like a soul tag seared into my skin. Not because I thought they were wrong, but because I knew they were right.

Like the Empress said, I was only alive because I'd gotten lucky.

The grip on my arm tightened as the man wrenched my wrist behind me. My hair fell in front of my eyes, and I made no move to brush it away so no one would see me cry.

My sister is dead, and I can't save her.

"Hey, hùnxiě!" Zheng Sili shouted.

I looked up. Zheng Sili had cast his bag of quail eggs to the ground, and was shuffling three alchemy stones in his palm.

"Don't!" I said. *They'll know you're an alchemist too,* I thought.

But Zheng Sili only rolled his eyes. "Get out of my way," he said. "I need a clear shot."

Then he reeled back and hurled the firestones at the guard. I jammed my elbow into the guard's stomach and twisted myself out of his grasp a moment before the firestones hit his face, flaring into a bright ball of orange flame that gnawed through the top half of his uniform, as if he'd been devoured by the sun.

I tucked Durian under one arm and pressed my hand to the other soldier's breastplates. The iron in my rings catalyzed the reaction, the metal of his armor bending into spikes that lanced between his ribs. He coughed and tumbled back into the other soldier, crushing him into the ground. I glared down at them, hands twitching with anger.

"Hùnxiě—" Zheng Sili said sharply, but he never finished his sentence, because a third guard appeared behind me.

I ripped three firestones from my bag, whirling around to grind them into his face, make all the bones collapse into his brain, blast his teeth away into a thousand shards, make him swallow his own tongue, anything to get him out of my way, to get back to Yufei.

But my fingers stopped a breath away from his face, firestones falling from my limp fingers, lost to the mud.

Why can't I move any closer? I thought, my fingers trembling, coldness spreading fast through my whole body, starting at my stomach, where it felt like I'd swallowed a ball of ice.

I dropped my gaze down, following the lean line of the guard's spear, which had plunged straight into my stomach.

White-hot pain swelled just beneath my rib cage, and when the guard yanked his spear back out, it felt like he'd sheared my soul to pieces.

My ears rang as I crashed to the dirt, distantly aware that a river of blood was spouting from my stomach, far too much of it to be safe, to be survivable. I had seen death many times, and I wasn't foolish enough to think this kind of wound could be healed.

Zheng Sili was shouting something, but I couldn't make sense of his words, my mouth welling with blood, choking me. I forced myself onto my side and it spilled hot and fast from my lips.

I'm not ready yet, I thought, helpless to stop the tears stinging my eyes. *I was supposed to save everyone.*

I imagined the way they would write about me, if they even cared.

The Scarlet Alchemist, who caused the death of all the royal alchemists and the last heir to the House of Li, then died on the street in a desert city. She didn't die protecting someone, or fighting for something important, but because she lashed out like a child, because she was never a royal alchemist, not really. Royal alchemists were cunning and wise and earned their place in the palace, but she was just a little girl who got lucky, until the day she didn't.

Being unique cannot make up for skill, or education, or talent, the

Empress had once said to me, as I'd knelt before her in a court-yard full of blood that had become my namesake. All of this time I'd lived beyond my death was stolen from other people, and finally, it had run out.

With a heavy thump, the world trembled, and the soldier lay on the ground in front of me, his face shattered in. It reminded me of the stand-in corpses the Moon Alchemist had used to fake the death of Hong's little sisters. Who had the bodies belonged to again? Were the real princesses all right?

Then warm hands were forcing me onto my back again, and Zheng Sili was above me, his stern face blocking out the searing white of the sky, his expression unreadable.

He grabbed the torn fabric of my dress and ripped it farther. Without thinking, I reached out to shove his hands away, but he brushed them aside as easily as falling leaves, and my hands dropped to the dirt while he ripped my dress wider. The ground felt wet and hot beneath me, Zheng Sili's hands now red gloves down to his sleeves.

How fitting for the Scarlet Alchemist to die covered in red, I thought, letting out a choked laugh. But the motion made my stomach clench, and I tossed my head back and gasped at the sudden surge of pain, my vision blurring.

There were the five gates of Chang'an, the yawning darkness. That was the first time I'd met death, and now it was reaching its hand out to me once more, welcoming me home. Was Yufei here? I tried focusing on her name, but the characters blurred together into a murky soup, a tarnished sky overhead eating my thoughts.

Coldness bloomed in my abdomen, burning ice and white light. "What did you *do*?"

That was Wenshu's voice, and the panicked sound was

enough to pull me back to the bright sun overhead. Zheng Sili pulled his hands back and peered down at me.

"That will stop the bleeding," he said, "but I can't fix internal damage."

"What do you mean you *can't*?" Wenshu said furiously. I caught a glimpse of the blue fabric of his robes, his white hands clutching Zheng Sili's clothes. "You're an alchemist, and you act like you're a great one. Alchemists can do anything if they sacrifice enough, so *fix her!*"

The rest of their conversation faded away as I melted into the dirt. The world flipped, and I was once again kneeling at the Empress's feet, collapsed against the gold tiles, my soul tag on the ground in front of me. *Fan Zilan, Fan Zilan, Fan Zilan*, I thought, clinging to the name like an anchor. But my name wouldn't be enough to save me this time.

I choked down a breath, the sky spinning above me, and realized I was in Wenshu's arms, his heartbeat so slow against my side, my own mockingly fast. I heard the sound of hoofbeats, then I tipped my head back just enough to catch a glimpse of Zheng Sili, eyes wide. I forced another burning breath down my throat, because if I was going to die, I would be damned if it happened in front of Zheng Sili.

He leaned forward and then someone was pulling me onto a horse, one arm braced across my chest to stop me from falling forward.

"Hold on, Zilan," Wenshu whispered, the words warm against my throat. I couldn't hold my head up anymore, and it rolled back against his shoulder. "I'm no alchemist," he said, "but I'll find a way to fix this."

CHAPTER THIRTEEN

I am standing on the street in Zhongwei, my neck arched, looking up at the white sky. The morning is too cold for my thin robes, and the air tastes of metal, the horizon spinning with desert ghosts.

"It's not my fault your stupid duck is so spoiled!" Zheng Sili says.

My gaze settles in front of me, where Zheng Sili has crossed his arms. A thin string—bright red—tethers his hand to Durian's leg.

"He was so noisy I couldn't sleep anyway. And if he stopped you two from sleeping, your brother would just collapse more often—"

"—which is already hugely inconvenient," I say at the same time as Zheng Sili, though his words are sharp while mine are dead leaves falling from a rotting tree, brought to my lips unbidden.

Zheng Sili blinks, watches me for a long moment. "How did you know what I was going to say?" he says.

But I don't know the answer.

This moment feels like I'm looking at it through a diamond

prism. Zheng Sili's words are a song I once knew. The morning has a pale tinge, all the colors weak as if stolen by the sun. Everything except the thread that Zheng Sili is holding, bright and brilliant scarlet.

I turn back to the main road, toward the sound of fighting inside the armory. Zheng Sili is speaking again, but the world has narrowed, and I see nothing but the open door. I brush past him like a silk curtain, and he can't stop me, he never could. I open the door, and there is no one inside, nothing but a wall plastered with flyers.

It is an illustration of a woman hanged from the gates of Chang'an, her bright red robes the same color as the thread in Zheng Sili's hand.

At the top, in bold black ink:

THE SCARLET ALCHEMIST IS DEAD

Of course she is, I think. *Everyone already knows that.*

The Scarlet Alchemist died in the throne room, at the feet of the Empress.

I turn around, but Zheng Sili is gone. Night swallows the city, wooden carts and red dirt walls inhaled by a sudden wave of darkness. Trees rise up to the sky, and I am standing at the edge of a riverbank, darkness just behind my heels, bone-white tree trunks and prickly black leaves before me.

There is a red thread tied to the ring finger of my left hand, and it pulls me forward. I am a minnow pierced through with hooks, dragged across the dark ocean of night.

I am lying in the streets of Chang'an, scarlet-red dirt and clay dust and lost dreams, and my mother is screaming.

The BLOOD ORCHID

My face is folded into itself, my teeth caught in my throat, eyes full of blood.

My father is speaking to me in a lost language, words that float away like dandelion parachutes, gone as soon as they leave his lips. Firm hands lift me up, no patience or warmth, cold and hard like the surface of the moon.

"Follow me," she says, and begins to walk.

I can no longer breathe, my chest seizing, and when I reach broken fingers to my throat, they tangle with bright red thread.

I am at the Empress's feet, my cheek pressed to a hot tile floor coated in blood, my soul tag on the ground in front of me.

The red thread is tangled and frayed in my fingers. It weaves across the floor, through puddles of blood and spilled pearls, and fastens tight around Hong's hand, where he lies dead on the floor, translucent skin and purple nails.

I can't move, can only shift the focus of my gaze from the prince's corpse to my own soul tag.

Su Zilan is what it's supposed to say. The merchant's daughter who was supposed to live and die in Guangzhou. The false name ripped from my spine because it was never who I was.

But that is not the name before me.

There are far too many characters, and when the wall of fire and burning flesh flares bright behind me, echoed in the puddles of blood, I can see the characters clearly.

THE SCARLET ALCHEMIST

I roll over, and I am in the sands of the Borderless Sea, wind pulling golden grains into my eyes, my muscles locked tight from venom, the sun devouring me in bright white overhead.

The Sandstone Alchemist watches me die, the snake curled

around his throat, golden eyes like two tiny suns. The red thread is gone from my fingers, and my brother is dead beside me, and the sun is opening its maw to swallow me whole.

This is just another way I was supposed to die, but I have always poured like sand through death's fingers, not solid enough for him to hold on to.

The poison courses through me like a river of fire, my hands so tight they're curled into claws, every muscle clenched so firmly that I can't even breathe.

The Sandstone Alchemist is supposed to leave me to die alone, but instead he stands over me, his eyes pure gold, his snake curled tight at his throat.

This isn't right, I think. *This isn't how it happened.*

The snake slithers down the Sandstone Alchemist's arm and lands in the sand, curling smooth patterns into the sea of gold until it's right in front of my face. It opens its mouth, its fangs bright moonstone.

The serpent's bite, I think as it draws closer.

My stones are spilled in the sand, my numb fingertips brushing across them, but I can't recognize them by touch alone like usual. They're just vacant rocks, no alchemy to be found.

The snake sinks its teeth into my throat.

My fingers close reflexively around the nearest stones. With my other hand, I grab the snake by its tail and wrench it away from me. Its fangs rip open my throat, a deep wound that bleeds hot and fast, soaking my dress in scarlet, pulsing loud in my ears.

I cast the serpent to the side and rise to my feet, my shadow eclipsing the golden sands. I unclench my left fist, and in it there are two bright red stones like drops of blood, like fang marks. The firestone that had once destroyed venom from inside of me, ripped it from my veins.

The BLOOD ORCHID

Red zircon.

I close my fingers around them like a promise, then look out across the desert. On the white horizon, a figure stands backlit by the sun, robes shivering in the breeze.

I woke to darkness.

Sensation came back to me in pieces—my feet numb and ankles tangled in blankets, an ache behind my eyes, a cool breeze shuddering down my spine. At the sound of breathing beside me, I jolted upward, smashing my forehead against something firm.

"What is *wrong* with you?" Wenshu said, along with a few more colorful words, one hand clamped over his eye. "Literally the first thing you do when you wake up is fracture my skull?"

I looked down at my clean robes—blue ones I'd never seen before. I tentatively touched my stomach, the memory of the spear still lightning-sharp. But the skin beneath my palms was smooth and unbroken, cool to the touch.

My eyes adjusted to the darkness, and I looked around at the small room—shelves packed with scrolls, windows dark with shadows of crooked branches that rapped against them, a futon laid out beneath me, a desk piled with jars of alchemy stones, glistening in the whisper of sunlight.

A thin wooden panel stood a few feet back from the door, blocking the light from the hallway but letting air pass through. The base was dark wood, but the center was a painted landscape of a ship far out at sea, mountains piercing through clouds in the distance. It was a yǐngbì—a spirit screen, that some people used to keep out ghosts, who supposedly couldn't move around corners. Most people built stone yǐngbì at the gates to their courtyards—I had never seen one in an interior room like this.

211

Whoever owned this house must have been very superstitious.

I turned back to Wenshu, who was watching me intently. "What happened?" I said.

Wenshu crossed his arms. "You got yourself skewered."

"Yes, I remember that part," I said, trying to untangle my ankles from the blankets. "And after that?"

"Zheng Sili stopped the bleeding, but you wouldn't wake up," Wenshu said, not quite meeting my gaze. "No one in Zhongwei wanted to risk helping an alchemist, so we followed the river until we reached Wuzhong and found you a healer who hadn't seen you *doing alchemy in broad daylight*."

I winced. That certainly hadn't been my brightest idea. Why had I even bothered? A memory itched at the back of my mind, but the moments leading up to being stabbed had faded away into a white fog.

"We tried two different healers," Wenshu went on, "but since Zheng Sili had sealed the wound, neither of them knew what to do for you. But there was one alchemist who saw us in the town center and agreed to help. We had no other options, so we brought you to her home."

It sounded like a stroke of luck, but I could tell from the uneasy grimace on Wenshu's face that it wasn't all good news.

"What's wrong?" I said, clutching my abdomen. "Did she destroy my organs or something?"

"Do you feel like your organs have been destroyed?" Wenshu said, raising an eyebrow.

I hugged a pillow close to my stomach, shaking my head. "I don't think so."

"Her alchemy isn't the issue," Wenshu said. "It's the payment."

"What did you give her?" I said, hands clutching the pillow

tight. Alchemists could be oddly pedantic about fair trades, and I knew Wenshu would have promised anything, even himself. "Gēgē—"

"All she wanted," Wenshu said, "was the ring."

My gaze snapped down to my left hand. I still wore my remaining iron rings, plus the gold ring the prince had given me the day he died, but the opal ring was gone.

"And you just gave it to her?" I said, so loudly that Wenshu shushed me, glancing over his shoulder.

"You would have died if I hadn't," Wenshu said flatly.

I groaned and flopped back down across the futon, my fingers twitching as if remembering the ghost sensation of the opal ring. I should have just kept it in my bag rather than worn it on my hand. Even someone with no knowledge of alchemy stones could tell at a glance that it was by far the most valuable thing we carried. It glimmered like a stolen piece of the moon, and the swirling inside the gem spoke to its great alchemical power. This healer alchemist probably thought she could sell it and buy a new house. It was a safer purchase than asking us for gold, because its value wouldn't fluctuate.

There was only one good thing about this situation: we'd found another powerful alchemist up north.

"Maybe we have another candidate for the Empress's accomplice?" I said, turning my head toward Wenshu.

Wenshu blinked quickly as if considering this. "Would she have healed you if that were the case? Doesn't she want you dead?"

"She wants me on a leash," I said, thinking back to the way Zheng Sili had leashed Durian. In my dream, the string had been red, like the red thread of fate . . .

Cold seized my body. All at once, I remembered the headline

on the flyer in the armory. How could I have forgotten? And how much time had passed since I was stabbed? Surely Yufei's soul, if it had ever been waiting at the river, was long gone by now. The chances of finding her soul had already been so slim, and now they were almost nonexistent.

"Gēgē," I said, grabbing his wrist. "There was a flyer, an announcement from Chang'an about the Empress."

"Oh, that," Wenshu said, rolling his eyes. "Yes, I saw that in your pocket when they gave me your clothes. I didn't know printing presses could reproduce illustrations so clearly."

I waited for him to say more, but he only sat down at the nearest desk and crossed his arms. Were we speaking the same language? Had he actually read the flyer?

"You know what this means?" I said.

He nodded. "It means we need to wrap up this business with Penglai Island as soon as possible so we can sort out the mess at the palace before there's a war of succession," he said. "And it means I need to be extra careful that no one recognizes me. Maybe I should grow a beard?"

"What about Jiějiě?" I said, my fist tight around the sheets.

"What about her?" Wenshu said, raising an eyebrow. "I'm sure Yufei will come back to the palace when she hears that we've returned."

"Come back?" I said. "Gēgē, the illustration—"

"*It isn't her!*" he said, slamming his fist on the desk.

I flinched, tugging the sheets tighter. A breeze rushed through the windows, tearing Wenshu's hair back, curtains billowing behind him. Facing away from the light, his brown eyes looked starkly black. For a single moment, as he looked down at me, I saw one raw glimpse of his anger, dark enough to devour the world.

He took a steadying breath as the wind died down, and when he opened his eyes, he looked calm once more.

"She wouldn't let this happen," he said, waving his hand as if waving a cloud of smoke from the air. "Besides, did you see the drawing? It doesn't look like the Empress. She's not even wearing shoes."

I said nothing, too terrified to argue with him. Because if he truly understood that Yufei was gone, he would hate me for it. He had left the palace for *me*, to help me fix my mistakes.

Something in my expression must have given away my thoughts, because he sighed and knelt back down on the floor in front of me.

"Do you really have so little faith in her?" he said.

I shook my head. "It's not about faith," I said.

"It is," Wenshu said, frowning. "I have faith in Yufei, and in you."

All at once, I understood. Even if Yufei was dead, Wenshu thought I could bring her back.

I shouldn't have been surprised. Thanks to me, Wenshu had only ever seen death as a temporary state, something I could fix for him given the right ingredients. I didn't know if he could even comprehend the permanence of death. He had never had to drag those he loved back from the other side. He had never held the corpse of someone he cared about. Death was an abstract idea to him, like the Confucian philosophy he studied.

"Show me a body, and I will mourn," he said. "Bring her corpse to me, and I will plan a funeral. But my sister is alive, and I will not mourn the living."

"Right," I said quietly. What else could I do but pretend to believe him? He thought I was the Scarlet Alchemist, the girl who would save the entire kingdom, and more importantly, our family. To him, this didn't change our plans. Either Yufei had somehow escaped and would return to us in time, or I'd bring her back once I got to Penglai Island. Slowly, I released my grip on the sheets. Wenshu believed Yufei would be fine in the end, and Wenshu was usually right.

"Where is Durian?" I said quietly.

Wenshu's jaw unclenched, perhaps relieved that I'd dropped the subject. "Downstairs, where Zheng Sili is entertaining the alchemist who saved you."

"And where are my clothes?"

Wenshu passed me a pile of clothing, surprisingly free of bloodstains. I gestured for him to turn around while I changed.

I rose to my feet, shaking the numbness from them, then smoothed down my dress. My face felt scraped raw, and I was sure that meant Wenshu had scoured it with a wet rag while I was asleep. "All right," I said. "I want to see what kind of alchemist managed to save me."

We passed through a long hallway of arched doorways on the way to meet the mysterious alchemist, and every single one was blocked with a painted yǐngbì—some showed terraced fields of rice, others misty mountains, and others twisting rivers that led to the sea, almost as if each door was a passageway into a new world.

"This alchemist is very superstitious," I said as we reached the staircase.

"You could say that," Wenshu said under his breath.

The temperature dropped steeply as we went down the stairs, the tiles sharply cold beneath my socks, the banister like ice against my palm.

"Aren't we still in the desert?" I said, looking over my shoulder at Wenshu, whose teeth were already chattering. "How is it this cold?"

"The alchemist said something about slate tiles retaining cold," Wenshu said, though I could tell from his expression that he wasn't convinced. He pointed toward the end of the first-floor hallway, where another yǐngbì blocked my view of the room. This one was not a landscape painting, but a scene in a dark pit carved from black rock, alight with red fire. Fanged monsters dragged naked figures across the ground, bound them with chains, and fed them into the depths of the pit. Religious conceptions of the afterlife had all but vanished in the golden age of alchemy, but I remembered Auntie So's stories about the ten courts of Buddhist hell, and this sure seemed like one of them.

I stepped around the yǐngbì, into the room.

The first thing I saw was Zheng Sili, seated on the floor, clutching Durian in his lap. His gaze snapped toward me when I entered, something close to a smile crossing his face before he carefully smoothed out his expression again.

Across from him, a young woman with hair the color of starlight sat on a wooden chair before a low table, where one steaming teapot sat surrounded by five small white cups. The wall behind her—in fact, all the walls in the room—were shelved, packed tight with glass jars that twinkled in the weak sunlight. The jars looked empty as far as I could tell, but each one had one or two colored ribbons tied around the neck. My breath fogged the air in front of me as I stepped into the room, the cold tiles numbing my toes.

The woman's eyes tracked me with an odd sort of intensity as I approached, the way my uncle appraised his clay creations. The sharpness of her gaze and the long mane of white hair over her shoulder made her look like a winter fox, ready to devour me.

As she raised a teacup to her lips, I caught a glimpse of the Arcane Alchemist's opal ring on her finger. On her other hand, she wore a gold ring with a bright red gemstone.

I drew to a stop.

Red zircon, I thought, my pulse hammering in my ears, the image from my dream echoed across my vision.

Before I could get a closer look, Wenshu nudged my shoulder, pushing me farther into the room. The white-haired woman set down her teacup and folded her hands in her lap.

"Zilan, this is the Silver Alchemist," Wenshu said, gesturing to the woman.

I stepped around the table and knelt down on the floor, pressing my face to the freezing cold tiles in a deep bow. "Thank you for saving me," I said.

"Alchemists are a dying breed," she said, her words light as silk. "I could hardly let you go to waste."

I lingered on the floor, my forehead chilled against the tile, for she hadn't exactly given me permission to stand up yet. "Well," I said, after an awkward stretch of time, "I'm grateful for what you've done."

"Indeed," the woman said airily. Then, at last: "Come, sit with me. I've been waiting to speak with you."

I peeled my forehead from the floor, blood rushing from my head, and sat down in a chair that creaked as if in agony beneath me, the sharp edge biting into the back of my thighs even through my skirts. Wenshu sat in the chair next to me, while Zheng Sili remained on the floor.

"I would ask how you're feeling, but I know that you're fine because *I* healed you," the Silver Alchemist said. "So please don't take my lack of concern for rudeness."

"Oh, I didn't," I said, leaning to the side so the sunbeam glaring off one of the jars wouldn't hit me in the eye. "What are all the jars for?"

"They're containers," she said, as if it should have been obvious.

"Yes, but what will you put in them?" I said. I must not have done a good job at sounding polite, because both Wenshu and Zheng Sili shot me warning looks.

The Silver Alchemist only raised an eyebrow, a slight smile curling one side of her face. "They're already full," she said.

The sunlight shifted through the window, lighting up the far wall of glass jars, each one undoubtedly empty. Wenshu's gaze could have burned a hole in the side of my face, but he shouldn't have worried—I knew when to drop a topic. It didn't matter to me how this alchemist wanted to decorate her house, only that she gave me my ring back.

"I'm very grateful for your help," I said, leaning around a servant who hurried to pour me a cup of tea, "but about your payment—"

"What does your duck eat?" the Silver Alchemist said, eyes fixed on Durian, who had hopped from Zheng Sili's lap and was trying to sit down on an empty tea saucer.

"Whatever we can find for him," I said, trying not to let the irritation at being interrupted show on my face. The rich had always talked down to me when I was a merchant, but it had been a long time since anyone had dared. "He eats fruits. Sometimes he finds bugs—"

"Servant boy!" the Silver Alchemist called.

At once, a pale boy appeared in the doorway, as if he'd been waiting somewhere close by.

"Go dig up some worms in the yard and bring them here," the Silver Alchemist said.

"Oh no, please don't go to that much trouble for us," Wenshu said, looking between the Silver Alchemist and the servant. "He doesn't go hungry, I promise. Besides, he probably can't eat whole worms."

"Cut the worms up when you find them," the Silver Alchemist said to the servant. "But not with the good knives, for Heaven's sake." She turned back to me and smiled, her teeth vivid white. "It's no trouble at all," she said, leaning forward and stroking Durian's head with one finger. "We have to find joy where we can these days, don't we?"

"I'll say," Zheng Sili said, downing the rest of his tea like a shot of alcohol and not even glancing to the side as a servant girl appeared, refilling his cup. There was a strange edge to his voice that I hadn't heard before, his words tight and precise.

I cleared my throat. "About your payment—"

"Shut up and drink tea, you're being rude," Zheng Sili said in Guangzhou dialect, then turned back to the woman with a practiced grin. "Sorry, she has trouble with northern dialects," he said. The back of his neck had broken out in sweat, his eyes darting nervously between me and my brother.

Part of me wanted to smack him, but Zheng Sili had rarely seemed so nervous, so surely there was a reason for it. He'd been waiting down here alone with the Silver Alchemist for a while, after all. Had he seen something we hadn't?

"I'm sorry to meet you under these circumstances," the Silver Alchemist said, leaning back in her chair. "The way alchemists are treated now is despicable. We should be proud of our powers, not cowering at the sight of swords. Alchemists built this kingdom, after all. The people are in our debt."

I took a sip of tea to hide my expression. I had never considered anyone in my debt just because I was an alchemist. If anything, I'd trampled over others to gain my position.

"Were you a royal alchemist?" I said.

The Silver Alchemist let out a sharp laugh. "I would rather pour sand in my eyes than serve the House of Li," she said. "And it's a good thing I didn't, isn't it? Now all the royal alchemists are dead."

Except for me, I thought. But the Silver Alchemist didn't seem to know who I was, and I saw no reason to enlighten her. "You don't like the House of Li?" I said instead.

The Silver Alchemist shook her head. "My family served theirs since before the Tang Dynasty," she said. "The men of that house were like my brothers, but they lacked innovation. I had so hoped that Empress Wu would create her own dynasty before her death, if only to seize power from men who took it for granted."

I picked up my teacup and sipped tentatively at the water that scalded my lips, sharing an uneasy glance with Wenshu over the rim. If this was the alchemist helping the Empress, surely she'd try to be a bit more subtle about her loyalties. Besides, she had a sharpness to her that I doubted the Empress would have appreciated. The Empress had wanted to rule alone, to surround herself with docile puppets who trembled at the sight of her. She was probably working with someone who she could blackmail, not someone tied to her through loyalty alone, which could be broken easily.

But even if she wasn't helping the Empress, she was still standing between me and Penglai Island.

"Can you ask her about my ring?" I said to Zheng Sili in Guangzhou dialect.

He tensed, smoothing over the motion by reaching for his cup. "Why me?" he said.

"Because you know how to talk to rich people."

That, and I didn't particularly want to pick a fight I wasn't sure I could win. If the Silver Alchemist had healed me, she must have been a very powerful alchemist.

"Is something wrong?" the Silver Alchemist said, frowning and looking between us.

"Ah, well, there is one thing we should discuss," Zheng Sili said, straightening up, his voice smooth and commanding in a northern dialect once more. "You see, my friend is a bit embarrassed by this whole situation," he said. "She's so sorry to have inconvenienced you, and feels that we've gravely underpaid you."

The Silver Alchemist waved her hand dismissively. "Let's not talk of money, it's an ugly matter," she said. "What's done is done."

"Well, unfortunately, I'm afraid it's a bit more complicated than we've let on," Zheng Sili said. "My friend comes from a rather . . . important family back home. We're traveling now, so we can't bring all our resources with us—you understand, of course—but she can give you a letter of credit for a much more appropriate amount. It would make her feel much better knowing that she's compensated you for your discretion. After all, it wouldn't do well for word of this to reach home. Someone her age, unmarried, and traveling with two men . . ." He glanced over at me, wincing. "It does raise certain questions."

I clenched my jaw and did my best to look ashamed rather than angry. I hadn't even known that letters of credit existed among the rich. It seemed Zheng Sili was good for something after all.

"I see," the Silver Alchemist said. "Well, in that case, of

course I can accommodate. What kind of host would I be if I sent you away with unease?"

I smiled politely, even though I wanted to slam my face into the table. Was this really how rich people talked to each other? So many words that meant nothing at all.

"There's just one small matter," Zheng Sili said, taking another sip of tea. "That ring she was wearing—it's truly worthless in all senses but a sentimental one. It was from her late mother, who came from a much humbler family. It would be embarrassing to pay you in such a cheap stone. Please allow us to provide you with something much more appropriate for all you've done."

For a long moment, the Silver Alchemist stayed still, as if contemplating the depths of her teacup. Then at last, a small smile raised the corner of one side of her face. She set down her teacup and folded her hands, fingers laced over each other, displaying the white and red rings, one a winter moon and one a bloody harvest moon. I narrowed my eyes to get a closer look, and sure enough, the red ring swirled like a scarlet sky.

"I did not gain the kind of skill I have by bumbling around this world in ignorance," she said. "Do not insult my intelligence. You and I both know exactly what this ring is."

"We didn't mean to insult you," Wenshu said quickly, shooting Zheng Sili a glare.

"No," the Silver Alchemist said, her glare sharp, silencing him, "you only meant to con me out of something infinitely more valuable than gold." She turned to me once more. "I am going to ask you a question, and if you lie to me, I will kill you. Do you understand?"

I swallowed, clutching my teacup, and nodded.

"What do you want with Penglai Island?"

CHAPTER FOURTEEN

The Silver Alchemist sat perfectly still as she awaited my answer. She wore no alchemy rings, or gloves, or anything that she could have wielded as a weapon. Here she was, completely unarmed, yet threatening to kill me.

This, more than anything, told me exactly how powerful she was. Alchemists did not make idle threats.

"There are people that I need to bring back," I said at last. Hopefully that was a vague enough answer to stop her from trying to kill us like the Arcane Alchemist, but truthful enough to satisfy her.

The Silver Alchemist stood up, stepping around the table. I drew back against the chair, but her arm on the armrest caged me in, her other hand gently cupping my face as she contemplated my eyes. Up close, her irises glinted with starry flecks of silver.

"There's someone you love," she said after a moment, drawing back and crossing her arms. "You would go to all this trouble for a boy? *You*, an alchemist? How pitiful."

My face burned. "It's not just for one person," I said, shrinking back against the chair.

The Silver Alchemist turned away with a sound of disgust, drawing a jar from one of her shelves. She caressed the side of the glass with the same gentleness that she'd held my face, staring intently into the jar.

"I had fifteen husbands, you know," she said.

Zheng Sili choked on his tea, spilling half of it down his robes.

"Not all at once, of course," the Silver Alchemist said, smirking at him. "Life is long."

"Not *that* long," Wenshu said, eyes bright and focused, the way he looked when he was studying Confucian texts.

I was sure that what he was thinking, but too polite to say out loud, was that it made little sense for a rich woman to remarry so many times. Once remarried, she would have lost all rights to her late husband's property. Poorer women often remarried out of necessity, but I'd always thought that the rich valued widow chastity and saw remarriage as something shameful.

"I thought I loved them all," the Silver Alchemist went on, holding her empty jar up to the light from the window, casting a rainbow prism across the floor. "Love is beautiful when it blooms, but it dies, like everything and everyone else." She lowered the jar, and the rainbow disappeared, the room pale once more. "There will always be another love," she said. "To risk everything for something so ephemeral is madness."

"If saving him is madness, then I lost my mind long ago," I said, rising to my feet. The chill from the floor had seeped deep into my bones, and I could distantly sense myself shivering even as my blood felt like it was on fire. "If you never would have saved any of your husbands, then you have no idea what love is."

The Silver Alchemist's grip tightened on the jar. "Some people cannot be saved," she said. Then she let out a tense breath, and when she turned back to me, her expression was even once more. "Regardless, there is no way back to Penglai Island," she said. "It was sealed with blood, and that is how it will remain, forever."

The Arcane Alchemist had said nearly the same thing, but hearing it from the Silver Alchemist's lips felt like a door had slammed shut in my face. Maybe the Sandstone Alchemist had truly gone mad and his transformation wouldn't bring me there at all. Maybe it would rebound and kill me instantly—a trap laid to punish anyone who dared try to find Penglai.

But there was only one thing that didn't make sense.

"I can't lie to you, but you can lie to me?" I said.

The Silver Alchemist raised an eyebrow.

"Hùnxiě," Zheng Sili said warningly.

My gaze dropped to the ring on the Silver Alchemist's hand.

Song of silver, the serpent's bite.

"You're wearing my ring," I said.

"*Your* ring?" the Silver Alchemist said, jaw clenched.

"The opal," I amended. "It won't give you beauty, the Arcane Alchemist said so himself. If it's not on his hand, then its only use is to unlock Penglai Island. If all you wanted was to stop me from going there, you would have destroyed it or hidden it while I was sleeping. But instead, you're wearing it."

The Silver Alchemist's eyes narrowed. Zheng Sili looked like he was about to pass out, while Wenshu's gaze darted around as if cataloging the exits.

"You don't want to stop me from going to Penglai," I said. "You want to go there yourself."

A dark smile crept across the Silver Alchemist's lips. "It's no wonder you took the Arcane Alchemist's ring," she said at last. "He's a fool."

She knows him, I thought grimly. Of course she did. Like the Arcane Alchemist, she must have been much older than she appeared. Marrying fifteen times hardly made sense for a wealthy young woman, but made a lot of sense for someone who had been alive for centuries, perfect and ageless from the waters of Penglai while her husbands grew old and died, one after another. She was one of the Eight Immortals, which was why the red zircon ring on her finger looked just as bright and alive as the Arcane Alchemist's opal.

"Well," she said, clutching the jar to her chest, "I suppose you want the ring back?"

Tentatively, I nodded.

"Then we have an issue," she said. "We've made an equal exchange. That's how alchemy works, isn't it?"

"I never agreed to your terms," I said.

The Silver Alchemist sighed. "I accepted the ring in exchange for your life. If you intend to take back the ring, then I must take back your life."

I let out a sharp laugh. "Many have tried," I said, jamming a hand in my satchel full of alchemy stones. "Only a horse has ever succeeded."

As I spoke, I brushed my fingertips over my remaining stones, mentally cataloging how many I had left. Zheng Sili had his fist in his green velvet bag, doing the same. But even now, the Silver Alchemist didn't reach for a single stone of her own. She turned away, completely vulnerable with her back to us, and ran her finger across a row of jars. She paused after half a row, her fingers hovering over a jar with a yellow and white ribbon around the neck. She carefully pulled it from the shelf, then twisted the lid off.

"Guān Rén," she said sweetly, setting the open jar on the floor, "I need your help."

Wenshu and I looked at each other in confusion. She thought her husband was . . . in the jar?

"Do you want to just hold her down while I take the rings?" I said quietly to Zheng Sili. There was no point in hurting her if she really was this helpless.

Before he could answer, the jar fell onto its side with a heavy *thunk*, spinning in circles on the floor, faster and faster.

A familiar scent knifed up my nose, making my stomach clench. I clapped a hand over my nose and backed up into Zheng Sili, who gagged into his sleeve. This was the scent of half-baked corpses that customers dragged into my shop in Guangzhou, the kind with maggots for eyes and skin that slipped right off flesh like a loose jacket. A body poisoned with rot, far beyond the help of an alchemist.

Abruptly, the jar stopped spinning, and a silvery mist crept across the floor. It shrouded the tiles and blurred the shelves, casting the whole room in cold gray. My teeth chattered harder as the mist numbed my ankles.

A dark shadow rose from the fog, stretching up the wall and spilling onto the ceiling before congealing into a dark figure in the center of the room.

A man rose unsteadily from the silver blur, his skin bruised blue gray from rot, his flesh falling from his body in wet chunks, eyes shrunken and dry like two tiny pearls deep inside his skull.

The rotting man shuffled closer, legs bumping the low table and jolting the teacups. At the touch of his flesh, the wood of the table rapidly turned wet and crumbled, as if unmaking itself. Even after it fell to the floor, it continued to rot, gnawed through with a sudden bloom of fungus, settling on the ground at last as wet dirt.

"Nope. No way," Zheng Sili said, already heading for the door. But the man lunged to the left and swiped a hand clumsily at him, making him yelp and duck behind Wenshu. I stood rooted in place, barely able to feel the alchemy stones beneath my fingertips.

What kind of alchemy was this? Presumably, if the yǐngbì in front of every door were any indication, this was some sort of ghost. I was no stranger to raising the dead, but I'd only ever been able to do so if I had a body to put them in once I restored their flow of qi. I supposed it was possible to manipulate a dead person's qi into another form, but that must have required immense alchemical skill.

I glanced at the red ring on the Silver Alchemist's finger, now so bright that it cast the entire room in a sinister red tinge.

The Arcane Alchemist had found a ring at Penglai that had let him push the limits of normal alchemy. Surely, the Silver Alchemist's ring could do the same. But rather than using its powers for incomparable beauty, she'd used it to trap the souls of the dead.

As the rotting ghost stumbled forward, the Silver Alchemist sat back down and lifted her teacup to her lips. "My husbands promised themselves to me until the end of time," she said, leaning back in her chair. "My alchemy still sings through them, honoring all that they were. This is the only way that love can be eternal."

Perhaps I was still half dead from the spear to my stomach, or perhaps I was too entranced by the thought of how powerful the red zircon must have been, but before I could back away any farther, the ghost lunged across the table.

He moved like a silk scarf tossed through the air, a smoothness to each motion governed not by the limits of the human body but by the flow of alchemy.

Before he could reach me, cold hands closed around my arm. Zheng Sili yanked me to the side so hard my shoulder nearly popped out again. He tripped over a low chair, and both of us tumbled to the floor.

The ghost had barely missed me, crashing into the wall instead. A flurry of moths appeared out of nowhere and gnawed through the paper murals of the wall he had touched, followed by fungus that devoured the wood behind it. A hole yawned open in the wall, letting in the screaming, sandy winds from the courtyard.

He barely touched the wall at all, I thought, recoiling against Zheng Sili, dreading what would happen if the ghost touched my bare skin.

I snatched Durian from the ground and shoved him into Wenshu's arms, then pushed him toward the door.

"Get out of here!" I said.

"You don't have to tell me twice," he said, hurrying away.

As I turned around, Zheng Sili slammed a couple of wood-stones against the banister of the staircase. With a surge of white light, the stairs shivered, the ground beneath them humming. The ghost and I both took a step back as the banister tore itself from its posts and unfurled like a great white serpent, needle-thin splinters raised along its spine. It fell heavily to the ground, scraping along the floor as it surged across the room, then seized the ghost by the ankle and yanked him to the ground.

It only trapped the ghost for a moment before his rotting

hands closed around the serpent's neck. Decay began to gnaw through it, winding in black ribbons across the surface.

Zheng Sili grabbed my arm and headed for the door, but the ghost rose to its feet before we had made it halfway there, forcing Zheng Sili to release my arm or lose his own. A handful of his robes burst into moths at the ghost's touch, tearing a hole in his sleeve.

"If you have any more of those demon eggs," Zheng Sili said, stumbling back into a shelf, "now would be a fantastic time to use them!"

Durian's eggs!

I'd nearly forgotten about them. I felt around my secret pockets, sure that the Silver Alchemist had emptied them while I was unconscious. But it seemed she'd only cared about the opal ring, because my fingers ran over the cool surface of the two remaining golden eggs.

Before I could grab them, the ghost slammed his palms into the floor.

Decay bloomed across the floorboards, rippling through the room. The floor beneath my feet vanished as insects devoured it, dropping me five feet down into the jagged foundations of the house, a mess of crooked planks and dirt.

Zheng Sili hopped over a chair and just managed to avoid the hole, crashing into a desk as the ghost approached. He quickly climbed over the desk, eyes darting around for an escape, now backed into a corner.

He shot a panicked glanced down at me before his gaze snapped back to the ghost, whose moldy fingers reached for his face. I pulled out one of the eggs, tightening my grip around it, then leaned back and hurled it at the ghost.

The egg smacked the back of the ghost's head with a hollow

clunk, smashing his face into the desk, then fell unbroken to the ground beside him.

Zheng Sili made a petrified sound as he hurried to stand on the desk and hop over the ghost, nearly falling into the hole as he landed. He knelt at the edge of the pit and held out a hand to help me up, but my sleeve snagged on a splintered floorboard and tugged me back.

The ghost hauled himself upright, snatching the egg from the ground, but it didn't so much as crack at his touch, as if made of solid gold. The other egg had shattered so easily, but this one seemed indestructible. I'd assumed all three of Durian's eggs were the same, but apparently I was wrong.

The ghost tensed his fist around the egg, as if he too was confused by its strength, but must have decided it wasn't worth the thought. He tossed the egg to the ground, where it spun in circles until it settled under a table, then turned his attention back to us.

The ghost lunged for Zheng Sili, who yelped and stumbled away from the edge of the pit, the front part of his robes bursting into a cloud of dust where the ghost's fingers grazed him.

"Hùnxiě, I'm about to lose all my clothing!" Zheng Sili shouted, falling halfway onto the tea table and sending cups spinning across the floor. The Silver Alchemist leaned to the side to avoid the spilled tea, but otherwise didn't react. "Unless that's what you want, *get out of that hole and help me!*"

"That is definitely not what I want!" I said, tugging harder at my sleeve until it tore free from the broken piece of wood, fabric splitting up to my elbow. I gripped the jagged edge of the pit and hauled myself onto the main floor, ignoring the splinters that stabbed into my palm and under my nails.

With my feet on solid ground, I reached into my pocket for

Durian's last egg. Maybe it wouldn't knock anyone unconscious like the first egg, but surely it would do *something*. Durian's birth had saved my life, so surely his eggs would help in some way.

I rolled to my feet and threw the last egg at the ghost.

It shattered on the side of his face, a bright burst of golden yolk seeping into the crevasse of his eye, chunks of shell sliding down his neck. He froze, outstretched hand suspended in midair.

Zheng Sili wasted no time running away. He ducked around the ghost and braced himself in front of me on the other side of the room. I spotted Durian's unbroken egg glistening on the floor and snatched it, stuffing it back in my pocket.

The ghost pressed a hand to his cheek, then pulled back and observed the stringy yolk between his fingers.

I knew right away that this egg was not the same as the one that had broken in prison. Instead of durian, the room began to smell of fire.

The collar of the ghost's filthy robes began to dissolve first, blackening and vanishing as if gnawed away by an invisible flame. Steam rose from his face, and darkness devoured the pale edge of his jaw, spreading fast across his teeth. The hole in his face screamed wider and wider, a rain of yellowed teeth clattering to the ground as his jaw dissolved, the darkness spreading fast across his eye socket. Over half his skull was now gone, revealing the cavern where a brain should have been. Instead, there was nothing inside but liquid silver dripping onto the ground.

The ghost clutched a hand to the hole, but yanked it away when the caustic yolk ate away at his fingertips, which quickly dissolved down to the wrist. He collapsed into the pool of silver and slowly oozed into it, the cream of his bones spilling across the uneven floors.

With a flurry of white silk, the Silver Alchemist finally rose to her feet and uncapped a glass jar, kneeling before the puddle. All that remained of the ghost rushed inside the glass and vanished as she twisted the lid, her lips pressed tight together.

"Disappointing," she said, holding the jar up to the light. "But then again, you always were."

She set the jar down next to the teapot, then grabbed another from the shelf, twisting the lid off. This time, we didn't wait around to see what would appear.

Zheng Sili grabbed my arm and yanked me around the spirit screen and into the hallway. The Silver Alchemist's footsteps grew farther away as we wound deeper into the labyrinth of her mansion.

"We need to find Wenshu Ge and get out of here," I said.

"You told him to get out, so if he has half a brain, he should already be outside," Zheng Sili said.

"And which way is out?" I said.

Zheng Sili grimaced, sliding to a stop as we reached the end of a hallway. "Back the way we came," he said.

"Wonderful," I said, flinching at the sound of approaching footsteps. The room to our left had a spirit screen painted with summer constellations, while the screen to our right was a dark and lightless forest.

"We're finding another way out," I said, stepping around the yǐngbì covered in stars and into the room.

This room had no windows, no source of light save for what spilled past the edges of the spirit screen. Just like the room where we'd had tea, the walls in this room were packed full of glass jars. I'd hoped for a door to an adjoining room, but of course we could never be that lucky.

Zheng Sili huddled closer to me and stepped on my skirts.

"Watch it!" I whispered, shoving him away. He tried to step back but tripped over a low table, falling against a shelf.

All of the jars rattled, tilting dangerously as he tried to right the shelf. I hurried over to help, but it was too late—two jars tumbled off the edge and burst on the floor.

"Shit," Zheng Sili and I whispered at the same time, backing quickly away from the shattered glass. After a few moments with no sudden surge of mist or rotting apparitions, I dared to relax my shoulders.

"Maybe she keeps her empty jars in this room?" I said.

"Either way, she probably heard that," Zheng Sili said. "We should go."

I nodded and took another step back, but instead of touching the yǐngbì behind me, I pressed against something soft and cold.

"Wait," a man's voice said, a hand closing around my wrist.

I tensed up, prepared for my flesh to start decaying and slough off, for holes to gnaw through my bones. But my skin only felt cold and numb, like my hand had fallen asleep.

I turned around and faced a young man, half translucent in the dark. Unlike the other ghost, he looked whole and human, save for his translucent skin. A young woman stood in the shattered glass a few paces behind him, gaze darting between me and Zheng Sili, her skin the same hazy tinge, as if both of them had stepped out of a dream.

I glanced at Zheng Sili, who was backed against the shelf, his face white.

"Where is the Silver Alchemist?" the man gripping my arm whispered.

I tried to pull my wrist away, and to my surprise, he released me easily.

"Please," the man said. "She'll kill you and keep you in one of her jars."

Zheng Sili laughed incredulously. "Yes, I think we've figured that part out already."

I glared at him, then turned back to the ghost. "Who are you?" I said.

The man pressed his lips together, looking mournfully over his shoulder at the woman, who was staring sadly at the ground.

"We don't remember our names anymore," the man said quietly.

I thought of Hong, slowly losing his memory in the river plane. Would he forget his own name one day? An ache bloomed in my chest at the thought.

"We were her friends once," the woman in the corner said. "A long time ago."

"How long are we talking?" Zheng Sili said, arms crossed.

"Are you her friends who went to Penglai?" I clarified.

"Yes," the man said, the word so quiet that I felt it more than heard it, a cold breeze stinging my eyes.

"So much for the Eight *Immortals*," Zheng Sili said. "Two of them are already dead."

"Four of us," the man said, grimacing. "The Silver Alchemist made sure of that."

"*Four?*" I echoed, my heart racing. There were only eight immortals, four were dead, and we'd met three of the living ones. That meant there was only one left we had yet to meet, and I prayed they had one of the stones we needed.

"Why did she kill you?" I said. "And who else is alive?"

The man opened his mouth to speak, but flinched at the sound of footsteps in the hallway.

"We don't have much time," he said. "You need to take her ring away. The red one."

"Easier said than done," I mumbled, readying a few firestones.

"She has many types of ghosts trapped here," the female ghost said. "They can do awful things. Be careful."

The footsteps drew to a stop just outside the door.

"Zilan?" Wenshu called from the hallway. "Where are you?"

"Let's go," I said to Zheng Sili, who nodded quickly and hurried from the room. I hesitated just before leaving, looking back at the ghosts of the two immortals standing pale in the darkness.

"She can't control you with alchemy like the others?" I said.

The man shook his head, smiling sadly. "Her alchemy can trap souls, but not control, them," he said. "Love does that."

I fished three firestones from my pocket. I didn't have many to spare, but I supposed I could make do without these ones.

"No reason to keep you here, then," I said, pressing the firestones to the yǐngbì. It burst into wood scraps at my touch, my fingernails cracking from the sudden surge of alchemy. I heard Zheng Sili swearing outside at the sudden spray of wood chips.

The ghosts stood stunned for a moment, then turned to each other and smiled.

"Thank you," the woman said, reaching for the man's hand. I nodded as they hurried into the hallway and stepped into the bright patch of sunlight that the window cast on the tiled floor. Their skin began to glow, as if drinking in the light, then their features grew softer until they faded into the glow, nothing but sunbeams and falling dust where they had once stood.

Wenshu and Zheng Sili stood gaping at the square of sunlight, hair covered in wood chips.

"Yes, go on and unleash strange ghosts on the world, that's

a great idea," Wenshu said after a moment, crossing his arms.

"I've unleashed far worse than that before," I said. "Where's the Silver Alchemist?"

"I don't know," Wenshu said, glancing around uneasily, "but let's not stick around to find out."

We moved quietly down the hallway, peering around every corner, but the Silver Alchemist seemed to have vanished just like the ghosts. After a few minutes, we reached a door beside a window that looked out across the courtyard. Wenshu peered through it, checking for signs of danger.

"I think this is our best bet," Wenshu whispered, waving for me to go first.

I moved to go through, but hesitated on the threshold. "Where's Durian?"

"What?" Wenshu frowned. He shook his head. "Come on, we have to go."

"Not if Durian is still inside," I said. "Where did you put him?"

Wenshu paused, his eyes bright the way they always were when he was thinking very hard. Zheng Sili stepped in front of him and elbowed him back.

"Zilan, we have to go," Zheng Sili said, grabbing my arm.

I tore away from him, drawing back against the wall. His words played again and again in my mind until I realized what was wrong, and all my blood pooled in my feet. "What did you call me?" I said.

"Zilan," he said again, frowning.

I shook my head, taking another step back. "You never call me that," I said. To Zheng Sili, I was always *hùnxiě* or *peasant girl*. I swallowed, looking between them, my heartbeat loud in my ears. Wenshu had forgotten about Durian, and Zheng Sili had forgotten to insult me.

She has many types of ghosts trapped here, the female ghost had said. I knew from Auntie So that there were ghosts who could cause blinding light or cavernous darkness, dry winds or noxious gas. There were even some ghosts who could transform into objects, animals . . . or *people.*

I'd let both Wenshu and Zheng Sili out of my sight, and we hadn't walked around any spirit screens since being reunited.

Except for this one door, which they wanted me to go through first.

"Where are they?" I said, drawing firestones from my bag.

Zheng Sili seized my wrist before I could activate them, bending it back painfully until the firestones clattered to the ground. "Come on, Zilan," he said, tugging me close to him. "You wouldn't hurt us, would you?"

I pulled back my other hand and punched him in the face.

"Ow, what the hell?" he said, stumbling back into Wenshu. "You would punch your friends in the face?"

"The real Zheng Sili knows that I already stabbed him and knocked his tooth out," I said, swiping my firestones from the ground. "You really thought using his face would deter me? That only makes it easier."

Zheng Sili sighed, then both he and Wenshu trembled as white light rippled across their bodies. Their familiar faces faded away, melting into faces I had never seen before—men slightly older than them, shoulders broader and expressions more stern and lined with age, hair tied up with headscarves tight across their foreheads. Like the immortals, their skin was transparent, the sunlight cutting through them.

"Women these days really have no class," said the one who used to be Wenshu.

"I'll say," I said, rolling my eyes and tucking my firestones into my other pocket, reaching for woodstones. The two stepped toward me, but I slammed three woodstones into the ground, and a new yǐngbì burst from the floor between us, halting them in their tracks.

I turned around, determined to search through every room of the house until I found the others, but a cold hand seized my throat.

The Silver Alchemist stood in front of me, crushing me back against the yǐngbì I'd just built. At her touch, a stabbing pain all over my body forced me to the ground. It felt like knives had been slipped between each of my ribs, my bones splintering apart, my veins full of thorns.

"Do you know how I healed you?" the Silver Alchemist whispered. Sound hurt, breathing hurt, light hurt, as if my whole body was nothing but a feral scream. My knees shook, and I slid down the wall, but she followed me to the ground, refusing to let go. "Silver is a waterstone," she said. "It has amazing healing properties, but inevitably, some of it ends up in your bloodstream. It filters out of your body in a few days, but for now, you're full of metal. My *favorite* metal. It practically sings to me."

I scratched at the screen behind me, the only thing keeping me from falling all the way to the floor and never getting up again. It felt like the Silver Alchemist was unmaking me.

With a sudden *splash*, the pain lifted all at once. I collapsed back against the wall, hot liquid at my feet.

I looked up at the Silver Alchemist, who was now soaking wet and steaming, glaring over her shoulder. Wenshu stood a few feet behind her, clutching an empty teapot. Zheng Sili stood behind him, grimacing as he peeled cobwebs from his hair.

"I told you to *get out of here!*" I shouted, hauling myself to my feet even though my knees trembled.

"You're mispronouncing *thank you!*" Wenshu said, tossing the teapot at the Silver Alchemist and disappearing back into another room. Zheng Sili took a step forward, but hesitated as a shadow crossed the doorway before us. All of us turned to the servant boy, clutching a plate of chopped worms in trembling hands.

"Ma'am, where would you like these?" he said.

Zheng Sili grabbed the plate and hurled it at the Silver Alchemist, who struck it down from the air, sending chopped worms raining down over us.

"Leave!" Zheng Sili said to the servant, who bowed and rushed into another room.

The Silver Alchemist grimaced as she wiped bits of worm from her face. "You know why I wanted to feed that abomination of a duck?" she said. "So he can get nice and fat before I eat him."

"Over my dead body!" Zheng Sili said, slamming three wood-stones into the ground. The wood panels rose up and opened like a jaw ready to devour the Silver Alchemist in its splintered teeth, but she slid behind my spirit screen and dodged the bite. I heard the *pop* of another jar opening and wasted no time running down the hall, Zheng Sili close behind me.

"Where the hell did you go?" I said.

"Some ghost shoved me into a disgusting basement," Zheng Sili said, taking a sudden left turn. "Then one of the immortals let me out a minute later. They're not a very cohesive group, are they?"

I laughed, skidding to a stop in front of a room without a spirit screen, sunlight bleeding through the windows across the kitchen table. I hurried inside, but the room darkened as shadows eclipsed the windows. Gray fingers stabbed through the paper and writhed through the lattice like hundreds of maggots.

"She's got the place surrounded with ghosts," Zheng Sili said, grimacing. "How are we supposed to escape?"

"Her ring," I said, thinking back to the ghosts of the Silver Alchemist's friends.

"Is now really the time to be pickpocketing?" he said. "I know you're poor, but—"

"It's where she gets her power, you moron," I said. "These aren't actually ghosts, they're alchemical creations. If we can take her ring, I think they'll go away."

"I hope you're willing to stake your life on that theory," Zheng Sili said as the Silver Alchemist stormed into the room.

"Got any silver in your body at the moment?" I said to Zheng Sili as I backed up, trying to put the kitchen table between us like a barrier.

"Not that I'm aware of," he said, tossing a few firestones in the air and catching them in his other hand. "Besides." He turned back to the Silver Alchemist. "Silver is a soft metal. I would never want to be named after something so weak."

The Silver Alchemist lunged forward, but Zheng Sili cast the firestones to the ground and a wall of flame scorched itself into the floor, encircling her. I remembered when we'd sparred in the courtyard back in Chang'an, when he'd drawn the same wall in moments and I'd despised him for it.

But the Silver Alchemist only cast a few waterstones to the ground, and with a flash of silver, the fire turned into a hissing curtain of smoke.

"Okay, new plan," Zheng Sili said, grabbing an iron pan off the stove and hurling it at the Silver Alchemist. It hit her nose with a wet crunch and sent her tumbling to the floor.

"Aren't you supposed to be good at sparring?" I said, grabbing a cleaver from the counter.

"She has more stones than us! It's a waste!" Zheng Sili said, sending a flurry of spoons raining down on the Silver Alchemist.

"*You're being a cheapskate now, of all times?*"

"Do you have a better idea, *Miss Royal Alchemist?*"

The Silver Alchemist tore off a section of her silvery robes and transformed them with a brilliant flash, a long whip appearing in her right hand. She struck out at Zheng Sili, who tumbled back into me with a startled yelp, both of us crushed against the window. The ghosts outside the window tugged eagerly at my hair, fingers and tongues lashing through the lattice. I yanked my hair out of their grasp, slamming a fist against the window and breaking a few fingers.

We didn't stand a chance as long as she was wearing the red zircon ring. One way or another, I had to take it.

"I need you to hold her down," I said to Zheng Sili in Guangzhou dialect. "I'm going for the ring."

He sighed, clutching a couple stones in his palm before I could see them. "If I lose any more teeth because of you, I'm sending you a bill," he said.

Then he dove for the iron pan on the floor. Blue light flashed, and when he rose again, he clutched an iron spear in both hands. Dodging the next strike of the whip, he stabbed the Silver Alchemist through the stomach. He planted his foot on the table and leaned his body weight into the spear until it crunched, pinning her firmly to the table.

"Now or never, hùnxiě!" he shouted.

I didn't waste a second more, grabbing the Silver Alchemist's wrist as she twisted and writhed. I tried to yank the ring from her finger, but it stayed fastened tight as if part of her body.

"It's *my* ring," she said, coughing out sparks of blood. "You can't take it."

I clenched my jaw, remembering Hong, the Moon Alchemist, the life that I'd had before I'd ruined it, the life that I could have again.

"Want to bet?" I said, picking up the cleaver and, in one clean motion, slicing all her fingers off.

She screamed, a river of blood rushing hot and fast across the table. Zheng Sili flinched at the sound, and the moment he backed away, she yanked the spear from her stomach, a burst of blood spraying across both of us as she fell to her hands.

I shuddered as I picked up her severed fingers, slid the rings off the broken ends, and slipped the bloody metal rings onto my own hand. As her burning blood raced down my wrist, a strange calm settled through my bones, the blood suddenly cool, the hum of powerful alchemy rising inside me once more. The sounds of scraping outside the windows grew silent, the fingers retreating from the lattice.

The Silver Alchemist slumped to the floor, clutching the wound in her stomach. She glared at me and opened her mouth as if to speak, but a torrent of blood rushed from between her lips, and she fell forward into it. She reached for the hem of my skirt, but I stepped back and her hand splashed against the tiles, leaving a bloody palm print. Her face was bloodless, lips blue.

I picked up the cleaver with numb fingers before I really understood what I was doing. This was the part where I was supposed to finish her off—she was dying anyway, and rage was still boiling through my veins, my heartbeat pounding all the way up to my skull, breath fast from adrenaline. She'd tried to keep me away from Hong, from the royal alchemists, from my siblings' real bodies.

But she'd also saved me.

Someone grabbed my sleeve. I nearly jumped out of my skin,

but it was only Wenshu. "Let's go," he whispered. *"Now."*

We ran through the back door, where Wenshu had already untied the horses. He grabbed Durian off the ground and stuffed him into a bag, then struggled to climb onto a saddle. Zheng Sili shoved him upright with one hand, then easily mounted his own horse and held out a hand for me. Before I could argue that I wanted to ride with Wenshu, he'd grabbed me by the wrist and hauled me halfway onto his own horse. Our horses took off, and I clung to Zheng Sili, afraid I would fall off at this speed.

"She'll come after us if she lives," Zheng Sili called at Wenshu over his shoulder.

"I cut the other horses loose," Wenshu shouted back. "She can chase us on foot if she wants, but she won't catch up."

I glanced over my shoulder at the mansion as we rode into the countryside, then down at the rings on my hand, my whole arm stained with the Silver Alchemist's blood.

Once, I'd thought my cousins heartless for wanting to leave even a single soul behind when we could have helped them. But the Silver Alchemist had saved my life and I had robbed and killed her. And yes, she had killed people, but so had I. Yet I was the one riding away, pretending to be a hero while she bled out on her kitchen floor.

My hand felt numb from the weight of the two powerful rings, my skin stiff from dried blood. Just like the first time I'd put on a silk gown to dine with the Empress, I felt like a child playing dress-up. But this time I wasn't pretending to be an aristocrat, but a great alchemist who deserved to carry such important stones. As soon as we found the third ring, everyone would expect me to do a transformation that would split the seams of the world and carry me to a mythological island—something I wasn't sure that even the Moon Alchemist was capable of.

Yet somehow, no one had asked me if I could actually do it.

They still believed in the Scarlet Alchemist who had seized her dream at all costs, and I couldn't bear to tell them that she was dead.

I turned my gaze to the approaching horizon and slipped the red zircon ring off my finger, examining it in the light of the setting sun. The zircon was a vibrant, bloody scarlet with deadly sharp facets, trapped red light pulsing within the stone like the slow but steady beating of a heart.

CHAPTER FIFTEEN

At first, I thought I couldn't find Hong because I was too distracted.

I stood on the river plane, my skin rubbed raw after Wenshu had scoured the Silver Alchemist's blood from my face. I'd used moonstone to absorb the blood from my clothes and carefully polished both rings until the bloodstains grew faint, but they still felt oddly warm on my fingers, like the Silver Alchemist's ghost was clutching my hand. I could still hear the sound of the cleaver slicing down, the snap of bone, the wet gush of blood.

I should have been happy to see Hong. I should have rushed through the forest to brag that I now had two of the three rings, that I would bring him home any day now. *Only one more ring to go*, I thought.

But the feeling that hummed in my chest was not something I wanted to share with Hong. I thought of the Sandstone Alchemist's transformation and felt like a bird that sensed the teeth of winter closing in, an unnamed longing to *flee and never look back* deep within my bones. Maybe all of my strength until now had come not from inside me, but from the other royal alchemists, who couldn't protect me anymore. I would have to find Penglai by myself.

My next step forward sank into wet ground, cold mud swallowing my ankle and numbing my toes. I'd been distracted and wandered too far from where Hong was supposed to be. I took a steadying breath and pictured his face, the way he always felt like the soft blur of dawn, pale colors and latent moonlight. I wanted him to soften all my colors, smooth away the bright flashes of worry that I couldn't seem to shake.

I trudged through the mud until grass whispered around my ankles once more, and at last, the fog parted, revealing the broad tree with Hong's rope around it.

I called his name and circled the tree, peering through the white fog, but Hong wasn't there. I clenched my teeth and swallowed down my panic, feeling for the end of the rope, praying I wouldn't find frayed threads and a severed end.

My fingers closed around the rope and traced it up, straight into the sky.

I craned my neck, looking into the misty canopy of dying trees overhead.

"Hong?" I called.

No one answered.

I rolled back my sleeves and lifted the hem of my skirt, then jammed my foot into a low branch and hoisted myself up into the tree.

Branches scored across my face, scraping lines into my forearms, wet and sharp beneath my fingers as my grip pulled away rotting bark. I climbed higher and higher, the air growing thin, the mist denser, until at last I found him.

Hong was pressed up against the trunk, straddling a thick branch and staring off into the distance, face turned away from me.

"Hong?" I said, edging carefully onto the branch below him.

His gaze snapped down toward me, as if he hadn't heard my undignified struggles to climb up. He reached down and grabbed me by the wrist, his rings burning against my skin. With strength I hadn't known he had, he hauled me easily up onto the branch, straddling him, then wrapped his other arm around me and pulled me close.

"Hong, what—"

"Something is down there," he whispered against my throat.

The words shivered across my skin. His hands trembled where he clutched my back.

"Something?" I said. "Like what?"

"Maybe an animal," he said, pulling me closer. He'd seemed so still before he'd noticed me, but now his whole body shook, as if my warmth had reminded him to be cold. "Maybe a person? I don't know. But I'm not alone here, Zilan. Aren't I supposed to be alone?"

I gripped his shoulders, unsure how to answer. Either his mind was truly unraveling in death, or the Empress had made good on her promise and was looking for him in the land of the dead. I wasn't sure which one was worse.

"Are you sure it's safer up here?" I said, casting an uneasy glance down at the forest floor shrouded in fog.

"I don't know," he said, resting his forehead against my collarbone, letting out a sigh, "but it's harder to fall asleep when I'm up here. I'm too scared to fall."

I said nothing, pressing my hands to his back, feeling the cavernous silence where his heartbeat should have been.

"I'm sorry," I whispered. Once the words left my lips, I realized I wasn't sure if I'd even said them since he'd died. They seemed so small and worthless compared to his suffering. "I'm sorry, I wish I could—"

"It's okay," he said, pulling back and smiling softly. "Can you just . . . stay here a bit longer? Please?"

I nodded and held him tighter. As a prince, he'd been good at putting on an air of confidence when it mattered, but death seemed to be eating through him like moths devouring the fabric within a dark closet.

"Of course," I said, holding him even though his coldness was bleeding into me, making me shiver.

It wasn't wise to stay for much longer, but I couldn't bring myself to leave. I was too exhausted—we'd already ridden deep into the night, past the first few closest towns, just in case the Silver Alchemist tried to come after us. If I fell asleep here, I would disappear in his arms, and that somehow seemed worse than telling him I had to go.

The leaves shivered around us, and from the ground below, I sensed a pull.

It was wordless, soundless, but I sensed it in the uneasy shifting of branches, the wisps of gray fog that murmured secrets across the forest floor. The wind picked up, a breeze rushing between us . . . and I felt it call for Hong.

He must have sensed it too, because his arms tightened around me, as if anchoring himself here.

"Zilan," he said, the word muffled into my shoulder. "How long have I been here?"

The words sounded so soft, so lost that I wanted to cry. I swallowed the feeling down before I spoke so he wouldn't sense it. What right did I have to sadness when he was the one trapped here?

"About a month," I said. "But I have two out of three rings now. It won't be much longer."

"Just one more ring," he whispered into my hair, as if making a promise himself. "Do you know where to find it?"

"I . . . haven't discussed it with the others yet," I said tentatively. A simple *no* felt too cruel to say out loud. "Zheng Sili is such a know-it-all, I'm sure he'll have a few theories."

Hong didn't respond, except to rest his head on my shoulder.

"I'll go over my father's notes again," I said, wishing I could promise Hong something more. I wondered, for the thousandth time, if the missing page would have saved us.

More than anything, I wanted Hong to say something, anything except this resigned silence, like he too had stopped believing in me. "Maybe we mistranslated something and we'll find a whole passage about a scarlet-winged tree."

"A what?" Hong said tiredly, finally lifting his head.

"*The child of Heaven, the scarlet-winged tree,*" I recited. "It's the next line of the transformation. But I don't know what—"

"The child of Heaven," Hong echoed softly, trailing off as if he'd already forgotten the second part. "Zǔfù?"

"Hm?" I said, tracing a hand down his hair, tucking it behind his ear. I had the strange sensation that he was breaking to pieces in my arms.

He sat up, his eyes suddenly bright. "My grandfather," he said firmly. "Emperor Taizong."

"Your grandfather," I echoed, frowning. "What does he—"

"When he founded the Tang Dynasty, he was called Tiānzǐ, Son of Heaven."

"Okay," I said, my mind spinning. I'd assumed the reference had something to do with mythology, but I supposed that its connection to the Mandate of Heaven—where the royal family believed they got their power—also made sense. "But we're looking for an alchemist."

Hong closed his eyes, frowning as if trying to remember something. "My grandfather died before I was born," he said, "but I remember my father saying he was very interested in alchemy, and very close with his alchemists, even when they seemed to be poisoning him with their concoctions. He never lost faith."

There was no record of Taizong himself being an alchemist, that was certain. Back when he was alive, alchemy was seen as undignified work, a new and unproven science.

I shook my head. "Even if it's referring to Taizong, that wouldn't help us. I can't go ask a dead man for his ring." I hoped that Hong was wrong, because the last thing I wanted was to go back to Chang'an to dig up his grave and pry the ring from his skeletal fingers.

"You could check the treasury?" Hong said. "If he had a ring he knew was valuable, he might have left it for my father."

I let out a stiff laugh, imagining myself going back to Chang'an and waltzing into the palace treasury. I'd probably end up stabbed again. "They don't let concubines poke around in there," I said. "Especially now that Yufei isn't there, I don't think I can just walk in."

"But you're not just a concubine," Hong said. "Remember?"

Right, I thought grimly. *I'm the Empress.* It felt impossible to imagine myself in such a position. I had spent my whole life standing in opposition to the rich, the family chosen by the gods. And now I was part of their history.

Far below us, the wind hummed once more, whispering his name in a language I didn't know yet somehow could understand perfectly. I didn't want to leave him again, but we were so painfully close to finding Penglai, to bringing him back for good, and if something was hunting him in the river plane, it wasn't wise to waste more time. "I have to go," I said, pulling away. "But I'll see you soon."

He smiled, but it didn't reach his eyes. "Soon," he echoed, the words soft, a gentle promise that the dead wind carried away.

"We are absolutely not going back to Chang'an," Wenshu said, clutching his pear like he wanted to bludgeon me with it. "Do you want to get skewered again?"

We all sat on the floor of our room, pears and grapes spread out on a cloth before us. We'd ridden half a day south back to Zhongwei, not wanting to stick around Wuzhong on the off chance that someone found the Silver Alchemist's body and started looking for her murderer.

Zheng Sili was peeling grapes for Durian while Wenshu sliced the pears. I turned to Zheng Sili, but his expression looked just as uneasy. I couldn't blame him—Chang'an was at least a week's ride south, not exactly somewhere to return to on a whim.

But I worried more about what we'd find when we eventually returned. I imagined the private armies tearing through the palace, overturning chests of jewels, storming through the duck ponds. It was dangerous to leave the throne empty for too long.

"The whole country is looking for us," Wenshu said. "At least out here, they can only go by a description and some illustrations. People in Chang'an have actually seen us. Not to mention that the Empress probably has more puppets there than anywhere else."

"It's not like we're safe up north either," Zheng Sili said, carefully peeling the skin off a grape.

"We'll have to return at some point," I said. "People need to know that the House of Li hasn't been wiped out."

"Yes, we'll return," Wenshu said, "once you've harnessed all the power of Penglai Island to make sure we win whatever fight we're walking into. Otherwise, all we'll do is *prove* that the House of Li is gone once they hang our corpses at the gates."

I groaned, flopping back against the futon and staring at the ceiling. The other reason, which I didn't want to bring up, was that if Yufei was alive, she would return to the palace once she heard that we were there. If she never came back, we'd know what that meant. Perhaps Wenshu didn't want to think about it.

"But where else can we look?" I said. "What else could *child of Heaven* mean?"

"Oh, it's definitely Taizong," Zheng Sili said, popping a grape into his mouth. He moved it to his cheek for a moment, then spit the skin loudly on the floor, followed by two seeds. "Your boyfriend is right."

"Taizong was not the first emperor to hold that title," Wenshu said, glaring at the discarded grape skin. "The Mandate of Heaven began in the Zhou Dynasty."

"Yes, which is way too old to make any sense," Zheng Sili said, picking something from his teeth. "The Arcane Alchemist said that when he and his buddies found Penglai Island, they came back with the idea for life gold. That was one century ago, not nine centuries ago."

"So it's definitely Taizong, who is buried in Chang'an, the one place we absolutely cannot go?" I said.

Wenshu grimaced but said nothing. Zheng Sili finally succeeded in plucking the piece of seed from between his teeth and cast it to the floor. "Maybe I could go?" he said.

Wenshu and I both turned to him.

"My face isn't as well-known as yours," he said, shrugging.

I pictured Zheng Sili knocking on the doors of the palace, picking grape seeds from his teeth. The private armies would behead him on sight.

"Is this some misguided ploy to seize the crown?" Wenshu said flatly.

Zheng Sili scowled. "My family hasn't laid the political groundwork for something like that. The Zhu family, on the other hand . . ."

I shook my head. "This is my mess to clean up," I said. "Besides, they wouldn't let you in, and you'd be executed if they caught you."

"And they'd let *you* in?" Zheng Sili said.

"If I showed them the right paperwork, they'd have to," I said. "Hong went ahead and preemptively married me."

Zheng Sili stilled, a grape falling from his hand. "You're already married?" he said.

I nodded, trying my best to ignore Wenshu, who had gone very still.

Zheng Sili let out a stiff laugh, swiping his discarded grape from the floor and starting to peel it. "Well, that explains why the Empress needs you," he said.

"Yeah, she needs me to make life gold," I said, frowning.

Zheng Sili blinked back at me as if I'd spoken a different language. "Oh, you actually don't understand?" he said. "Sorry, I forget you're a peasant sometimes."

Wenshu drove the knife hard into the next pear, stabbing the blade straight through the fruit into the floor, glaring pointedly at Zheng Sili.

"Watch your fingers," I said to him, then turned back to Zheng Sili. "Why does me being married to a mostly dead prince change anything?"

"*Because,*" Zheng Sili said, "it changes the order of succession. The wife of the emperor outranks his mother. If he dies and there's no one else in the House of Li, then the crown goes—"

"To me," I finished quietly.

That was why it wasn't enough for the Empress to kill "the prince" and take my sister's body for herself. She needed proof of my death as well, or her claim to the throne would be illegitimate. Since there hadn't been a wedding, no one would know at first, but anyone who wanted to challenge her legitimacy wouldn't have to look very far. She needed me back in Chang'an to die publicly.

But now that the Empress was supposedly dead, what did she expect to do? Have me resurrect her and tell everyone that she'd dabbled in the very life alchemy that she'd forbidden? There would be an uproar.

My next breath caught in my chest. Of course the Empress wouldn't do something like that. She might have wanted her own body back at first, but now, surely she wanted *mine*. It was the only legitimate way to keep the throne she'd worked so hard for.

I pictured the red thread of fate tying me to the Empress, pulling me closer across the river plane, drawing my whole soul into her until my bones, my blood, my heart belonged to her.

You and I are tethered, and death can never sever that thread. I will always find you.

Wenshu staked his knife into the ground and rose to his feet. He looked between me and Zheng Sili like he wanted to say something, then turned and grabbed his coat, slipping on his shoes.

"Where are you going?" I said.

"Out," he said stiffly.

Zheng Sili picked up Durian and carefully edged away as if sensing Wenshu's temper. I rolled my eyes and hurried to grab my own coat, nearly losing my fingers when Wenshu slammed the door in my face. I yanked it open and hurried after him.

Wenshu was already halfway down the hall, but ignored me when I called for him. I caught up to him just in front of the inn, grabbing his shoulder, but he shrugged out of my grip and pulled up his hood as it began to lightly rain.

"What's wrong with you?" I said.

He let out a sharp laugh. "What's wrong?" he said. "Other than the prince marrying you without your consent and making you a target?"

I rolled my eyes. "It's not that bad," I said. "We would have been married eventually, and I was already a target."

"Do you hear yourself?" Wenshu said, finally turning around, raising his voice so much that nearby merchants paused to stare at us. I grabbed Wenshu's sleeve and pulled him into an alley, but he yanked out of my grip. "Am I not allowed to be angry for all that he's done to our family?"

"That's not fair," I said. "Nothing that happened at the palace was his fault."

"No, nothing could ever be his fault," Wenshu said, glaring down at me. It was strange to see the prince's face contorted with such uncharacteristic anger.

"Why do you hate him so much?" I said. Wenshu stiffened but didn't answer. "He doesn't hate *you*, you know. Even though he has every right to."

"And why would he have that right?" Wenshu snapped.

"Because I chose you over him!" I said. How could Wenshu

not understand that? He'd once told me he was scared of losing me to the prince, yet here was the irreconcilable proof that he never would. How could he overlook that so easily?

Wenshu's expression darkened, his jaw tense. "No," he said quietly. "You didn't. I chose *you*."

CHAPTER SIXTEEN

The rain fell harder, a rushing sheet of it forming gray walls all around us, sealing us in our tiny world inside the alley.

"I saw you," Wenshu said quietly. "In the river plane."

"You remember that?" I said. I hardly remembered much of it myself beyond grabbing his hand and pulling him to the surface.

He nodded. "I remember drowning," he said. "It was like my whole life had turned to water and was filling up my lungs. But then it was gone, and I was lying in this muddy riverbed with a stone wall behind me. I sat there in the dark and waited for you. I knew you'd come eventually."

He looked past me, into the sheet of rain. "But so much time passed, and you didn't come. I called your name, but I couldn't even hear my own voice. I could see through my own hands, like I was made of mist. The forest was so loud, it kept calling for me, and after a while I couldn't ignore it anymore.

"I walked into the forest, and it got darker and darker. But then I heard footsteps, and when I turned, I could see you in the clearing. I called out for you, but you still didn't hear me. You kept walking past me, and that's when I realized you weren't there for me at all. You were looking for the prince."

He trailed off, gaze dropping to the ground.

He must have seen me wading through the darkness before I truly knew who I was going to bring back. Alchemy was driven by intention, and without a crystal clear goal, I'd been lost in the woods for what felt like hours.

"For a moment, I thought of just letting you go to him," Wenshu said, his words quieter now. "Maybe I should have. But I needed to make sure you and Yufei were all right on the other side. So I ran up to you and took your hand, and that was when you finally noticed me."

That part I remembered. The darkness had dissolved, and suddenly my brother was standing before me, as if surfacing from a dark sea. I'd taken his hand, and the haze of the river plane had evaporated.

"I thought you would return for the prince afterward," Wenshu said, glaring at his feet. "I didn't realize you were choosing between us. But it wasn't a choice, because I decided for you."

I shook my head. "That's not how it works."

"It's obvious that you wish I was him, Zilan," he said, finally meeting my gaze. "Everyone can see it. You spend half your time with the prince at the river, and the rest of the time you walk around like a kicked puppy. You never looked this sad, even when your mother died."

I wondered, fleetingly, if Wenshu was right. I had never consciously wished that it was Hong and not my brother standing beside me, but alchemy had a way of unspooling all the lies you told yourself, revealing the truths you tried to ignore. I'd been so happy for the brief moment Hong was back in his own body, but that was only because I worried about him waiting in the darkness, wasn't it? I didn't want my brother dead any more than I wanted Hong dead. I had faced an impossible choice.

And somehow, even when I'd chosen Wenshu, it wasn't enough for him.

I took a steadying breath, clenching my teeth against the onslaught of angry words that wanted to rush out. Wenshu had never been asked to choose between those he loved, except for the time when he'd kicked me out and chosen to protect Yufei over me. He'd apologized, but it wasn't something I could easily forget.

Everyone I loved was either dead or hated me. I wished I could go back to a time before I was anyone of importance, before anyone had expected any more from me than to sell míngqì in a tiny shop in Guangzhou and not complain that no one wanted to marry me. If no one expected me to save them, I could never let anyone down.

"I don't understand what you want from me," I said, fists clenched. I knew it wasn't what Wenshu wanted to hear, but in that moment, I didn't care. "I brought you back, even though it meant I might lose Hong forever. I'm trying to get your body back. And somehow, I still did something wrong?"

"That's not what I'm saying," Wenshu said, frowning.

"Then what are you asking me to do?" I said, raising my voice against the roar of rain. "Go back in time and find you faster in the darkness? Wait to mourn my betrothed until after you're asleep? I have a lot more important things to worry about right now."

"Well, at least you're being honest now," Wenshu said. "I'm always the last person you think about."

"*I gave up Hong for you!*" I said.

"And I wish you hadn't!" Wenshu shouted back.

I stilled, suddenly too aware of the coldness of the rain on my robes, the searing heat of my anger extinguished in an instant.

"I would rather you left me for dead than let me live this way," he said. "Because every time you look at me, I can tell you wish I was someone else. I don't want to live my life indebted to him, always knowing that I'm not enough for you."

I shook my head. "That's not what I said."

"You didn't have to say it," Wenshu said, turning away.

"Gēgē, I want you here with me," I said. Surely he knew that much was true.

But he only glanced over his shoulder, his expression so perfectly even and cold, like he didn't know me at all. And there, once more, was the proof that I had ruined another precious part of my life. There was so little left that I hadn't destroyed.

"This conversation was pointless," he said, turning away. "Let's go."

Then without another word, he headed back into the rain. I pulled up my hood and hurried after him, sure that there was something more I was supposed to say to reassure him, but with no idea where to begin. There were no words in the universe that could explain how much I cared for my brother, and trying to choose the right ones was like parsing the perfect grains of sand from a vast desert. I'd thought Wenshu too pragmatic to need any reassurance, but I would have to think of something. Maybe Zheng Sili, with his expensive education, could help me come up with something eloquent.

Wenshu stopped suddenly. I bumped into him, peering over his shoulder to see what was going on, but could see nothing but the rain in front of us.

"What is it?" I said.

He glanced over his shoulder, then shook his head. "Nothing," he said, taking off quickly.

At first, I thought he was taking a winding path back to the inn, but he drew closer to the city center and farther from our room. I could smell bread even through the rainstorm, and just when I was starting to think that food would most certainly solve all of our problems, Wenshu drew to a stop again. This time, he rolled up his sleeve and examined his arm.

"What is it?" I said.

He turned and showed me his forearm. There was nothing but pale skin and the purpled scar of his soul tag.

"I know you hate my handwriting," I said, "but—"

"No, *look*," he said, shoving his arm closer to my face. "Goose bumps."

"Do you . . . want my coat?" I said, feeling like we were speaking two different languages.

He shook his head. "I'm not cold."

"Then why are we stopping?"

He glanced over my shoulder, then turned and looked behind him, drawing closer to the wall of the closest building. This startled, fearful look—like a deer ready to lope off at any moment—looked almost exactly like Hong.

"I feel unsettled," he said, "but I don't understand why."

That certainly was unlike Wenshu. He was logical if nothing else, and did nothing if there wasn't a reason for it. He had never been prone to random anxiety. That sounded more like Hong, who had always been running for his life. Maybe some of his instincts remained in his body and not just his brain.

"Do you see something?" I said.

"No, that's the problem," he said. "I can't explain it, but I feel as if we're being followed."

"Then let's go," I said, grabbing his wrist. If Hong thought we should flee, I wouldn't question it.

The rain began to pick up, destroying any hope of hearing footsteps behind us and obscuring the whole street in murky gray. If we were being followed, I didn't want to lead them right back to where we slept, so we took a winding path around the city, the rain quickly soaking us through.

"Do you still feel it?" I said, my teeth chattering from the cold rain.

Wenshu only nodded, his face pale. I was starting to worry he was going to collapse again soon, and I'd be left defending his limp body from an unknown assailant.

I yanked him into an alley, tucking us both under an alcove at the back door of a restaurant beside a pile of compost.

Why are you running? I asked myself, the thought sharper than the burst of cold rain that gushed down from the gutters onto my head. *You are the Scarlet Alchemist.*

But was I really? I thought of the way Hong had looked at me, like he no longer believed I could truly bring him back.

Wet footsteps approached the mouth of the alley, then drew to a stop. My heartbeat hammered through my bones, and the shame I felt at my fear was more harrowing than the fear itself.

Get up, Zilan, my father's voice said. But I couldn't move, shivering hard beside the pile of rotting fruit.

Maybe the Silver Alchemist had somehow survived and caught up to us. Or maybe it was just another one of the Empress's puppets come to drag me back to Chang'an in chains so I could hang from the gates.

To my horror, Wenshu rose to his feet.

I yanked his sleeve, but he pulled away, heading straight for the stranger.

This, at last, forced me to my feet. I wedged myself in front of Wenshu, squinting through the barrage of rain, reaching for three firestones.

But as I drew closer, I realized this couldn't be the Silver Alchemist. This figure was much smaller, their fingers too thin and pale. That was all I saw before a gust of wind pulled at their hood, and in the darkness of the alley I caught a glimpse of two golden eyes.

I raised my firestones, but Wenshu seized my wrist.

"You walk too damn fast," the stranger said.

The words felt like falling into a frozen sea. I knew that silvery smooth voice, the same one that haunted my dreams.

In the darkness of the alley, the stranger pulled her hood down, and I stood face-to-face with the rain-drenched Empress Wu.

"Jiějiě?" I said the word so quietly that I wasn't sure if she'd even hear it over the roar of the rain.

The Empress locked her gaze with mine, but her expression hardly changed save for a raised eyebrow, and yes, that was the Yufei I knew—the girl with so few facial expressions that neighbors whispered about how she wore a porcelain mask instead of a face. The Empress was like a painting, a thousand stories behind her eyes, but Yufei had always looked like she couldn't bother to expend the energy to change her expressions.

"Why were you sitting in rotten fruit?" she said.

I let out a sharp, delirious laugh. "Why were you sneaking around like you wanted to mug us?" I said.

"The whole country knows my face and thinks I'm dead," she said. "I couldn't exactly pull my hood down from three blocks away and shout your name."

I crushed her into a hug that punched her breath away, and

even though it felt wrong to be wrapped in the Empress's bony arms, to hear the Empress's traitorous heart beating against my own, in that moment it didn't matter what form my sister took as long as she was *here*.

Wenshu crossed his arms, scanning her from head to toe. "You should really try to tell us *before* you fake your own death, not after," he said.

"Where was I supposed to send the letter?" she said, raising an eyebrow. "And I was in a bit of a hurry."

"I guess I can forgive you this once," Wenshu said, pulling her into a hug the moment I stepped back.

Under the awning, she told us how she'd watched from her window as the private soldiers finally broke through the main gates of the palace. She'd managed to hide herself in a potato barrel in the cellar and remain undetected while the soldiers killed all the servants trying to flee. After the soldiers gave up, she'd swapped clothes with a dead servant and left the body in the dungeon staircase, where it looked as if she'd fallen and broken half her face off. She fled through the tunnels and wandered through the wet darkness.

"Which, by the way," Yufei said, "are impossible to navigate. You know how long it took me to find my way out of there? At least a day. I was starving by the time I got out."

"That's sort of the point of the tunnels," I said, clinging tight to Yufei's arm, even though both of us were shivering from the rain.

"You did a pretty convincing job of faking your own death," Wenshu said, arms crossed. "Except for one thing."

She raised an eyebrow. "Oh?"

"There were no shoes on the illustration of the Empress," Wenshu said. "You never walk around the palace fully dressed but barefoot. The Empress's shoes were too small to fit onto a random corpse, weren't they?"

Yufei smirked. "The opposite, actually," she said. "The shoes were too big, and they fell off when the soldiers dragged the corpse outside."

"You knew?" I said, smacking Wenshu's arm.

"I told you the shoes were suspicious!" Wenshu said. "And I told you not to worry about it!" He turned back to Yufei. "So how did you find us?"

"You sure didn't make it easy," Yufei said. "It took me forever to figure out you were traveling with three people instead of two. Which, by the way—who's the servant boy?"

"He's not important," I said. "Are we really that easy to track?"

"Zilan is," Yufei said.

I froze. *Me?*

"The vendors always remember you," she said. "Two aristocrats buying plain congee and yóutiáo every day? It stands out."

I grimaced. I'd grown up eating congee for breakfast simply because it was always there—meats and vegetables were sometimes scarce as the seasons changed, but we always had rice, so we always had congee. Eating it reminded me of sitting in the kitchen with Auntie So while she brushed my hair back.

But I supposed it was considered a poor man's meal, something an aristocrat probably wouldn't buy plain, if at all. They were more likely to eat it when ill, in which case they'd order their servants to make it for them.

"Once I knew where you'd been, there weren't that many inns to check, and the innkeepers could always be . . . *persuaded* to tell me if you'd stayed, or if they'd heard you talking about where to go next, or, at the very least, which direction you rode off in."

"Did you torture them?" Wenshu said flatly.

"Only a little," she said, shrugging. "Now, are you actually sleeping in this compost pile, or did you find somewhere to stay?"

Zheng Sili did not appreciate the unannounced return of the Empress.

He braced himself in front of Durian like a human shield and hurled a shoe at Yufei, who smacked it out of the air before spotting the pear slices on the floor and popping three in her mouth at once.

Zheng Sili froze, another shoe in hand, looking between me and Wenshu.

"If that really was the Empress, the first thing you would attack her with is a *shoe*?" I said.

He blinked, slowly lowering the shoe. "That's not . . ." He shook his head. "Of course it's not the Empress. I forgot you stuff people inside other people like human sausages."

"Gross," Yufei said through a mouthful of fruit.

I rolled my eyes, sitting down beside her. "This is my sister, Yufei." She waved in acknowledgment, popping a grape in her mouth alongside the pear slices. "Yufei, this is Zheng Sili, who is supposedly an alchemist who can actually fight with stones instead of shoes."

"This is so weird," Zheng Sili said, dropping onto the bed. "You imprisoned me. You were hanged."

"Nope, wasn't me," Yufei said.

"Yes, I obviously understand that," Zheng Sili said, glaring. "Well, this is great. We're walking around with the undead Empress, the Crown Prince, and the last royal alchemist. As if we weren't memorable enough already."

Yufei coughed, pulling a piece of grape peel from her mouth and casting it to the floor.

"You're not supposed to eat the peel," Zheng Sili said, angling away, like he thought she might eat him as well.

"I obviously didn't mean to," Yufei said, still chewing. "I'm hungry, okay? I didn't get a chance to pack a ton of snacks before fleeing for my life."

He tensed, his eyes brightening. "I don't suppose you brought anything from the treasury with you on your way out?"

"Of course I did," Yufei said, wiping her hands on her skirt. "I needed gold. You think anyone gave me passage north for free?"

"Did you bring any rings?" I said, grabbing her arm. Maybe we wouldn't have to go all the way back to Chang'an after all.

Yufei shook her head. "Just some gold headdresses."

My heart sank, my fingers loosening around her arm.

"You sold gold headdresses from the treasury?" Zheng Sili said, looking physically pained by the words.

"Not *whole*," Yufei said. "I'm not an imbecile. Everyone would think I was a thief. I broke them into pieces."

Zheng Sili let out a strangled sound, turning his gaze to the ceiling as if asking the gods for help. "Those are pieces of history—"

"I can't eat gold," Yufei said flatly. "Well, I guess some people could, but not me."

Zheng Sili looked to me as if I would object, but I only shrugged. "I'm sure the royal family still has plenty of gold."

Zheng Sili's lips pinched together. He pulled Durian into his lap and started stroking his back, like he wanted to think about absolutely anything else.

"We're looking for a ring that is most likely in Chang'an," Wenshu explained to Yufei.

"And you're positive that Taizong didn't happen to share the

KYLIE LEE BAKER

location of this ring with his precious grandson?" Zheng Sili said to me.

I shook my head. "Taizong died before he was born."

"Can't you raise the dead?" Zheng Sili said. "Isn't that your whole thing?"

"He would be a skeleton," I said.

Yufei paused as if actually considering it. "Have you ever tried resurrecting a skeleton?" she said.

"Don't answer that," Wenshu said before I could speak. "I don't want to know. Someone a hundred years dead wouldn't have a brain, so I doubt he would be that helpful."

"And yet we keep Zheng Sili around," I said, glaring at him.

He scowled. "Some resurrection alchemist you are. The one time it would actually be helpful to talk to the dead, and you can't do it."

I crossed my arms rather than admit he was right. We didn't need to give Taizong a whole new body and life, just ask him one simple question.

Besides, the dead didn't need a body to speak. I thought of Hong waiting on the river plane, of the way I'd been able to touch the Moon Alchemist's past along the river of her soul, even though she was dead as well. Maybe I could visit Taizong's river as well. I doubted I'd find a rushing stream there after a century of death, but maybe I could find a single drop of water trapped in the air or the soil, some small ghost of his past that lingered. That was all we needed, after all—one brief memory.

I turned to Zheng Sili. "We're going to need some rope."

CHAPTER SEVENTEEN

The three of us stood side by side on the gray sand of the river plane, looking up at the flat sky and white coin of the moon overhead.

"So this is how you do it," Yufei said, staring in wonder up at the moon. "I should have studied alchemy. This is way more fun than reading about Confucius."

"Fun?" Zheng Sili echoed, arms crossed. "Alchemy isn't about fun."

"Again, we're comparing this to Confucius," Yufei said.

With Chang'an in shambles, what little time we had was running out, and I wanted help looking for Taizong in the endless forest of this plane. I had a feeling someone that long dead wouldn't simply be sitting around in human form, waiting for me. It was more likely that I'd have to dig through the dirt for clumps of moisture left behind from his river.

Zheng Sili, despite how annoying he was, probably would be able to help. And of course Yufei had refused to be left behind.

Zheng Sili looked down at Yufei with distaste, then opened his mouth to say something he would probably regret, but I yanked the rope and forced him to uncross his arms before he could.

"Don't be a snob," I said. "It's not like you've been here before either."

"Yes, shame on me," he said, as the wind picked up in a sharp howl, blasting our hair back. "It's practically a summer palace."

Still, he knelt down and stared with wonder into the river. He reached a hand forward.

"I wouldn't do that, unless you want to see all of my brother's life," I said.

He drew his hand back, frowning. "I can't imagine it's that exciting, but he'd probably murder me, so I will refrain."

"How wise," Yufei said, reaching out to touch one of the prickly pine needles.

The trees shifted in a cool breeze, and all of a sudden, Yufei vanished. The rope on my right wrist pulled taut, sending me spilling into the mud. I tried to stand up, the rope still dragging me forward, but I'd pulled Zheng Sili's rope with my other arm, and he fell over on top of me, crushing me down with a muddy splash.

"Jiějiě, *focus!*" I called out into the darkness, elbowing Zheng Sili behind me.

At once, the rope went slack. Yufei stood over me once more, looking bewildered as she pulled me up by a muddy sleeve.

"I don't know what happened," she said, gazing out across the forest.

"You move through this place by desire," I said. "We need to all think of the same destination, or we're going to get separated."

Yufei said nothing, winding the rope around her wrist a few times so the loose end was shorter. Zheng Sili grumbled and wiped mud from his robes behind me.

"Get over it," I said. "It's not even your real clothes."

"Shockingly, eating spirit mud tastes almost exactly like eating real mud," he said, glaring at me.

I took a steadying breath and turned to the sky. "Just think about Emperor Taizong," I said.

"What about him?" Zheng Sili said. "I never exactly saw his face."

"His name," I said. "Just close your eyes and imagine you're writing his name into the sky."

Zheng Sili glanced unsubtly in Yufei's direction. "Can your sister write?"

Yufei raised an arm to smack him, but I held her back. "Yes, all of us can write, asshole," I said.

"It's a valid question for peasants," Zheng Sili said, crossing his arms.

"We're not peasants!" I said, yanking on the rope to force him to uncross his arms again. "Can you shut up for five seconds?"

He looked like he wanted to say more, but mercifully closed his mouth and looked to the sky. I took a deep breath and curled the rope up in my palms—if their minds wandered, I'd rather have rope burn on my palms than have my shoulders yanked out of their sockets.

I took a steadying breath and focused only on the sensation of the ground beneath my feet, the all-consuming darkness that made my eyelids grow heavy, as if nudging me toward a deep and eternal sleep. With my next exhale, I imagined a fine brush in my hand, painting the characters of Taizong's name across the sky.

I took a step forward.

The ground whispered fast under my feet, like each step carried me a hundred miles. The stinging wind rushed past us, whipping my hair back, sealing us in a tunnel of screaming air.

I knew we were drawing closer when the winds grew quiet enough that I could breathe once more. I drew to a stop, the ground jagged and frozen beneath me. Then I opened my eyes and lurched backward.

I stood at the precipice of a dark and endless canyon. My toes just barely hung over the edge, the wind rushing up from the chasm in a high-pitched scream. While the living and the newly dead had running rivers or withered riverbeds, the place of Taizong's soul was a ribbon of vast nothingness that had been ripped out of the ground.

I knelt down, the rope going slack as Yufei and Zheng Sili knelt beside me, peering into the darkness. I extended my hand, and the air parted like lukewarm water, ribbons of invisible silk tangling around my fingers.

I glanced over my shoulder, where the forest should have been, but there were only thousands of dark holes in the ground where the trees used to be. Out into the horizon, the sky was a lightless whisper of silver that bled into black. The darkness rendered Yufei and Zheng Sili's faces papery white and gray, as if this place had stripped us of all our colors, extinguished the memory of light.

I turned back to the river of nothingness and leaned closer. Yufei gripped my arm as if to hold me back, but I only used her as an anchor to lean farther across the yawning chasm, extending my fingertips out into the night, where the darkness seemed to shroud them completely.

Something brushed across my hand—a tiny spark of brightness, perhaps a silverfish glinting over my knuckles. I jolted back, the sensation like a needle driven up under my nail. But as the pain bloomed bright, the lights of the main dining hall in the palace of Chang'an flashed across my vision.

I had only ever seen the empty hall shrouded in a haze of incense, but the vision before my eyes was bright with jewels, warm with laughter, the sharpness of ginger knifing up my nose, so vivid in contrast to the nothingness around me.

Then the light glinted away, and the image was gone.

"There are residual memories," I said, pulling my hand back, examining where a single drop of water tracked down my palm, running down my wrist—moisture pulled into the air, trapped in clouds, thin and distant remnants of the river that used to be the Emperor's entire life. Death could never erase anything completely.

Yufei took my wrist in her hand, pulling it closer to her. Under the gray light, I realized that the nail of my ring finger, where the water droplet had landed, had turned purple as a corpse. She prodded at it, and I watched the nail flash white from pressure before darkening to purple again.

"I don't know about this," Yufei said.

"Me neither," Zheng Sili said. "This definitely feels like a place we're not supposed to be."

"Because we're not," I said, frowning. "All kinds of life alchemy go against the natural order of the world."

A cold breeze shivered up from the base of the canyon, like a wintery sigh.

I handed Yufei and Zheng Sili the ends of the rope that I'd gathered. "Hold on tight. I'm going in."

"In *there*?" Yufei said, raising an eyebrow. "Into the death pit?"

"It's not a death pit," I said, kicking my shoes off so I could feel the moisture on as much of my skin as possible. "Just give me thirty seconds or so?"

I turned to Zheng Sili, but his expression was hard to discern in the colorless light. He let out a sigh and wound more of the rope around his hand.

"Your brother will blame me if I come back with a corpse on the other end of this rope, you know," he said.

"I know this is hard to believe," I said, dangling my legs over the edge, "but there are things in this world that I fear more than my brother."

Then, before I could change my mind, I dropped down into the darkness.

For a moment, it was like falling into a dream, my limbs wrapped in velvet darkness, sparkling drops of water like whispered stars around me. My feet landed on soft ground, but the rope on my wrists remained loose, even though I could no longer see Yufei or Zheng Sili above me, a world away.

Slowly, Taizong's memories came to me.

I was sixteen, a boy who lived in a house of gold but would never be the emperor. I sat outside the hall where my brothers studied, watching the shadows from the lattice windows carve diamonds onto the gold tiles. At high noon the diamonds filled with sunlight, and I tried to hold the bright reflections in my hands but never could. Instead, I lay on top of them and let the sun carve into me as well, make me golden, make me bright and perfect. But it would never work, because second sons are safeguards, and third sons are shadows, and I only existed where the light could not reach.

I was twenty, and a woman with silver hair pressed golden lips against my throat. She was a song of silver, her words honey that dripped down my collarbone, her promises congealing into hope. She whispered to me about a world that did not yet exist, but maybe one day could. I stayed up late imagining, and for a while, I kept that dream secret and perfect inside of myself. No one saw me, so no one noticed the universe I carried inside my ribs.

I was twenty-eight, and the world was paved with gold. There was stinging sunlight and parched dirt and armor with the weight of a thousand kingdoms on my back, the gates of Chang'an open wide before me. The sky was white and the horizon red, phoenix trees the color of blood shivering around me, shedding their crimson leaves like bloody rain. *The scarlet-winged trees.*

That was the day the world changed.

I was high in the scarlet trees, hidden among the bloody leaves, and my brothers were on the ground, approaching the gates.

I clutched the bow slung over my shoulder, the arrow meant to kill my brothers. Both of them were here, but neither of them saw me tangled amongst the red leaves, because they had never really seen me, not even once.

This was how they were supposed to end. If they died, I would be the crown prince, for there was no one else left. It was a simple choice that would change everything, something I'd long decided, and yet . . .

My hand trembled and the arrow fell, stuck in the branches below me, lost.

I thought of the woman with silver hair, the world we found, the ring we made together. It sat on my finger then, burning.

I dropped down from the tree. My brothers drew their swords, then lowered them when they realized it was only me. They would not raise a sword to someone they did not fear. After all, I was unarmed. I was small. I was so very close to being forgotten forever.

They spoke to me, but I did not hear. I pressed my hands to the earth, and everything began to bleed.

Alchemy rushed into the ground. It devoured the roots of nearby trees, squeezed scarlet sap from their trunks, wilted their branches to ashes. Groundwater rushed up from deep beneath the soil, pulling apart the tiled pathway. Flowers abandoned their petals, walls shivered into sand, the burning iron of earth metals drew up as if purged, and the world was red and red and red forever.

My brothers fell to their knees, and the tiled ground unlatched like a jaw full of jagged golden teeth, devouring them. And at last there was silence across the shattered courtyard, and what remained of the broken world belonged to me alone.

I was thirty-five, a commander at war, and the world trembled beneath my palms, for it feared me at long last. The fields before me were sharp with bones, the sky shattered with screams. *I am the Son of Heaven, I am Tengeri Qaghan, I am the Earthquake Alchemist.*

I was fifty-one, and the world was gray, and the light was gone, and my son was standing over me. He reached for my hand, and that was how I knew that all things were coming to an end. I thought he was there to say goodbye, but instead he slid the ring from my finger, the one that a woman with silver hair had forged with me long ago. I reached out for him, but all I could see were golden diamonds, sunlight I could never touch, bright red leaves falling down and down and down into darkness.

The ropes yanked me up. I splashed into mud, its coldness shocking me awake. Yufei and Zheng Sili looked down at me, both talking over each other so loudly I couldn't make out their words.

My body no longer felt like my own, my skin borrowed and

loose, my bones shuddering even though I didn't feel cold. Yufei took my hand and rubbed it between hers, a burning warmth spreading through my fingers. I sat up and the world spun, so I latched on to Zheng Sili's sleeve to stay upright.

"Are you all right?" Yufei said.

"She's not dead, at least," Zheng Sili said.

That much was true, but I didn't know how to answer Yufei's question. My whole body was still too numb.

Taizong was an alchemist, I thought. Even Hong hadn't known, which meant the royal family had kept it a secret even amongst themselves. The House of Li had always spoken of Taizong as one of the greatest emperors China had ever seen, and now I knew why.

He had a ring, just like the Arcane Alchemist and the Silver Alchemist.

Come to think of it, the woman in Taizong's memories was definitely the Silver Alchemist, though she'd looked younger than I remembered. Somehow, they had known each other when Taizong was alive.

I managed to pull myself upright, letting go of Zheng Sili's sleeve.

"Gaozong took the ring," I said, breathless. "When Taizong was on his deathbed, Gaozong took it. He must have known what it was."

Zheng Sili groaned. "Great. Another dead guy?"

"A fresher corpse this time, at least," Yufei said. "Maybe his river won't eat us alive?"

I looked back out across the black expanse of Taizong's life, flashes of it rushing through me in tiny shocks. The world hummed, somehow delighted in my discomfort. After all, I wasn't supposed to be here.

"We can try tomorrow," Yufei said hesitantly.

I thought of Hong sitting up in the trees, too scared to sleep. It didn't matter how tired I was—he hadn't slept in weeks. I shook my head. "Let's go while we're already here."

"Are you sure?" Zheng Sili said.

I stood up on legs that I could hardly feel. My nails were cracked and black, my skin prickled with goose bumps, like I'd been stabbed with a thousand thin needles. "The hardest part is over," I said.

Yufei held my hand, and Zheng Sili stood close beside us. I took a deep breath, thought of Gaozong's name, and led us forward into the darkness.

The ground began to hum. The sound of wind picked up as the trees rushed past me, the world breathing us into our new destination. The cracked earth softened beneath my feet, my shattering footsteps now barely a whisper. The wind began to quiet down, and slowly, I drew to a stop and opened my eyes.

We stood before a racing river. The sky had brightened from a murky darkness to a hazy morning gold. Fish glinted down the stream like diamond shards in the perfectly clear water.

Normally, when I revived the dead, I had to walk around the barren riverbank until I found the dam where their qi had stopped. The only time I'd visited a flowing river was when I tapped into my own qi, or my brother's.

I turned to Zheng Sili. "Were you thinking of Gaozong?" I said.

"Obviously," he said, frowning. "I'm not illiterate."

I knelt down by the river and stuck a finger in, at once shocked through with the burst of light and life like a solid slap across my face. I wrenched my hand back, frowning in disbelief at the silvery fish rushing through the waters, the endless torrent, the swaying kelp and whispering sands just beneath the surface.

"What is it?" Yufei said, drawing closer. "What's wrong?"

"The rivers of the dead dry up quickly," I said, "but this one is still flowing."

Zheng Sili frowned. "What does that mean?"

I stared at my own distorted reflection in the churning waters, mockingly clear. "It means that Gaozong is still alive."

Zheng Sili turned to me, expression pale. "Are you sure?"

"Look at the river," I said, sitting down heavily at its edge.

"He had a public funeral," Zheng Sili said, shaking his head and backing away. "Who did you bury if it wasn't the Emperor?"

"The corpse of one of the guards," I said, shrugging. "We never found the Emperor's body."

Then why the hell did you think he was dead?

I started to answer, but the words died on my lips when I realized how foolish they would sound:

Because the Empress said so.

"Why would the Empress lie about this?" I said, my fingers clenched in the dirt. "She didn't want Gaozong to die until he changed the line of succession to put her first, and he never did. Doesn't his fake death make her life more difficult?"

"Maybe she doesn't know?" Yufei said.

I grimaced. I'd learned the hard way how dangerous it was to assume that the Empress was ignorant about anything at all, especially something happening right under her nose.

There was little the Empress didn't know, but every now and then, someone deep in the palace managed to surprise her. When I'd eaten the pearl and torn out her throat, and when the Moon Alchemist had smuggled the princesses out through the tunnels, saving the last of the House of Li. So maybe someone had rescued the Emperor from the brink of death and smuggled his corpse away?

"Actually, this tracks," Zheng Sili said.

I turned to him. "It does?"

He nodded. "A powerful alchemist has been pseudo-resurrecting the Empress into corpses all over the country. The son of another great alchemist is mysteriously dead after stealing a magical alchemy ring, yet there's no body. Think about it."

"You think Gaozong is the alchemist helping her?" I said. "The Empress kept him sick for a century. Why would he go back to her?"

Zheng Sili shrugged. "Maybe she's blackmailing him."

I didn't know enough about Gaozong to say if that made sense, but I knew there weren't many other living alchemists powerful enough to help her. At least not any that she trusted. I remembered the man who had attacked me at the river when I'd been expecting the Empress, eyes bright with life gold. Perhaps that had been Gaozong.

The ropes on both my wrists suddenly tightened, yanking my arms backward. Yufei let out a surprised cry, so I yanked her end of the rope first, then Zheng Sili's end, drawing them both out from the darkness.

"Could you focus before you rip my arm off?" Zheng Sili said. "That one was definitely your fault."

I wanted to yell at him, but he was right. I'd been thinking about the Empress, which was dangerous in a place like this. My own mind could deliver me straight to her. Hopefully I hadn't drawn too close.

I turned back to Gaozong's forest, but the vibrant trees were suddenly bare and withering, melting into the foggy darkness.

The rope on my left wrist went slack. I turned, expecting Yufei beside me, but instead, a loose length of rope spiraled on the ground, the end cut and frayed.

All tension in my right wrist disappeared, and suddenly I was holding two frayed rope ends in my hands, both my sister and Zheng Sili gone.

The fog swirled around my ankles, so thick it almost felt like cold fingers caressing my skin. Far away, in a swirled haze where the forest should have been, two pinpricks of golden light pierced through the darkness. Slowly, they drew closer, and all I could see were two round, golden eyes.

I took a step back, then another, then turned around and ran. The frayed ropes dragged behind me, rapidly unspooling into wispy white ribbons.

But in the darkness, I'd forgotten where I was. My next step wasn't met with ground under my feet but the freezing surface of a river that swallowed me whole.

While the river of Taizong's soul had felt like clinging to driftwood in an empty sea, the river of Gaozong's soul felt like drowning a thousand times. The entire river seemed to pour into my mouth at once, filling my lungs, stabbing into my ears, silt scraping across my open eyes.

A bright flash of sunlight trapped in the arc of a sword, festering wounds and burning flesh, armor that glints like dragon scales, and thatched roofs that scream with fire. A palace of yawning darkness, rammed dirt walls built higher and higher, deep graves in red dirt, concubines in pink silk, maps of bright blue ocean, kingdoms across the sea, death so far away and dreams so very close.

The images blurred together into a nauseous tide of colors,

years spinning by in moments. There was grass under my bare feet and metal scorching my palms and warm lips pressed to my cheek and so many sensations all at once that my skin felt flayed apart.

The ring, I reminded myself, clinging to that one bright thought. That was the only part of Gaozong's life that mattered to me.

When I exhaled, the whirlwind of sounds evaporated, invisible hands floating away from my skin. The world smelled of flowers and spring mornings.

I opened my eyes.

I was standing in the quiet yard of a convent cast in white stone, cicadas chirping far away, a fountain bubbling softly in the center. In its pure waters, the reflection of a young man stared back at me. I thought at first it was Hong, but the jaw was too broad, the shoulders too square, the gaze too sharp—Hong did not have harsh edges like men who had seen battle—this had to be Gaozong.

A small figure in plain white robes knelt on the ground, praying, facing away from me.

I took a step closer, dead leaves cracking under my feet. The figure went still at the sound, then slowly looked over her shoulder.

Her eyes were a warm brown instead of the gold I remembered, but she had the same comet-bright smile, the same glint of hunger behind her eyes. She turned completely and bowed.

"Don't," Gaozong said, kneeling before her, reaching out for her hand. "You will be my empress. You bow to no one."

Falling in love with Wu Zhao was a bit like falling into open sky.

In palace silks, she was the brightest flower in every garden, and at night her eyes were twin stars. Her words whispered in my ear might as well have been the words of a god, for they carved themselves deep into my heart, became the sacred promise of my soul.

She is that first sharp blade of light that breaks across the morning sky, she is the comet that rakes across the darkness, she is my forever. I will build an eternal world for her.

I recognized, distantly, that I was drowning in Gaozong's thoughts. They filled my lungs until they burst, stole away every thought that was once mine. She was everywhere and always, her hands the touch of comet tails searing my skin, her dreams like bright new skies.

I clenched my fists, clinging to whatever scraps of my own mind remained. There was the Empress waving me closer, and her hair was more vibrant than all the night sky, tangled with constellations of flowers. And there was her pearl necklace, the one that had once snapped and spilled pearls across the throne room on the day she died. I clung to that thought, the image of her grinning before a wall of fire, then dying between my teeth, blood and salt and dreams that would never come true.

I tried to get a good look at the ring on Gaozong's hand, but the edges of the memory blurred, dissolving when I tried to discern any details.

Then I was standing atop the gate, looking down across a kingdom of gold, and Hong—no, Gaozong—was looking at me like the world was mine. I looked down at my yellow silk dress, the color only the empress and emperor could wear. The hands were not mine, too thin and small. Such delicate hands that would one day kill so many.

"Anything you want, it's yours," Gaozong said.

"Anything?" I said. And the words were maybe mine, maybe

hers. Alchemy had once made me the same promise. "You may come to regret those words," we said.

I held out my hand, and he didn't even hesitate, laying his palm on top of mine, clasping our fingers together.

And there it was at last: a red diamond wrapped in the embrace of a golden phoenix, tight around his ring finger. The ring stolen from his dying father, who used it to seize the palace for himself.

The ring that I had definitely seen before.

The world dissolved, an eclipse of night crashing over Chang'an, Gaozong dissolving into ashes at my feet. Nothing existed except for the blazing, clear image of the ring.

I remembered that jewel tangled in my hair as Hong held my face. He had worn that ring in the river plane, which meant he had died wearing it.

I had a vague memory of Wenshu returning all of Hong's jewelry to me when he'd woken up in his body, but I couldn't remember what I'd done with it. I definitely hadn't packed it for our journey, which meant it was surely back in Chang'an, in the palace under siege.

We would never find it.

It was such a small jewel, and if it hadn't been crushed under the feet of soldiers, surely it had been stolen in the raids and sold for its value in gold. I'd held it in my hands, and then I'd lost it.

I clawed my way out of the riverbank, falling onto crooked roots that jabbed into my ribs, barely registering the pain. I stared at my palm where Gaozong had laid his hand in mine, wishing I could wrench the ring from his finger. But this world was not the real world, and its treasures were only an illusion of light.

Except . . .

I sat up straight, remembering the restaurant in Baiyin where the Empress had ambushed me and my brother. I'd attacked her in the river world, and when I'd woken up, I'd found her broken pearls still clutched in my palm.

Maybe objects in the river plane began as tricks of light, but in the hands of an alchemist, they didn't have to stay that way.

I took off running before I could even see, tripping over broken branches, repeating Hong's name in my mind in a panicked loop. The soft, fertile ground of the river of Gaozong's life quickly withered and tightened with coldness, until at last I was standing by the same forest where I'd met Hong so many times.

The rope arced into the sky once more, exactly the same as the last time I'd visited. I grabbed the lowest branch of the tree and scrambled up and up, bark scraping my palms raw. How high had he climbed?

The clouds thickened into an impenetrable gray cloud as I climbed higher, each branch its own island in the sky. I nearly fell down when I reached out for a branch and missed, but a cold hand closed around my wrist and yanked me up to the next branch.

"Hong—" I said, but my words died on my lips.

Perched on the highest branch, the Empress held the frayed end of the rope in one hand.

"Hello, Scarlet."

CHAPTER EIGHTEEN

I jolted back and nearly toppled all the way down, but the Empress grabbed the front of my dress and yanked me onto her branch, like I weighed no more than a dream.

I shoved away from her and backed up against the trunk, clutching the bark to steady myself.

"Where's Hong?" I said. "What have you done to him?"

The Empress examined the rope in her hand, running a thin finger across the threads on the frayed end. The fog blurred her features, her golden eyes the only thing that didn't wave and shiver in this colorless plane.

"You can't keep secrets from me, Scarlet," she said at last. "I would think, after all we've been through together, you could at least tell me the truth. You owe me that much."

I closed my eyes, trying to think of Hong, hoping the river plane would deliver me to him, but the sky seemed to erase his name as soon as my thoughts carved it overhead, like he didn't exist at all. I dug my fingers into the bark and tried harder, but the landscape stayed stubbornly still. There was nowhere to go. He wasn't here.

"You can't kill him here," I said at last. "His soul lives here, not his body."

The Empress raised an eyebrow, looking up at me in surprise. "Can a soul not break just like a body?" she said. Then she dropped the end of the rope into the spiraling darkness of the forest floor. "I'm not here because of Hong," she said. She closed her eyes, her lips mouthing words that I couldn't decipher. After a moment, I realized she was counting. "Thirty-five thousand, eight hundred and twenty-four," she said. "That's how many times my name is written on the skin of peasants in Guangzhou."

I tensed, already sensing where she was going with this, but not wanting to say it out loud, to make it real.

"You specialize in death, don't you, Scarlet? How many people do you think each of those peasants could kill before they're subdued? I suppose it depends. The children probably can't kill as many as the adults."

"You don't have that many bodies," I said, shaking my head, not wanting it to be true. "There aren't storehouses full of corpses in Guangzhou. And how long would it take you to resurrect them one by one? That's not a real threat, and you know it."

The Empress laughed, the sound echoing back cruelly a thousand times in the cage of the sky. "I know this is very hard for a child to believe," she said, "but you don't know everything about alchemy."

She reached into her pocket and withdrew three red and white stones, presenting them to me in her palm.

"Recognize these?" she said.

Of course I did. It was chicken-blood stone, the kind my father had theorized was the key to resurrection, the kind I'd used to bring back the dead a hundred times over, the kind that had helped me win at my final alchemy trial where I'd become the Scarlet Alchemist.

"It's an incredibly powerful stone," the Empress said. "I was impressed the first time I saw you use it, but your methods were primitive."

She pressed her palms together, grinding the stones between them. They crumbled apart easily, for they were firestones and destruction was their natural state. She opened her palms, which were stained with pale red powder, then tilted her hand and let it fall in a crimson snow over the forest floor.

"I think you know as well as I do that activated alchemy stones work well if ingested."

I tensed, thinking back to the first time I'd tried to kill the Empress. I'd tried putting one type of activated stone in her morning tea and the second in her afternoon tea. When the stone types combined, they were supposed to kill her. But of course, the Empress had seen through my plan easily, and the second dose had never arrived.

"What are you saying?" I said. "That you'll make all of Guang-zhou eat chicken-blood stone?"

"Not at all," she said, grinning. "I'll make them *drink* it."

I shook my head, drawing back. "I don't—"

"I think the Pearl River is my favorite," she said, as if I hadn't spoken. "It's much cleaner than the Cháng, but of course, some degree of filth is inevitable when it comes to peasants."

I clutched the branch, mind unspooling, sure I was going to fall all the way down. The Pearl River sliced through Guangzhou. My cousins and I had waded into its muddy banks to collect clay. It was where people fished, bathed, and drank. If she poured chicken-blood stone into it, then surely all of Guangzhou would be exposed at one point or another.

"You gave me the idea, Scarlet," the Empress said, grinning. "Activate the stone, and it works even if the alchemist isn't around."

"Those people aren't dead," I said. "You can't just cram two souls into a living body."

"Maybe *you* can't," the Empress said. "But if it comes down to me and a peasant, I always win."

Just like when Wenshu took his body back from Hong, I thought, cold horror rippling through my blood. Surely the people branded with the Empress's name would have no idea what was going on. They wouldn't know they were supposed to fight for their own bodies. The Empress, with all her determination, would simply rip their souls out of their bodies and cast them into the river plane.

"I've been playing a long game, Scarlet," the Empress went on. "Thirty-five thousand people are just waiting for my command. I'll make sure they start with this one little míngqì store by the shore."

I lunged for the Empress, hoping to knock her clean out of the tree. Maybe it wouldn't hurt her permanently, but it would still be satisfying.

But she caught my wrist and wrenched it to the side before I could reach her. I managed to grab another branch with my other hand, barely catching myself. The Empress ground the heel of her gold shoe onto my fingers.

"If I were you, I'd start listening," she said.

I clenched my jaw and nodded. She lifted her heel from my fingers and I quickly hauled myself onto the closest branch, glaring up at her.

"I know you're uneducated, so let me be abundantly clear," she said. "Guangzhou is not an important city to me anymore. There is nothing it has that another city cannot offer me, and I will sacrifice it a thousand times over to get what I want. I will wipe it off the map, and where it once stood, there will be a red sea filled with the blood of peasants like you."

I thought of my auntie and uncle, who wouldn't stand a chance if one of the Empress's undead soldiers burst into their shop. So many people had died for me already, and now an entire city would be next.

"What do you want?" I said, my voice so small and pathetic, everything the Empress knew that I was beneath my title.

The Empress smiled. "Now, that's the kind of question you should be asking," she said. "First, you will return to the palace in Chang'an."

"It's under siege," I said dully. "They'd imprison me before I made it to the front gate."

"You think I can wipe out an entire city but not a couple of peasant soldiers in my palace?" she said. "Chang'an is mine. I will clear the way for you."

I tightened my grip on the bark. "You have so much power over Chang'an, yet you let a couple 'peasant boys' hang your body?"

She clenched her teeth. "I was a bit preoccupied with an errant alchemist," she said. "And, as I'm sure you know, they did not hang *my* body. But regardless, once in Chang'an, you will schedule a public execution for Hong."

"*What?*" I said. "On what grounds?"

"Treason," she said airily. "For turning his mother in to the private armies because he wanted to hold power alone. He was always so shortsighted. But don't worry, you won't be around for that part."

"And why not?" I said, trying my best to keep my voice even.

"First," she went on, "you will meet with Gaozong, who will remove your soul and replace it with mine."

I clenched my teeth. I'd known that this was what the Empress wanted, but hearing her finally say it still made my breath come short and sweat break out across my forehead. I imagined her wearing my skin like a dress, saying cruel words with my lips.

"The Scarlet Alchemist—the new empress—will then order the hanging of her beloved prince, and become the sole emperor of China."

"Emperor?" I said.

"Yes," the Empress said, her eyes blazing. "Empresses must share power. Emperors do not. I will be the first and last female emperor."

My grip tightened on the bark. I closed my eyes and took a steadying breath, feeling like I was going to tumble into the broken black sky.

"Am I supposed to believe that you'll show mercy to Guangzhou if I obey?" I said.

The Empress made a dismissive gesture, like my words were flies to swat away. "Guangzhou's existence does not threaten me, and its erasure does not benefit me. Its only value to me right now is that *you* value it. There is no reason to destroy parts of my empire to spite a dead girl."

She shifted, her shadow falling over me, an eclipse of black and gold.

"My husband will be waiting for you in my throne room at dusk in one week's time," she said. "If you haven't done everything exactly as I've described by then, I will pour chicken-blood stone into the Pearl River, and you can say goodbye to Guangzhou forever."

"But that's hardly enough time to make it back to Chang'an!" I said.

The Empress only smiled. "Then you'd better hurry."

I opened my eyes to the wood slats of the ceiling at the inn, halfway convinced that all of it had been a dream. But Zheng Sili and Yufei were looking over me, both talking frantically.

I sat up and rubbed my eyes, trying to make sense of their words.

"Where did you go?" Yufei demanded.

"*Me?*" I said, frowning. "You two are the ones who got sucked into the forest!"

"We ended up in some sort of cave," Zheng Sili said. "I don't know what happened, but eventually it spit us back out here, only you wouldn't wake up."

"And neither will Wenshu Ge," Yufei said.

I glanced down at Wenshu, who was lying still on the ground. I shook his shoulder, but he didn't react at all.

I sank back against the wall and buried my face in my hands, trying to think as Durian pecked at my feet.

"Zilan?" Yufei said tentatively. "Did you at least find the ring?"

I shook my head and hugged my knees tighter, not wanting to look up because I already felt tears dampening my skirt. The ring didn't matter anymore. We were never going to make it to Penglai, because Wenshu and I were going to die in Chang'an.

Yufei knelt in front of me, pushing my hands away and cleaning my face with her sleeve. She whispered words that I was sure were meant to comfort me, but all I could see was the setting sun through the lattice window behind her, another day passing, the sky a sharp and brilliant gold.

CHAPTER NINETEEN

In the end, there wasn't a choice.

As soon as Wenshu awoke and I told him and Yufei what the Empress was planning for Guangzhou, they went pale and quiet. Even Zheng Sili, who I'd half expected to willingly hand over my hometown or at least argue why we should consider it, hadn't said anything.

"We should head back and think about a plan on the way," Wenshu said. "It will take us a week, at least. If the Empress sees that we're not even trying to make it back on time, she might act preemptively."

"And once we're in the palace, maybe we can look for the ring?" Yufei said.

"Yes," I said quietly, even though I doubted we'd find it.

"We're not going to die," Wenshu said, as if sensing my thoughts. "Stop looking so morose."

I glanced at Zheng Sili, who was oddly silent.

"You don't have to come," I said to him.

He looked up in surprise. "Where else am I supposed to go?" he said.

So we bought another horse, extra provisions, and by the afternoon, we were headed south toward Chang'an.

Traveling to the capital had once been my greatest dream, but now it felt like approaching my own funeral. The days spun by all too quickly, the setting sun a mocking reminder of how little time I had left and what would happen if I didn't think of a plan before we got there. What could I do that wouldn't put all of Guangzhou at risk? We could try to kill Gaozong, but surely the Empress would just take that as permission to kill everyone in Guangzhou. One wrong move, and tens of thousands of people would die.

What would the Moon Alchemist do? I thought, staring up at the fat almond of the moon as we rode closer to the capital. I tried to imagine her riding beside me.

I wouldn't have gotten into this mess in the first place, she said in my mind. *I know better than to bring the dead back.*

Unless you're being threatened by the Empress, in which case you'd do it for centuries, I thought wryly.

She shot me a deeply unimpressed look. *There are ways to fake death with alchemy*, she said.

The Empress specified that he needs to be hanged, I thought. Public executions were usually more drawn out and torturous, but I supposed the Empress wanted to make sure I didn't trick her—it was difficult to fake a hanging.

It's impossible *to fake, not* difficult, the Moon Alchemist corrected me.

I supposed I could always resurrect Wenshu into another body, but the damage would be done—the prince would be dead in the eyes of the people, and everything would still hinge on me somehow surviving. Plus, I wasn't particularly keen on watching my own brother get hanged.

What about the girls I sent to the convent? the Moon Alchemist said.

Yiyang and Gao'an—the Emperor's daughters by another concubine—were still safely hidden away. But Gao'an was in a coma, and Yiyang was only a child. She could challenge my claim to the throne if she wanted to, but surely the Empress would have her killed the moment she came out of hiding. If two highly trained alchemists couldn't even find a way to stop the Empress, how could I expect a child to do it?

I don't think they're going to get me out of this one, I thought.

The sound of hoofbeats grew louder, and suddenly Zheng Sili was riding next to me, the image of the Moon Alchemist dissolving.

"It helps to look forward when you're riding a horse, you know," he said. "You almost trampled a pit viper."

"Sorry if I've got a lot on my mind," I said. "You know, having to hang my brother and become the Empress's eternal puppet in a few days and all."

"Technically, *you're* the Empress, you know," he said.

"Don't remind me," I said, gripping the reins tighter.

"You'll have at least one day of being the Empress in the palace before Wu kills us all," Zheng Sili said. "You're not looking forward to it?"

"No one will take my orders," I said stiffly. "Well, I could boss you around, I suppose."

"You've always done that."

"You've always done that, *Empress*," I corrected him.

"Gross," Zheng Sili said, wrinkling his nose. "I refuse to call you that."

"I suppose you could call me Zilan," I said. "You know, my name?"

"Zilan," he echoed. He let out a dry laugh. "The girl with a servant's name is the Empress," he said, shaking his head in wonder. "Who would have guessed?"

"Not me," I said, turning my face to the moon.

"I guess you could call me Sili Ge, if you wanted."

"Don't make it weird."

"Right," he said quickly, nodding. "Of course." Then he straightened his shoulders. "When all this is over and Wu is dead, I expect you to fulfill your promise and make me a royal alchemist."

"I don't think I ever actually promised that," I said, smirking. "You just assumed that I'd agreed."

It was nice, for only a moment, to imagine a way this ended in which all of us got what we wanted, everyone alive and happy, every dream fulfilled.

"It was implied," Zheng Sili said.

"How optimistic of you, to think that you'll actually have a job at the end of all this."

"I mean, we only have one more ring to find, and we're going to its most likely location," he said. "From there, it's a straight shot to Penglai, eternal salvation, all problems solved, right?"

I laughed sharply to hide the nervous clench in my stomach. "Yeah, that's the plan."

"And what are you going to do about the last line?"

I frowned. "The last line?"

"*Together at last, the shadow makes three*," Zheng Sili said. "Please tell me we don't need to wait for a full moon or something."

"What are you talking about?" I said. "There's three stones. Isn't that all that last line means?"

Zheng Sili sighed heavily, rolling his eyes. "Sorry, I forgot you never went to school. It's a reference to a Li Bai poem, obviously."

"*Obviously?*" I said. "What kind of alchemist studies poetry?"

"A well-rounded one?" he said. "It's a poem about a man drinking under the moon, all sad and lonely."

"Like you?"

He shot me a withering glare. "But he's not actually alone," he went on. "He has the moon and his shadow."

"Those hardly count as people," I said.

Zheng Sili opened his mouth to respond, but someone shouted behind us.

I looked over my shoulder, tugging on the horse's reins. Zheng Sili pulled his horse to a stop easily, but I struggled to make mine slow down. Behind us, I could see the horses pacing, Wenshu struggling to dismount, Yufei crumpled on the ground.

Zheng Sili reached them first, hopping to the ground and turning Yufei on her back. I all but fell off my horse while trying to dismount, catching myself on my hands in the dirt.

Zheng Sili looked up at me as I approached, Wenshu's foot still caught in the stirrup. "I think this is the same thing that happened to your brother," he said, his expression tight.

I tried all my usual tricks to wake Yufei, but no matter how much I shook her, she remained stubbornly limp.

"We have to keep moving," Zheng Sili said after a few minutes, glancing at the horizon. "I'll ride with her."

"No, I'll do it," Wenshu said, scowling.

"You want to drop her and crack her skull like an egg?" Zheng Sili said. "What could I possibly do to your sister while on a moving horse?"

Wenshu grumbled but relented, lifting up Yufei to pass her to Zheng Sili after he mounted his horse. We rode toward the city once more, this time in silence.

We approached the gates of Chang'an the next day at dusk.

Zheng Sili pulled Yufei's hood over her face—explaining the Empress's sudden resurrection would be difficult when life alchemy was strictly forbidden. But Wenshu and I had no reason to hide anymore—we were heading home to die. If word got back to the Empress, all the better.

The guards at the gates of Chang'an turned to us as we strode to the front of the line on our horses. They frowned as if prepared to scold us, but they held Wenshu's stern gaze, eyes flickering between me and him.

"Your Highness?" one of them said.

Wenshu made a gesture for him to step back and rode through the gate. The crowd murmured all around us, slowly backing away.

I remembered the first time we'd entered Chang'an, running from the guards who now cowered before us, our broken sandals sinking into red dirt roads, only a few coins to our name. Now the crowd parted for us, the streets lighting up with whispers as we rode toward the palace.

As we drew closer, the dirt began to darken from pale red to deep scarlet, the soil softer beneath our horses' hooves. A woman's corpse, just beginning to rot under the hot sun, swung from the central gate as we passed beneath it.

The front gate of the palace had shattered open, the guards lying in pools of blood, their throats slit. So this was how the Empress had "cleared the way" for us.

We dismounted once we reached the palace grounds, our feet splashing in bloody puddles. Zheng Sili and I quickly repaired the gate with a couple waterstones. It wasn't enough to keep out any true threat, but it hardly mattered—the private army that had laid siege to the palace was long gone.

The palace had been carved open like a gutted pig. Most of the golden brick walls of the inner courtyard were now clumps of rocks and powder, gaping open to reveal the scorched interior. On foot, we led the horses deeper into the palace, through the garden where all the prince's ducks used to live, but now there was nothing but a hole in the earth and wilted lily pads, the grass scorched yellow.

The center of the palace was in better shape, aside from the bloody footprints and the lingering smell of salt and smoke. The Empress had killed her entire family just to live in this palace, and then she had destroyed it.

Yufei remained asleep, so Wenshu went off to find a bed to place her in. Zheng Sili took Durian off to what remained of the western duck pond, promising to draw water up into it. I lingered by the inner courtyard and looked to the sky, where the sun was melting into the horizon. We had one more day until Gaozong would meet me.

I tied up my horse and headed for the treasury without a word, trailing bloody footprints behind me, the ground so spongy from blood that it felt like living, fleshy tissue beneath my feet.

I should have known by the door ripped from its hinges, but still I crossed the dark threshold, igniting three firestones in my hand.

The treasury was empty.

Shelves had toppled over and lay in pieces on the ground. There were holes in the wall where paintings had been mounted, tables overturned, remnants of glue where wallpaper had been torn off.

Something glinted in the darkness. I rushed forward, irrational hope swelling in my chest as I knelt down on the ground to get a better look.

A single pearl lay in the corner, covered in dust. I clutched it between my palms and sat down heavily.

"Zilan?"

I didn't turn around, closing my eyes against the prince's voice. Footsteps drew closer.

"It's not here," I said quietly. "The private armies probably raided the palace the day they came for Yufei. It could be anywhere."

Wenshu said nothing, but I could sense him lingering behind me.

"I can try to teach Zheng Sili how to resurrect people," I said.

"In one day?" Wenshu said softly.

"I don't know if the Empress knows he's involved," I said. "Maybe he can hide for a few months, then find a way to bring us back?"

"Zilan," Wenshu said, and I could sense the anger in his voice even if I couldn't see his face. "You mean you want to let the Empress kill us?"

I turned around, frowning. "Of course that's not what I *want*," I said. "But what else am I supposed to do?"

"You beat the Empress once," Wenshu said.

"I didn't!" I said. "Don't you see that? She only let me think that I beat her. I don't see a way out of this one, do you?"

Wenshu said nothing, his shadow stretched long in the doorway, so sad and silent that for a moment he looked exactly like the prince.

"I can't gamble with other people's lives anymore," I said quietly, turning back to the wall. I thought of the ghost villages trampled by private armies, the prison full of alchemists half my age, the immortals who had died for doing nothing but chasing a dream at all costs, just like me. "This is all my fault. Maybe this is what I deserve."

Wenshu let out a sigh, then his footsteps slowly came closer until he drew to a stop behind me, paused for a moment, then shoved me to the ground.

"Hey!" I said, sitting up and turning to him. "What are you—"

"*Fan Zilan*," Wenshu said. The prince's voice had never spoken to me so sternly, and the harshness of it made me flinch. "You are the Empress of China."

"I'm not—"

"You already are," he said, his eyes blazing, "and you are giving up on your people."

"What do you expect me to—"

"If this were Empress Wu, the last thing she would do would be to *roll over and die!*" Wenshu said.

"Better me than our parents!" I said, tears burning down my face. "Better me than everyone in Guangzhou!"

Wenshu crossed his arms. "And what about everyone you swore to bring back?"

I shook my head, wiping my face with my sleeve, but the tears kept traitorously falling. Why was he being so cruel? "I tried—"

"You're not trying *now*," Wenshu said. "You're moping."

"Am I supposed to apologize for feeling bad that people died for me?" I said, rising to my feet.

"They didn't die for *you*, Zilan!" he said, throwing his arms up. "Is that really what you think? Are you actually that self-absorbed? They died because they believed in a better world than this one, not because you asked them to. They'd been planning this long before you came along."

I shook my head. "They trusted me."

"And you ruined everything," Wenshu said, crossing his arms.

I blanched, my mind suddenly blank. "Gēgē—"

"Is that what you want me to say?" he said, his eyes dark. "You want me to help you punish yourself even more? You seem to be doing enough of that on your own."

"It's the truth."

"And so what if it is?" Wenshu said. "You tried. Now try again, and do it right this time."

I let out a sharp laugh. "You say that like it's easy."

"It's not easy," Wenshu said, "but you're Fan Zilan."

I couldn't help but smile, wiping my tears away with my sleeve. At least he hadn't said *you're the Scarlet Alchemist*. My brother truly believed in me, and he wasn't the type of person to sit back and let a fool handle matters of importance.

"Mèimei," Wenshu said gently, the word for *little sister* that he hardly ever used, "we'll figure out another way."

"Right," I said quietly.

I must not have sounded convinced, because Wenshu sighed and sat down in front of me, then pulled a rag from his pocket and started to scour the tears from my face.

Just behind him, the setting sun had lit up the throne room across the courtyard in glowing gold, the doors hanging open and swaying in the wind. We were so close to where I had lost everything. I could still see the Empress towering over me while I gripped the bars of my cage, her golden eyes sun bright.

Hong will be dead within the hour, she'd said. *Then the people will learn of the tragic passing of their beloved prince and emperor, in that order.*

What have you done with him? I'd said.

My breath caught in my throat.

I froze, recalling with perfect clarity what the Empress had said next. I could still see her crimson lips forming the words, echoed by her reflection in the pool of blood that glowed from the blazing wall of fire behind her.

She had already told me how to defeat her.

Maybe she hadn't realized it at the time, or maybe she'd thought I wouldn't have noticed. But, like everyone else, she had underestimated me.

I ducked away from Wenshu's cloth and jumped to my feet. "Gēgē," I said, "get some scroll paper and an inkstone. I need you to draft me some legislation."

CHAPTER TWENTY

The crowd gathered for the royal announcement at high noon.

Though I couldn't bring myself to look at them from the balcony, I could sense as our audience grew from the nervous whispers and unanswered questions just beyond the gates.

They had seen the gallows.

Wenshu had paid some carpenters to build them that morning, in full view of the main road. As the day wore on, more and more people had gathered, curious who they were for. It was exactly what we wanted—for people to see, for word to get back to the Empress that we were following her orders.

Many people had seen the prince return yesterday. They probably expected him to punish the private armies for destroying his palace. They didn't know they were about to witness the dawning of a new era.

I sat alone in the throne room on the Empress's throne, looking out the open window. From this height, I could see nothing but the sharp flash of sunlight and the faint ghost of the nearly full moon against the blue sky. In the memories of past emperors, the sky had always seemed so much clearer, like an open expanse of Heaven. But to me, Chang'an had always seemed like a cage, a flat blue ceiling slowly lowering to crush us all.

The Scarlet Alchemist—who had ruined China—was somehow now its sole ruler. It hardly seemed fair, though I supposed fairness was a childish concept among royalty.

Once, Hong had told me in my own dialect how he would rebuild the world when his mother was dead, stripping the wealthy of their life gold, sending food and hope to the south. I had inherited the kingdom in his place, and instead of fulfilling his promise, it had crumbled in my hands.

I gripped the edges of the throne, the sun shifting so its rays were searingly sharp across my face.

Perhaps I would never feel that I was enough of anything to rule this country. But somehow, it was mine, so I had to try.

The door opened, and my chest seized up. *It's Gaozong,* I thought. But it was only Wenshu.

"Are you ready?" he said.

I shrugged. "I don't have much of a choice, do I?"

He said nothing, stepping fully into the throne room. He crossed his arms, looking me up and down.

"We'll have to get you some etiquette lessons when this is all over," he said. "You're sitting on that throne like a monkey."

Heat rushed to my face as I uncrossed my legs, setting my feet on the floor. "Is that really our biggest problem?"

Wenshu smiled, though his eyes had no light behind them. "No," he said. "But I look forward to the day that we can worry about small problems again. It will all be over soon, right?"

I could hear the sharp edge to his question. *This will all be fine, won't it, Zilan? You promise?*

"Right," I said, not meeting his gaze.

There were a lot of ways this plan could go wrong, leaving

both of us dead within the hour. But we had no other options.

Wenshu nodded stiffly. "I'll get started," he said, turning to leave.

As he reached for the doorknob, the shadows fell in stripes across his back, and I was struck with the feeling that this was the last time I'd ever see him. I'd felt that same strange premonition the day I'd left Auntie So and Uncle Fan back in Guangzhou, the same childish fear that once they were out of my sight, they'd vanish forever.

But today, that was a real possibility.

"Wait," I said.

Wenshu hesitated, his hand on the doorknob, looking over his shoulder as he waited for me to speak.

Don't go, I wanted to say, even though I knew how childish it would sound. But I had never gotten to be a child. Just this once, I wished I could sit here in my brother's arms and let someone else fight monsters in my place. *Stay here with me, so there will be no last time for us,* I wanted to say. *I don't want to ever say goodbye to you again.*

"Alchemy relies on the intentions of the alchemist," I said instead, the words stiff, practiced from my studies with the Moon Alchemist.

Wenshu raised an eyebrow. "Is this really the time for an alchemy lesson?" he said. "I'm not sure how this is relevant to me."

"You said that I didn't choose you," I said quietly, and I could sense from the sudden stillness in his posture that he knew exactly what I was talking about. "I don't always know what's in my heart," I said. "It's the reason Durian's a duck. I wasn't consciously trying to make a duck, but I was thinking so much about the prince and his overfed ducks with ridiculous names, and some part of me must have found it endearing enough that

I wanted a duck of my own." I chanced a glance up at Wenshu, whose expression was unchanged. I took a deep breath.

"When I went to the river of souls that day," I said, "I didn't know whether I was going to bring you or Hong back at first."

Wenshu's face twitched, and I knew it was probably the wrong thing to say, but there was no going back now. "I love him," I said. "I love both of you, and I shouldn't have had to choose."

Wenshu shook his head, turning back to the door. "I don't want to hear about—"

"Alchemy knows what's in your heart," I said, ignoring him. "*You* are my heart, and that's why you're here now."

Slowly, he turned back to me. "I forced you," he whispered. "You don't have to lie to me. I know you love the prince more."

I stepped down from the throne, because I didn't want to talk to him as the Empress, but as his sister. "The way I love Hong is different," I said, gently taking his hand. "I wouldn't have been able to resurrect you if it wasn't what I wanted the most. I could have dragged you all the way to the surface and knocked on the door until my fingers broke, but it never would have opened. It is alchemically impossible for me to love you less than Hong, because you're here."

Wenshu's lip twitched with the ghost of a smile. "You're using science to prove your point now?"

"Is it working?"

Wenshu let out a stiff laugh. The sadness had smoothed out of his features, but he still looked distant.

"You have been with me all my life," I whispered. "I can't imagine a world where you don't exist. I don't want to live in that world."

"Really?" Wenshu whispered, the most delicate word I had

ever heard him say. My heart broke for how uncertain he sounded, like he truly feared my answer.

"Yes," I said. "Promise me that I'll never have to live that way again."

At once, he closed the distance between us and wrapped his arms around me, crushing me against his chest. That was how I knew, in a way words could never express, that he understood.

"I won't leave you," he said. "Not for anything."

I laughed, hugging him tighter. "You've already died on me twice."

"Well, nobody's perfect," he said. "And one of those times was arguably your fault."

I pulled back and smacked his shoulder.

"You're starting to take after Yufei," he said, grimacing and massaging his arm.

"What about me?"

We both turned to Yufei, who had stuck her head through the door.

"Nothing, just that you're unreasonably strong," Wenshu said, turning to her.

"Thanks," she said, shrugging. "Come on, if you want to be out of here before Gaozong comes, we have to go."

Wenshu nodded, casting me a glance over his shoulder.

"Etiquette lessons," he reminded me. "Next week, all right?"

"Yes, Gēgē," I said, smiling in a way that I hoped looked convincing.

"Go destroy her," Yufei said from the doorway.

"Yes, Jiějiě."

Then they both turned, and the door swung shut, leaving the room in cold shadows and silence. This part I would have to face alone, at least at first. Zheng Sili would be waiting in case I needed help, while Yufei would stay with Wenshu to protect him.

I leaned back against the seat of the throne, imagining how the Empress might have sat. Slowly, I uncrossed my legs, planting my feet firmly on the ground, resting my forearms on the gilded armrests, the cold making me shiver.

Come on out, Gaozong, I thought. *I'm ready.*

The sun fell lower in the sky, the angle sharp through the windows, the light too bright to look at from where I sat. Still I didn't move, squinting through the blades of sunlight until at last, the door opened once more.

I remembered Gaozong's face from the memories I'd borrowed when drowning in his river, and seeing him now felt like my dreams had come to life. He and Wu Zhao had stood on the very same balcony just across the room—when he was young enough that he looked almost exactly like Hong—and he'd promised her the world. Now he was trying to deliver on his promise.

I could still see the echoes of his century-long sickness in his papery complexion, the darkness around his eyes. But despite the signs of age, they still held the dangerous gleam that I'd seen in Taizong's vision, when he'd slipped the ring from his dying father's hand.

He hesitated in the doorway, looking me up and down.

"It is customary to bow to the emperor, you know," he said, a soft smile at the corner of his lips. His eyes were so kind, so like Hong's, that it would have been easy to trust him if I hadn't known better.

"There is no emperor here," I said, crossing my legs. "And I already held your funeral."

He let out a sharp laugh, stepping fully into the room and closing the door quietly behind him.

"I suppose that, technically, I should be the one bowing to *you*," he said. "Imagine that."

"Stranger things have happened in this palace than a merchant girl sitting on a throne," I said.

He smiled. "Oh, I can see why she likes you," he said. He stepped forward, examining me. A chill rippled through my bones, and I tried my best to remain still, to not give away my fear, even when I felt like a piece of merchandise he was appraising. After all, he was imagining the body of his future wife.

I examined the alchemy rings on his hand, bright blue diamonds, jade bands, purple amethyst. It was a diverse array, a good—albeit needlessly expensive—assortment. He clearly was no amateur alchemist.

"I suppose you'll do," he said at last, crossing his arms. "You're no Wu Zhao, but then again, no one is."

I barely resisted the urge to slap him. "I was your son's concubine," I said. "Do you not see how strange that is?"

He shrugged. "Wu Zhao was my father's concubine first."

My expression crumpled. "And people think *my* family is weird."

"Your family certainly is remarkable," he said, leaning forward and cupping my cheek, running a calloused thumb across my lips. "Peasants do not normally live such loud lives."

"For the thousandth time, I'm not a peasant," I said, turning my face away.

"You're not anything anymore," Gaozong said, his eyes darkening. He reached for his satchel of alchemy stones, and I pressed back against the throne, my heartbeat loud in my ears.

"Why did she fake your death?" I said. "Am I at least allowed to know that before I die?"

"She didn't," he said, eyeing my throat. "There are herbs that can slow breathing and pulse, mimicking death for a time," he said. "A physician was loyal to me and helped me escape."

"And yet you returned to her after she kept you ill for over a century?" I said.

Instead of answering, he knelt down before me, the gesture so sudden that I flinched. *The Emperor of China was on his knees in front of me.* I was so stunned that when he reached out a hand for my arm, I extended it to him without question. Gently, reverently, he rolled up my sleeve, examining the soul tag that I'd carved in this very room. *Fan Zilan.*

"It is difficult to stop loving someone, even if they hurt you," he said quietly, the gentle words breathed across the pale skin of my wrist.

"She killed all your children."

He sighed. "I don't expect you to understand," he said, his thumb rubbing softly across my scar. "Royalty survives because we love our kingdom above all else. My father killed his brothers to become emperor, and in turn, he was the best ruler our country has ever seen. None of our hands are clean. A clear conscience is a privilege of people who do not have power. If you have a soft heart, you lose everything, and the country falls to someone far worse than you."

"*She killed all your children,*" I said again.

Gaozong shook his head, drawing a blade from his pocket. "If your plan was to talk me out of this, it won't work."

"And what will she do with you when she's empress?" I said, leaning away from the crisp gleam of his knife in the sunlight.

"She already tried to dispose of you once."

"That was when I wasn't useful to her," he said. "I can hardly blame her for that."

He held my wrist, his grip suddenly bone-crushing. "Here is what you must understand, Fan Zilan. You can stand beside greatness, or you can be crushed beneath it. We have both made our choices, and we will live—or die—by them."

Then he sank the knife into my skin.

I flinched, reflexively trying to pull away, but he held me tight as, stroke by stroke, he carved *Wu Zhao* into my right arm, a fresh crimson mark compared to the wrinkled purple scar of my own name on the other arm. Blood ran down the armrest of the throne, pooling on the floor.

"Thank you for looking after Hong," Gaozong said quietly, releasing my wrist. He grabbed my other arm, the one that said *Fan Zilan*. "Please give him my regards."

Before I could answer, he drew a clean line straight through my soul tag.

I tensed, fists clenching, toes curling, jaw clenched. I went limp in the chair, breathing shallowly, gaze locked on the ceiling.

That was what was supposed to happen when you damaged someone's soul tag.

That was what Gaozong, who had performed so many thousands of resurrections, would expect to see.

That was what would have happened, if he'd actually cut through my soul tag.

But there was another, carved cleanly between my shoulder blades, courtesy of Wenshu, activated by Zheng Sili that morning.

I stayed still and limp while I heard Gaozong shuffling through a bag of stones. I didn't even flinch when he pressed a warm, disgusting kiss to my parted lips.

"We're almost there, darling," he whispered. Then he pressed three stones to the new soul tag, and my whole body filled with light.

Both soul tags flared up in white-hot agony, the new one on my left wrist glowing as if my blood was full of light. My vision fractured, one eye fixed on the dark rushing river, the other staring back at Gaozong's expectant face.

Stay grounded, I thought, clenching my teeth against the burn. I folded forward, and Gaozong caught me, lowering me to the floor with reverence. The new name on my wrist burned brighter, and my bones seized up, joints locked tight. Deep in the labyrinth of my mind, someone was pounding their fist against a door, and it took all of my strength to keep it shut.

I hadn't known exactly how this part of my plan would unfold. Wenshu had described the sensation of sharing a body as *trying to peel off your own face*, though I suspected the Empress's soul would be much harder to extract from a body than Hong's.

I had once clung to my body with no soul tag at all, fought for it with all my strength. It was too tall and wiry and looked not enough like my siblings, but it was *my* body, not a puppet for the Empress to possess.

I opened my eyes, and I was standing on the river, the Empress on the other side, the scarlet current rushing between us, sparks of blood splashing into the air. She met my gaze, her eyes filled with so much raw hate that it scorched me to the bone.

Then the Empress was behind me, one hand yanking my hair, the other hand clawing at my face, trying to unpeel me like a fruit. Sharp nails caught on my lips, cold fingers in my mouth, rings clinking across my teeth.

Get out.

The words hummed through my bones, a chill that made all my muscles seize up in agony. I caught a flash of Gaozong's concerned gaze, then there was only darkness and mud, silt and bones between my teeth, the Empress's hand on the nape of my neck.

I threw a hand back and raked my nails across the Empress's face, leaving three red scratches across her skin, smearing her lipstick down one half of her face like a lopsided snarl.

I turned my head to the sky and tried to trace the characters for my own name into the air, to cling to nothing else but that.

I am Fan Zilan, I thought, again and again and again.

I was the merchant girl from Guangzhou, the girl who lived on the road of pig's blood, covered in clay dust, the flower who was meant to die in winter. I was the sister of Fan Wenshu and Fan Yufei, the daughter of a great alchemist from the west, brash and uneducated and sharp.

I was the girl who forced her way into the palace even when no one believed that I could.

Men were golden thread around my fingers, lies like poetry, bloodstains and screams and gold. And there was Gaozong, taking my hand and looking out over our city, my city, my kingdom.

I tensed up and realized the Empress had pressed me up against a tree, her hand at my throat. *Those aren't my memories*, I thought. Our minds were melting into each other.

A blunt pain hammered through my skull, and through my skewed vision, I caught a glimpse of Gaozong on the floor of the throne room, Zheng Sili looming over him.

I need to hold on until Zheng Sili can kill Gaozong, I reminded myself. This was my only job—to occupy the Empress while Wenshu and Yufei did their job outside, and Zheng Sili took care of Gaozong. If I failed, all of them would die.

I am Fan Zilan, I thought, but the words came quieter now, the Empress's hand choking the breath out of me, her hands like solid gold.

It was bright summer, and I was gathering mud to make clay back in Guangzhou, throwing a handful at Wenshu.

I was wrapped in white, a discarded concubine praying in a convent, waiting for greatness to find me once more.

I was studying by moonlight, my sister offering me a bite of cucumber while I traced my fingers over my father's notes in a language long lost to me, the embers of a dream slowly glowing brighter.

I am . . .

My thoughts reached out, drowning hands clawing for shore, but the name slid through my fingers and turned to mist.

I was alone in darkness among sweaty blankets and blood, clutching my newborn daughter too tightly against my chest, weighing my dreams against my own heart.

I wanted *more*.

The men who had underestimated me, used me and thrown me away—all of them would suffer. They could rot in dungeons, grow like mildew into its wet stones, dissolve into darkness. Because I had earned this title, this dream, this life.

I am the Empress.

I let out a breath, the tension leaving my muscles like a cool wave sighing over my whole body.

I opened my eyes, and I was sitting on my throne, watching as my husband dispatched the commoner. He had the boy pressed down against the ground by the throat, three stones crushed against his chest. The stones dissolved in a blaze of red light—alchemy could truly be beautiful beyond measure—and the boy's eyes went wide. He coughed and sprayed blood across

Gaozong, tiny pearls of it splattering against my dress.

But I didn't mind at all. Red was my favorite color.

"You have to destroy his body completely, or some worm will find a way to bring him back," I said. That was all that alchemists were—wet bugs crawling through dirt, refusing to die.

Gaozong looked at me with those round, helpless eyes that told me I would have to do everything myself, like always.

"Do I need to be clearer?" I said. "Cut his head off."

Gaozong frowned. "But I'm out of firestones."

I rolled my eyes. Alchemists were truly spoiled with their power. Gaozong wouldn't know how to wash his own feet without alchemy. "Then find something sharp."

He stood up and bowed, hurrying out of the room. He always obeyed my direct orders, which was desirable to an extent, though for once I wished he'd have a single intelligent thought of his own.

Like my favorite alchemist.

I looked down at her hands—my hands—caked in dirt, crooked and split nails that I would need to have Gaozong fix later. I ran a hand through my coppery hair, grimacing at the dirt and blood tangled in it. At least my dress was silk, but travel had dulled the vibrant red to a muddy brown. The girl was too wiry, her edges as sharp and gangly as a newborn deer, though I supposed that was the inevitable consequence of growing up on a peasant's diet. I'd taken worse bodies before, and there was little I couldn't fix with time.

I looked in the mirror, and a sudden wave of sadness rushed through me.

After all this time, she was gone.

The thought should have elated me. In only weeks, she'd

unmade everything I'd spent a century building. She was a needle slipped under my nail, a relentless annoyance.

But how long had it been since anyone so interesting had crossed my path?

Eternal youth had seemed so promising at first. Rulers fell because they grew old and weak, but I was neither, and my reign would last forever.

But after a century, all the colors in the world had begun to look dimmer. A sunset was a sunset, each as dull as the one before. I could no longer taste food, barely registering sensations of cold and hot on my skin. When I read, the words blurred together into a swirl of ink because I hardly cared for them at all. I'd begun to wonder what the point of living forever was if the life I had finally won was truly so dull.

Until *she* arrived.

From the moment I saw her, I despised her. She fought like a rabid wolf, gnashing teeth and foaming spit and blood and hate that burned fire-bright in her eyes. What right did a peasant girl have to that kind of blazing fire, but not me?

I supposed, in a way, she would always be with me now.

I ran a delicate hand down my face in the mirror, fingers ghosting over my split lip. But even wearing her face, somehow I didn't look like her at all.

Her eyes had burned like summer stars, but my own eyes looked flat and empty without the blaze of life gold igniting them.

The doors opened, and Gaozong returned with a sword hefted over his shoulder.

"Execution's about to start," he said. "You could probably still get a good view."

I grinned, feeling a spark of warmth inside me for the first time in a very long time. I clung to it, let it fill my chest. "I love a good execution."

"I know you do," Gaozong said, leaning forward as if to kiss me over the scholar boy's body, but I turned my head, and his wet lips grazed my jawline.

"Don't kiss me until you finish what you started," I said. Then I turned and strode from the room. It wasn't every day you got to witness your son's execution. This was the last step, and everything would be mine at last.

I strode out to the balcony, where the crowd was gathered far below, their nervous murmurs like a drug. I loved the taste of anticipation, of fear.

Hong was standing on the lower balcony, tense and fidgeting like always, a gleam of nervous sweat on his brow. He shifted and said something to a person in the doorway, adjusting something tucked under his arm. As he turned, I could make out the shape of a scroll.

I frowned. All the excitement I'd felt moments ago pooled hot in my feet.

Something was wrong.

What purpose was there to bring a scroll to his own execution? Traitors did not give speeches. They did not get final words, not in my kingdom. His hands should have been bound, not holding a scroll. What did he think he was doing?

He unfurled the scroll, the sun bright across the words at the top.

I squinted and read the title once, then twice, and as I slowly began to understand their meaning, I felt as if a sudden darkness had eclipsed the bright courtyard.

In a flash, I shoved away from the window and rushed down

the stairs. Gaozong was busy throwing the alchemist boy's body out the window, but I shoved him aside and yanked the sword from his belt. He let out a sound of surprise.

"What's wrong?" he asked, but I was already running for the lower level. The sword was too heavy for me and pulled at my shoulder as I hauled it alongside me, but I couldn't trust Gaozong to do anything right. He'd said that they'd prepared for the execution, that the announcement had been made, that everything was in place. But there was no one competent in this palace. No one but me.

And, apparently, Scarlet.

I let out a sharp laugh as I turned the corner. As always, she was keeping things interesting.

I ran through the main hall, toward the front balcony where I'd seen Hong.

The title at the top of his scroll ran again and again through my mind on an endless loop, the words burned into my vision.

With a single document, they were trying to strip me of all the years of work Gaozong and I had put into folding this country into the palm of my hand. I hated that they even had that kind of power, but sadly, the rules of alchemy could not be bent, not even for me.

And how well it would have worked, if only their little sister had won. They thought they would end me with a few words, but this was what would happen instead:

The whole country would witness the Scarlet Alchemist executing her own husband before the words could leave his mouth. They called me *Scarlet* for a reason, after all. I looked beautiful drenched in blood.

Hong would fall before the kingdom he never wanted, and at

last, I would win. I was the Empress, a title I had earned at the cost of absolutely everything, and a peasant girl would not take that away from me.

I am the Empress, I thought, approaching the doors, my sword clutched tight in my right hand. It was so much heavier than I'd expected, but I wouldn't let go of it for all the world.

I am the Empress.

The thought repeated, a battle cry that reverberated through my bones. I reached for the door handle, but my hand slipped away, fingers grasping at empty air as if the earth had tilted off its axis. Suddenly there were two door handles, one of them a trick of light. My vision doubled, bright diamonds of sunlight searing through the windows.

I am the Empress.

And I realized, too late, that the thought was not my own.

I fell to the marble floor and crashed straight through it into mud.

And there was Fan Zilan standing over me, backlit by a sky that used to be gray but now was gorgeous crimson, spilled blood and rage. I grappled for Gaozong's sword, but my hands were empty.

She clutched the blade in both hands, unwavering as she pressed the tip to my throat.

"*I* am the Empress," she said, this time in her own voice, her eyes a gorgeous fire of red and gold.

Despite everything, as the blade rose, I felt a smile curl my lips.

I was not the kind of person who died.

I was not the kind of person who failed.

I did not lie in the mud at anyone's feet, especially not a merchant's daughter named after a worthless flower.

But if I had to end, and there was only one thing I could see at the end of my long life, this was what I would choose:

A girl who burned like a comet across the sky, who thought the world could be hers, as I once did.

Until next time, Scarlet, I thought, as she struck down and tore the world in two.

CHAPTER TWENTY-ONE

I fell against wooden doors, and they opened outward with no resistance, spilling me onto a balcony. My cheek slammed into warm tiles, the sword clattering beside me, the angle of the setting sun knife-sharp in my eyes.

Voices called out for me, but I couldn't answer at first, too busy reminding myself how it felt to move each finger, to curl my toes, to draw in air. My skin felt foreign, like I'd pulled on someone else's robes and found the sleeves too short.

Hands closed around my arm and pulled me upright. Yufei was frowning at me as if searching for something in my eyes.

"Is everything all right?" she said.

Wenshu was standing over us, unfurled scroll in both hands as he stared unsubtly at the sword beside me covered in blood. People murmured in the street below, confused at the delay.

"Have you done it yet?" I said.

Wenshu's gaze snapped back to me. "Not yet."

I rose to my feet, ignoring Yufei as she tried to steady me. My legs felt numb, but I managed to take two steps toward

Wenshu, holding out my hands.

"I want to do it," I said. "Please, let me do it."

He raised an eyebrow, scanning me from head to toe. "Are you sure?" he said. "You look a bit . . ."

I looked down at my robes, which were spattered with blood. One sleeve was torn from the wrist up to my shoulder, fluttering like a wing behind me. I tasted blood on my lips, and my hair blowing freely around my face told me that all of my hairpins had fallen out.

But none of it mattered.

There was no longer any reason to hide, or lie, or pretend I was anyone else but a merchant from Guangzhou.

I held out my hands expectantly. Without another word, Wenshu passed me the scroll.

He turned back to the crowd. "Empress Fan Zilan has an announcement to make," he said, before stepping back and nodding to me.

The crowd murmured uneasily at my title. I couldn't blame them—there had been no wedding or coronation. But far stranger things had happened in Chang'an than someone like me.

I clutched the scroll tight in my hands, leaving scarlet fingerprints on the fresh paper. As I drew closer to the edge of the balcony, the vastness of the crowd suddenly overwhelmed me, all their expectant eyes pinning me down.

I had never given any sort of formal speech. I wasn't Zheng Sili, who knew how to speak eloquently. The words on the paper before me seemed to blur together.

But I didn't need them. I already knew what they said. These were perhaps the most important words I would ever speak in my life.

Once, only one floor above here, the Empress had stood over me in a room soaked with blood, and told me Hong would be dead within the hour.

What have you done with him? I'd said.

I've been thinking of posthumous names for Hong, she'd said, as if she hadn't heard me. *We can call him Emperor Xiaojing, even though he was never really emperor, but I think the people would find it endearing.*

I remembered that moment so clearly because the very concept was foreign to someone of my class—merchants had the same name in death as in life.

But people that would be remembered—like the royal family—received new names after their deaths.

Taizong had been known as Li Shimin when he was alive, and Gaozong had been Li Zhinu. They'd received both posthumous names and temple names so the people could worship them long after their deaths, and those new names eclipsed their old ones, all but erasing them. It was disrespectful to call them their common names once their temple names had been established.

Wu Zhao had branded her name onto thousands of people, thinking it guaranteed her safety in the afterlife.

But very soon, Wu Zhao would not be her name anymore.

I took a deep breath and straightened my back.

"As many of you know," I said, my words wavering, "the Perpetual Empress Wu Zhao has passed away. As such, in the tradition of great rulers before her, we must give her a posthumous title."

The crowd began to whisper, people turning to each other in confusion. In the distance, the corpse that was not Yufei or Wu Zhao swayed in the wind.

Wenshu had thought all night about the Empress's new name. As funny as it would have been to name her something she would have hated—perhaps a commoner's name, like mine—it would likely confuse the people who had no knowledge of all her treachery. Posthumous titles were signs of respect, and if they felt the name was disrespectful, they might not use it.

"From this day forth," I said, "the name Wu Zhao shall no longer be spoken in this kingdom. From now on, we will remember her as Empress Consort Wu Zetian."

The characters for *Ze Tian* meant "Ruler of Heaven," an appropriately pretentious name for someone of her status, though I was secretly thrilled to cement her title as empress consort rather than empress regnant—she had only ever ruled with power borrowed from the Emperor, not in her own right. If anyone asked, we'd say that her name was inspired by the Zetian Gate that led to the second palace in Luoyang, but it had another secret meaning—she would never again rule anything on earth, but she could try her luck in whatever world awaited her after death.

A notice about her new name had already been sent to all the other circuits in China. It would take time for the public to forget the name Wu Zhao entirely. But, as of this moment, her name had officially and irrevocably changed.

"May her soul rest in peace," I said, because that was something an empress was supposed to say when someone of importance died. But I knew her soul wasn't resting peacefully because I'd just sliced it to ribbons and hurled it into a river. It wasn't her physical body, so surely she was already piecing herself back together. But soon, every door she'd built for herself would slam shut in her face.

I lowered the scroll, and as I looked across the kingdom that now belonged to me, I knew that Wu Zhao was truly gone.

Part of me had always known that her "death" in the throne room hadn't been her end—I had sensed her in every shadow, every creak of old wood in the ancient palace, every cold and starless night. But this time, as I'd brought my sword down, the look in her eyes had been different. It was the same expression that the Moon Alchemist wore upon her death—the face of someone who knew they were about to meet their end.

I looked down at my hand, imagining the red thread of fate that had long tied us together. I could almost see its shorn end blowing in the wind, the thin string at last severed.

Goodbye, Wu Zetian, I thought, a strange lightness filling my chest. Long ago, I had sworn to myself that I would be the end of her story, that I would pry her kingdom from her withered hands. At last, I had kept my promise.

The sun sank just beyond the Buddhist temple on the horizon, crossing that thin threshold from afternoon to dusk with a fiery orange glow, and the crowd began to fall.

The first woman collapsed in the front row, her sun-scorched face suddenly gray, jaw slack as she fell to the dirt. A guard tried to lift her up, but her limbs had locked tight, as if long dead.

Someone screamed from the middle of the crowd, and the sea of bodies pushed outward, forming a circle around a man collapsed on top of another.

The crowd began to wilt, people toppling headfirst into each other, tripping others as they tried to flee and found themselves climbing over bodies. The crowd pushed outward, the street swelling with panicked screams and cries for help as they trampled each other in their haste to escape.

I turned to Wenshu and Yufei, who stood speechless at the railing beside me.

Was this because we'd changed her name?

I'd assumed that at least a small percentage of the city would be her walking corpses—either bodies that Gaozong had taken from the stockpiles in the dungeons, or peasants that he'd killed and resurrected with her name carved into them. I'd known that those people would "die" when I changed Wu Zhao's name, for they would only be empty shells. But I hadn't anticipated this many.

"Gaozong killed all these people by himself?" I whispered. The guards were trying to control the crowd below, but could do little to fight the crush of fleeing people.

"The Wei River is just beyond the walls," Yufei said, staring stone-faced at the chaos below. "Maybe she already put chicken-blood stone in it."

"But she only threatened to do that in Guangzhou because of me," I said, clutching the banister. The crowd had finally begun to clear, revealing the trampled corpses like squished red grapes in the dirt.

Wenshu shook his head. "She wanted everything, Zilan."

The doors opened behind us, and a flustered looking guard threw himself into a bow at Wenshu's feet.

"Your Highness," he said. "What are your orders?"

Wenshu grimaced. "I'll handle this," he said, waving for the guard to stand up and leading him back into the palace.

I turned back to the street below, the echoes of screams from far away rising to the red sky. This was supposed to feel like a victory, but even when she was gone, the Empress found a way to destroy.

At least she could never come back, as long as Zheng Sili had taken care of Gaozong . . .

Zheng Sili.

All at once, I remembered seeing the throne room through the Empress's eyes.

Zheng Sili fighting with Gaozong.

Zheng Sili covered in blood.

Zheng Sili falling from the window.

I shoved away from the railing, tripping over my skirts.

"Zilan?" Yufei said, steadying me.

But I pulled away and ran past her, down the empty hallways. The Empress's path was scored into the soft golden tiles—a thin scratch where she'd dragged Gaozong's sword.

I burst back into the throne room, but Zheng Sili's body was gone, a pool of dried blood beneath the window.

I drew back at the sight of Gaozong, barely catching myself on the doorframe when Yufei ran into me.

But Gaozong was unconscious, collapsed only a few feet from the window. When he didn't react to the sound of the door slamming behind us, I drew closer.

I knelt down at his side. He had no visible injuries, and his chest rose and fell with slow, deep breaths. I pulled out a knife and pricked it under his chin, but as a drop of blood rolled across his throat, he didn't so much as twitch. I sheathed the knife and tugged his eyelid up, examining the vast emptiness in his pupils.

The door opened once more, and I heard Wenshu whisper something to Yufei behind me.

"His soul is loose," I said, frowning and rolling up his sleeves. When I couldn't find a soul tag, I gestured for Yufei to help me and we rolled him onto his stomach, slicing open the back of his robes. But still, there was no soul tag on his spine.

"Are you sure he's dead?" Wenshu said.

I shook my head. "I didn't think he was, but why else would his soul be loose?"

Wenshu rolled up his sleeve, offering me his wrist with his own soul tag. "Why don't you go find out?"

I jammed a hand into my bag, fishing around for firestones. My gaze lingered at the pool of blood by the window.

"Jiějiě," I said, "can you look for Zheng Sili? Maybe there's enough of him to bring back."

Yufei nodded and tightened her scarf over her face, then took off running.

I turned back to Wenshu as he sat down beside me, digging my last three stones out of my satchel and pressing them to his arm.

Emperor Gaozong, I thought as the world dissolved and the forest breathed me in.

I landed on all fours at the river where his soul should have been. Only days ago, it had been filled with fish and plants and racing waters, but now there was nothing but a murky riverbed with dying fish writhing in the mud and river plants lying in limp green puddles.

What happened to him in the last ten minutes? I thought. Had his soul been reliant on the Empress's in some way? I didn't know any alchemy that would do it, but Gaozong had already showed me that there was a lot about alchemy I still didn't know.

I walked onward until the riverbed curved sharply to the left, and in the darkness, I could just barely make out a dam.

"What on earth?" I whispered, laying my hand against it.

I had broken through many dams to resurrect people back in Guangzhou, which was how I knew right away that this one was different.

When someone died, a dam of rounded gray stones appeared, cutting off the body's qi. Only chicken-blood stone and alchemy was powerful enough to break through it.

But this dam was made of dark wood with jagged edges, the same as the trees that had once surrounded the river. I glanced to the edge of the forest, where only stumps remained.

Someone made their own dam, I realized. Gaozong's life had been cut off from the inside.

"Zilan?" said a voice behind me.

For a moment, I didn't turn around. The river plane was cold and cruel and didn't want me here. This could only be a lie, something that bloomed from the desire in my heart.

"Zilan?" he said again.

And despite all the reasons I knew I shouldn't, I turned around.

Hong stood on the other side of the riverbank.

I remembered the first time I saw him standing on the Road to Hell back in Guangzhou, so out of place in his clean purple silk and golden shoes, like he'd stepped out of a fairy tale. Somehow I had known, even then, that my life would forever change when I spoke to him.

Standing in front of me now, he looked just as lost as he had back then, the same wide and haunted eyes, like a deer that would lope off if startled. But this time, when his gaze met mine, all the fear vanished. He smiled and stepped down the slope.

I rushed forward and met him halfway. The sticky mud trapped one of my shoes, and I fell forward, but Hong caught me with a laugh and held me to his chest. I crushed him against me, my heartbeat so loud and fast I was sure he could feel it in his bones.

"I'm so sorry it took me so long to find you," I whispered into his shoulder. "I looked for you, I swear I tried, but I couldn't—"

"Couldn't find me," he said, pulling away gently, a soft smile on his lips. "I know. I was hiding."

"Hiding?" I frowned, disentangling myself from him. "Didn't the Empress take you?"

He shook his head, his hand sliding down to lace his fingers with mine. He turned around, gesturing to a young girl standing on the lip of the riverbank.

In the dim light of the forest, it took me a moment to recognize her. The last time I'd seen her had been in the prince's blood-soaked closet, where she lay limp in my arms, her soul still trapped in the river plane.

"Gao'an?" I whispered.

"Hi, Zilan," she said, smiling.

This was the prince's little sister, the one I'd sworn to bring back once I made it to Penglai Island. I'd tried to revive her after the Empress's monsters had ripped her throat out, but I'd failed, leaving her soul trapped in this plane. She was the first in a long line of failures on my part, but at least she didn't seem angry.

"Gao'an is very good at hiding here," Hong said. "She found me and helped me hide when she saw the Empress drawing closer, but unfortunately that meant hiding from you as well. I didn't mean to deceive you, but it seemed preferable to letting the Empress capture me."

"She never had you," I said, shaking my head in disbelief. I was a fool to believe anything the Empress said. Hong must have been long gone by the time she'd found his tree and hidden there.

I turned to Gao'an. "How did you know to hide here?"

She frowned, crossing her arms. "Well, I didn't exactly want to wander into the afterlife."

I glanced at Hong. "I mean, it's very difficult for people to not do that," I said delicately. "Unless they're trained alchemists."

Gao'an raised an eyebrow, her frown deepening.

"*You?*" I said. "You're an alchemist? Just how old are you?"

"Ah, Zilan," Hong said quickly, taking my hand. "Apologies, I don't think I ever fully explained this to you. Yiyang and Gao'an are not as young as they appear. They are actually my older sisters."

I sighed, closing my eyes. I should have guessed—the royal court already had a laundry list of morally questionable practices. Feeding little girls life gold to keep them young and cute for decades wasn't uncommon among rich families.

"I'm not quite at the level of a royal alchemist," Gao'an said, uncrossing her arms, "but my mind is disciplined enough to stay grounded in a place like this, and to look out for others."

For others?

I remembered Zheng Sili and Yufei disappearing into the darkness when we'd come here together, the forest that had called my name and reached for me just before I'd fallen into Gaozong's river.

"Were you the one who hid Yufei and Zheng Sili?" I said.

She nodded, smiling proudly. "I tried to help you too, but you ran away from me and fell in the river."

I laughed, shaking my head in disbelief. "Well, thank you for trying," I said. "And for protecting Hong when I couldn't."

Hong smiled and ruffled her hair, but she quickly swatted his hand away.

I glanced back at the dam. "And I suppose both of you did this?"

Hong nodded proudly. "Gao'an used metals in the earth to bring the trees down with alchemy. It took a bit longer than we hoped."

"It's impressive," I said. "I never thought to do this. I didn't know you even knew he was alive."

"He came here often to visit the Empress," Gao'an said, wrinkling her nose. The fact that Gaozong had ordered her mother—Consort Xiao—executed probably had something to do with it.

I looked to Hong. Though he'd never been that close to his father, he hadn't wanted to leave the palace without him. Surely he still cared for him.

As if reading my thoughts, he shook his head. "It's all right, Zilan," he said quietly. "When I was hiding with Gao'an, I heard my parents talking. He knew that the Empress had killed me, but he didn't . . ." He paused, as if selecting his next words carefully. "He never asked why, or how, or where I was. He was never upset with her for it."

"Hong," I said gently, squeezing his hand.

"It's fine," he said, as if trying to convince himself. "I knew what our family was like, Zilan. I've always known. It was foolish of me to think my father was any different."

"You're not foolish for hoping there is good in people," I said. If Hong had been as cynical as me, if he'd looked at me and seen nothing but a brash merchant girl, then we would have been strangers forever.

The prince adjusted his grip on my hand to hold it tighter, and at once I felt the cold press of his rings on my skin. I pulled back and took his hand, my gaze falling to his red diamond ring, wrapped in the wings of a golden phoenix.

"This is it," I said, squeezing his hand. "This is the last ring, Hong."

His eyes went wide, then he pulled away and tore the ring off like it was on fire, setting it in my palm.

"This is the last piece?" he said, the words so quiet, as if afraid to be wrong.

"Yes," I said. "The next time I see you, we'll be in the palace together."

My words sounded more confident than I felt—after all, I still hadn't tried the transformation to bring me to Penglai Island, but I could give him nothing else but hope. He pulled me close, tight against his chest.

"We'll be home," he whispered into my hair.

For a moment I said nothing. I had never considered home to be anywhere but Guangzhou. But here and now, with Hong's arms wrapped around me and the word *home* echoing across the darkness, I realized it had never felt more true. This was my home—with Hong, with my family.

I took a steadying breath and pulled back gently.

"I have to go help Zheng Sili," I said.

"Of course," Hong said, releasing me. "See you soon?"

I nodded, taking a step back that felt like a thousand miles, and opened my eyes.

CHAPTER TWENTY-TWO

Wenshu wouldn't show me Zheng Sili's body.

He and Yufei had found it floating in the pond below the window of the throne room, but by the time I made it out there, nothing was left but red water and stained dirt. I stood at the edge of the pond and stared at my crimson reflection, the surface oddly frothy.

"Where is he?" I said, sensing Wenshu lingering behind me.

"Yufei handled it," he said quietly.

But that wasn't what I'd asked. "Tell me where you put him," I said.

Wenshu grimaced. "Zilan, there's no point. You would have needed a whole new body to bring him back."

"You're not an alchemist," I said, clenching my teeth. "You wouldn't know."

I'd expected anger, but his expression shifted into something pale, almost pitying. "Zilan," he said, "please trust me on this one."

I wanted to argue further, to demand that he bring me to him. Didn't he know I'd handled half-melted corpses with rot foaming from their mouths before? I wasn't a child who needed to be shielded from anything, and how dare he treat me like one? But my throat closed up and my eyes felt traitorously wet, so I said none of it. Instead, I turned away, staring back at the scarlet pond.

"You can just add him to your tab when you get to Penglai," Wenshu said. I knew he was trying to sound lighthearted, but his words made my throat clench with nausea.

"Did you know that when I first met him, he asked if my dress was made of diapers?" I said, letting out a dry laugh. "It was technically the same fabric as diapers, so I guess he wasn't wrong, even if he was an asshole."

I looked to Wenshu for a response, but he was staring at me strangely, so I went on, inexplicably determined to fill the silence. "I made him eat one of his teeth," I said. "The other alchemists hated me for it, but I don't regret it. I won't pretend to regret it just because he's dead. He deserved it."

"Zilan—"

"And who the hell feeds eggs to a duck? Who takes someone else's duck for a walk? He would have let a little girl die in jail, but he cared about a *duck*."

"Zilan."

"He owes me a drink," I said. The wind picked up, and my dress fluttered in scarlet silk around me, so I hugged myself to hold the fabric down. I didn't feel the cold at all. "That's probably why he died. So he could worm his way out of it."

Wenshu's shadow fell over me. I turned as he offered me a small green silk satchel. "I found this in his pocket," he said quietly.

It took me a moment to recognize it—it was the satchel I'd bought for Zheng Sili in Baiyin to hold his alchemy stones. I took it without thinking, tipping the contents into my hand.

A single grape fell into my palm. The kind he'd fed to Durian.

I stared at it for a long moment, the rushing river of my mind grinding to a halt.

Then I let out a laugh, closed my eyes, and clenched my fist around the grape. It burst, cold juice seeping between my fingers, twisting in sticky ribbons down my wrist. My hand shook, and I squeezed harder and harder until the flesh oozed out, then relaxed my hand and stared at the split skin and pale white flesh. Everything—and everyone—was so fragile.

"Zilan, we're going to bring him back," Wenshu said, wiping my tears with his sleeve. "We're going to bring all of them back. We have the rings now."

"Right," I said quietly, holding tight to his unwavering belief in me, because Wenshu only believed in things that were probable.

He wiped my hand clean with a rag, then waved for me to follow him back into the palace.

Yufei was sitting on the floor of one of the main hallways, eating bread. Her hands, normally dirt-stained, were suspiciously clean. She waved for us to sit down and nodded to a basket of breads and fruit on the floor in front of her, probably gathered from the storage cellars. The hall was one of the only parts of the palace with walls still intact, other than the throne room, which none of us wanted to revisit.

The sight of the Empress's body hunched over a pile of food, cheeks filled with bread, was so undignified that I couldn't help but laugh. "All the dead are waiting for me, and you want to take a snack break?" I said.

"Dead people can't get any *more* dead," Yufei said, "but bread will get stale."

"And you're about to open a whole new world," Wenshu said, tossing me an orange. "I think you deserve a snack."

I smiled even though my face felt stiff, then looked down at the orange and began peeling it so I wouldn't be expected to say anything else. My stomach felt like it was clenched into a tight fist. I peeled the fruit slowly, letting my hair fall over my lap to hide my trembling hands, and ate even though I could taste nothing but blood.

The hours wore on, and the shadows devoured the hallway. I'd been trying to make the transformation work all evening without so much as a spark. Now the food basket was no more than fruit pits and orange peels, and the hall was so dark we could hardly see each other. Wenshu complained and tried to light the hall torches, but I warned him that if the transformation rebounded, they might set the whole palace on fire.

The only light in the whole room came from the three rings on my right hand.

The dragon's white eye, the faceless night,
The song of silver, the serpent's bite,
The child of Heaven, the scarlet-winged tree,
Together at last, the shadow makes three.

This was everything my father had died trying to find. But now that I had all the pieces, I didn't know what to do.

"If this is gonna take much longer, I'm getting more food," Yufei said.

I couldn't blame her for getting impatient. For the last hour, I'd knelt on the floor, trying to clear my mind and think only of Penglai Island, carving the words into the sky of my mind like I did in the river of souls. I could hear the rushing water of my qi somewhere far away, just waiting for me to tap into it, but couldn't quite bring myself to try.

"You're stalling," Wenshu said.

I opened my eyes, glaring at him. "I'm trying my best."

"No, you're just sitting there meditating," he said, crossing his arms.

"And how would you know?"

He rolled his eyes. "Because," he said, "when you do alchemy, your hands glow and your face pinches in like you're eating something sour."

"Pardon me if it's a little hard to open an entirely new world with two people staring at me," I said, fists clenching, rings pinching my skin at the tightness. He and Yufei always acted like alchemy was easy, just a simple matter of throwing the right rocks together and watching what happened.

Wenshu sighed dramatically and turned around, staring out the window. "Better?"

"Everything's better when I don't have to look at your ugly face."

"Again, this is not my face," he said. "You're still stalling."

Yufei sighed and turned around, fidgeting with the hem of the Empress's dress.

I looked down at the rings as if they'd reveal the answer to me, their facets mockingly beautiful and bright. *You have the most powerful rings in the world, and you don't know what to do with them?* they whispered.

I closed my fist and looked to the gold ring Hong had given me when he was alive, which I'd moved to my left hand. I twisted the cold metal and tried to think only of what I'd promised him, what I'd promised all the alchemists. But rather than stoking fires of determination, I only felt my stomach hollow out with nausea.

It doesn't matter if you're nervous, I thought. I wasn't Zheng Sili, who had the luxury of performing alchemy under perfect conditions. People were depending on me.

I closed my eyes and focused on the sound of the running river. It rose louder and louder in my ears, devouring all sound. Darkness closed in overhead, the cool golden tiles softening into wet dirt.

I was kneeling once more at the river of my own qi.

Finally, I thought, letting out a tense breath. I pressed my hand with the three rings into the water.

Take me to Penglai Island, I thought, with all the authority of an empress. I flooded my mind with intention, feeding the river with the kindling of that deep and desperate want—the River Alchemist and Paper Alchemist laughing with me in the courtyard, Hong kneeling before me and clasping the ring in my hands, Zheng Sili blushing furiously when I caught him walking Durian. The river began to surge around me, the storms within the jewels spinning faster.

My chest felt light, like I was full of brightness instead of bones, only tethered to the ground by the weight of my shoes. I was so perilously close to unwinding all of my mistakes, healing all the scars I'd left on the world. I saw the River Alchemist ripped to pieces, organs spilled across gold tiles, Hong's throat weeping blood and eyes darkening, the smashed grape in my hand that was all that remained of Zheng Sili.

The rings began to heat up, scalding my fingers. I plunged my hand deeper into the river, hoping its coolness would soothe the burn, but the heat only grew, searing down to the bone. I was clutching a comet in my hands as it devoured my flesh.

I yanked my hand away from the river and landed on my back in the hallway, the tiles beneath me melted into a pool of liquid gold and black sludge. I tore the burning rings from my hand and tossed them to the floor, where they spun in glittering circles.

Wenshu and Yufei grabbed my arms and dragged me out of the pool of melted gold onto a patch of clean tile, both shouting questions at once that I didn't know how to answer.

I pressed my palms to the cool floor, soothing the ghost of a burn.

Yufei seized my wrist, examining my palm, but it was clean and unscarred. "What happened?" she said.

"I don't know," I said, my voice shaking. "It . . . it didn't work."

"What do you mean, *it didn't work?*" Wenshu said, expression sliding into a frown.

"I mean I messed it up and it spit me back out!" I said, yanking my hand from Yufei.

"I don't understand," Wenshu said. "We have all the stones, don't we? So what's the problem?"

I clenched my fist, hanging my head and biting back the words I wanted to scream at him. "Me," I said at last, the word so small that I wasn't sure if he would even hear it.

"What does that mean?" Wenshu said, not even bothering to hide the impatience in his voice. Of course he was tired of waiting for me to fix everything—he wanted his body back, his life back, and I was supposed to give it to him. I was the Scarlet Alchemist, pride of the south, the youngest royal alchemist in Chang'an, and I was supposed to be able to do anything.

"It means *I can't do it!*" I said.

Yufei blinked quickly, tilting her head like she didn't understand. Of course she didn't. None of them understood.

"Of course you can," Wenshu said, rolling his eyes like I was just a child throwing a tantrum. "You're a royal alchemist, you—"

"*I'm not good enough!*" I said, the words I'd been terrified to admit ever since we'd set out for Penglai. For so long, I'd clung to that hope of fixing everything I'd ruined, wiping my past clean. But I was more destructive than any private army, for every time I created, I destroyed ten times as much. "You have no idea how advanced this alchemy is," I said. "I don't know if the Moon Alchemist could even do it."

"Why didn't you say so?" Wenshu said, his scowl deepening. "If you didn't think you could actually get to Penglai, then what the hell have we been doing the last few weeks?"

"*What else was I supposed to do?*" I said, tears pooling in my eyes. "I have to fix everything I've ruined or I . . ." My hands twitched, wanting to grab something, but there was nothing but melted gold and scattered rings. I gripped my hair, wishing I could tear it out, but a hand gently pulled my wrist and fingers laced with mine.

Yufei knelt in front of me, the Empress's clean skirts soaking through with melted gold. "You're supposed to tell your jiějiě when you don't know what to do," she said.

I shook my head. "I thought maybe, with Zheng Sili, we could do it together. But I don't think I can do it alone."

"You're not alone," Yufei said. Then she scooped the rings from the floor and slipped the red diamond onto her finger.

"What are you doing?" I said.

She tossed one ring to Wenshu, who caught it with a frown, then handed the third to me.

"You told me that using three people makes a transformation more stable," she said. "You told me your alchemy could run through us for your resurrections."

"Yes, but I understood resurrections," I said. "This is dangerous."

"If it's dangerous, then why the hell were you doing it alone?" Wenshu said, jamming the ring onto his finger. "You're the youngest. We're supposed to protect you, not the other way around."

He grabbed Yufei's hand, then held his other hand out to me, gesturing impatiently until I took it. Yufei held my other hand, and the three of us knelt in the wet pool of gold.

"Do it again," Wenshu said.

I hesitated, my palms damp between them. "What if—"

Wenshu gripped my hand harder, crushing my fingers, cutting off my next words. "What's the worst that could happen?" he said. "We die? Been there, done that."

"Or I somehow mess up and destroy the whole world," I said.

"It's a pretty awful world, anyway," Yufei said, shrugging. "Don't alchemists want to raze it all down and start again? Now's your chance. End the world, Zilan, I dare you."

I cracked a smile, tightening my grip on their hands. "Okay," I said. "One more time."

I took a deep breath, then reached for the sound of the river.

I knew at once that this time was different.

Alchemy rushed like white lightning through our arms, stinging through our veins. I could tell from the way Wenshu and Yufei stiffened that they felt it too.

Our rings suddenly blazed star bright, casting red light on the ceiling. The gold tiles beneath my knees dissolved into a sparkling mist. A ringing began in my ears, an angelic hum like the vibration of a crystal drinking glass, the whole universe clicking into alignment. The river roared louder in my ears, its waters crashing into the hallway, shockingly cold as the ceiling fell away to a starless night sky.

Together at last, the shadow makes three.

I'd assumed it was the joining of the three stones that opened Penglai, but perhaps it was three souls, three hearts with the same dream, intention clear and bright. Just as Zheng Sili had said, the man in the poem wasn't actually alone—he had his shadow behind him and the moon above him.

Take us to Penglai, I thought. The river inhaled the words and began to rise.

Waters wrapped around me in warm ribbons, my whole body suddenly so relaxed that I almost let go of my siblings' hands. As if they could sense it, both of them tightened their grip around me as the current lifted us off our feet.

The water carried us forward into warm darkness, its touch like silk as it ferried us forward. It felt nothing at all like drowning in the river of life, but rather like falling slowly into a dream.

The waters set us delicately on soft ground and retreated, cool waves kissing over our feet, warm light cast over our faces. The air smelled of summer, years spent splashing through cool mud with my cousins and sharing half a dragonfruit on the front stairs and hunting for summer constellations. The memories scorched away all my fears, just as my father's notes had said.

It is a place of no pain, or hunger, or winter.

"Zilan," Wenshu said, tugging my sleeve. "What are you waiting for? Look where we are."

But I waited a moment longer, too aware that I was balanced on the precarious edge between dreams and reality, the moment when a wish became truth. Nothing could ever be as beautiful as a dream. At least, that was what I'd always believed.

I opened my eyes.

CHAPTER TWENTY-THREE

Sunlight had never felt so gentle on my face. It was like my mother cupping my cheeks in her hands and saying, *You are my whole world*. My toes sank into sand as soft as silk, a warm bath of it molding to the shape of my feet.

We were standing on a shore, the waters around us spanning all the way to the horizon, clear with shifting sunbeams. The waves captured the gentle light, sparkling far out to the horizon. I could make out glimpses of colorful fish and bright coral beneath the surface, swaying dreamily in the waves.

Over my shoulder, parasol trees cast the island in shade, the shifting leaves carrying the scent of fruit and salt. Cottony cloud formations dotted the pale blue sky and gathered around a mountain peak in the hazy distance.

All the aches I'd felt from travel, and thirst, and worry had melted away, leaving my body warm and pliable as clay, yet somehow lighter than it had ever been before. I looked down at my clean hands, no dirt or blood beneath my nails. I wore robes of white silk that fluttered in the breeze, rippling behind me.

I turned to Wenshu and Yufei, who looked like ghostly versions of themselves, their scratched and sunburned faces once again smooth, hair clean and untangled.

"Wow," Wenshu said, eyes wide as he turned to look out across the sparkling sea, then up at the mountains that faded into lavender high above us. "You were right, Zilan."

"About what?" I said, my own voice an ethereal echo.

"Penglai Island is real," he said.

I shoved his shoulder. "You never thought it was real?"

He shrugged. "You have to admit, all this"—he gestured to the bright island before us—"is a bit unlikely."

Yufei was already wandering off toward the tree line, pulling a pear from a low-hanging branch.

"Can we live here?" she said as I approached, her mouth full of fruit, juice dripping down her neck.

It would have been easy to say yes. Something about this place seemed to block out all of my fears. My life before I'd come here was only a series of facts as if read from someone else's story, meaning little to me: I was an orphan. I could never see my aunt and uncle again. My cousins and I were dead. The royal alchemists had died because of me. All of these things were truths, unchanging and inconsequential as the pull of the tides. They carried no innate meaning.

"Let's look around first," I said to Yufei, because I couldn't bring myself to say *no* when I didn't want to leave either.

I sat down at the pebbled edge of a river that wound through the trees. Here, the water ran so smoothly that it was almost like a shimmering pane of glass, reflecting back all of the sky.

My reflection looked so much younger than I felt inside, though I couldn't pinpoint exactly why. Perhaps the island had stripped the anger from my eyes, polished the scrapes and scratches away.

Wenshu sat beside me and took a pear from Yufei, leaning against me as he cataloged the clouds and the shapes of the mountain.

"I suppose alchemy isn't all bad," he said quietly, "if it can create a place like this."

"And food like this," Yufei added. "Do you think there's animals here? What do you think a Penglai bird would taste like?"

"I doubt you can kill anything in a place like this," I said. "I think that's the point. Nothing and no one here can suffer."

"Animals don't suffer when I kill them," Yufei said. "I make it quick."

"There's enough fruit here to last a lifetime, so maybe work your way through that first," Wenshu said, shoving another pear in her face.

I turned back to the water, which flowed downhill toward the sea but didn't ripple over rocks and plants like a normal river. Instead, it seemed to wave like a piece of silk in the wind, emanating a soft haze of light. I reached a hand down toward the clear water, and when my fingers broke the surface, the world flashed away.

I squinted through the searing sunlight, and when my vision cleared, Wenshu and Yufei were gone.

In their place, a group of people sat around the river, staring into its muddy surface.

I tried to step forward, to ask them what was going on, but it was as if I had become part of the whispering river, the shifting leaves, the twisted roots. I was everywhere—a bird looking down over them, blades of grass swaying beneath them, nothing and everything all at once. I had no body, no voice to call out.

Footsteps descended the incline, and the Sandstone Alchemist appeared around the bend.

His face looked much younger than the man I'd seen, the brightness of the island casting him in vibrant color, compared to the pale and sun-starved man I'd met underground. He met the gazes of the others, then looked up at the mountain from where he'd come and shook his head.

"If anyone finds out about this—"

"They won't," said a woman's voice. And I recognized the lilt to her words before I even noticed her face. It was the Silver Alchemist, unchanged by time, kneeling before the river.

To her left, a young Taizong stood with his arms crossed, hovering close to the Silver Alchemist. I remembered how she'd appeared in his memories, how she'd given him the ring that he'd used to bring down his brothers and become emperor. My gaze dropped to his hands, but he wasn't wearing a single ring yet.

Another man straddled a low tree branch beside them, hidden in the shadows. I was sure I'd seen him before, but couldn't place where until he spoke.

"He can't keep his mouth shut, you know he can't," the man said, rolling his eyes.

The Arcane Alchemist, I thought. His face was plain and unmemorable, so this must have been before he'd done the transformation that gave him his beauty. But he still had the same sharp, pompous voice.

Two women and two men sat nearby the first four alchemists in the clearing, their posture stiff, gazes darting around as if afraid to look anyone else in the eye. There was some great difference between the four alchemists I had met and the four I hadn't, though I didn't yet understand what it was. As the trees shivered in the breeze and sunlight lanced through them, I recognized the two nameless ghosts I had met in the Silver Alchemist's house.

"I don't see how you can be so unbothered," one of the strangers said, a pale young man who looked about as enthused as a soggy sheet, watching his reflection in the rushing current.

"And I don't see how you're so morose," the Arcane Alchemist said. "You're the one who wanted to know where alchemy came from."

Where alchemy came from? I glanced up at the mountain peak, where the Sandstone Alchemist had descended from. My father's scrolls had alluded to the source of alchemy hidden on Penglai Island, the reason alchemy had flourished in China and not the rest of the world.

It seemed they had found it.

The stranger shook his head, as if disagreeing with his own reflection. "I didn't think—"

"What were you expecting?" Taizong said, and even now, when he was young, he had the voice of an emperor, the Son of Heaven. His low words shook the ground, the flare of anger in his eyes like a comet scorching into the earth. "Alchemy is the greatest power this world has ever seen. You thought that would come at no cost?"

"How can we possibly use alchemy anymore?" the Sandstone Alchemist said at last. "Knowing the cost, I can't—"

But Taizong kept speaking, ignoring him entirely. "We need this power in my kingdom," he said.

"*Your* kingdom?" the ghost woman said. "You're not even the Crown Prince. What makes you think China will be yours?"

Taizong jerked a hand up at the mountain. "With this kind of power—"

"We could destroy anything," another one of the strangers said, a young woman with dark, haunted eyes. "Without meaning to, we could shatter the whole world."

"And then we could build a new one," Taizong said, waving his hand dismissively.

The Silver Alchemist slammed a fist into the tree trunk, and the whole world shivered, knocking half the alchemists off their feet, though I couldn't feel the vibrations in the ground at all. She looked up with a grin, showing her empty palm.

"Only one earthstone," she said. "Alchemical power is amplified here, so close to the source. Imagine what kind of transformations we could do."

"I don't want to imagine it," the woman at the back said. "We should never have come here."

The Silver Alchemist and Taizong shared a knowing look.

"Fine," Taizong said after a long moment. "It would be a waste of breath to argue further. Your mind is made up."

The Silver Alchemist looked between the nameless alchemists, her gaze settling on the Sandstone Alchemist. "What about you?" she said.

He shifted from foot to foot. "Does it matter?" he said. "The rule of three. You don't need me."

Need him for what? I thought, at the same time one of the strangers voiced the thought aloud, though it went unanswered.

"Unlucky number four," the Silver Alchemist said, shrugging.

The Sandstone Alchemist grimaced, looking between Taizong, the Arcane Alchemist, and the Silver Alchemist with a pained expression. He let out a sigh, then stepped across the shallow end of the river, standing on the side with the four nameless alchemists.

"How disappointing," the Silver Alchemist said.

But the Sandstone Alchemist didn't respond. Instead, he reached into his sleeve, pulled out a keenly sharpened blade, suddenly the brightest point in the dark gray plane, and sliced a clean line across the closest woman's throat.

I wanted to draw back, to cover my own throat reflexively, but I was the soil drinking her blood, the blade at her throat, the unforgiving coldness of the sky above, and I could do nothing at all.

The woman clutched the wound, falling to her knees. One of the strangers reached for her, but blood was already rushing through her fingers. She fell forward, landing face-first in the river, clouds of red spilling into its clear waters.

The three other strangers stared in disbelief, looking between the dead woman and the Sandstone Alchemist.

"*Why?*" one of them said, taking an unsteady step back.

But the Sandstone Alchemist didn't answer. His hands trembled as he cuffed blood spatter from his face, then dropped his blade and turned away.

"Finally," Taizong said, rolling his shoulders and drawing his sword.

The other three tried to flee, but each of the alchemists grabbed one and hauled them back to the river.

Taizong smashed one of the young men's heads against a rock until his face crushed inward and he fell limp, gurgling in the shallow waters. The Arcane Alchemist stabbed the other man in the stomach, stepping back in surprise when the man continued to fight, yanking the knife from his own abdomen. He took a wide swing at the Arcane Alchemist, who only laughed and kneed him in the stomach. When he folded forward, the Arcane Alchemist held him facedown in the river until he fell still. The Silver Alchemist forced the last woman to the ground and pressed her knee into her throat, leaning harder and harder until the woman's face turned blue.

When she stopped struggling, the Silver Alchemist rolled her body into the river, and the world fell quiet once more. The four remaining alchemists looked to each other, the river between them now rushing red.

"We shouldn't have done this," the Sandstone Alchemist said quietly, still staring out to the sea.

Taizong scoffed. "Spare me your judgment. You're just the same as us."

"It wasn't supposed to be this way," the Sandstone Alchemist said, his voice distant, the words so soft that the song of the wind nearly overpowered them.

"If you understood alchemy, you would have known that this was inevitable," Taizong said, jaw clenched.

The Sandstone Alchemist's expression slid into a frown. "I understand alchemy."

Taizong shook his head, taking a thundering step closer. "You think of alchemy as pretty lights and party tricks and sparkles, but that is not alchemy's heart. Alchemy is for destroying the world and rebuilding it all over again. It's dirty, and cruel, and unfair."

The Sandstone Alchemist looked like he wanted to argue, but his gaze drifted to the top of the mountain, his eyes glossing over once more. *What had he seen there?*

"What did you think we would find on Penglai Island?" the Silver Alchemist said, crossing her arms. "You want the power of alchemy, but you don't want to pay for it? You just want to look away while other people pay the cost for you?"

"*They were my friends!*" the Sandstone Alchemist shouted, whirling around. For the first time, he sounded as enraged as when I'd met him in the desert.

"They were *our* friends!" the Silver Alchemist said, tears cutting through the bloodstains on her face. "That's the only reason this works. It's not a sacrifice without love."

"You love alchemy more than you ever loved them," the Sandstone Alchemist said.

"And, apparently, so do you," the Arcane Alchemist said, nodding to the river.

The Sandstone Alchemist shook his head. "That's not why I did this."

The river began to glow, changing from a murky red brown to a color like liquid sunlight.

"It's now or never," Taizong said, pulling a clear stone from his pocket. The Silver Alchemist and Arcane Alchemist did the same, and the three of them stepped down into the golden river, turning back to look at the Sandstone Alchemist.

"Are you coming?" the Arcane Alchemist said.

After a moment, the Sandstone Alchemist nodded and stepped into the water.

It hadn't seemed that deep before, but the alchemists quickly sank down to their chests, their faces blurred from the brightness of the river.

The Silver Alchemist held her hand above the water, ribbons of starry gold wrapping gently around her wrists, spinning in comet tails across her thin fingers. The stone in her hand glowed pure white, the color slowly fading into red zircon, the ring that I had cut off her hand.

Taizong's ring glowed scarlet, while the Arcane Alchemist's ring glowed pearly white. A silver haze enveloped the four corpses, dragging them under the surface. They rose again as glowing bones that floated toward the sea.

"What is he doing?" the Arcane Alchemist whispered to Taizong, frowning at the Sandstone Alchemist.

He was standing in the water, staring at his reflection in the brilliant gold, unmoving.

"Well?" said Taizong, his booming voice jolting the Sandstone Alchemist out of his reverie. "What power are you going to ask it for?"

"I don't know," the Sandstone Alchemist whispered.

"Didn't you think about it beforehand?" the Silver Alchemist said.

"I did," the Sandstone Alchemist said, "but now I'm not so sure." The river beneath him rippled, his tears diamond bright as they fell from his face into the golden glow of the river.

"Are you actually *crying*?" the Arcane Alchemist said, reeling back.

The Sandstone Alchemist didn't answer. His next tear turned black as it hit the water, the darkness spreading fast as the current carried it downstream. The other alchemists scrambled out as the river rapidly turned the color of a starless night.

"What did you *do*?" the Silver Alchemist said. "Are you trying to ruin this place?"

"No," the Sandstone Alchemist said. "I'm keeping it safe from people like you."

The world began to tremble, the ocean churning in the distance. Then the black waters rose and wrapped around the other alchemists, dragging them back out to sea. They screamed and clawed at the grass, but the unrelenting pull of water was too strong, and eventually the ocean silenced their cries.

The Sandstone Alchemist took a deep breath, and when he exhaled, he was standing on a shore of pale sand and cloudy skies, a port city murmuring behind him, lanterns lighting one by one as darkness fell. He was no longer standing on Penglai Island, but somewhere real and sharp and imperfect, nothing at all like the impossible beauty of Penglai. He looked out across the horizon as if searching for something, but there was nothing but an unbroken expanse of sea.

I reeled back, my hands wet and freezing cold, Wenshu and Yufei each gripping one of my arms as they pulled me back from the river.

"What's wrong?" Yufei said, her grip bruising around my wrist.

I turned away, sinking my fingers into the soft soil to ground myself.

I understood, all at once, why the Sandstone Alchemist had tried so hard to keep me away from Penglai.

He understood as well as I did that powerful alchemy could rend the world in half if it fell into the wrong hands, as it had with the Empress. Of course he hadn't trusted someone like me with that kind of power.

But if he'd gone so far to hide Penglai away, why had he kept any sort of instructions for how to return? The fact that they were written down meant they were intended for someone else. Perhaps it was in case he ever changed his mind?

"I think I figured out where all these rings came from," I said at last, turning back to the river where the bodies had fallen. I dipped my fingers into the river once more, feeling for latent alchemical energy, but could sense nothing but cool, clean water. The other four alchemists had gained incredible, inexhaustible powers from this island by sacrificing their friends. What kind of sacrifice could I give in order to bring back a dozen souls?

I pulled away from my siblings, looking between the three

rings we'd stolen, then up at the mountain peak where the Sand-stone Alchemist had descended from.

The source of alchemy.

Surely, if there was anything in the world that could bring back all the long-lost dead, it was up there.

I hesitated a moment before rising to my feet. The Sandstone Alchemist had used his sacrifice to keep this place hidden away. Surely that meant this place was awful, that this sort of alchemy wasn't meant to be used.

But so many people were waiting for me, trapped in the river of souls. I could hardly turn back now.

I rose unsteadily to my feet, pointing at the mountain. "I need to go up there," I said.

Slowly, we trekked into the forest. The leaves felt like silk brushing past my face, the hum of insects like distant bells. Each pebble glimmered, a marvel in and of itself, every flower and grain of sand and cloud overhead perfectly shaped, as if crafted by the hands of the gods.

At last, we reached a small cave, cool with shade, where the stream disappeared into darkness. I stepped under the blanket of shadows, emerging in a small stone room where the water swirled in a small pool on the ground.

On its surface bobbed a transparent sphere, like a planet made out of the thinnest, most delicate glass. Inside it, storm clouds of every color swirled, the same as inside all of the other alchemists' rings. The air rang like the faint echo of a gong, my bones buzzing from the force of it. My rings felt warm, and my soul tag burned. The Silver Alchemist had said alchemical power was heightened on Penglai Island, but this was the only place I could truly sense it.

Here, at the source of alchemy.

"Zilan?" Wenshu said, his shadow eclipsing the doorway, casting the room in darkness.

Just beyond him, at the opening of the cave, I caught a glimpse of a figure standing on the golden sands, far below.

Who else is with us? I thought. But when he moved from the doorway, the figure was gone.

I shook my head and knelt down at the water's edge as Wenshu and Yufei lingered uneasily behind me. Whatever the Sandstone Alchemist had seen, it had changed his mind about alchemy. Once I learned its source, I could never unsee it.

I took a deep breath and sank my hands into the water.

CHAPTER TWENTY-FOUR

I am standing in a village that no longer exists.

The sky is an unsettled gray, the taste of an impending storm on my tongue, pinpricks of cold rain over my face and open palms. The houses of this fishing village burst like plum blossoms from the green hills, south sides hugged with moss, red lanterns echoed in ruby reflections across the cove. It is the kind of quiet, perfect beauty that can only exist in memory.

To my left, the ocean hums. The villagers are hiding from some nameless fear, whispering behind their locked windows.

I come from a world of fierce monsters and evil empresses, and I expect a great sea beast to claw its way up to the shore. Perhaps a creature of legends, something fearsome beyond measure.

But what happens next is much worse.

From the east, the ocean begins to rise.

As if the sea is a great blanket that someone has peeled up to peer underneath, it grows taller and taller, the dark abyss of the deep ocean yawning as it approaches. It stretches taller than the village, taller than the whole world, blacking out the gray sky until there is a lightless cage of sea overhead. And then, at last, it crashes down.

The wooden bones of the village shatter, lanterns extinguished in an instant, foam and black sea rushing toward me. Thatched roofs are carried away, carts tumbling over themselves, children screaming before they're sucked underneath. The water seizes me, crushes me in its cold hands, slams me against the side of the building. It drags me along the village streets until my chest screams for air. The ocean releases me at last when a metal support beam from the roof skewers my spine, splitting me in half.

I am lying in a field of blood, face-to-face with a dead soldier. The earth is cracked and sun-scorched beneath my palms, trembling from hurried footsteps. Someone trips over my legs, another person stomps down on my fingers, but I barely feel the pain because I am the earth and the roots, I have always been here, this is where I will die.

The face of the man across from me is streaked with tears that cut like white scars through blood and dirt, and I want to look away but cannot move. I try to draw in a breath, but it gurgles in my throat. There is a spear at the base of my neck, hot metal lodged in my windpipe, blood spilling hot and fast, wetting the parched dirt. I have died many times and know there is never any dignity in death, but knowing is different from feeling, and in this moment I am both scorched alive by the sun and drowning inside myself.

I am so very close to home.

It is night, and the cicadas are screaming in the tall grass around me, and there, at the end of the path, candlelight is burning through the windows.

I clutch a handful of bayberries as I fall to my knees, then my face, unable to catch myself. The hunger is a beast that has built its nest deep in my stomach, carving me apart from the inside. But these berries were the only ones in a flood-drenched field, all I have to show for my day, and I will not eat them for all the world. Even when the pain in my stomach settles deep between my ribs, an ache that grows and grows until it consumes me, and the cicadas are so loud, they are all that I can hear, the starless sky all that I can see.

I am the fever that burns through small children at night, blooming scarlet across their cheeks, reaching in and stealing their breath from their mouths.

I am the smoke that chokes the sky after lightning strikes, the simmering embers that devour thatched roofs.

I am the tiger's teeth as they bite down on a child so very far from home.

I am the earthquakes that rip the earth to pieces and the corpses that fall into its fresh chasms.

I am the bones of all the planets.

I am silence.

I am the end.

And at last, I am standing on golden sands, a firm hand closed around my wrist, yanking me to my feet that no longer feel like mine, all of my bones borrowed, skin stolen.

"Zilan," a man's voice says.

And when my vision settles and I find myself kneeling in the desert, I look up at a pair of bright green eyes.

The man in front of me was a foreigner, skin pinkish and pale like uncooked jellyfish, his hair coppery under the desert sun.

He said my name again, and the tones were wrong, but I understood anyway because this was a voice I had always known.

"Bàba?" I whispered.

He smiled down at me, and the sight was so new yet so familiar, and I knew even before he answered. I had died so many times that my memory was a patchwork quilt, but I was certain that I had seen him before.

"How are you here?" I said.

He looked at me sadly for a moment, and I wondered if he didn't understand Chinese. He'd named me Zilan, after all. Only a foreigner would give a child that name.

But his next words came in unsteady Guǎngdōng huà, my first language.

"Penglai Island amplifies alchemical power," he said. "It allows me to manifest here in ways I couldn't before."

"And where is *here*?" I said.

He looked out across the sands, not unlike the desert of Lanzhou, though this one somehow felt flat, as if the world dissolved at the edge of the horizon.

"In your mind," he said.

"Then where are you really?" I said, my fists closing in the sand. "I'll come find you."

He let out a sharp laugh, shaking his head. "I am in an unmarked grave just beyond the outskirts of Chang'an," he said softly.

I turned away, unable to bear the pitying look on his face. I had known my father was probably dead, so I wasn't prepared for the swell of disappointment, the way my throat closed up and tears burned at my eyes. Maybe some small part of me had always hoped that, since I had never seen a body, he wasn't truly dead. Resurrection alchemists never really believed in endings.

He took my hand, kneeling in front of me. "That is where my body is," he said, "but my qi runs inside of you, so I'm with you as well."

He placed a hand on the inside of my wrist, feeling my pulse. Our heartbeats drummed in sync, the gentle hum of alchemy between us like one long, unbroken river. Of course, he'd died because I'd devoured so much of his qi after he'd resurrected me, so part of him was inside me forever. Perhaps his voice that I'd heard had never been my imagination at all, but the part of him that still lived within my soul.

"I've been trying to reach you ever since you left in search of Penglai Island," he said, "but it's a bit hard to break through."

He waved his hand across my lap, and there were the loose sheets of his notes that I'd read over so many times as I'd tried to retrace his footsteps. He placed a new, cleaner sheet in my hands, and I knew from the writing at the top that I had never seen this one before.

"I had this one with me when I died," he said.

I skimmed over the unfamiliar words, then placed the paper in the sand beside the others.

This was the missing page.

I'd thought it wasn't that important, since I'd managed to find my way to Penglai Island without it, but I was wrong.

"I don't understand," I said at last, a coldness settling in my stomach despite the desert sun overhead.

He folded his hands in his lap, staring off into the pale horizon as if considering his next words.

"What did you see when you touched the source of alchemy?" he said at last.

Hesitantly, I told him about the typhoons, the war, the starving children in the fields. Once I started, I felt like I couldn't stop talking, needing to tell him about each and every instance of suffering, for keeping those moments secret inside me felt like a betrayal. Though it was only an illusion of alchemy, I knew these people had been real, their pain had been real.

When I finished, he nodded knowingly, staring toward the horizon as if seeing past it.

"Alchemists are born from suffering," my father said at last. "Suffering helps alchemy to grow, and in turn, more people suffer."

The Moon Alchemist had said as much when she was alive. Every rule of alchemy confirmed it, right down to its most central rule: *You cannot create good without also creating evil.*

Alchemy was China's greatest good, and year after year, it had deepened our suffering. Greed had led to starvation and disease, then war, and now a city in ruins.

Maybe at first, China hadn't suffered noticeably more than anywhere else in the world. But a century into our reliance on alchemy, the suffering was deepening, and the country was creaking apart like a house after a typhoon. The villages were torn apart by private armies, the capital in shambles, the royal family dead.

"It's going to get worse, isn't it?" I said.

"Yes," my father whispered.

How much can one country suffer? I thought. At once, I imagined a kingdom ravaged by civil war with no one to claim the throne, armies fighting until there was nothing left but bones and blood, no people to rule over.

I thought of all the small and insignificant ways I'd used alchemy—to mend my clothes and freshen fruit and untangle knots in my hair—maybe, somewhere across the country, it had caused small suffering in equal measure. A child falling and skinning their knee, an old woman burning her tongue on hot soup, a mother looking for her last piece of fruit, only to find it swarming with fruit flies.

Carefully, I folded the paper into fourths, closing it in my fist.

"I need to think," I said.

My father nodded. I stood up to leave, unsure what to say to him. I'd been curious about him for so long, but I remembered so little of my life before my first death that it felt like I was parting ways with a stranger.

"Just so you know," I said over my shoulder, "Zilan is a terrible name for a child."

He laughed. "But orchids are so beautiful."

"That's not the point. There are more important things than beauty."

"Indeed," he said. "In fact, do you know what Confucius said about orchids?"

I shook my head. Confucius had been Yufei and Wenshu's area of expertise.

"Confucius admired the way orchids survived in harsh environments," my father said. "In the mountains, where the terrain is rocky and roots cannot penetrate the earth, they grow in the trees. *The orchid grows where others cannot*, he wrote."

He raised his gaze to meet mine, and something in his eyes was deeply sad despite the soft smile on his face.

"That is why I named you Zilan," he said. "I have always thought orchids were beautiful, not because of their color, or shape, or patterns, but because they endure."

The sands began to swirl around my feet, the sun brightening overhead. I opened my mouth, knowing I should say something, but unsure what.

"Do not say goodbye to me," he said, smiling. "I'm not going anywhere."

Then the sands rose up into a golden cloud, and the last thing I saw was his green eyes.

I was kneeling in the cave once more, the sphere held delicately between my fingers. I set it back down in the water as Wenshu and Yufei converged on me.

"What did you see?" Yufei said, tugging at my sleeve.

"Did it tell you how to bring everyone back?" Wenshu said.

In the doorway behind him, the sands were still and golden once more, no sign of a figure on the horizon.

I shook my head, rocking back on my heels, a piece of paper still clenched in one fist. I closed my hand tighter, hoping they wouldn't see it.

"It was a lot to take in," I said quietly, not quite meeting their gaze. "I need time to think about this. I want to be careful, to not make any mistakes."

It was exactly what Wenshu wanted to hear, so I wasn't surprised when he nodded and offered me a hand to help me up. "We can always come back tomorrow," he said.

Yufei seemed reluctant, but her skirt was still filled with pears, so she didn't protest. "Like I said, the dead won't get more dead."

"You just want to go back because there's no meat here," Wenshu said.

I tucked the paper in my pocket, and we joined hands around the pool. I closed my eyes, allowing the perfect island to peel away to darkness, soft sand giving way to hard tiles and a cold night.

We sat once more in the empty hallway, surrounded by bread crumbs and fruit peels and night. This world seemed so sharp and unpleasant compared to the gentleness of Penglai, my every footstep so jarringly loud on the tile floors, the night air thick with the smell of smoke and blood.

I told Wenshu and Yufei I was going to sleep and hurried back to my old room in the alchemy compound. I waited another hour, feeding seeds to Durian, then slipped on my old shoes—the reed ones I'd first brought to the palace—and headed for the tunnels.

I emerged onto the streets of Chang'an, my hood pulled low to shield my face.

The city smelled of blood and the faint beginnings of rot. Carts rolled down the streets carrying limp bodies, the wards left open long after sunset so they could pass through. I didn't know where we could even bury this many bodies at once. Surely the gravediggers were already working day and night.

I thought, wryly, how lucky it would be if I were a míngqì merchant right now, making a fortune on all the funerals.

But this was not the heart of the city's pain.

I walked toward the western ward, where my cousins and I had stayed when we'd first arrived in the city, too poor to afford to stay anywhere else.

Here, the streets were near deserted.

Of course, the poorest ward was where the Empress would have branded her name onto the most souls in exchange for food or money or empty promises. Wind whispered through the streets, carrying the scent of decay. Doors and windows hung open, revealing shadowed interiors—I'd heard that some families had died all at once, and the cleaners had to break their doors down to remove their bodies before they started to smell.

The streets had a dark tinge to them that I knew all too well as blood, some of it pooling in the drainage ditches, a muddy red soup. I saw my reflection in it, a scarlet contrast to the clear waters of Penglai Island.

I am the Empress, I thought.

Even though this wasn't solely my fault, it was my responsibility now. Half a city gone, perhaps even half a country gone. Surely Guangzhou looked the same. Even if the souls possessed by the Empress hadn't been used as an undead army to wipe the city off the map, thirty-five thousand were still dead.

I returned to the throne room and sat down in the Empress's chair—my chair—and imagined a world where the joy of Penglai Island existed here for everyone, forever.

But that had always been a foolish dream. Penglai Island, the place of no winter or suffering, had been bought in blood. That kind of happiness was never free.

I walked to the room to where my cousins were sleeping and lit a candle. They would be angry at me for waking them, but they would be even angrier if I left without a word.

I shook Yufei first, but I knew at once from the stiffness in her limbs that she was not asleep.

I shook her harder, but she stayed limp and unresponsive. I moved over to Wenshu, but he was the same.

I sat between them, feeling the entirety of the world roaring between my ears.

"Wake up," I whispered, even though I knew no one would hear me. I was eight years old again, alone in my room with their corpses. Last time, Yufei hadn't woken for nearly a day, and Wenshu's attacks were getting more frequent. One day, surely, they would never wake up at all, their souls lost somewhere far away like Gao'an's.

All because I had broken the rules of alchemy, used it to tether them here for myself. Everyone in the world suffered, but I'd thought myself exempt, tried to bend the world to please me, to worm my way out of sacrifice, out of suffering.

Durian lay sleeping above the covers, so I picked him up, pressed a kiss to his head, and set him down on top of Wenshu, where he fell back asleep.

I picked up the rings from the table and slipped one onto my hand, the others onto my siblings' fingers, then lay down between them like when we were children sharing the same bed. I took their hands in mine and closed my eyes.

This time, I returned to Penglai Island alone.

CHAPTER TWENTY-FIVE

Once again, I stood on the golden shore. The sunlight tried to strip away all the pain I felt, but I clung to it like it was driftwood in a nauseous sea. I replayed the faces of those I loved, imagined their names written in the immaculate sky.

I ascended the mountain, brushing away silky leaves and soft sugar sand until I sat in the cave once more. Its waters flowed silently downhill, through the river where the other alchemists had died, into the vast expanse of sea.

The other four alchemists had made a sacrifice to this water and harnessed the island's amplified power for their own purposes, then forged it into rings that seemed like miracles, but were only an equivalent exchange. Now it was my turn.

I sank my hands below the surface.

What will you give me? the water whispered, the sound humming through my bones.

The river didn't wait for my answer. Alchemy could only be controlled with clear intentions. If you didn't make an offering, it took what it wanted.

The water rose over the edge of the pool, filling the cave with cool, shallow water that soaked my skirt. The glass sphere bobbed on the surface, but remained in the center like a buoy.

What will you give me? it said again.

Have I not given you all of me already? I thought.

Weeks in the Borderless Sea, snake bites and sunburns and a whisper of a dream chased across a country. Days of my finite life spiraling away, blood under my fingernails, my friend lost. But alchemy did not take prepayments or letters of credit like the rich.

I closed my eyes and imagined the rest of my life, the gates of Chang'an rebuilt, standing side by side with Hong as he was crowned emperor, his perfect voice promising a future better than anything his mother could have imagined.

I was sitting in the palace garden while Yufei waded into the pond, splashing clear water at Wenshu, who was trying to read his scroll. Ducks bobbed in the water, and sunlight filled the pond with diamonds. Hong appeared behind me with a head of cabbage under each arm, tearing off pieces for Durian.

The Moon Alchemist held my hand and guided it up to the night sky, helping me wrap my hand around the perfect full moon. I clutched it close to my chest, and its bright light cast the courtyard in white as the River Alchemist and Paper Alchemist watched in awe.

Auntie So and Uncle Fan were sitting in the shade of the courtyard while Yufei served them tea and suspiciously half-eaten cakes, their cheeks flushed red from health.

The western ward of Chang'an roared with the bright lights of a carnival, bread passed out for free, and no one had to beg for scraps when it was over.

And because there was no life gold in this perfect future, I began to age. My hair turned gray, my skin growing thin and translucent. But through it all, there was always Hong, standing beside me, believing in me.

This, I thought, *is what I'll give you.*

I breathed the alchemy into my bones, and when I opened my eyes, a perfect diamond had appeared in my palms.

My own stone of Penglai Island, like the rings of the other four alchemists. Sure enough, the gem swirled with light, like a raging blizzard of alchemical potential trapped inside.

I'm going to save them all, I'd once said as I set off from Chang'an with my brother. Now I let that determination swell inside me, writing it across the sky of Penglai Island the same way I wrote the names of the dead in the river plane, desire pulling forth the stone's power.

The walls of the cave fell away like ashes, and the sky opened up in all directions, a brilliant violet light somewhere between a day's beginning and a night's end. The dawn breathed above me, pulsing with the beat of my heart.

Then the sky unspooled, and I could see the faces of those I loved in the same perfect clarity that I used to see their names, and that was how I knew my sacrifice had been accepted.

The Paper Alchemist and River Alchemist were caught in the waters of the river plane, tossed along the current. They crashed into a shore that was no longer dark skies and black dirt but golden sand, the firm and imperfect earth of the real world.

Then there were Hong and Gao'an, walking hand in hand through the forest, hesitating where the darkness ended and the world unfolded into the main hall of the palace, bright with blood. They shared a glance, then took off running toward it.

Then Zheng Sili, hopping down from a tree, looking highly inconvenienced but otherwise fine, as the darkness around the river faded away. He turned toward the horizon, where Chang'an was only a speck of gold in the distance.

Then at last, there were Wenshu and Yufei, sitting up in bed under the moonlight, their clothes suddenly too large for them, wearing the faces I had known all my life. Wenshu gasped and clapped a hand over his mouth when he saw Yufei's face, pointing her toward a mirror. She tripped over her long dress and crawled toward it, tentatively running her fingertips over her cheek, ghosting over the face of Fan Yufei, her eyes that were no longer blazing gold but warm pools of brown.

Once, I had promised to bring back the entire house of Li, my parents, everyone who had died for me.

But I was only one person, and I could already feel my sacrifice wearing thin. I was not arrogant enough to think that my life was worth every life in the world. That dream was just another one that would die, tossed into the current. Another type of suffering I would have to endure like everyone else.

"Scarlet," said a voice behind me.

The name no longer felt like mine, but I turned all the same.

There, at last, was the Moon Alchemist.

She was just as I remembered her—beautiful and terrifying like an endless sea, her long braid like the end of a dagger, her eyes full of autumn light. Once, I'd thought I'd never see that light again.

"I told you to be careful," she said, crossing her arms. "This wasn't exactly what I had in mind."

"I'm sorry," I said, even though I wasn't, since my choices had brought her back to me.

"You're not," she said, her eyes cold.

I sighed. "No, I guess not."

I looked down at my hands, now only a whisper of color, a slant of light. "You should go quickly," I said.

The Moon Alchemist shook her head. "I already told you I

didn't want to go back. I'm glad, though, that I got one last conversation with you, to tell you how foolish you are."

I laughed. "I'm glad too," I said. "Though sorry to disappoint you."

She frowned. "Disappoint me?"

"I'm sure there was a better way to go about all of this," I said, staring at my rippling reflection. "I'm sure you would have done it differently. You always knew the answer."

When she didn't respond, I looked up. She was frowning at me like I was a problem she couldn't solve. "How would you have fixed everything?" I said.

She shook her head and sat down beside me, staring out across the sky. "Not everything can be fixed," she said.

I laughed. "I'm not sure if that's supposed to make me feel better or worse."

"Not everything is about you," the Moon Alchemist said. "Some things just are."

I moved closer to her. "I've missed you," I said quietly.

I knew she wouldn't answer, so I turned away and placed all three of the rings in a bowl, along with the diamond I'd just forged. With the quick touch of a couple firestones, the bowl began to heat up, and the stones melted into a silvery soup.

"What do you think all the power in the world tastes like?" I said, trying to sound casual, but the Moon Alchemist didn't laugh.

"Like gold, I bet," she said at last.

"So, awful?"

"Like you would know," the Moon Alchemist said, a smile at the corner of her mouth.

"I know exactly what it's made of, and none of it is food," I said, smiling even though I tasted tears.

Before I could stop myself, I pressed the bowl to my lips and tipped my head back, the liquid burning down my throat. I did it partially to make sure the rings would never find their way back to the outside world—Penglai's only keys were locked inside— and partially to give myself the strength for what came next.

My father's note fell from my pocket, and I didn't have to unfold it to recall the words that were now etched across my soul.

I once thought that the greatest act of love was to traverse the lines drawn by fate himself, to hold on tight even as death pulled us apart.

But that is its own kind of selfishness.

I will do something even greater for them.

I will give them a world where suffering makes us stronger but does not destroy us, where pain can be overcome. Because if things continue as they have, then this world will not be worthy of them and all of their light.

I will find the source of alchemy, and I will destroy it.

"I can't imagine a world without alchemy," I whispered as the stones settled warmly in my stomach. I tried to imagine it was Auntie So's congee, that she was here with me.

"It was a better world," the Moon Alchemist said, taking my hand. "A less exciting one, but a better one."

"What would you have been, if not an alchemist?" I said.

She looked to the sky, considering her answer. "Perhaps a very strict mother, or a very angry librarian," she said at last. "And you?"

"No one," I said. "Isn't that funny? I was born to be an alchemist. My father only came to China because of alchemy. I was saved once because of alchemy. It was my greatest dream."

The Moon Alchemist hummed, a sound I knew so well that it brought a smile to my lips. It meant *don't you dare interrupt me, I am selecting my next words of wisdom.*

"Alchemy was always just a tool for you to help others," she said at last. "Alchemists want to rebuild the world around them so badly that they would give anything. In that sense, you are the only true alchemist there ever was."

She placed a hand on my head, brushing down my hair.

"Stop stalling," she said. "You know what comes next."

I nodded, leaning forward and picking up the glass sphere from the water, setting it in my lap. Up close, it looked like an entire universe of lights, colors never before perceived by human eyes, lifetimes and landscapes and dreams.

I held it steady with one hand, then pulled out Durian's last egg from my pocket. The Silver Alchemist's ghost hadn't been able to break it, so I could safely say it was one of the strongest materials I'd ever encountered. Wenshu had said that Durian was evil, and surely his eggs were proof of that—toxic fumes and flesh-eating sludge, and now, the ability to destroy alchemy forever. Did that mean that what I was about to do was evil?

I closed my fist around the cold metal.

You cannot create good without also creating evil, I thought. Likewise, you cannot create evil without also creating good. Durian's first two eggs had been weapons—undoubtedly evil. But maybe this third one was the good that balanced them out.

Maybe this was a mistake, like so many other mistakes I'd made ever since I became an alchemist. It would help the world, but it would hurt people in the process.

I took a deep breath and decided that this would be my last mistake.

This time not made out of ignorance, or guilt, or regret, but out of a great love for this world and all the people in it.

I swallowed, my hands shaking. "What comes after the river plane?" I said.

The Moon Alchemist shifted closer to me, setting a warm

hand on my back. "The end," she said.

The words should have terrified me, but a strange calmness settled through my bones. Everything had an endpoint. I had always known that. It was only the rich who had gorged themselves on life gold who had been foolish enough to believe otherwise.

"That sounds . . . perfect," I said at last.

I raised my arm, my palm sweaty, and brought the egg down on the glass sphere.

I only heard the crisp sound of shattering glass before a blaze of white washed away my vision. The island was breaking apart, blasted away by star fire. All the agony of the world rushed through me, igniting my blood, singing through my bones.

And for one breathless moment, I was sitting on a hill back in Guangzhou, my brother to my right and my sister to my left, a thousand stars above us.

"What if we went to Chang'an as scholars?" I said.

Wenshu laughed, the sound sharp, echoing across the valley. "*Us?*" he said. But I knew, even then, that his words weren't truly doubtful. He just needed one of us to say it first, to believe.

"What's so funny?" Yufei said. "I hear the food is good there."

"I hear the streets are paved in gold," I said.

"They can't be. They would get dirty too fast," Wenshu said, crossing his arms. "I suppose we'll just have to see for ourselves one day."

"One day?" I said.

Wenshu nodded, and Yufei bit the other half of my rice ball out of my hand. In that one beautiful summer night, our dream was whole and unbroken, untouched by the cruelty of the world. Perhaps that new sapling of hope was the greatest currency an alchemist could offer to the hungry jaws of alchemy. Nothing more than the whispered beginnings of a dream.

CHAPTER TWENTY-SIX

Li Hong, Emperor of Tang

Once, death was my greatest fear.

When you live in a court of eternal life, where everyone's skin glitters with gold, their bodies slowly calcifying into statues, you are raised to believe that death is the worst thing that can happen. For people like us, death means sacrificing power. It means crossing into an After that is inevitably less gilded and glorious than this life.

But death was much simpler than I thought.

After I died, I passed lonely nights on the banks of a river with no temperature, an endless ribbon of time with days I no longer counted, a moonless sky, and soundless woods. I was a whisper of wind between silver grass, the pale reflection of moonlight cast across a pond.

I only remembered my name when she came to visit me.

I saw her and then there was light, and the shadows had sharp edges, and the river was once again cold on my feet, and I was something and someone separate from the blur of endings. I never told her that when she left me, I could feel myself growing roots into the cold earth, colors fading into the forest. I never wanted her to know, to hurt for me more than she already did.

But even death has an endpoint.

One day, the walls of the forest fell away, and I was back in the palace where I had died, my sister's hand in mine. My home was crumbled and ruined, but it was *real*, I was real, feeling as if I'd spent the last month dreaming.

Upon my arrival, the royal alchemists were already giving orders that I was all too glad to take. They wrote laws for me to sign that they promised would fix the country, and I trusted them because Zilan had, because following their orders felt like following hers.

Zheng Sili appeared among their ranks on the second day, clutching a full written proposal as to why he deserved to work in the court even though he could no longer do alchemy. He'd only gotten through the first sentence before I told him to save his breath, that he could stay here as long as he liked. He was Zilan's friend, so he was mine.

I think all of them knew that I was a dreamer, not an emperor. They seemed all too prepared to have me as their puppet, and for the time being, I couldn't bring myself to care. The only order I gave was to send ships out to the Bohai Sea, the last place that had mentioned Penglai Island in any written record.

Even without alchemy, the royal alchemists destroyed the private armies within a week. They offered the peasant soldiers more money to work for the palace, distributed food to the poorer districts, and declared the hiring of private armies illegal, punishable by death regardless of one's class. It only took one public execution before the aristocrats realized, with horror, that they would be punished like peasants for disobeying.

Soon after, I officially became the emperor. I dressed in yellow robes that once were only for my father and watched the crowd of my sparse city bow to me with a reverence I didn't deserve. That same night, the Paper Alchemist reported that the ships in Bohai had returned empty-handed.

"Send them out again," I'd said, leaving no room for comment.

Day by day, the world began to shift.

From my window, I watched as the shattered rooftops of Chang'an were retiled, as the rain washed away the bloodstains, as the market stalls were repaired and the pear trees lining the canals flowered once again. The palace walls were rebuilt with clay, the bloody ponds drained and replaced with fresh water, and soon it was hard to see that anything had changed at all.

But I sensed the newness of this world in small ways that no one else would believe.

At first, I noticed that rain would only fall at night, the clouds scattered by morning, the sky more blue and open than I'd ever seen it in my lifetime. The moonlight seemed sun-bright every evening, casting the palace in silver light. The plum blossom trees in the courtyard flowered even though it was the middle of summer.

I asked the magistrates how the other cities under their control were faring, and they told me that the homes had been rebuilt, the dead buried, extra rice safely delivered. Disease and disquiet had tapered off, and for now the world was calm.

Of course, that was exactly what they would tell a new emperor, even if it was a lie.

So I sent Zheng Sili out to do a circuit of the northern cities in my place. He returned a week later and confirmed that what the magistrates said was true.

There were no signs so drastic that I could fully attribute it to the loss of alchemy. But life gold had taken nearly a century to destroy China, so surely it would take just as long to recover. This was only a quiet beginning.

"Thank you," I whispered as I knelt in the alchemy courtyard, knowing she wouldn't hear it. My palace of a thousand rooms was so empty that I could hear the wind twisting through the lattice windows, humming over the still ponds, dying as the sound hit the clay walls. At night, I listened for footsteps in the grass, but they never came.

I told the Fans that they could stay in the palace, but they insisted on finding their own housing. I imagined that to many, the palace walls would forever look like they were stained with blood, but as the emperor, I couldn't run away.

Perhaps I would go down in history as the worst emperor that had ever lived. In the dawn of my reign, alchemy had vanished.

But I trusted Zilan, always. She once told me that alchemists wanted to rebuild the world and start again. Perhaps this was how she wanted to do it, the way others before her had been too afraid to attempt.

The ancestral shrine of the Wu family had a great many visitors in the months after the reconstruction. I couldn't blame them, as few knew what my mother was like in person. They could only see the streets paved in gold, which, under my reign, were quickly tarnished by footsteps. I stopped by there on occasion to pay my respects.

My mother once said that we laughed at the dead for their failures, but I didn't feel like laughing when I saw her carved out of stone, people crying at her feet. Her stone visage looked so much kinder than she ever had. I looked at it and imagined a world in which she hadn't felt the need to trample others on her path to power, in which she could have lived as she was. Maybe, without alchemy, that world would come into being.

On the day before my wedding, I lingered too long at her temple. After a few weeks passed, my sisters convinced me that Zilan had been right—it was dangerous for the last heir to the House of Li to be unmarried. My sisters were not interested in ruling, and their claims to the throne were tenuous enough as it was.

It seemed more reasonable now that the bodies had been buried, the streets cleaned, the city of Chang'an so much quieter than before, but somehow I didn't mind the quiet. It gave me the same feeling as standing in the retiled palace courtyards, where all the dead plants had been uprooted and new seeds planted that hadn't yet broken the surface. For now, it was nothing but wet soil and hope.

With all the rites established and a perilously long investigation process to ensure I wasn't accidentally marrying my own relative, I bowed to my veiled bride before a crown of aristocrats who cared nothing for either of us, trying not to squirm under their gazes as we ate dinner before them, then finally retreated back to my room.

"I'm not consummating anything, just so you know," she said once the door shut. "I ate so much food I think I'm going to explode."

She reached for her veil, but I gently took her wrist.

"Let me at least do this properly," I said, picking up the wooden dowel that one of my advisers had given me that morning. I slid it beneath the veil and lifted it back, over her head.

"Finally," Zilan said, smiling as she peeled back the rest of the veil and cast it to the floor.

Ten days after the disappearance of alchemy, a merchant ship had found Zilan on an island in the Bohai Sea.

I would have traveled out there to meet her immediately if the royal alchemists hadn't argued for hours that it would destabilize the country once more, and that they would bludgeon me unconscious to stop me if necessary. Her siblings had no such qualms and raced across the country to meet her halfway.

It was another week before she returned, and I knew at once that something was wrong.

Her eyes were vacant, her words quiet and far away. She looked at me only fleetingly, always talking just past my shoulder, as if staring beyond.

One night I found her sitting in the shallow water of a courtyard pond, watching Durian swim under the moonlight. She didn't react as I approached, but I knew she heard me because she became very still. Moonlight spilled across the silk of her dress, painting her in stony white.

"I don't believe any of this is real," she whispered.

I waited to see if she would continue, but she only dropped her gaze to her lap.

"How can it not be real?" I said.

"Because all of this," she said, gesturing to the palace behind her, "this life that I get to have, it's worth so much more than just losing my alchemy."

I watched her for a moment longer, then slipped my shoes off and knelt in the pond beside her. She moved as if to stop me, but I was already sitting in the cold pool, blue silk floating around me.

"You don't think it's a fair exchange," I said. "You're worried something worse is coming."

She nodded, hugging her knees. Durian swam toward me— his human food dispenser—and pecked at my hands.

"Maybe you did die," I said, petting Durian, who turned and

swam away when he seemed to realize I didn't have any food. Zilan stared at me, waiting for me to continue.

"The Scarlet Alchemist died," I went on. "You lost your alchemy, your dream."

"Everyone lost their alchemy," she said.

"Yes, and everyone gets to live in a better world because of it," I said. "Maybe, instead of one person paying the ultimate price so that everyone can be happy, everyone carries just a little bit of the pain. Maybe it's enough that you were willing to pay. Maybe that's the good that wipes out all the evil."

Finally, a smile rose to Zilan's lips, soft and bright as a blooming orchid. She turned away so I couldn't see it.

"That's nice," she said, "but that's not how alchemy works."

I shrugged. "Alchemy doesn't work at all anymore."

She smacked my shoulder gently, then scooted closer and leaned against me. It was the first time she'd touched me since I'd hugged her upon our reunion.

"You're right about one thing," she said. "The Scarlet Alchemist is dead. I never want to hear that name again."

"Because my mother gave it to you?"

She nodded, pressing herself closer.

"Well, empresses typically receive new titles," I said. "We could come up with something for you."

She seemed to consider this for a moment, then shook her head. "I don't want a new title," she said.

"But I thought—"

"I want to be Fan Zilan," she said. "I have always wanted to be Fan Zilan."

"As you wish," I said, pulling her close. "*Empress* Fan Zilan, if that's all right."

Now, in our room, as she removes her veil and wipes the

makeup from her face with her sleeve, my Empress at last, I can't help but think that her smile in this moment is something that will last forever. Even though life gold is gone, this moment is etched into my soul.

"I don't really know how to be the Empress," she says, wrapping her arms around me, her head against my chest, listening to my heartbeat.

"That makes two of us," I say. "Mother wasn't the best example."

"I'm probably going to be very irritable and tedious until I find some new hobbies," she says. Then, softer, as the wind snuffs out one of the candles, casting us in quiet, secret darkness: "I don't really know who I am without alchemy."

I hold her tighter. "I don't know either," I say. "But let's find out together."

She looks up and pulls me into a kiss.

Tomorrow, I am sure that I will have to think about the many people who would like to see both of us dead, who will challenge our claim to the throne, who will try to avenge the loss of alchemy. But that is a problem for the morning.

I will never tell this to Zilan, but I think that maybe the alchemists had it all wrong from the start.

Maybe the key to eternal life was never gold, or youth, or an island free of pain and suffering, but just the dream of tomorrow that can never be extinguished, a hope that endures even when its leaves are wilted, purple petals unfurling without fail in the morning sun.

HISTORICAL NOTE

Penglai Island and the Eight Immortals
Penglai is a mythological island which no one has found (yet), but the earliest Chinese emperor, Qin Shi Huang, believed it contained an alchemical elixir of immortality. He sent ships out to the east of China to find it in 219 BCE[1] but none of them ever returned.[2] Similar quests continued up through the fourth century CE, when books such as *Records of Ten Islands within the Sea* (海内十洲记) repopularized the idea of mythical islands of immortality.[3]

The Eight Immortal alchemists in this book are inspired by the Taoist concept of the Eight Immortals—a group of immortal humans who lived on Penglai Island and popularized the idea that anyone could attain immortality by strictly following

---

1   Cornelius C. Müller, "Qin Shi Huang," in *Encyclopedia Britannica*, November 20, 2023, www.britannica.com/biography/Qin-Shi-Huang.

2   Tony Allan and Charles Phillips, *World Mythologies: Ancient China's Myths and Beliefs* (New York: Rosen Publishing, 2012), 108.

3   Bin Luo and Adam Grydehøj, "Sacred Islands and Island Symbolism in Ancient and Imperial China: An Exercise in Decolonial Island Studies," *Island Studies Journal* 12, no. 2 (2017): 9, doi.org/10.24043/isj.19.

Taoist teachings.[4] Much like the final "elixir" that Zilan drinks, the Taoist elixirs of immortality in the Tang Dynasty were well known to be poisonous, often made from mercury and arsenic.[5]

Emperor Taizong and Emperor Gaozong of Tang
The real Emperor Taizong was the second emperor of the Tang Dynasty. As one of the immortals correctly points out, he was not born as the Crown Prince, but rather was the second eldest son of the emperor. He became a respected general after capturing Luoyang for his father, after which his elder brother and one younger brother plotted to assassinate him. Taizong killed them both (most likely without an alchemical earthquake) and told his father, Emperor Gaozu,[6] which all but forced Gaozu to abdicate in Taizong's favor.[7] The battlefield that Zilan sees in Taizong's memories is a reference to his victory over the Eastern Turkic Khaganate in 630 CE, from which he attained the title Tengeri Qaghan, or Khan of Heaven.[8]

Wu Zetian was one of Taizong's concubines, and was sent to a convent after his death. When Taizong's son Gaozong became emperor in 649 CE, he brought Wu Zetian back to the palace as his own concubine. The latter part of his reign was defined by

---

4   Allan and Phillips, *World Mythologies: Ancient China's Myths and Beliefs*, 109.

5   Charles Benn, *China's Golden Age: Everyday Life in the Tang Dynasty* (New York: Oxford University Press, 2002), 289.

6   Dennis C. Twitchett, "Taizong," in *Encyclopedia Britannica*, October 6, 2023, www.britannica.com/biography/Taizong-emperor-of-Tang-dynasty.

7   Isenbike Togan, "Court Historiography in Early Tang China: Assigning a Place to History and Historians at the Palace," in *Royal Courts in Dynastic States and Empires: A Global Perspective*, eds. Jeroen Duindam, Tülay Artan, and Metin Kunt (Netherlands: Brill, 2011), 171, www.jstor.org/stable/10.1163/j.ctt1w8h2rh.13.

8   Jonathan Karam Skaff, *Sui-Tang China and Its Turko-Mongol Neighbors: Culture, Power, and Connections, 580–800* (New York: Oxford University Press, 2012), 120.

his submission to Wu Zetian's political desires.[9]

Just as he tells Zilan in the throne room, the real Gaozong was gravely ill at the end of his life, and was (temporarily) saved by his physician in 683 CE through acupuncture that cured his blindness. Wu Zetian strongly objected to the procedure, but Gaozong overruled her. He died later that same year.[10]

Posthumous Names

The infamous empress who is today most widely known as Wu Zetian (武則天) was in fact not called this name until after her death—Wu Zetian is her posthumous title. These titles were bestowed on scholars or officials (or their wives) by family and friends, a practice that began in the Zhou Dynasty. Rulers of ancient China generally also received temple names—such as Taizong and Gaozong—to be recorded in the grand temple on ancestral tablets,[11] but Wu Zetian never received this honor.

Emperor Xiaojing—the name that Empress Wu considers giving Hong after his death—is the actual posthumous name of the real Li Hong, even though he was never emperor. This name was bestowed on him by Emperor Gaozong, not Wu Zetian.[12]

Li Bai

The poem that Zheng Sili refers to in the final line of Zilan's transformation is "Drinking Alone under the Moon" by Li Bai,

9   The Editors of Encyclopedia Britannica, "Gaozong," in *Encyclopedia Britannica*, January 1, 2023, www.britannica.com/biography/Gaozong -emperor-of-Tang-dynasty.

10 Benn, *China's Golden Age*, 232–33.

11 Irena Kałużyńska, "Linguistic Composition and Characteristics of Chinese Given Names," *Journal of the International Council of Onomastic Sciences* 51 (2016): 177, doi.org/10.34158/ONOMA.51/2016/8.

12 X. L. Woo, *Empress Wu the Great: Tang Dynasty China* (New York: Algora Publishing, 2008), 90.

one of the most well-known and respected poets in Chinese history. Li Bai was commonly referred to as a *zhexian* (谪仙), meaning *banished immortal*, by those who appreciated his work. He frequently referenced the moon in his poems, which he believed was a home for immortal beings.[13] The stanza Zheng Sili refers to reads as follows, as translated by Herbert Giles in 1901:

> *An arbour of flowers*
> *and a kettle of wine:*
> *Alas! in the bowers*
> *no companion is mine.*
> *Then the moon sheds her rays*
> *on my goblet and me,*
> *And my shadow betrays*
> *we're a party of three.*[14]

The Downfall of the Tang Dynasty

In chapter fifteen, Zheng Sili remarks that he can't seize the throne because his family hasn't laid the political groundwork for it, unlike the Zhu family.

In the real world, the Zhu family seized the throne from the House of Li in 907 CE, when Zhu Wen deposed Emperor Ai, a fifteen-year-old puppet emperor who Zhu had placed on the throne after assassinating the previous emperor, Zhaozong of the House of Li.[15] Thus, the Tang Dynasty came to an end.

---

13   Ha Jin, "The Poet with Many Names—and Many Deaths," *The Paris Review,* January 23, 2019, www.theparisreview.org/blog/2019/01/23/the-poet-with-many-names-and-many-deaths.

14   Herbert A. Giles, *A History of Chinese Literature,* Project Gutenberg (New York: D. Appleton and Company, 1901), www.gutenberg.org/files/43711/43711-h/43711-h.htm#Page_143.

15   Emily Mark, "Tang Dynasty," in *World History Encyclopedia* (World History Publishing, 2016), www.worldhistory.org/Tang_Dynasty.

ACKNOWLEDGMENTS

It seems that every time I start to write a sequel, I think to myself, "Why did I ever agree to do this?" and then by the time I get around to writing the acknowledgments, I think, "Why didn't I make this a trilogy?"

In other words, the process of writing a sequel feels insurmountable, but is made so much easier and ultimately rewarding by the hard work of so many people behind the scenes.

Thank you as always to my agent, Mary C. Moore, for believing in this series first, for making all my dreams possible, and for giving this book its name!

Immense thanks to the whole Inkyard team for bringing this series to life and launching book one with so much enthusiasm. This book would not exist if you all hadn't believed in me back in 2020. Inkyard left an incredible mark on the world, and I wish nothing but the best for the whole team.

I am forever grateful to everyone at HarperTeen who welcomed me and put so much hard work into *The Blood Orchid*. Especially Emilia, whose edits made this book exponentially better. I am so proud of what we've made together.

Thank you to my UK team at Hodderscape for giving Zilan such a warm welcome in the UK, as well as FairyLoot for enchanting so many readers with a gorgeous special edition.

I'm also grateful to all the booksellers and librarians who championed this series, hand-sold it to customers, encouraged patrons to read it, and chose it for your book clubs. Thank you as well to all the book bloggers, BookTubers, BookTokers, and Bookstagrammers who do a tremendous amount of unpaid labor in this industry to support the books that they love—please know I never take you for granted.

Thank you to my writing buddies Van Hoang, Yume Kitasei, Rebecca Kim Wells, Karen Bao, and Rory Ursula for giving me great suggestions when I got stuck writing this book, fielding my complaints, and passing around publishing tea with me. Writing is a solitary job at times, but having you all in my community makes it worthwhile.

Thank you to my friends outside of publishing for listening to me talk about how secretly wild this industry is, for supporting my dreams so enthusiastically, and for sending me pictures of my book whenever you see it on shelves. Even when we're far apart, I feel your love and support with me always, and it motivates me to keep making you proud.

And of course, thank you to my parents, who made this career possible with their love and faith in me.